SILENTCIDE 2

VENGEANCE

Kill or be killed while US senators die.

WITH 145
ONLINE PHOTOS OF
ACTION SCENES IN
21 CITIES IN
4 COUNTRIES

A SUSPENSE THRILLER BY

RICHARD EBERT

ENCIRCLE BOOKS™
RICHARD EBERT NOVELS

Encircle Books™
The publishing imprint of
Encircle World Photos, LLC
Saint Paul, Minnesota

ISBN: 979-8-9895711-3-0 (Hardcover)
ISBN: 979-8-9895711-4-7 (Paperback)
ISBN: 979-8-9895711-5-4 (E-book)

Library of Congress Control Number: 2024913318

First Encircle Books™ edition: September 2024

Printed in the United States of America

Encircle Books™ is a trademark of Encircle World Photos, LLC

Cover photos: Lincoln Memorial – Richard Ebert; Eyes – Adobe Stock/JuanM
Cover design: Rafael Andres
Author photo: Lisa A. Crayford

Author website: www.RichardEbert.com
Author email: Author@RichardEbert.com

This book is for my family with all of my love.

145 Online Photos for Silentcide 2

145 online photos show *Silentcide 2* action scenes
in 21 cities in 4 countries.
Each photo annotated by a footnote number in the book.
All photos and descriptions by Richard Ebert.

Three Ways to See Photos

Author website: RichardEbert.com. Look for *Silentcide 2* cover.
Click "145 Silentcide 2 Photos."
Scan QR code at the end of a chapter.
See entire photo gallery:

Scan QR code below

ONE

MONITORING QUÉBEC CITY, CANADA

Friday

Death was imminent. Watching would be divine.

Irene Shaw tingled with anticipation yet portrayed dispassionate elegance. Heaven forbid the hired help detect anything but her poised control over the pending termination of Chris Davis and Anna Monteiro. Their demise was long overdue yet rapidly approaching. The ambush promised to be splendid vengeance.

Irene's intense blue eyes focused on four large monitors suspended over an ornate marble fireplace. Each live video showed the view of a killer's bodycam or rifle-mounted camera. Two assassins had been stationed for over an hour at the north end of Terrasse Dufferin,[1] a quarter-mile promenade overlooking the Saint Lawrence River. The third had been conducting surveillance of Old Québec City[2] from a high-rise until recently ordered to reposition in the south. The fourth showed a ham sandwich being eaten at Tourny Fountain while the targets toured the adjacent Parliament Building.[3]

The trap was almost ready. Irene detested waiting. Yet perfection required patience.

A handsome young manservant approached her, paused to be acknowledged, then delivered a third dirty martini in a frosted Baccarat crystal glass. "Thank you, dear," Irene said with a suggestive smile. She ogled Pierre's retreat from the Ops Room of her

Philadelphia mansion while fondly recalling their last tryst. Then she placed a Sicilian stuffed olive on her tongue, withdrew the ivory cocktail skewer with her perfect teeth, bit down, and savored the zesty burst of gin, bitterness and blue cheese. Life's simple pleasures were often the best. Excessive wealth paid for every other indulgence.

While placing the stemware on the Louis XV period end table, Irene's bejeweled fingers spasmed. She cursed the sign of weakness. Arthritic hands were among a growing list of physical imperfections that had been accelerating since her sixtieth birthday twelve years earlier. Managing or masking her body's degeneration was increasingly time consuming and expensive. Yet aging was just another formidable adversary to defeat. Irene was accustomed to winning.

In subservient silence, an elderly Vietnamese manicurist used an embroidered washcloth to pat dry the splash of martini before it seeped into the table's rosewood inlay. The woman then retrieved a fresh towel for the top of the portable cosmetic workstation, gingerly lowered Irene's hand again and resumed airbrushing her fingernails. The illegal immigrant was a gifted artisan, nonjudgmental and discreet.

Irene Shaw stole a glance at the full-length dressing mirror. A few tufts of silver-white hair needed to be ushered back into the French bun. She admired the taut pink skin stretched over high cheekbones. Her authoritative eyes were accented by layered mascara, long lashes and dark microbladed eyebrows. Yet her neck needed a nip and tuck. She must remember to ask her assistant to make an appointment with the cosmetic surgeon. He was always booked months ahead. The doctor's scalpel was sheer genius.

Irene's thoughts shifted to Chris Davis, her protégé for the last twenty-eight years. Since he was orphaned at ten years old, she had meticulously honed his skills for silentcide, the art of undetected killing. Along with his younger sister, Michelle, they had become an outstanding team, far exceeding initial expectations. They had rarely failed to execute a silentcide commission on time and without repercussions from police. Their near-flawless record was remarkable. Irene had envisioned the siblings becoming heirs to her murder enterprise ... until recently.

For some reason and without warning, Chris Davis had become rebellious. A simple disobedience would have been distasteful yet manageable. A bold resistance against her authority could have been dealt with harshly and then forgiven.

Yet his increasing acts of defiance were much deeper, reprehensible and unpardonable. Chris had refused to kill his assigned target, Anna Monteiro, because he had become infatuated with her. The police were also investigating his rogue actions in three cities. The needless body count was now at five. Worst of all was the avenging conspiracy: he had plotted to kill Irene.

His audacity was outrageous. The consequences would be severe. Soon, Chris Davis would lie in a pool of blood. Simultaneously, Anna Monteiro would die on this last day of the extended deadline as promised to the client. Two birds, one stone, and marvelous retribution. Plus, the spectacular slayings would be a stern warning to potential malcontents in her network of assassins. You don't screw with Irene Shaw.

"Ms. Shaw," came a booming voice from the computer screen on the nearby Baroque writing desk. Jürgen van Oorschot was the middle-aged head of Phonoi, the group named after the Greek personification of violent murder. His square chin, thin lips, bulbous nose, and narrow menacing eyes beneath a black crewcut created a fierce appearance.

"Yes, dear." Irene acknowledged the ruthless man.

The former mercenary replied, "The targets have left the Parliament Building and are heading toward the promontory."[4]

A glance at the wall monitors confirmed the news. Camera four – from the man discreetly tracking the couple – showed them strolling on the lawn at Plains of Abraham Park. Camera three was a shaking view of Porte Saint-Louis[5] along the old city wall as a sniper hurried toward his newly assigned position. The noose was tightening.

Irene looked down at the Vietnamese woman. "I'm afraid we'll need to suspend this for now, dear."

"Yes, ma'am," the nail technician said while pushing aside the cosmetic station. She graciously lifted one of Irene's feet, causing the Garra rufa fish that had been feasting on dead skin cells to dart wildly within the ichthyotherapy tank. After Irene's second foot had been dried, the manicurist helped her into designer slippers, bowed, and humbly left the room. The closing door echoed off the mahogany walls, crown molding and coffered ceiling.

Irene retrieved the martini, plodded across the Persian rug, sat down in the Chippendale desk chair and adjusted her floral silk dress. She took a sip, relished the harsh warmth sliding down her throat, then took another. The emerging buzz blended perfectly with rising endorphins.

On monitor four, Chris and Anna appeared to be admiring the western wall of La Citadelle de Québec[6] – a British fort built after the War of 1812 – until they abruptly stopped walking. Anna handed Chris a cell phone, stared for a moment, then curiously hustled away. Was she pissed? Had the lovebirds been arguing?

Irene asked into the computer screen, "Are you seeing this, Jürgen?"

"Yes, Ms. Shaw," the commander of the assassination team replied into the boom mic on his headset.

"Where's she going?"

"On her present course, there is only one way she can go," he said with a reassuring voice, "and that's directly into the kill zone. The boys will be waiting for her."

Irene insisted, "They shouldn't fire a single shot until she is reunited with Chris. Understood?"

"Understood," he said with a nod.

Perhaps Jürgen understood, but did those idiots behind the triggers?

Irene intently watched Chris talking on the phone. He was animated, perhaps agitated, while pacing back and forth. His free hand alternated between waving wildly and rubbing his short blond hair. The conversation was obviously intense. Each ticking minute was putting greater separation between Chris and Anna.

Equally bad, the sniper on camera three was finally in position and getting camouflaged, but the unassembled rifle was still in the backpack. He was hideously slow.

A queasy feeling emerged in Irene's stomach. The mission was cracking, maybe crumbling. She sensed another failure, similar to Monday's assassination attempt on Chris at his house in Saint Paul that had cost Irene two people. Continued failure was unacceptable. "Where's Monteiro?" she demanded to know.

Jürgen calmly replied, "She's jogging along Governors' Promenade."

"Do you have eyes on her?"

"Yes, we have cameras along her path."

"That wasn't a rhetorical question, damn it. Show me."

The top two monitors switched to views of the half-mile board-walk[7] suspended between the massive citadel walls and a 330-foot drop-off. The narrow walkway was filled with meandering tourists. Anna was nowhere to be seen.

"Where is she?" Irene asked with escalating agitation.

"She should be appearing on monitor two just about …" After a lengthy pause, Jürgen added, "Now."

Forty-one-year-old Anna Monteiro jogged by with an effortless stride. Her black pixie haircut, fresh delicate face, olive complexion and sturdy build were a disgusting display of youth. Irene resented how the entitled hussy had bewitched Chris and turned him into a traitor. Killing him meant the loss of an outstanding asset and the collapse of her succession plan. What a waste!

Irene's eyes narrowed to slits while staring at video feed four. Chris was still on the phone. Who the hell was he talking to?

The plan now seemed hopeless. To be successful, Chris and Anna needed to enter the trap together. Irene was ready to abort when Chris suddenly ended the call, pocketed the cell, and began running down Avenue du Cap-Diamant. Within fifteen seconds, he leaped onto a platform and disappeared down a ramp.

"Tell your man to follow him," Irene commanded.

"He is," Jürgen said as monitor four showed bouncing movement.

"Hell, I can go faster than that. Get his ass in gear."

Before the tracking assassin reached the entrance of Governors' Promenade, Chris was seen on monitor one dodging summer tourists as his pace on the elevated boardwalk intensified. His androgynous facial features were red with exertion and determination. A minute later, monitor two showed him sprinting along a straightway beneath the enormous base of the fort. The tracker was hopelessly behind as his labored breathing grew louder over the speakers of the Ops Room. The man would never catch the prey. And the sniper on camera three was still assembling his rifle. At this pace, he'd be unprepared for the first shot.

The incompetence outraged Irene. After gulping the rest of the martini, she hurled the stemware toward the fireplace. The shattering glass startled the Afghan hound sleeping on the camelback leather couch.

"I'm sorry to have disturbed you, Brutus, my dear," Irene said with a comforting tone.

The fifty-five-pound purebred shook his long silky coat and circled twice before plopping down to resume his nap.

Irene aimed her wrath at Jürgen. "Your men three and four are bungling amateurs. Complete dolts! They're totally unfit for the high standards of Phonoi. I want them dealt with after this mission is over. Got that?"

"Yes, Ms. Shaw."

"Are your other two men ready?"

"Yes, Ms. Shaw."

"For god's sake," she bristled, "stop saying 'Yes, Ms. Shaw' and show me what they're seeing."

"Yes, Ms. Shaw," Jürgen habitually replied, flinched at his mistake, then switched the video feeds on monitors one and two.

Camera one was a bird's-eye view of Terrasse Dufferin. The sniper was positioned within scaffolding along the main tower of Fairmont Le Château Frontenac, an iconic railway hotel and late nineteenth-century landmark. The entire 1400-foot length of the promenade was visible below him. Camera two was from a man on the ground at the Samuel de Champlain Monument.[8] He was pretending to watch a street performer while awaiting orders to advance to the flash point.

"Jürgen, give me a full zoom on camera one." Within a millisecond, she added, "Do it now." When his response was too slow, she took control.

She pushed the command button on the desktop, placed headphones on her coiffed hair, raised the mic to her scarlet lips, zoomed in on monitor one, and began issuing commands. "Number One, see that long staircase at the far end of the boardwalk? Anna Monteiro will be coming down any minute. Number Two, start moving now and be prepared to engage. Number Three, for god's sake, stop screwing around. Lock and load your damn weapon. Number Four, move your sorry ass. Acknowledge."

The word *copy* simultaneously boomed into her ears four times. The team knew who was now in charge and the penalty for disappointing her. They were no doubt hyped up.

"Brutus," Irene cooed to the Afghan hound. "Come to Mama." The aristocratic dog sprung off the couch, lumbered over, and placed his long snout on her lap. "Such a good boy," she said while stroking the flowing hair on his ears. The love of her life always calmed her agitated temperament. "Mama will take you for a nice long walk after this nasty business is done. I promise." The animal's chocolate-brown eyes sparkled with approval.

"Visual on target B," came the announcement from the sniper on top of the hotel.

Irene concentrated on monitor one. Anna had passed the landing of a very tall staircase and was coming down the last flight of forty stairs. She was moving quickly. Was she trying to escape Chris? Or was this simply an obnoxious display of her daily obsession with running?

Regardless, she was jeopardizing the ideal point of attack in the center of Terrasse Dufferin unless Chris caught up soon. It was also essential that all four guns be in position for the deadly crossfire. But Chris was off camera and only one killer was in range and ready.

The pending debacle was infuriating. Anger pulsated across her forehead.

Irene watched as the crowded boardwalk modified Anna Monteiro's pace, forcing her to weave among the throng of people. She was walking parallel to the second sniper, hidden in the brush behind a long wooden toboggan slide used during winter. Within thirty seconds, she appeared on his camera. Her back would soon become the perfect target for a .30-06 cartridge.

"Where the hell is Chris?" Irene bellowed at Jürgen while slamming her fist on the desk. With a startled whimper, the Afghan slinked away.

"Any second now, Ms. Shaw," was his totally unsatisfactory answer.

The delay was excruciating. Rapid heartbeats echoed in her eardrums as she clenched her jaw. The rage was blazing until the sniper atop the hotel reported, "I've got eyes on target A."

There, on monitor one, was Chris. He was bolting down the staircase, pushing people aside as he jumped down two stairs at a time.

The strategy was working. The mission was a go.

An intense calm swept over Irene. With composed authority, she confirmed the assignments. "Number One, your target is A. That's Chris Davis. Number Three, your target is B. That's Anna Monteiro. Number Two, you'll verify they're dead and finish them off if needed." She didn't bother giving instructions to Number Four. It was doubtful the fat sloth would arrive before the carnage was over. "Are my assignments clear?"

In her headset she heard, "One, affirmative. Two, affirmative. Three, affirmative."

"Good. Now hold your fire. I repeat, do not fire until my command."

Chris leaped onto the boardwalk, sprinted for fifty feet, appeared winded, stopped, cocked his head, searched the crowd, then began yelling something in desperation. If he was calling out for Anna, she either couldn't hear or was ignoring him.

Time to execute.

"On three, gentlemen," Irene announced while staring at Chris and Anna on the monitors. "One. Two."

An instant before Irene said, "Three," Chris doubled over with his hands on his knees as if gasping for breath from running. The bullet intended for him hit a teenager. Anna had suddenly turned around and was beginning to wave. The abrupt stop caused an elderly couple to bump into her. An old man spun violently from the velocity of a bullet before collapsing.

Chaos ensued. The crowd scattered. Screams of terror. Most people ran up a small hill lined with historic cannons. A few crouched or lay flat on the boardwalk. Some hid under benches. Anna plus two others took cover beneath a decorative cast-iron gazebo[9] overlooking the river.

Irene was inflamed by the incompetence. "Keep firing!"

Successive bullets slammed into the base of Anna's kiosk and ricocheted off a nearby ornamental fence. It was impossible to see if Anna had been hit.

Monitor one showed Chris climbing up the wooden slats of the toboggan slide[10] as chunks of debris exploded around him. He leaped into the foliage and disappeared. Immediately, the video feed of the sniper on the ground began gyrating. Sounds of a fight blasted in Irene's ears.

Then an eerie silence. Chris's furious face filled monitor three. "Hi there, Irene," he said with contempt. "Your time is coming soon, dear. Very, very soon."

Irene shrieked, "Number One, start firing into position three."

The hotel sniper said, "I don't have a visible target, Ms. Shaw."

"I don't give a damn. Empty your magazine. Now."

A series of bullets shattered trees, bushes and rocks as fast as the sniper could work the bolt, refocus and squeeze the trigger again. The sound was deafening.

Suddenly, his camera tumbled until coming to rest beneath a scaffolding platform. A splash of blood covered the lens. Now both snipers were down and presumed dead.

The bodycam of the killer from the north showed him racing down the boardwalk while approaching the kiosk. He had a two-handed grip on the company-issued SIG P229 pistol and was taking aim at Anna. As his index finger slipped into the trigger guard, he was blown backward. Chris had claimed another victim using the commandeered sniper rifle.

Irene was stunned by the debacle.

The last functioning video displayed the surveillance tracker reaching the bottom of the staircase. He was wheezing and coughing as he held out his weapon.

She shouted, "Number Four. Team is dead. You're alone. Chris Davis is on the hill behind the toboggan slide. He's armed. Anna Monteiro is in the next kiosk. Make this happen!"

A successful outcome seemed doubtful.

Irene leaned within inches of the desktop computer screen and berated Jürgen. "Your plan sucked. A real shitshow. We'll discuss this later."

Despite his attempt to remain stoic, Jürgen's battle-hardened face turned ashen. "Yes, Ms. Shaw."

Chapter One: Québec City, Canada

Photos 1–10

TWO

Québec City, Canada

The boyish face of Chris Davis was contorted by angst and concentration. The firefight had lasted less than sixty seconds yet felt like an eternity in hell. The crosshairs of the sniper rifle were still focused on the third gunman lying face down on Terrasse Dufferin. Chris was prepared to deliver a final kill shot if needed. The man didn't twitch. A spreading puddle of crimson was seeping into the wooden slats.

Using the high-powered scope, Chris scanned for additional assailants. The boardwalk was mostly deserted. Only a few tourists still cowered with paralyzing fear. An elderly woman was sobbing over the fallen man who had taken the bullet meant for Anna.

At the far end of the promenade, near the hotel, two policemen had their sidearms drawn. They were on guard but not advancing, no doubt waiting for backup. A distant siren wailed. Another joined the chorus. Soon police and SWAT would surround the area.

The window was closing fast to find Anna and escape. Perhaps three minutes remained. Maybe less. He assumed she was still hiding beneath the kiosk. He prayed she had survived the onslaught.

Chris frisked the dead sniper next to him, found his pistol, checked the chamber of the SIG P229, and was preparing to leave the brush. He stopped. Strained breathing was advancing on the other side of the adjacent toboggan slide. It could be someone returning to the scene, but that was doubtful. Or perhaps it was the teenager who had been shot. But a decade of survival training dictated the unseen person be treated as a potential combatant.

Chris waited until the footsteps passed in front of a small utility shack, then he slithered down a retaining wall. Fast reflexes caught a tumbling rock before it hit the ground. He paused. Listened. The cadence of the person's cautious pace had not changed. Safe to proceed. Chris ducked below the toboggan slide and approached the opposite side of the shack. His handgun led the way.

Nearby was a grossly out of shape man. His back stretched a hideous sport coat. Bulging arms held an outstretched pistol. Beads of sweat rolled off his glistening bald head. He was peering around the shack in search of an adversary, oblivious to the pending assault.

Chris removed the slack from the trigger until his finger met resistance. Additional pressure would release a 9mm round. He debated, then commanded, "Don't move."

The gunman flinched but obeyed the order.

Chris continued, "You can drop the gun and live, or you can die. So you have to ask yourself, is it really worth dying for Irene?"

With a shaky voice, the man said, "She'll have me killed if I surrender."

"Maybe, maybe not. But I'll kill you right now if you don't."

The assailant hesitated before lowering the gun to the ground and kicking it away.

"Good choice," Chris said. "How many on your team?"

"Four including me."

"Then you're the last man standing. Turn around." As he did, Chris waved at the man's bodycam and blew his nemesis a kiss. "You lost again, Irene." He then stared at the tense assailant and said, "Now run like hell back up those stairs. If you return, you're dead." After a second of indecision, the man scrambled over a trail of bloody footprints presumably left by the wounded teenager who had managed to flee.

Chris stuffed the sniper's pistol behind his shirttail. He picked up the man's weapon, released and pocketed the magazine, ejected the chambered round and threw the gun into the trees. He then bolted toward Victoria Kiosk. Anna was squeezed into the corner between a lamppost and the fence. She was huddled in a fetal position with arms covering her head. Two other people hid beneath benches. They were terrified but unhurt.

"Anna, thank god you're all right," he said while holding out his hand. They shared an impassioned embrace, grateful to be alive. He thought he had lost her. For over two weeks, he had fantasized about having a future with her. The feelings had been mutual. She was everything he had ever hoped for but never expected to find. Nor did he deserve. That pipe dream would soon be shattered. This was probably the last time she would ever hug him. He didn't want to let go. "Are you okay enough to leave?"

Anna protested with wide-eyed panic, "But what if it's not safe yet?"

"It's safe," he said, trying to remain calm while suppressing his worry of being caught. He draped her arm around his shoulder, held her waist and began leading her across the boardwalk.

The elderly woman begged for help. Chris debated, weighed the risks and chose the right versus the smart thing to do. He released Anna, knelt down and examined the old man's shoulder. The bullet appeared to have shattered the clavicle before exiting. Blood loss seemed minimal, yet his complexion was sickly gray, breathing was rapid and his bluish lips were quivering. Slipping into shock could be fatal.

"Your husband will be fine," Chris said for reassurance yet doubted the prognosis was accurate. "Press his jacket on the wound, elevate his feet with your purse, keep him calm, and medical help will be here soon. Sorry, but that's all I can do."

Anna looked concerned for the frightened couple as Chris jumped up, grabbed her hand and led her up a small set of stairs through a crowd of gawkers. Moving briskly was critical but not too fast to attract attention. They had to disappear before the police sealed the perimeter. Multiple sirens were now approaching; two had already stopped. The lone gunman could also be circling back. Maybe it had been a mistake to spare his life, but Chris was tired of killing.

"Aren't we going to the hotel?" Anna asked, pointing to the valet entrance a short distance away.

Chris held her shoulders. Anna's expression was numb. Her gorgeous brown eyes darted with anxiety. She needed a haven soon to decompress from the ordeal. That wasn't going to happen. He was about to traumatize her further but wanted to delay the inevitable as long as possible. "No," he said. "Going to the hotel is risky. Shots were fired from there. Let's keep moving. Can you do that?"

"Yeah, I think so," she said with uncertainty.

They dashed along a footpath in Governors' Garden and hustled down Rue Haldimand until reaching Rue Saint-Louis,[11] one of the city's oldest streets. Instead of entering the intersection, he led them through the door of an underground parking lot.

"Where're we going?" she asked between gasps of continued fear.

"We're driving out of here."

"But why? I'm sure we're safe now."

"We're not. Trust me."

"How do you know?" she asked tentatively.

Chris scrambled for a plausible answer without adding to the litany of lies he had told her since their first discussion on the Caribbean cruise. The lies had to end sometime, yet he wasn't ready to divulge the truth. "Because I saw the face of one of the gunmen. He could be coming after me."

"Do you think he followed us?"

"I don't know, but let's not stand around to find out."

As he led her down a row of parked cars, they kept vigilant for a possible attacker. When they reached his late-model Ford Explorer, he slid between the adjacent car, opened the passenger door and said, "Hop in." He was surprised she didn't. He turned to face her.

Anna was in shocked disbelief. "Chris, is that a gun beneath your shirt?"

"Yes," he reluctantly admitted.

She started inching away from the SUV. "Were you one of the shooters?"

"At the bad guys, yes."

With hesitation, as if hoping for any acceptable explanation, she asked, "Are you some kind of undercover cop or agent?"

He considered saying yes. It was the easy answer. He opted for the truth. "No."

Anna turned to run.

He grabbed her arm, just hard enough to detain her without being aggressive, then immediately released the grip. With a tone meant to sound soothing, he said, "Anna, I know you're scared. I'm scared, too. But our lives are in danger until we leave the city. So please, just get in."

"No, no, no, no, no," she repeated with outstretched palms. "Get away from me."

"If I do that, I can't protect you. And that's all I'm honestly trying to do. You've got to trust me."

"I used to trust you implicitly," she said with eyes ablaze. "But not now. I don't know who the hell you are."

Struggling to defuse her distrust, he said, "You're right. You don't. But deep down, I'm still the guy you thought you knew. So please, let's go."

"No," she said with defiance.

Chris considered pulling out the pistol to coerce her. But even if he aimed the barrel at the ground, the abhorrent action would shatter any potential for renewing trust. Instead, he removed two small photos from his pants pocket. They were blurry surveillance images of himself and Anna. Some of the handwritten letters on the words *Target A* and *Target B* were smeared with dried blood. "See these? We were the targets of that firestorm."

Her mouth gaped. "Where did you find them?"

"In the backpack of one of the snipers."

She dared to ask, "How did you get them?"

"After I stopped him from shooting at you."

"Oh my god," she exclaimed while stumbling backward. "You mean you …"

"Yes, I killed him and two others. It was either them or us. But one is still out there. So you can either come with me or go back outside. But if you do" – he held up her bloodstained photo – "you'll be dead within hours. These people will stop at nothing. Whatever you decide, I'm leaving now."

Anna was motionless with distress and doubt.

Gaining her cooperation seemed hopeless. The longer the delay, the greater the chance of getting caught. Fleeing was paramount. He walked around the car, got in the driver's seat and started the ignition. "Please close your door so I can pull out," he said with a calm yet firm voice.

Ten seconds passed before she reluctantly got in the car.

"Good. Now keep your head down."

Chapter Two: Québec City, Canada

Photo 11

THREE

QUÉBEC CITY, CANADA

Anna immediately regretted getting into the SUV. Had the locking car doors sealed her fate? Was she trapped inside with a dangerous man who had conned her? For nearly three weeks, she had a growing infatuation for Chris, thinking maybe, just maybe, he was the one. Now, all illusions of romance, compatibility and trust were shattered. Chris Davis was a killer. Worse yet, she was the target of the bloodbath and apparently still in peril. But was the biggest threat outside the car or behind the wheel? The distress was suffocating.

When Chris spoke, she flinched. "Inside the glove box is a mesh bag," he said. "Would you grab it for me, please?"

Her fingers struggled with the simple task of pulling up the latch, opening the compartment door and retrieving the bag. Inside were sunglasses, a short brown wig, and a lower-face mask consisting of oversized ears, sideburns and a well-trimmed beard. Chris put them on with practiced ease. The transformation was stark. He was unrecognizable. Wearing a disguise was clearly a uniform of his profession, whatever the hell that was.

She cowered when he reached into the backseat and grabbed two shirts. One he wore. The other he offered to her with an apologetic expression. "I'm sorry, but please cover yourself with this and stay low, at least until we are out of the city. It's for your protection."

She complied, yet the request felt sinister. Equally ominous was the black handgun wedged next to the driver's seat.

As the car moved through the parking lot and up a ramp, Anna hoped to scream for help to the cashier at checkout. Unfortunately, there was no attendant. Chris used a credit card to pay before exiting.

At the next stop, she considered fleeing. The neighborhood must be swarming with police. But among them was another gunman. He probably also had her photo marked as Target B. If she jumped out now, could she be dead soon?

The SUV meandered through the clogged streets of Old Québec City while Anna's mind raced with indecision and dread. The eddy of conflicting scenarios vacillated between hope and doom.

Is Chris really trying to protect me? Or is the plan to kill me, too? If so, why didn't he pull the trigger in the parking lot? That would've been fast and easy. Maybe he's not a threat. Didn't he risk his life to rescue me on the boardwalk? He even took time to help the old man who had been shot. So maybe he really is trying to keep me safe. Sure, that's got to be it. He couldn't have faked his emotions for me all this time, could he? Am I that bad at judging people? Is he that good of an actor? Think of all the times we were alone together. Was I vulnerable then too? Maybe. Oh my god, probably. Perhaps he's driving to a remote location to dump my body. Escape now before he gets onto the open road. It might be the only chance to survive.

Anna mustered the courage to act. She expected her voice to be compelling but the words tumbled out with a babbling whimper. "Chris, I'm going to be sick. Pull over."

"Okay," he said with urgency. "But I'm on a busy street. Hang on a second."

"I can't. It's going to come. Hurry."

She lifted her head and squealed as Chris swerved onto a sidewalk, plowed over a flowerbed and bounced into a parking lot. She bolted. He pursued. The chase ended in seconds when her wobbly legs betrayed her. Anna tumbled onto the lawn of a tree-covered park in front of Gare du Palais.[12] The historic, château-style train station seemed almost deserted.

Chris knelt down and asked with compassion, "Are you hurt?"

"No," she managed to say while fighting back tears, "but I'm scared. Petrified. Just let me go. Please."

"I will. Just give me ten minutes to explain. That's all I ask. Afterward, if you still want to leave, you're free to go. I promise. Okay?"

The question hung suspended. He didn't press for an answer. Instead, after a quick glance left and right as if searching for onlookers or threats, he unexpectedly removed the disguise. The man she thought she knew reappeared. There was no obvious deceit in those once-charming aquamarine eyes. His expression seemed conciliatory, his tone was nonthreatening, he appeared unarmed, and the way he held her hand was oddly comforting. Plus, the safety of passing cars and a few pedestrians was less than fifty feet away. A single scream for help could save her. She decided to hear him out.

He sat down on the grass, took a breath as if collecting his thoughts and gnawed his lip before making eye contact. He seemed nervous. "Anna, listen, I understand your inclination to run. Hell, inclinations two through twenty will also be to run to the police when you hear what I have to say. But they can't protect you, at least not for long. You'll be dead soon because the people hunting for you are unrelenting. And today you saw only a fraction of their firepower."

The repeated prediction of her pending death was traumatizing. A flash of crippling anxiety exploded in her chest and brain. Anna struggled to speak. "Why? I don't understand."

"Because there's a contract out on your life. It's already been extended once. The second deadline was today."

"But I'm a nobody," Anna said, as if pleading for clemency. "I don't have enemies. Who'd want me dead?"

"George Henniker," Chris said flatly.

George was the conceited owner of a hedge fund who Anna had regrettably dated a few times and slept with once. Six weeks ago, she suspected George was trolling for insider information on Longfellow BioSciences, a biotech company where she had been vice president of marketing until a few days ago. To test his ethics, Anna had cryptically misled him by claiming she would have something to celebrate on their next date. It seemed like a harmless ruse at the time, but the deception triggered retaliations.

First, George made drunken threats outside of her Boston brownstone and was thrown into the drunk tank overnight. Days later, he spray-painted "BITCH" on the front door and shot her dog, Blue, through the bay window. He was later arrested and awaiting trial. As terrifying as those assaults had been, they paled in comparison to the attack on the Terrasse Dufferin boardwalk about a half hour ago. Learning George had hired someone to kill her was incomprehensible. "I know George was pissed, but why would he want me dead?" Anna asked in bewilderment.

"Because your misleading statement prompted him to make a twenty million dollar bet that Longfellow was going to announce positive clinical trials for curing cancer. When the negative news went public, George lost over ninety-five percent within days."

"But George ran a good-sized hedge fund," Anna rationalized. "Surely he could absorb a single bad investment, right?"

"No, because his firm had made other bad investments. Lots of them. The portfolio was hemorrhaging. His richest clients were leaving in droves. He was facing bankruptcy. Your perceived insider tip was his last salvation. When it blew up, George blamed you. He wanted revenge. That's when he arranged for a professional killer."

"How do you know all of this?" she asked.

"Because I spent considerable time researching George."

When she and Chris had first talked in the Dominican Republic, he had claimed to be a cybersecurity expert. Therefore, it seemed plausible he could illegally access George Henniker's financial information. "You mean you hacked into his firm's computer system?"

"Yes, because I wanted to learn his motives for threatening you."

"Okay, so if George took out a hit on me, wouldn't the contract be canceled when he died last week?"

"That's what I thought too."

Anna detected something menacing in his statement. She wanted to be wrong but feared the worst. She resisted asking another question to learn the truth. She looked away.

Chris obviously sensed her dilemma. He gently lifted her chin, paused to study her anguish and appeared remorseful while saying, "If you're wondering if I shot George, the answer is yes."

"Oh my god," she said while inching away. "George was despicable. But still, how could you do such a terrible thing?"

"Because, at the time, it was the only way I could think of to protect you."

"So you learned about the contract on my life in his computer?"

"No." Chris paused before adding, "I knew about the hit a week before the cruise."

"How could you? Unless …" She stopped, suddenly terrified she knew the answer.

Chris closed his eyes and tightened his jaw. The question seemed tormenting. He started to say something, then stopped. The delay spiked her anxiety. After a long exhale, he said with a pained expression, "Anna, here's the horrible truth, the worst thing I have to tell you." He paused again. "I was ordered to fulfill the contract."

"You mean kill me?"

Chris's nod was almost imperceptible.

Anna was paralyzed, frozen in disbelief. A pounding pulse assaulted her ears. Every nerve misfired. Survival instinct screamed escape, yet her muscles were unresponsive. Her stomach convulsed. She gagged twice while gulping down waves of vile saliva but couldn't vomit. Her body shook as if having a seizure.

Chris gently touched her shoulder. "Breathe," he said. "Deep breaths."

She recoiled before trying to stand. When her legs refused to cooperate, she raised her knees, clenched them tightly, lowered her head and prayed to endure the trauma. Death seemed certain, either by Chris, an unknown gunman, or her body's reaction to fear.

Chapter Three: Québec City, Canada

Photo 12

FOUR

QUÉBEC CITY, CANADA

Chris was helpless watching Anna suffer. Telling her the truth was more devastating than he imagined, despite rehearsing this discussion countless times. But her reaction was totally predictable. Hoping for anything else was naïve. Frankly, it was surprising she hadn't already run off screaming. Judging by her crumbled posture on the park lawn, she was either too scared to move or was resigned to her fate. Probably both.

Perhaps he should let her go. She'd never feel safe with a former lover who was actually a deceiving, lying assassin assigned to kill her. That was an impossible expectation. Besides, the chances of saving her were minimal, probably nil. So why make her suffer the delusion of being protected? The situation was hopeless. The only solution was to give her a sense of freedom during the precious little time she had left.

"Anna," he said softly, "I know this will sound trite, but I apologize for everything. I'm truly sorry."

There was no response. She remained cowering.

"So I am going to leave you now." He dreaded having to say the final word. "Goodbye."

As he picked up the disguise and stood, she lifted her head. Hatred distorted her blanched complexion and swollen eyes. "You're a bastard, Chris, you know that?" she shouted. "I can't believe you slept with me while actually assigned to kill me!"

"Keep your voice down, will you?" he pleaded while looking around to see if anyone overheard.

"Or what? You'll shoot me now?" she bristled.

How could he calm her down? "I have no intention of harming you, Anna. Just the opposite." He sat down again and scooched close, hoping the proximity would lower her volume, before beginning his contrition. "But you're right. What I did was despicable. I'm despicable. But I never had a choice."

"That's bullshit. How could you not have a choice to kill people?"

"I'm not sure you'd understand."

"Try me. And this time, spare me your lies."

Where could he start? How much could he reveal? He opted for a novel approach: the truth. "Well, I was coerced into this role at the age of ten."

She scoffed. "You expect me to believe you were some kind of child prodigy at killing?"

"No," he said, dismissing the biting retort. Her anger was well deserved, and it was doubtful an explanation would help, but it was worth a try. "My stepfather was a savage brute, probably in the Philly mob. One night in a drunken rage, he tried raping my little sister until my mom fought him off. While he was strangling Mom to death, I hit him with a baseball bat. They both died."

"So your parents didn't die in a car accident like you told me?"

"No," he said with an apologetic tone. He waited a downbeat before continuing. "Anyway, that night, a defense attorney named Irene Shaw took total control of my life and my sister's. She sheltered us in a foster home for two years before sending us to an Amish farm to become elite assassins. For a decade, we were brainwashed, browbeaten and constantly threatened into compliance. For the last sixteen years, Irene has maintained that iron grip on us."

"So, I take it you and your sister are not estranged, right? That was just another lie. Instead, you work together to kill people?"

"Yes, but most of them are scumbags."

"So that's how you categorized me?" she asked with bitterness.

"God no. I'm the scumbag here. Everything about my life sucks. I hate it, and myself. So, when I got to know you during the cruise ... I don't know, something snapped. For the first time, I decided to rebel by refusing to kill you. But that decision violated Irene's number one rule: do exactly what she says or die."

"So that's why she sent those gunmen today?"

"Yes, but that's only part of it. On Saturday when I flew to Pennsylvania, she threatened to kill me three times execution style before killing Lionel, my old childhood instructor. Then on Monday, two assassins attacked me at home in Saint Paul. I barely survived the shootout. Another assassin was assigned to kill my sister."

Anna seemed to be reeling from the long list of violence. "Why would this Irene person want your sister dead?"

"Because we're partners. In Irene's eyes, if one of us betrayed her, we both did."

A hint of sympathy crossed Anna's face. She asked with hesitation, "Did your sister die?"

"No, but I thought she had until today when she warned me about the attack."

"Was that the Michelle who called when we were standing at the fort?"

"Yes."

"Thinking your sister was dead explains your somber mood all this week," Anna said, almost to herself, then seemed scared again. "But you're saying Irene won't stop until all three of us are dead?"

"Yes, or until Michelle and I get to Irene first. Anna, you don't need to be any part of our mission. I promise. But none of us are safe until Irene is gone. After that, you can resume your life."

Sounding exasperated, Anna asked, "But why can't you just report this woman to the police? Or is that too simple?"

Shaking his head, Chris responded, "That won't work, because Irene is one of the best criminal defense attorneys in Philadelphia.

She knows every trick in the book for concealing evidence and avoiding prosecution. Besides, that also risks exposing everyone in her network who, like us, have been coerced into this life." Chris absently picked grass off his pant leg as he reckoned the stark reality. "And even if she went to prison – which seems highly unlikely – she'd keep pulling strings until she got her revenge. Nope, there is only one way to stop Irene Shaw."

While wringing her hands, Anna asked, "But won't your vengeance against Irene be risky?"

"Sure, but it's riskier to just wait around until she strikes again like today. I'd rather manage the risk on our terms."

Anna's brows tightened, as if absorbing the severity of the dilemma. Both options were deplorable. Going on the offensive seemed to have slightly better odds. "I don't mean to sound unappreciative, but why would you jeopardize your life, and your sister's, to save mine?"

"The answer to that started when I began doing surveillance on you in Boston."

"You mean you tracked me for days before we met?" she asked with an ingenuous tone. "Do you know how creepy and invasive that is?"

"Yes, but please just let me finish, okay?"

She remained quiet, struggling to contain her indignation.

The first part of what he was about to explain wasn't the whole truth, but it was close enough. "I quickly sensed you were a good person, but I had to know for sure. That's when I booked onto your cruise with the hopes of getting to know you." The next part he could say with all sincerity. "During that first night we had wine together, I quickly began to admire you. Soon I believed in your passion to cure cancer. I concluded you deserved a future."

With sardonic anger, she asked, "So that's when you decided it was okay to sleep with me?"

"No, the first time wasn't planned. It was totally unexpected.

Remember how standoffish I was? But when it happened, I admit, it was incredibly selfish."

"You're damn right it was," Anna said with disgust.

"Yes, but every day afterward – on the ship, in your home, in San Francisco, and here in Québec City – my feelings for you deepened. You're incredible. Our time together gave me a glimpse of how my life could have been. But I haven't had a future since I was ten. So I decided I was willing to risk mine in order to save yours and the millions of cancer patients you're dedicated to saving."

Her stoic reaction was hard to read. She stared at him without blinking.

Explaining more would be fruitless. He could never justify what he had done, even to himself. Hopefully, he had revealed enough to warrant some modicum of trust about his intentions to save her life. "There you have it. You can hate me, condemn me and fear me. All of those feelings are justified."

Anna remained stoneface.

After a tormented exhale, Chris struggled to continue. "So now you have two choices. One, you can walk away and call the police. With a full description, it won't take them long to arrest me. But while I'm safe in prison someplace, you'll be defenseless. Your second option is to come with me until this is over. But you can leave anytime. I'll never try to stop you again."

Instead of responding to the choices, she gave him an inquisitive glare. Whatever she was about to say or ask, he sensed it was pivotal to her final decision.

Anna blurted out, "Did you have anything to do with Jessica's death?" Jessica was Anna's friend who had been with her on the Caribbean cruise. Two days after their vacation, Jessica died of an overdose at her home in San Francisco by taking a Midol intended to kill Anna. The tablet had been tainted with carfentanil, a drug ten thousand times more potent than morphine.

"No," Chris said with every technique he had been taught for telling undetectable lies. This was one confession he could never divulge. Nor could he ever explain about the failed attempt to murder Anna during the cruise.

While studying him, she asked again, "Are you sure?"

"Yes. What happened to Jessica was tragic, but I had nothing to do with it."

She didn't say she believed him. But her intensity softened.

"Listen," he said. "I know you must have a ton of other questions. But right now, we've got to move. At least I do. I'm going back to the car. I'll sit there for five minutes. If you don't come back, I'll drive off. All I ask is you give me a head start before calling the police."

"Fine," she said softly with a noncommittal expression.

He stood up, gave her a quick look, returned to the SUV and set the timer on his watch. When he glanced back to where they had been sitting, Anna was gone. Because of the obstructed view — parked cars, bushes and trees — he couldn't tell if she had walked or run away. Regardless, he planned to give her the full five minutes.

The wait was interminable. A lot could happen in five minutes, and none of it good. Two minutes would have been better. One would have been best. When the timer beeped, he turned on the car. The gambit had failed. No doubt the police would be searching for him soon. Escaping was imperative.

Before backing up, he checked the rearview mirror. Anna was approaching the car. When she reached the driver side, she motioned to roll down the window. "If this is going to work," she said, "you've got to be honest with me going forward. No more lies. I mean it. If I detect one, or even suspect one, I'm gone."

"I hear you."

She scowled. "That's not an answer, Chris. Tell me you promise."

"I promise," he said, knowing he had immediately broken the pledge. Some secrets could never be revealed. But the volume of lies could be substantially reduced.

She assumed an authoritarian stance with hands on her hips.

"And things will be different between us from now on. You're strictly my bodyguard, nothing more. Got that?"

"I understand," he said, realizing any hope for an ongoing relationship as lovers was now impossible.

With a gasp of resignation, she proceeded to the passenger side and hesitated before getting in. "One more question before we go."

"What's that?"

"I'm assuming Chris Davis is not your real name."

"You're right. It's Danny Ritchie. But no one – not even my sister – has called me that in over twenty-five years."

"Okay," she said, buckling her seat belt. "Let's go. But take damn good care of me."

"I plan to."

"That's not good enough. I'm counting on you to keep me alive."

FIVE

COPENHAGEN, DENMARK

Forty-Four Years Ago

A ray of midmorning sunshine intruded through a slit between the designer double drapes, streaked across the dark bedroom and assailed Irene Shaw's closed eyes. An irritating way to awaken prematurely. "Damn it," she sighed, resigning to get up and start another day of vacation in Copenhagen, Denmark.

She swept aside the duvet, stepped out of the four-poster king bed, and shuffled naked toward the hotel robe discarded in haste on a chair the night before. The Egyptian cotton felt scrumptious around her slender, five-foot-eight frame. She pulled out her dirty-blond hair from the collar, let the mane cascade midway down her back, then took a moment to leer at the exposed backside of her sleeping companion. Lionel Jørgensen was a stud.

What began as an intoxicated one-night stand had evolved into a five-night fling. A decadent pattern had evolved. Irene's sole obligation each evening was to have an elaborate dinner with her father and his gold-digger fiancée. The couple typically dismissed Irene around ten thirty so they could retreat to another night of passion in his sixteen-hundred-square-foot suite at d'Angleterre,[13] a five-star hotel dating back to the eighteenth century.

That gave Irene about a half hour to prepare. At eleven, there would be a gentle knock on the door of her luxury suite. The sound always prompted a tingle of anticipation. Within minutes, clothes would hit the floor and the debauchery would begin. Few words were ever spoken. None were needed. After ninety minutes, Lionel would discreetly leave while she rolled over in satisfied slumber. The arrangement was ideal.

Last night was different. They talked for hours between romps and snorts of cocaine. To her surprise, she discovered this muscular bad boy was intelligent, interesting and ambitious despite his lack of education, wealth and refinement. The slaughterer from Kødbyen – the Meatpacking District of Copenhagen – would never be accepted in Philadelphia's elite social circles. This epitome of masculinity was everything the cocksure professionals she typically dated pretended to be but could never measure up to. Father would be horrified to learn an unskilled foreign laborer had repeatedly ravished his twenty-eight-year-old only child. All of these factors made the forbidden fruit delicious. She fondly called her lover "Great Dane."

Irene plodded to the bathroom, admired her elegant face in the mirror, turned on the coffeepot and lit a Virginia Slims cigarette with a gold-plated Rollagas lighter. Outside the window was Kongens Nytorv; for a Saturday morning, a surprising number of people and cars bustled around King's New Square. Flanking the city's largest square was Det Kongelige Teater[14] where Father had purchased tickets for the Royal Danish Ballet in the evening. The performance promised to be exemplary, assuming she could tolerate the grating voice and mannerisms of her future stepmother. The floozy was only five years older than Irene.

Two massive arms encircled Irene's waist from behind. For such a big man – Lionel had to be at least six feet four – his approach was surprisingly stealthy. "Good morning," he said while affectionately kissing her on the head, then pressing close. "I hope you slept well."

She sensed his body heat and wondered if he was nude. She

hoped so. "You realize a girl needs more than a few hours of beauty sleep, right?"

"I get it." His deep, throaty Danish accent was titillating. "So finish your smoke and let's go back to bed."

"I said sleep, not sex." She feigned a protest.

"Sounds perfect. We'll just switch the order," he said with a laugh while turning her around.

At thirty-one, Lionel was physical perfection, from his tufts of uncombed blond hair to his Nordic blue eyes, square jaw, and a body resembling a Hellenistic deity sculpted from white marble. That marvelous chest was hairless, smooth and hard. Every large muscle was chiseled. They had to be natural; he couldn't possibly afford anabolic steroids.

She unabashedly gawked as a blush of excitement swept across her neck and jaw. This feeling was unnatural. She normally intimidated men with her beauty and svelte figure, then relished their nervous reactions. Now she risked appearing as a giddy schoolgirl. That was unacceptable. Maintaining control in every situation was essential.

When Lionel's hand began slipping inside her robe, she grabbed a finger and yanked it backward. "No," she said sternly, then took another drag of the cigarette. "I promised Father I'd have brunch with them. So you have to leave. Now."

"You've got to be kidding me, right? You'd really rather be with them than this?" His smile was salacious as he looked down at himself, acting justifiably proud.

Of course the answer was no, but she couldn't succumb. She would always be the dominant one, in this and any other relationship. That was nonnegotiable. It was time he learned his place. "Whenever I say no, that's exactly what I mean," she said sternly. "You'll always respect that without hesitation and without being told twice. Is that understood?"

"Sure," he said flatly while stepping back. After an inquisitive stare, Lionel shrugged and turned toward the bedroom.

As he walked away, Irene wondered if Lionel could be manipulated into solving a major problem.

+ + +

As expected, brunch was hideous. Although the food was exceptional, Charlotte was insufferable. Too much of everything, especially makeup, perfume and cleavage. Equally deplorable was her father's doting behavior, his incessant laughter at her lame humor, and his lecherous stares. It was sickening to watch the head of a prestigious law firm act like a horny frat boy, especially over a woman nearly twenty years his junior. Irene could hardly wait to escape.

Back in her suite, she ditched the conservative black dress for a formfitting pink paisley halter top that left little to the imagination. The bell bottoms of the button-fly blue jeans flared above open-toe sandals. A touch of blush and her signature red lipstick completed the carefree yet risqué ensemble. Only three hours had passed, but she looked forward to the rendezvous with Lionel. It was the first time they would be out in public since they'd met at a discotheque. She wondered if she would be as charmed seeing him in daylight fully clothed.

Irene was purposely twelve minutes late to arrive at Nyhavn.[15] New Harbour was established in 1670 as the main canal into the inner city. Recently, the old quay was transforming into restaurants, bars and clubs, and a lively haven for tourists and locals.

Lionel leaned impatiently against the Memorial Anchor, a maritime tribute to sailors who died in World War II. He wore an unbuttoned polyester shirt revealing an imitation gold chain, plus plaid bell-bottoms and pointy-toe leather boots. There was no way these were his normal clothes. He obviously wanted to impress her. The sentiment was endearing, but she'd never tell him.

His face brightened upon her approach. He obviously approved of her suggestive attire and strut. He went for a kiss on the lips. She gave him a cheek instead. Ignoring the rebuff, he asked, "How was brunch?"

"Food was great. The company sucked. What a nightmare," she declared, then added with a chuckle, "We should've stayed in bed." She grabbed his hand. "Come on, let's not ruin our afternoon talking about them."

They meandered on the cobblestones along the quay's "Sunny Side" in front of a row of colorful seventeenth-century townhouses. The crowd was equally vibrant. Lionel explained the history of the harbor and the docked wooden sailing ships. He pointed out the nineteenth-century homes of fairytale writer Hans Christian Anderson. Then he ordered two pints of Carlsberg Pilsner at an outdoor café. The taste was crisp and hoppy. The lager glasses sweated in the afternoon heat. The conversation was delightfully mindless.

Lionel relished his self-appointed role as tour guide while describing Amalienborg Palace,[16] the four winter residences of Danish royalty. He was equally knowledgeable about Frederiks Kirke,[17] especially the church's grand copper dome and interior Baroque artwork. It was fun hearing his pride about the city's landmarks.

Her enjoyment soured when they reached the *Little Mermaid*[18] sitting naked on a boulder along the waterfront. The famous bronze statue reminded Irene of her adversary, Charlotte. This could be the impetus to lure Lionel into doing her bidding. Irene spat in disgust. "That bitch."

Lionel was startled. "What? How could you not love the *Little Mermaid?* She's the symbol of Copenhagen."

"Don't get me started," she responded with a huff.

Lionel began following the bait by asking, "Seriously, what's the problem?"

"You really want to know?"

"Maybe," he said with hesitation.

"Fine. Let's find someplace we can talk."

At an isolated bench along the tree-lined waterway of Churchill Park,[19] Irene began a tirade. "All my life, my father has groomed me to run his law firm. It was his dream and my nondebatable career path. First, the finest education, along with clerking for two of Philadelphia's best judges. Since getting my master's in criminal law, Father has mentored me in the practice. I've had to work my ass off. I also had to tolerate sexist behavior and accusations of nepotism. Okay, that's fine. I can deal with that crap because someday I'll inherit everything."

Lionel's blank stare suggested he wasn't following all of this, but she didn't care. He was the only person she had ever vented to. The release felt liberating, especially knowing that ranting to a temporary plaything was free from repercussions. And, if she judged him right, the upside potential was huge.

She continued, "Then, along came Miss Fake Tits. It wasn't long before my mom learned he was having an affair, but she didn't feel threatened. She told me the tryst was like letting Father have a shiny new sports car. It was fun for him to play with but would never replace the practical car. That is, until nine months ago when the practical car mysteriously drove into a tree."

"Oh my god. Was your mother hurt?" he asked.

"Worse. Killed instantly. The police ruled it an accident, but I know in my bones Father hired one of his thug clients to tamper with the brakes."

"Could they prove it?"

"Hell no. He pulled every string to bury the investigation before burying her. And now, in six weeks, this conniving witch will become the new, blushing Mrs. Shaw. She'll tolerate the old man's lust until he dies, then get rich by stealing everything from me."

"You've tried talking him out of it?"

"Of course, many times, but the bastard won't listen. He says he loves her and I should too. That was the whole purpose of this summer vacation. It was my chance to get to know Charlotte. He wants my approval. Boy, has that backfired."

Lionel reached out to comfort her. With genuine sincerity, he asked, "What can you do about it?"

"Nothing. I just hope to God the will and prenup will leave me some crumbs. I'm telling you, Lionel, my entire future is screwed. I don't know what to do. I'm frantic." With misty eyes, Irene moved in for an empathetic embrace, then waited for his response while feigning tears. With luck, her dilemma would coincide with his ambitions.

The wait was interminable. Hopefully, he was contemplating a bigger plan than just being a manly shoulder to cry on. She dared not speak first.

"You know," he said cautiously, "in my neighborhood, we live by the motto 'an eye for an eye.' Maybe that's something to think about."

She smiled. The bait was taken. Time to set the hook. Pulling away to confront him, she asked with a manufactured horror, "What are you suggesting?"

"I don't know," he said slowly, then stopped as if deciding whether to cross the line. "Maybe, just maybe, something could happen to the girlfriend's face."

That was all the confirmation Irene needed. The rest of the conversation could be devoted to negotiating the conspiracy details. "You'd do that for me?" she asked coyly.

With a still-cautious tone, he said, "I suppose so." Then he sat upright, as if gaining confidence. "Sure, you're talking to a guy who sledgehammers cattle all day. I'm used to getting my hands bloody."

"That might work," she said absently, as if seriously considering the plan. "But no, wait, there's a big problem with that. Father's libido would soon find another money-grabbing tramp, and I'd be right back where I started. There's got to be a better way."

The silence was deafening as Lionel contemplated his reply.

Did he have the balls to take the next step? Or would he leave her hanging?

"Well," he said before pausing, then cautiously continued, "the other way I can think of is to have the driver of the shiny sports car hit a tree."

Irene reeled back as if shocked. "Are you saying what I think you're saying?"

"Sure, it's the only way to really fix your problem. That's what you want, right?"

She decided to stop acting coy and close the deal. "What would you get out of it? Money?"

He said with intense certainty, "No, citizenship."

"What's that supposed to mean?"

"You're a smart gal. Figure it out." He leaned deep into her space. "Listen, I want out of this hellhole. There's nothing here for me. I want to live in America."

She tried pacifying him by saying, "Well, I know lots of lawyers. Maybe I could find one to help expedite your green card."

"Cut the crap, Irene. That'll take forever, and I won't wait that long. No, I want the fast route, a sure thing. Let's get married." It wasn't a proposal. It was a demand.

"Are you fucking serious? That's never going to happen."

Lionel jumped to his feet. "Then enjoy your life of poverty. See you later."

"Where're you going?"

"I'm leaving, unless you drop this fucking damsel-in-distress act. Listen, I didn't go to your prissy schools, but I'm more street smart than you'll ever be. I can smell a con artist from a mile away. And at this distance, your act smells like cow shit. If you want to become partners, let's talk. Otherwise, piss off."

Irene was flabbergasted. She had grossly underestimated him. He was more intuitive and ballsy than any man she had ever met. It was strangely erotic.

Perhaps this marriage of convenience could be a win-win. She wouldn't have to tolerate marrying some egotistical bastard who always felt superior to women. She'd never have to use her ovaries; kids were wretched and would distort her figure. Nobody would ever have to know about her arrangement with Lionel. Of course, he'd never be her equal, but maybe close. And having a pseudo-partner she could control could come in handy. Best of all, she'd become instantly rich. *Yup, do this.*

Without acknowledging his insults or ultimatum, she said, "From what I remember, it takes about three years after getting married to become a citizen. I propose this be strictly transactional." She added with a sly grin, "With benefits, of course. You can find a job, pay your expenses, and live in the guesthouse of my father's mansion. And a prenup will limit your payout after the divorce. That's the best I can do."

He rolled his eyes – probably for dramatic effect – but she could tell the proposal sounded attractive.

Instead of agreeing, however, he said, "You realize, of course, if you don't hold up your end of the deal, then you'll be the next one hitting a tree."

"I totally understand. Heck, I'd do the same thing."

He studied her for a second before concluding, "Okay, then, I think this will work." He sat down on the bench with a smug look of satisfaction.

"Good. Now put down your damn sledgehammer. My father is no cow at the slaughterhouse. I've seen his law firm defend lots of criminals, and the stupid ones always end up in prison. So this can't be messy, nor some flimsy-looking accident. It has to be done silently, as if he died of natural causes."

"You mean a silentcide?"

She tilted her head at the odd-sounding word, then said, "Exactly."

Chapter Five: Copenhagen, Denmark

Photos 13–19

SIX

"**M**agnificent," Michelle Barton murmured while savoring the intricate details inside Basilique Notre-Dame,[20] the architectural pinnacle of Old Montreal, Canada. During her sixteen years as a silentcide assassin, she and her brother, Chris Davis, had traveled to countless cities. There was no question this interior – with a kaleidoscope of ribbed canopies, Gothic arches, carved balconies, sculptures and columns, plus a spiral pulpit and ornate altar with pinnacles – was among the world's grandest churches. Touring the basilica had been worth the hour-long wait among an annoying throng of summer tourists.

The thirty-six-year-old reluctantly slipped oversized sunglasses back over her deep-blue eyes to partially cover her wholesome, makeup-free face. A droopy sunhat and auburn wig concealed Michelle's long, sandy-blond hair and shadowed her high round cheeks. A billowing smock dress hiding her long-legged figure completed the disguise. The goal was not to be recognized by any of Irene Shaw's henchmen on the remote chance they had discovered her flight into Montreal the night before. Excess caution was always essential to staying alive.

A couple of fingers nonchalantly touched Michelle's, interrupting her focused admiration of the seven-thousand-pipe Casavant organ. "We've gotta go," Ansel Meehan said. His deep voice matched his solid, six-foot build. His grin lit up after blowing a puff of air in her ear. Those engaging, faded-blue eyes sparkled with mischief.

He had always been playful with his little foster sister while sharing a home with her and Chris. Over a period of two years – when she was eight through ten – Ansel had lifted her from the depths of despair after the violent death of the siblings' parents to the happiest and most secure she had ever been. She had idolized Ansel as a mature big brother – he was four years older – then mourned his abrupt disappearance when she and Chris were banished to an Amish farm by Irene Shaw. Unbeknownst to them at the time, Ansel had been sent to another farm. They had all been trained as professional killers.

They hadn't seen each other for twenty-six years. Michelle had assumed Ansel was dead until he unexpectedly showed up near her home in Minneapolis a month ago. Since then, their relationship had grown complicated. She wanted Ansel back in her life but was uncertain if she wanted a friend, another brother, a confidant, a protector or a romantic partner. During the last six days, their feelings had drifted toward amorous, yet a conflicting guilt had prevented them from crossing that threshold.

Michelle doubted Chris would approve. Hell, he absolutely wouldn't approve. But she had told her brother she was going to start asserting her independence to define a better life. He had promised to accept that. She planned to hold Chris to his promise. Her involvement with Ansel would be the first test. The disclosure would probably be contentious.

At the top of the basilica steps, Michelle scanned Place d'Armes[21] for potential threats. The main square was jammed with people, street entertainers and food carts, but no one seemed ominous. Her sweep ended when she spotted Chris standing a hundred feet away in front of the seventeenth-century Saint-Sulpice Seminary,[22] the city's second-oldest building. He was wearing his Ted Collins disguise consisting of a brown wig plus neatly trimmed sideburns and beard.

Michelle raced forward. The embrace was spectacular. She never wanted to let go, even when her hat began tumbling down the street. Who cared? She was ecstatic to see her brother after two violent attempts on his life within less than a week. "God, I'm glad you're alive," she said through tears of happiness.

"You, too," Chris said softly while tightening the hug. "Thanks for coming here so fast."

"Of course," she said. "We're here to help."

Michelle felt a pistol in the back of his belt, concealed by a windbreaker. Chris rarely carried a gun. He must be really nervous, which was totally justified after yesterday's attack in Québec City. She considered saying something about it but didn't.

The emotional moment was interrupted when Ansel walked up, carrying the hat. Chris lunged at his former foster brother. He sucker-punched him on the face and the side of the head. Ansel staggered backward – more surprised than hurt – and assumed a defensive position.

"Chris!" Michelle yelled at her brother's uncharacteristic outburst. "What the hell are you doing?"

While shaking off the knuckle pain, Chris seethed, "That's for his two clandestine meetings with you that were supposed to be kept secret from me. Worse yet, on Monday, he made me listen on the phone while he pretended to shoot you. You have no idea the pain that caused me this week thinking you were dead."

"That's fair," Ansel said, rubbing the red mark emerging from the groomed stubble on his chin. "But if you try it again, be prepared for a bloody fight."

"Stop it, you two," Michelle intervened. "Just settle down and relax. Got it?"

The men unclenched their fists yet remained physically taut, prepared for another round if needed.

Michelle said with disgust, "That was a pitiful way to greet each other after twenty-six years. You'd think a reunion between foster

brothers would be joyous, not a street brawl. Now lower your tes-
tosterone and let's talk this out."

"I'm not going to apologize," Chris said with defiance. "I was sure
he'd killed you. Letting me think that was deplorable."

"It was," Ansel agreed. "One hundred percent deplorable. But in
my defense, Irene insisted I meet Michelle alone to test her loyalty.
And when the two of you started plotting to kill Irene, I was told
in no uncertain terms to kill Michelle or else. Irene's ultimatum
was very clear. But I couldn't do it," Ansel said with a shrug. "That's
when Michelle and I hatched a plan to warn you about the attack
at your home while I fired the gun over the phone. The ruse made
Irene think Michelle was dead and I had followed orders. That gave
us some cover to be on the run for a few days."

"And in all that time," Chris said with an inflamed tone, "you
couldn't call and tell me my sister was alive?"

"We wanted to," Ansel said. "We really did. But we were afraid
our computers and phones, or yours, were compromised. We didn't
want to risk disclosing your location or ours."

Chris seemed unconvinced. "Why the hell should I trust you?"

"Because number one, I didn't kill your sister. And number two,
I asked a Phonoi facilitator to learn if and when Irene tracked you
down. I grew up with Tonya on the farm, so we're best friends. At
great personal risk, she's the one who told me you were going to be
attacked yesterday in Québec City."

Michelle added, "And if Ansel hadn't told me to warn you, then
you and Anna would be dead now. You could at least thank him
for that."

"Thank you," Chris begrudgingly said.

Michelle got more annoyed. "That's the most pitiful display of
appreciation I've ever heard."

"Of course I'm appreciative," Chris said. "But that still doesn't
excuse what he did. Hell, we were the Three Amigos once. As kids,
I remember him saying, 'Us orphans have to stick together because

we're the only family we got.' A trusted family member would've warned us from day one that Irene was gunning for us rather than sneak around behind our backs."

Ansel nodded in shame. "I agree. I messed up, big-time. I hope you can forgive me. I'd like the three of us to trust each other again."

Chris seemed reluctant to accept his apology. "So tell me this. Does Irene think you're still loyal to her or gone AWOL?"

"Probably the latter. I've been radio silent since Monday, so I suspect she's added me to her most-wanted list."

Chris continued the inquisition. "If that's the case, then why aren't you wearing a disguise like us?"

Ansel's only attempt to conceal his identity was a baseball cap pulled tight over his short, wavy black hair. Michelle had observed her foster brother wasn't as innately cautious as she and Chris. Perhaps it was a sense of immortality mixed with defiance and a touch of bravado.

"Because I'm probably the low man on Irene's kill list," Ansel answered. "I doubt there's a big manhunt for me at the moment. On the other hand, Chris, you're enemy number one, especially after killing five of her people this week in self-defense."

Chris stared at his older foster brother as if trying to read his soul. "Okay, I'll buy your answers for now." After another tense pause, he added, "But it'll be a very, very long time before I trust you."

"Yup, that's fair," Ansel said.

While extending his hand, Chris said, "Okay, let's move on."

The men shook. Michelle sensed the gesture was more of a cease-fire than a peace accord. She didn't dare tell Chris anytime soon about her evolving affection for Ansel. That disclosure could rekindle another fight. Perhaps it was best to cool the budding romance until things settled down. Hopefully, Ansel would agree. She tried changing subjects to a safe ground by asking Chris, "Where's Anna? I thought she'd be with you."

"She's back at the hotel sleeping."

Ansel asked with a judgmental tone, "You left her by herself?"

"Yes, she'll be fine," Chris assured him.

Michelle asked, "Did you tell her anything about who you really are?"

"Yeah, mostly everything."

"Seriously?" Ansel asked, looking perplexed.

"I had to. She was already guessing the worst, so I had to start telling her the truth."

"And you really think she's not talking to the police right now?"

Chris's brow twitched with irritation. "She promised she wouldn't."

"And you believe her?"

"Absolutely," Chris said with indignation. "I trust her more than I do you."

"Boys, boys, boys, dial it back a notch, will you?" Michelle's admonishment sent them into neutral corners, at least for the moment. Then she asked, "How's Anna doing after yesterday's ordeal?"

"Traumatized, of course," Chris said. "Who wouldn't be? And she's really scared she'll be attacked again."

Michelle asked, "Are you sure yesterday's assassins were also targeting her?"

"No question about it. I found surveillance photos of us marked Targets A and B on one of the gunmen."

"But that still doesn't make sense if George Henniker ordered the hit and he's been dead for a week, unless …" Michelle paused while thinking. "Unless, like Irene said, George wasn't the client after all."

"No," Chris said. "He definitely was. There's no question about it. Irene's lie is just part of her endless mind games and chronic need for dominance. She probably also hopes I'll have to watch Anna die first."

"What I don't understand is," Ansel said, "if you're so worried about another attack soon, maybe you should have driven further away than Montreal."

Chris snapped back, "Or maybe I had to get the damn car off the road in case the police were searching for it."

Michelle was incredulous. "Are you two going to bicker over everything? For God's sake, you're not grade schoolers anymore. Grow up. If the four of us are going to survive this ordeal, we're going to have to work together. So cut the crap. Now."

Chapter Six: Montreal, Canada

Photos 20–22

SEVEN

Saturday

Anna Monteiro was trapped in a cocoon of crippling fear. Since checking into adjoining hotel rooms the previous afternoon, Chris had honored her request to be alone. The moment he closed the connecting door, anxiety attacked with a vengeance. Rapid breathing. Pounding heart. Twitching muscles. The sweats with an uncontrollable sense of pending doom.

For over an hour, Anna shivered on the couch. A drink from the minibar tasted caustic. None of the food from room service was appetizing except a few green grapes. A hot shower was soothing, but the grim helplessness returned before she toweled dry.

Trying to sleep was hell. After turning off the lights, the silent blackness swallowed her into an ominous abyss. Turning the lights on offered little relief. No position in bed, no attempt to think pleasant thoughts, and no pleas for sleep blocked the gruesome memories of gunfire, panic, screaming, and blood oozing on the boardwalk. The mental onslaught cycled over and over on an endless loop all night. Equally traumatic was trying to process the horrifying revelations about Chris and the threat of being killed by relentless assassins. When she rarely slept, the nightmares were horrid.

Anna awoke buried deep below the covers curled tight in a fetal position. The bedsheets were damp. After a few moments of consciousness, nausea was overwhelming. She rushed to the bathroom, dropped to the floor, felt her stomach churn and her throat contract before vomiting. The third bout caused a back spasm.

A cold washcloth helped some. She couldn't brush her teeth because her toiletries and luggage had been stranded in their Québec City hotel room. Chris arranged to have their belongings sent to Longfellow BioSciences, her former employer in Cambridge near Boston. He also promised to take her shopping for replacement clothes. For now, she wore a robe and used a mini bottle of mouthwash to rid herself of the putrid taste of vomit.

Anna dreaded looking at the ghastly image in the mirror. The black pixie hair resembled a bird's nest. Brown eyes were red and puffy. Skin tone was gray. Her small athletic figure was slumped and shaking. She was too exhausted to cry.

While plodding back to bed, she saw a note had been slipped below the door of the connecting rooms. The message read:

> Good morning –
> Hope you're feeling better. I have some errands to run.
> Will return by 1:00. Feel free to order room service. I'll
> see you soon.
> Chris

Strange, but she had never seen his handwriting before. The cursive penmanship reflected Chris: precise and organized. Looking at the clock radio revealed he would return in less than an hour. Was this her chance to escape?

She gently knocked on the connecting door, then cautiously turned the knob and entered his room. Chris wasn't there. The main door to her room was locked from the inside. Outside was a Do Not Disturb sign. He must have placed it there. The hallway was empty. Running away would be easy, unless this was some kind of trick.

Her pulse elevated while she contemplated the decision. Then another wave of nausea provided the answer. She crawled into bed, clutched the pillow and tried controlling the anxiety. The barrage was relentless. The room was quiet and safe, yet every nerve was raw. There had to be a way to break the self-destructive anguish.

Anna turned on the TV. The CTV Noon News was already in progress. Against a backdrop of the Centre Block, the main building of the Canadian parliamentary complex, a solemn anchor said, "In regional news, the body of US Senator Richard Tomlin will be flown home to the state of Wisconsin today. As we reported yesterday, the senator died unexpectedly in Ottawa during a meeting regarding the future of the Keystone XL Pipeline among a contingency of Canadian and US lawmakers. The cause of death is unknown. The prime minister has ordered all flags be flown at half-mast in honor of Senator Tomlin."

Then a video montage of police cars, ambulances, frightened crowds and fluttering police tape followed. "In Québec City, authorities are still investigating yesterday's horrific shooting on Terrasse Dufferin. Three people were killed and two injured. One of the unidentified victims is listed in critical yet stable condition. Unconfirmed sources suggest the three victims were professional ..."

Anna turned off the TV, stumbled to the bathroom and retched. The cold toilet bowl on her cheek provided some solace, yet she struggled to regulate her breathing.

"Stop this!" she shouted. "Stop it now! Get a grip on yourself. Do something."

She did. There was no way Chris was going to see her in this pitiful condition. Anna put on yesterday's clothes. They were a wrinkled mess but better than standing around in a hotel robe. There was nothing on the room service menu worth vomiting over. She needed comforting. She needed to talk with Mom.

Instinctively, she reached for her mobile phone, then froze. Chris had warned her to keep the cell off because Irene's team may be able to trace it. The same rule applied to credit cards. He claimed Irene had found their location in Québec City when Anna used a card to check in to the hotel. Tracking phones and credit cards was a common theme on TV and in movies, yet it was hard to imagine such technology existed among a network of assassins.

Was this a Chris power play for control? Screw it. The hotel phone is probably safe.

Anna dialed the number and anxiously waited for her mother to pick up.

"Hello."

"It's me," Anna said. She felt better already.

"Hi, honey," Donna said. "It's great hearing your voice. What's up?"

"Not much, just wanted to say hi. Where are you and Dad now?" When Anna's parents weren't living at their homes at Cape Cod, Naples, Aspen or Boston, they were exploring the world.

"We're still at the Cape. We hate missing summers here; you know that. How's work going?" was Mom's standard question.

Anna hesitated. She didn't want a long, dragged-out conversation about another upsetting topic. What she needed was mindless chatter to block the angst of reality. But she couldn't say everything was fine. "Well, um, Longfellow was acquired on Monday by Fármaco, the big cancer pharma company."

"Does that create new opportunities for you?"

Anna nibbled on a nub of a fingernail. "Well, no, I was laid off."

"Oh, honey, I'm so, so sorry." Donna's tone switched from sympathetic to indignant. "That's gratitude for you, isn't it? You gave everything you had to them as a startup, then they cashed in and cut you loose. That's unconscionable." Next, the worried mother kicked in. "How are you doing?"

"Fine. I'll be fine," Anna said, justifying the white lie. "It gives me a chance to think about my career."

"Don't worry, honey. This is no reflection on you. I mean that. Companies will line up to hire you." Then Donna asked with concern, "In the meantime, are you going to be okay? I mean, moneywise."

Anna chose not to explain how her stock and severance package was worth about a million dollars. Given Anna's current problems, she was in no mood to hear Mom's celebratory zeal. "Yes, I have some money tucked away. Don't worry about that."

"Well, if you need some cash to tide you over, there's no shame in asking, hear me?"

"Thanks, Mom. But really, I'm fine. I took this week off to explore Québec province."

"That's great, honey. What a lovely part of Canada. Your dad and I love it there." The worried mom returned. "But, oh my gosh, I hope you weren't anywhere near that awful shooting in Québec City. It's been all over the national news."

"I heard about that too, but no, I'm fine. Really." *Okay, that counted as a bald-faced lie.*

"Well, good. The trip should help clear your head. Have a wonderful time. Say, I can't talk long because we're entertaining guests."

"I'm sorry. Why didn't you tell me you were busy?"

"No problem, you know I always love hearing from you. Say, before I go, did you get my email yesterday about a sergeant somebody – sorry, but I can't remember his name – from the San Francisco police calling? He's been trying to reach you and wants to talk again about the death of your friend from the cruise. What was her name again?"

"Jessica."

"Yes, that's it. Anyway, he'd like you to call early next week. He also needs to speak to that nice young man you met on the cruise."

Anna's pulse spiked. Why was the recreational drug overdose of her friend causing such a lengthy investigation? Was Jessica's family still implying she had something to do with it? And why question Chris? He only met Jessica one time on the ship. "I got your email, Mom," Anna said but hadn't because her laptop had been left behind in the Québec City hotel room.

"That's good. Okay, honey, sorry but I really have to go. Great talking with you. Have fun. And if you get the chance, please send a postcard. Love you lots and lots."

"Love you too, Mom. Say hi to Dad for me."

"Will do. Bye."

The disconnecting call cut Anna's lifeline. Now she had something else to worry about.

Anna felt captive. Claustrophobic. She desperately needed fresh air.

She cautiously looked down the hallway. It was empty. Each step she took from the room until exiting the hotel, she worried about being attacked again. On the street, she was on nervous alert for anyone suspicious. Anxiety was the only guardian.

Two blocks away, she saw a pair of patrolling policemen. She squeezed her eyes, gritted her teeth, hesitated, then decided to approach them.

EIGHT

Saturday

I rene Shaw glared with disdain at the full-length painting of her father. He was a vain son of a bitch. So was her grandfather, portrayed on the other side of the extravagant mahogany fireplace in the Ops Room of her mansion in Elkins Park, a northern suburb of Philadelphia. She scoffed at the men's pompous smiles. Irene had grown the Shaw legacy far beyond their wildest dreams. If they were alive today, imagine their shame at being bested by a woman.

A glance in the mirror revealed an errant gray hair on her black Dior dress. The diamond necklace and matching bracelet glistened below the Waterford chandelier. The timeless power outfit was perfect for the intimidating conversation ahead. She loved holding court.

When there was a knock on the door, she said, "Just a minute," while hustling behind the Baroque desk. This position would be as threatening to the accused as if appearing before a hanging judge. Control equaled intimidation. "Enter."

Her manservant, Pierre, opened the door and announced, "Your guests have arrived, Ms. Shaw." After a wave of her hand, he stepped aside, allowing four men to cross the threshold.

"Thank you for responding to my summons, gentlemen," she said gravely.

Everyone knew where they were expected to stand. Front and center were the leaders of her two assassin divisions. Flanking them from behind were her bodyguard, Frank, and chauffer, John. All of them wore black suits with white shirts and conservative ties. The expensive attire did little to soften their brawn.

Irene opened with a saccharine smile. "Let's start today's chitchat with you, shall we?" she said to Jürgen van Oorschot, the head of Phonoi, the group who specialized in violent death. "Anything new to report?"

"I'm happy to say we've located Ms. Monteiro," Jürgen said. His uneasy stance belied his enthusiastic announcement. Perspiration was beading on his broad forehead and upper lip.

"And how, pray tell, did you do that?" Irene asked.

"We intercepted a call she made to her mother and traced the origin back to a hotel in Montreal."

Irene was delighted by the news yet remained stoic. There was no way she was going to give Jürgen credit for finally doing his job, especially after his deplorable management of the shootout in Québec City. "And is Chris with her?"

"Ms. Monteiro didn't reference him by name, nor are any of his known aliases registered at the hotel, but we assume they're together."

"You realize," Irene said, "that the word 'assume' makes an 'ass out of you and me.'" She chastised herself for using the worn-out proverb. Her retort should have been pithier. "What has Ansel said about it?"

"Nothing so far," Jürgen responded.

Irene raised one eyebrow with displeasure. "Have you reached out to him?"

"Of course, Ms. Shaw. But we haven't heard from him yet."

Irene snapped back, "He should've responded immediately. So where's he now?"

"His last known location was Milwaukee."

With growing irritation, Irene said, "I explicitly asked where he is now, not where he was."

"I'm not sure," Jürgen said sheepishly. "He turned off his cell phone and laptop last night, so we haven't been able to track him today."

"Isn't that against strict protocol?"

"Normally, yes. But remember, Ansel has to maintain his cover that he's severed all ties with you and Phonoi."

That seemed like a plausible explanation, but Irene wasn't satisfied. "Is there a chance he's defected?"

"No, ma'am. Based on his daily reports this week, he continues to gain Michelle's trust while she thinks they're successfully hiding from you. She's also unaware if Chris is dead or alive."

"That's preposterous," Irene countered with a sneer. "Those siblings would stop at nothing to learn each other's fate. They'd find some way to communicate. So if Ansel had been doing his job, he should've been the first to learn when Chris was in Québec City and now Montreal."

"That's true," Jürgen said, "but only if Michelle has been talking with Chris. We have no evidence that's the case."

"Just because you're unaware doesn't mean it's not happening. In fact, Mr. van Oorschot, isn't it also possible Michelle is withholding information from Ansel or, worse yet, they're now working together?"

"Perhaps," Jürgen said weakly while staring at his feet.

"*Perhaps*," she repeated his word in mockery. "Or perhaps you should stop using the royal 'we' and admit you're solely responsible for this untenable situation. In my opinion, this is another example of your habitual incompetence, isn't that right?" Irene relished watching the giant man squirm.

Jürgen visibly struggled over how to answer the question. He tried sidestepping the insult by saying, "I have no reason to doubt

Ansel. In fact, so far, he's been implementing your instructions to the letter, Ms. Shaw."

Since learning Chris had talked Michelle into plotting to kill her, Irene had hoped to salvage Michelle as an asset. She was a consummate rule follower, incredibly reliable, and a masterful silentcide assassin. Michelle's only Achilles' heel was her emotional dependence on her brother. Irene had hoped to shift Michelle's reliance to Ansel so they could potentially become partners after Chris was dead. That goal was unlikely from the start but worth pursuing. It seemed increasingly improbable now. Yet Irene needed hard evidence of Ansel's betrayal before deciding to kill the pair, along with Chris and Anna.

In a voice reserved for crushing the credibility of a hostile witness at a trial, Irene said, "Mr. van Oorschot, I'm going to ask you this one last time, and I advise you to consider your answer carefully. Are you one hundred percent certain Ansel remains loyal to me while building Michelle's complete trust?"

"Yes, Ms. Shaw," he said without hesitation. "I'm absolutely confident of it. He's one of my best."

Irene had learned everything she needed to know. It was time to deal with her utter disdain for Jürgen. "Your confidence means nothing to me, Mr. van Oorschot. Frankly, less than nothing. And from what I've witnessed recently, being among your best is a very, very low bar. Your continued ineptness cost me two people during that hideous gunfight with Chris in Saint Paul. He also managed to kill three more in Québec City despite an overwhelming ambush that you personally orchestrated." Irene thrust her hand forward while continuing her rant. "That's five dead assets. Five! Count 'em. One, two, three, four, five. Those deaths are on you."

Jürgen winced before saying, "Yes, Ms. Shaw. I take personal responsibility for those mishaps."

Irene cackled while leaning back with arms crossed. "Isn't that swell. You're finally taking personal responsibility. But I think calling them mishaps is a bit of a misnomer. A more apt description is major fuckups. Don't you agree?" She relished watching her victim cower.

Through a tortured expression, he managed to say, "Yes, Ms. Shaw."

"And by the way, did you ever find that dolt who surrendered his firearm to Chris in Québec City?"

"No, Ms. Shaw, but we're still looking for him."

"That's nice," Irene said with scorn. "Well, I'll tell you what, Mr. van Oorschot, you can stop worrying about it. That's no longer your problem."

"I'm sorry, Ms. Shaw, but I don't understand." Yet his fretting eyes suggested her doomsday message was abundantly clear.

"Of course you don't, dear. You have a chronic inability to grasp the obvious. So let me explain this in very simple terms. You're officially relieved of your duties." While Jürgen babbled something in his defense, she turned her attention to the bodyguard and the chauffeur. "Frank, John, would you please escort Mr. van Oorschot outside to the inner courtyard?"

"Yes, Ms. Shaw," they said in tandem while extracting their pistols from their suit coats.

Jürgen began pleading when two SIG P229s were aimed toward his skull. "Ms. Shaw, I know I screwed up. But please let me fix this. Please!"

"That won't be necessary, dear," she said in a condescending tone, then chastised him. "Now don't lose your last shred of dignity by begging. It's most unbecoming of a professional. I suggest you exit like a man."

Irene watched as Jürgen was ushered across the room through a French door. She mentally gave him credit for accepting his fate. Watching someone plea for mercy was so distasteful.

When the patio doors slammed shut, the Afghan hound lifted his head from the couch. With his mouth agape and his tail between his legs, the dog stood to peer out a window to the courtyard, then flinched at the single gunshot.

In an attempt to sooth the distressed pet, Irene whispered, "Now, now, Brutus. Everything's fine. Go back to sleep."

The dog's chocolate-brown eyes seemed alarmed. Despite his large size, the hound was very sensitive, one of his many endearing qualities. Brutus cocked his head, whimpered, circled twice, then lay down again. Irene hoped the dog would not need to resume the anti-anxiety meds.

Without further acknowledgment of what happened, Irene turned toward Wolfgang König, who had patiently stood at attention during the ordeal. He was the leader of Thanatos, the division named after the winged Greek god of nonviolent death. The early-forties brute had short black hair, a flat nose dominating a square face with protruding chin, and deep-set cruel eyes. He was an ideal mercenary: efficient, ruthless and subservient.

"Wolfgang, my dear. Thanks for your patience. It seems I'm in kind of a pickle here." She asked a rhetorical question, "Can I count on your help?"

"Of course, Ms. Shaw. I'd be honored to help in any way I can."

"Excellent. Until Mr. van Oorschot's replacement is identified, I'd like you to lead both groups. Your first priority is to clean up your predecessor's mess. Start by learning the status of Ansel. I want you to determine, without a shadow of a doubt, if he's loyal or gone rogue."

"Yes, Ms. Shaw."

"But if you learn he and Michelle are in cahoots or, worse yet, they're in Montreal and Ansel doesn't report it, then talk with me first but expect their employment will be permanently severed. But it has to be done with finesse this time. Those god-awful gunfights are bad for business. Understood?"

"Perfectly."

"At the same time, find some way to quickly take care of Chris and his pathetic girlfriend without losing more of my people. Can you do that?"

"Yes, Ms. Shaw. One of my silentcide specialists is still in Ottawa after dispensing with Senator Tomlin. I'll make the assignment immediately."

"Excellent. Speaking of which, it goes without saying how important that commission is to terminate the other US senators. You must not lose focus on it. For any reason."

"Of course," he said dutifully.

"Finally, review all of the current commissions of Phonoi and make certain they are implemented flawlessly. We can't disappoint any of our clients while we're busy doing our housekeeping."

Irene walked around the desk and patted Wolfgang's broad shoulder. "I know this will be a burden, and your role as Preceptor on the farm may temporarily suffer as a result. But I have full confidence in you. I promise not to hover. Just don't disappoint me."

"You won't be disappointed, Ms. Shaw." He paused before asking, "Is there anything else?"

When she stroked his ruddy cheek, Wolfgang flinched. "No, dear, that's all for now."

He nodded, then walked out.

She glanced out a window. In the courtyard, John and Frank were rolling Jürgen's body in plastic. There were splatters of blood on two of the dozen white lion sculptures at the base of the marble fountain. Did they need to be reminded to clean up that mess? No, they were inherently meticulous. This was such an untidy business at times.

The Afghan hound stirred when Irene sat on the leather couch. She used a long floppy ear to clear some crud from his tired brown eyes. His snout was completely gray. Her once flamboyant puppy was getting lethargic and senile. He had been a gift to herself on her sixtieth birthday. "Such a good boy," she cooed while stroking his head. She couldn't bear the thought of losing her only remaining companion, but that time would arrive soon. Hopefully, the dog would die peacefully in his sleep.

Her thoughts drifted toward her former companion. She missed Lionel. Mourning his passing was painful. One week ago today, she had ordered the execution of the bloated, drooling vegetable in a wheelchair. One bullet to the back of the head. He did not deserve to further endure his undignified existence. Lionel had suffered enough for the eight years since inhaling a debilitating poison during a botched silentcide. The euthanasia had been an act of love. The loss was still gut-wrenching.

NINE

Walking down Notre-Dame Street East through the center of Old Montreal was tense. Typically, Chris carried his Nikon D850 when visiting a foreign city. He would have preferred to be photographing historic landmarks they passed such as Montreal City Hall.[23] Instead, the camera had been replaced with a SIG P229 behind his belt.

Equally unsettling was the presence of Ansel Meehan. The last time Chris had seen his former foster brother – his real name was Kevin twenty-six-years ago – was the summer before Ansel entered high school. As a sixth grader, Chris had admired his muscles, athletic ability, relaxed charm and good-natured smile. Chris wanted to be just like him, versus being the scrawny kid that bullies called "the Albino."

Ansel still had those enviable traits. Hell, he was also downright handsome. Yet Chris sensed something was off. Chris had stayed alive by trusting his gut. Also seared into his survival instincts was the first lesson Irene Shaw had taught him on the Amish farm. She had said, "Never trust anyone, regardless of how well you think you know them."

Besides, why had Michelle brought Ansel to Montreal? The conspiracy against Irene was their mission. They didn't need him. And the stakes were too high to partner with someone suspicious. Chris reluctantly decided to give Ansel some slack, if only for Michelle's sake, but the leash would be short.

There was an eerie silence as the threesome entered Chris's hotel and rode up the elevator. The walk down the hall was edgy. Ansel had repeatedly contended it was a mistake leaving Anna unattended. As Chris found his room key, Ansel asked for the second time, "You sure this isn't a trap?" When the question went unanswered, Ansel readied his Glock 17. Tensions spiked as Chris opened the door.

The room was empty. "I told you so," Chris said. "Now put down the gun."

"Not until you check out next door."

With disgust, Chris said, "If the first thing Anna sees is that damn gun, she's going to freak out."

Ansel's compromise was to hide the weapon behind his back.

Chris gently knocked on the door of the connecting room. "Anna," he said. "It's me." There was no answer. As he cautiously pushed it open with his foot, Ansel readied his weapon again. Chris reached back for his. The creaking hinge was unnerving.

The room was a mess. Trays of uneaten food. Piles of Kleenex near the couch. Unmade bed. Crumpled robe. The distinct smell of vomit. Chris chastised himself for not being there when she needed emotional support.

"Where's your girl?" Ansel asked with apprehension. "You said she'd stay put."

"Look around here," Chris snapped back. "She's obviously traumatized. I'm sure she just stepped out for some fresh air or something."

"Or ran out to call the cops."

Chris asserted, "I told you before, she wouldn't do that."

"Listen," Michelle said calmly to her brother, "I know you have confidence in her. I get that. But with all the pressure she's under, she's liable to do anything."

Ansel added, "And I'm not going to stand around waiting to see what that 'anything' might be."

"Then go," Chris said with ill temper. "The both of you. I'm waiting until she gets back."

When they heard a key card being inserted into the slot, Ansel swiveled into a shooter's stance. Chris jumped in front of his sister first, then assumed the same position. Both handguns were aimed at the door. They braced for a shootout. Chris regulated his breathing to assure an accurate kill shot.

The door slowly opened. Anticipation spiked. As Anna entered, she screamed. The screech was horrific. In horror, she turned and escaped down the hallway.

Chris handed his SIG to Michelle before running after Anna. She was frantically hitting the down button on the elevator. Her eyes were ablaze. He tried approaching in a nonthreatening way. His hands gestured to calm down, that she was safe. She studied his face as if reading his intentions, then began to regain her composure.

Chris said to her in a low voice, "I'm so sorry we scared you. Are you okay?"

"No, Chris," she said with distress. "I'm petrified. What do you expect? I just stared at two guns aimed at my head. What the hell was that all about?"

With a contrite tone, he said, "When your room was empty, we thought maybe you had gone to the police and they were storming the room."

"And then what? Another gunfight. Jesus!" She shook her head with disdain. "Trust me, Chris, I thought about going to the police. In fact, I almost did. But I remembered you saying they couldn't protect me for long, so why escalate things? I also promised you I wouldn't. And unlike some people I know, when I say something, I don't lie."

The chastisement was well deserved. There was nothing appropriate to say in his defense. The only option was to endure the berating.

With elevated intensity, she said, "And I seem to recall you said

I was free to go anytime I pleased. So I used one of my get-out-of-jail-free cards. But if you must know where I went" – she held up a small white plastic bag – "I went on a wild shopping spree at the pharmacy to buy extravagant things like toothpaste. Do you want to conduct a search?"

"No," he said with downcast eyes.

"And another thing," Anna said as the tirade continued, "who the hell are those people in my room?"

"My sister and former foster brother."

"What are they doing here?"

"They've come to help. I can't fight Irene alone. I need them. Frankly, we need them."

"When were you going to tell me they were coming?"

"We just made the arrangements late yesterday afternoon after you said you wanted privacy in your room. I respected that, and we haven't talked since. Did you want to go back so I can introduce you?"

She reluctantly agreed.

When they went inside Anna's hotel room, Michelle and Ansel were in a relaxed conversation. The unease had dropped precipitously. Fortunately, the guns were out of sight. Chris said, "Anna Monteiro, this is my sister, Michelle Barton." Michelle flashed a welcoming smile while the two women shook hands. "And this is Ansel Meehan, my former foster brother."

Ansel's greeting was rigid. While staring at the plastic bag Anna was carrying, he asked, "Were you out shopping?"

"Yes," she responded as if no further explanation was needed.

He said, "I hope you didn't use your credit card."

Anna stiffened. "No," she assured him. "Chris warned me not to."

Ansel replied, "Good, because that's how they traced you to Québec City."

She became irate. "Had I known at the time that assassins were trying to find me, maybe I would've paid for the hotel in cash."

"Okay, okay," Chris said while stepping between them. "Things are getting off on the wrong foot. We're all kind of jumpy here. Ansel, can you give us a minute?"

Michelle supported her brother by saying to Ansel, "Why don't you go next door to Chris's room and we'll be there in a little while."

After Ansel left, Anna turned to Chris. "What's his problem?"

"Nothing," Chris answered. "He's just worried Irene will find us again. So forgive him if he came off a bit brash."

"If you ask me," Anna said, "I'd call him rude. He sure makes a lousy first impression."

Michelle tried being peacemaker again. "Once you get to know him, I'm sure you'll like him. He's a good guy."

Anna's brow tightened. "Am I right in assuming he's also an assassin?"

Michelle's acknowledgment was almost imperceptible.

"And that's your definition of a good guy? Because that's not what I'd call it." Her denunciation hung suspended.

Chris was proud of Anna. Despite the traumatizing situation, she had no reservations about speaking her mind. Her inner strength was one of many traits he respected. He had never met someone so self-assured.

While putting the pharmacy bag down on a coffee table, Anna barely broke eye contact with Michelle. Anna slightly cocked her head as if struggling with a thought, then blurted out, "Have we met before?"

Michelle's evasive answer was, "Yes."

"On the cruise, right?" Anna snapped her fingers. "Yes, that's it. But where?" she asked herself. "I've got it, you were that goth woman I talked with at the pool."

Again, Michelle simply said, "Yes."

Anna stepped closer as if facing off with an adversary. "So all that ghastly makeup was just a disguise. While you were chatting me up, you were actually conducting surveillance."

"That's right," Michelle said with a hint of contrition, probably feeling guilty that she had actually been trying to poison Anna at the time.

"I see compulsive lying runs in your family." Anna then spun around to Chris. "Why didn't you tell me your sister was on the cruise?"

"It was implied when I told you she was my partner."

"That's bullshit, Chris. I explicitly told you not to withhold anything."

"I swear to you, I'm not. We only talked about a half hour in the car before you fell asleep with exhaustion. There wasn't time to tell you everything. This is complicated."

"No, 'complicated' is a relationship status on Facebook. This one is hell. A living hell. I've slept with an assassin. A few tried killing me and more are on the way. And now I'm surrounded by two more. This just keeps getting better and better. And then you have the audacity to ask if I'm okay?"

The silence in the room was deafening.

Anna's fists pressed against her mouth, as if stifling the urge to scream again. Her eyes were closed tight. She rocked nervously from foot to foot. Chris sensed she was on the verge of a breakdown. It was terrifying to watch and to be so helpless.

After a moment to regain her composure, Anna rubbed her face, then stood tall. While glaring at Chris and Michelle, she asked, "What happens next?"

Chris reluctantly said, "We don't know. We haven't had time to develop a plan yet."

"Well, why don't the three of you stay in the next room until you figure this out. In the meantime, just leave me alone. All I want to do is brush my teeth and go back to bed."

Chapter Nine: Montreal, Canada

Photo 23

TEN

CHICAGO, ILLINOIS
Thirty-Six Years Ago

I rene Shaw was intrigued by the invitation to a one-hour meeting in Chicago after receiving an anonymous call at her law firm promising a half-million-dollar case. High-profile criminals tended to be cautious and cryptic before retaining a defense attorney. Talking to an intermediary who was short on facts yet high on urgency was not unusual.

A first-class paper ticket arrived by courier that afternoon. Early the next morning, after landing at O'Hare, a private helicopter whisked her to Meigs Field Airport at the eastern edge of downtown. A driver took her less than a mile to Adler Planetarium,[24] put the Lincoln Town Car in park and handed her a pager. "Take this," he said, "and wait for instructions. By the way, you'll have to go outside because the skyscrapers interfere with reception."

Irene stepped out of the car and into a puddle of icy slush. "Shit," she cursed, knowing her red-soled leather pumps would be ruined. Standing at the tip of Northerly Island[25] along the shore of Lake Michigan, she was assaulted by a frigid mist and raw wind. Hairs from her French bun flapped wildly. Makeup began running. The stylish yet thin designer coat might as well have been a sieve. "Screw this," she mumbled and was about to call it quits when the pager dinged. It simply read: Shedd Aquarium.[26]

When getting back in the car, she demanded, "Turn up the damn heat."

"It won't make any difference," the driver said while pointing. "Your next stop is about two blocks away."

Again, she endured the bitter windchill for about five minutes. The insufferable delay was repeated outside of the Field Museum of Natural History.[27] Her fingers and toes were stiffening. Her polished, professional appearance resembled a drowned rat. She shivered from the cold and bristled with rage when a stretch limo pulled up beside her. The tinted window on the driver's side rolled down. "Ms. Shaw?" the man asked.

"Yes," she said through chattering teeth.

He jumped out, performed a cursory pat down – that was infuriating – then opened the side door. "Please enter," he said.

There was no ladylike way to get inside. She hiked up her dress, struggled not to hit her head, and flopped down on a leather seat facing two white-haired men wearing three-piece suits. The bastards looked warm and comfy. She looked like hell. "Was that some kind of damn endurance test?" she bellowed. "Or are you both sadistic?"

The eldest, who resembled a retired banker, emitted a chuckle. "We apologize. We expected your driver to be the one to wait outside, not you. He will be appropriately admonished."

Irene suspected the humiliation had been designed to demonstrate their dominance. "That's swell," she snapped back. "In the meantime, I'm suffering from hypothermia here."

He leaned back and knocked on the privacy window. "Harold, before pulling away, do you have a blanket for Ms. Shaw?"

"Yes, sir."

While the driver fetched a blanket, the first man turned up the cabin heat. The second poured some coffee. She used the time to assess the potential clients. They smelled of old money. They were nearly twice her age.

She had come this far and survived the tribulation. There was no sense pissing them off before hearing what they had to say. But she was going to gain control and remain in charge. "So what's with all this cloak-and-dagger crap? Couldn't we have met in your office?"

"No," the first man said flatly.

"Why not?"

"Because this meeting never happened. And we had to make sure you weren't being followed or wearing a recording device."

"I'm sure you've heard of attorney-client privilege," she said with a condescending bite as the limo entered Grant Park. "I'm bound to keep our conversation confidential."

"That's nice in theory. But we're not taking any chances. By the way, I am Mr. X. And this is Mr. Z." The latter resembled a cerebral, boring accountant.

Irene said, "I have to tell you, all of this is ridiculous. A first-year research clerk on my staff could identify your real names in about ten minutes."

Without responding, Mr. X opened a briefcase, pulled out a manila envelope and handed it to Irene. She undid the string on the flap and looked inside. She was astonished.

"That's one hundred thousand in US municipal bearer bonds," he said matter-of-factly. "They're unregistered and untraceable. They're yours if you assure us of absolute anonymity. I'll give you another if this meeting goes well and we reach an agreement regarding your assignment. Finally, upon successful completion of your services, there are three identical packages earmarked for you. Now then, will you accept our apologies for your earlier inconvenience? If so, let's talk."

They had Irene's full attention. "I'm listening."

Mr. X leaned forward with elbows on his knees while entering the negotiation phase as a consummate executive. His body language was poised yet intense. "A high-level acquaintance of ours has put us in a compromising position. We have very few options to resolve this unfortunate predicament, and all of them are costly and frankly unsettling."

"Then I assume your acquaintance needs excellent defense counsel like myself?"

"That is one alternative we considered but probably the least attractive option. No, we'd like to avail ourselves of your other expertise."

She instantly knew where this conversation was headed. Listening to his cryptic words was entertaining, but she wanted him to spit it out. She had no intention of blinking first. "I'm afraid you'll have to be a bit more specific," she said while sipping the hot coffee and savoring the warmth on her fingers.

Mr. X sighed before trying again. "We understand you have a unique ability to make unsavory problems go away quickly and discreetly."

"Meaning?"

Mr. X became annoyed. "Ms. Shaw, with all due respect, I have zero tolerance for you playing coy. We must have complete deniability. So either acknowledge what I'm asking, or I'll have Harold dump you back into the cold."

"I understand," she said, knowing he wanted someone dead. This aspect of her law practice was gaining popularity among her desperate criminal clientele.

He flashed a Cheshire grin. "Good. Now I sense we're on the same page."

She forced a return smile while wondering if Mr. Z was ever going to join the conversation or just sit there with a blank stare. "So does this acquaintance have a name?"

Mr. X handed her another envelope from the briefcase. Inside was a color 8x10 photo of a distinguished elderly man wearing a black cassock with a scarlet fascia, zucchetto and shoes. "This is Cardinal McPherson," he said somberly. "During his long tenure with the Church, he's ... well, let's just say His Eminence has demonstrated an affinity for young, vulnerable people. Until recently, his history of indiscretions has been contained. That's about to change. Settlements with nondisclosure agreements are no longer adequate. Reassigning him to the Vatican leaves the festering problem here. We're seeking a permanent solution."

"This sounds like a Church problem."

"It is, but they're buried in denial and resist proactive solutions."

"Then why does it matter to you?"

"Let's just say Mr. Z and I represent a concerned group who make frequent contributions to Sunday collection plates. We'd like to see our financial interests continue to support the Church's good works and not be squandered on frivolous and scandalous litigation."

"That's most noble of you," Irene said, unable to resist the verbal jab. After a prolonged sip of coffee, she asked, "Is there a timeframe?"

"Yes, two weeks."

Irene raised an eyebrow at the impossible deadline, then said, "That's tight but doable."

"Good," he said, leaning back to relax. "Any other questions?"

"Can I ask who referred me?"

"No, you may not," he said.

"Then how do I know this isn't some kind of trap?"

He displayed impeccable teeth. "Like you said, ask your industrious research clerk to check us out."

They had the upper hand. The cards were close to their chest. But she was being paid well to take the risk and be subservient. "Okay, then," was all she had to say to seal the deal.

"Then we have an agreement," Mr. X said with a self-satisfied smirk. He gave her another envelope of bearer bonds. "The third envelope will be delivered when the assignment is finished. Two more are yours only if your resolution is done with flawless discretion and without any – and I mean zero – repercussions of any kind within three months. Am I clear?"

"Very."

"Good, then our meeting is concluded. We will not meet again."

Mr. X knocked on the privacy window again. After it slid down, he said, "Harold, we're done here." Then facing Irene, he added, "We'll drop you off in just a minute. Another car is following behind and will pick you up immediately. No waiting this time. You'll be back to O'Hare soon. By the way, how was the coffee?"

"Bitter," she said, "but at least it was warm."

"Marvelous," was the last word he spoke.

They rode in awkward silence across the Michigan Avenue Bridge.[28] As she stepped out in front of the Tribune Tower, Mr. Z surprisingly spoke. "Nice meeting you, Irene."

✦✦✦

After landing in Philadelphia, Irene returned home. She showered, reapplied her makeup and slipped into a one-shoulder red cocktail dress with stiletto heels. Then she grabbed a chilled bottle of Dom Pérignon from the wine cellar along with the two manila envelopes.

Normally, Irene would have summoned Lionel to the mansion. But there was something inherently raunchy about visiting her ex-husband at the guesthouse. She burst through the front door unannounced. He was sitting at the kitchen table, reading the sports section of the *Philadelphia Inquirer* while sipping his customary end-of-day Jack Daniel's. He looked divine wearing faded blue jeans and a black muscle shirt.

Lionel's eyes swept over her – lingering at certain places – while grinning with approval. His reaction was more powerful than any verbal compliment. "What's the occasion?" he asked.

She said smugly, "I had – no, I take that back – we had a very lucrative day in Chicago today, so we're going to celebrate."

"Can't wait to hear about it," he said, then pulled two Baccarat champagne glasses from the cabinet. She'd left them there because she refused to drink from his mismatched collection of juice glasses.

He popped the cork, mouthed the top to catch the overflow, laughed when bubbles went up his nose, then poured. "To good news," was the extent of his toast.

"Follow me," she said while grabbing his hand and leading him into the bedroom. She was a bit upset seeing the crumpled sheets, but nothing was going to dampen her excitement as she scattered the bearer bonds on the waterbed.

"My god!" Lionel exclaimed. "What's all that for?"

"Your services have hit the big time, my friend," was how she began describing the Chicago meeting. She ended by saying, "But for this to work, we're going to have to up our game."

"What's that mean?" he asked with a scowl.

"Let's be honest here. Up until now, the jobs you've done have been effective but lack a certain – what should I call it? – finesse. Besides, nobody's really cared about the people you've neutralized, so the police didn't try too hard to solve the cases. But this one is different, really different."

"I still don't know what you're driving at."

"Well, remember back in Copenhagen when you mixed the cow tranquilizer xylazine with my father's cocaine? And how the medical examiner never detected it so ruled his and Charlotte's deaths as a tragic overdose? You were onto something back then. You called it a silentcide. That's what we need here. To induce the cardinal's death so it looks like it's from natural causes."

Lionel began pacing the room. "That's a tall order, Irene. How are we going to pull that off?"

"Dr. Nathan Yasin," she said with confidence.

"Who's that?"

"He's a local pharmacist who was charged for creating and filling fraudulent drug prescriptions. I got him off on a legal technicality last month, but his license has been suspended for three years. He's a dorky-looking nerd – only about yea high – but also brilliant, greedy and indebted to me."

"Okay, so where does he fit in?"

"That's the beauty of this," Irene gushed. "With his knowledge of medicine and drugs, along with your skills in planning and implementation, together with my contacts within criminal networks, we make a dream team."

Lionel cocked his head while thinking. At first, he seemed skeptical, then appeared to gravitate toward the idea. "That might work," he said cautiously.

Irene approached so she could stroke the stubble on his jaw. "I understand your hesitation. Really, I do. Let me talk to Yasin first about this Chicago commission without naming names. After that, you'll meet him. If we're all comfortable, we'll test him out. Then, if it succeeds – and I know it will – we'll cash in big within two weeks. From there, we can really ramp up this business."

Lionel stared down at the bearer bonds, looked back at Irene, hesitated, then raised his glass and smiled. "To the riches from silent killing," he said as a toast.

Chapter Ten: Chicago, Illinois

Photos 24–28

ELEVEN

Montreal, Canada
Sunday – Present Day

Michelle woke from a fretful sleep feeling anxious. She knew Irene would attack again. The she-devil was omnipotent. The only unknown was when. Being in fearful high alert was emotionally crippling and physically exhausting. There was no escaping the dread.

She had hoped being reunited with Chris would be rejuvenating. It wasn't. Although thrilled he was alive, Michelle still resented her brother for jeopardizing her life in order to save Anna. How dare he go rogue and alienate Irene while keeping Michelle in the dark. Had they killed Anna, everything would be normal now. Yes, their prior lives were deplorable. But being alive was better than being dead.

The previous evening, Michelle, Chris and Ansel had spent three contentious hours conspiring over how to kill Irene. The boys kept arguing about techniques. Chris advocated stealth approaches. Ansel suggested shock and awe. Michelle had been more of a referee than an integral part of the planning. Whatever was going on between them was childish.

After the meeting, she and Ansel had retreated to their separate hotel rooms. An hour later, he had knocked on her door with a handful of mini liquor bottles, a bucket of ice and a charming smile. Her emotions tingled while her discipline told him it wasn't wise to risk being caught by Chris. The real reason for turning Ansel away was one kiss would accelerate to a point of no return. She wasn't sure she was ready and didn't trust her self-control.

Michelle's thoughts then drifted toward Anna. She was the innocent victim. Shot at. Betrayed. Alone. Petrified. She might need someone to talk to. Michelle leaped out of bed wearing cotton pajamas and started to get dressed.

♦♦♦

Michelle lightly knocked at Anna's hotel room door and watched as the peephole darkened. The door cautiously opened but remained secured by the safety chain. "What do you want?" Anna asked with suspicion.

Michelle replied, "To talk. Can I come in?"

"Are you working?"

"What does that mean?"

With rancor, Anna said, "You know, conducting recon on me like you did on the cruise."

"No, nothing like that. I just want to see how you're doing."

"Did Chris put you up to this?" Anna asked with bitterness.

"No, he doesn't know I'm here."

The door closed. Michelle waited and wondered. While turning away, the door slowly reopened. The depressing room was cluttered, foul smelling and dark except for a bedside light. Anna pulled the robe tight across her waist, began picking up a few things, said, "Screw it," then flopped on the couch, pulling one leg beneath her. Her face was gray, her lips were white, and her intense eyes looked sickly.

Michelle cleared a spot on a chair before asking, "Are you okay?"

Anna snapped back, "If you can't answer that by looking around, then you're not as smart as Chris says."

Michelle ignored the slight. "I know you're feeling scared, but ..."

Anna's expression contorted with anger. "You have no damn idea what I'm feeling, so stop pretending you do."

Resisting the urge to match Anna's intensity, Michelle calmly said, "Listen, you know the fear you've had the last couple of days? Well, believe me, I've lived with that my whole life."

"I doubt that. You're an assassin, for god's sake. You're used to all this bullshit."

"No," Michelle said, shaking her head, "you never get used to the fear I've had."

"Like what?" Anna asked with defiance while clutching a throw pillow.

Now Michelle got angry. "Okay, you really want to hear about fear? Then here it is. My earliest memory as a child is being constantly beaten, molested and later raped by my drunken stepfather until Chris and I killed him while he was murdering our mom. I was so scared and full of hate that I stabbed him, over and over and over again. Nightmares still plague me. I was eight at the time. Only eight. Think about it. What was your life like at eight?"

Anna was visibly shaken. Her jaw tightened. A leg swayed back and forth. Lips were quivering.

Michelle continued the rage. "Since that night, we've been under Irene's control – and I mean absolute control – except for two years in a foster home we shared with Ansel. After that, Irene drugged us, staged our deaths, and kidnapped us to an Amish farm. In that living hell we were brainwashed, manipulated and threatened every day for a decade. For ten long years, we had one choice: learn to be assassins or die."

Michelle's heart was racing while reliving each crippling trauma. "And if that wasn't bad enough, for the last sixteen years, we again had one choice: kill or be killed. And if you think I'm kidding, there's been only one time when we – or should I say Chris? – defied Irene's orders. That was because of you. Since then, we've been repeatedly attacked and lived in mortal fear. And that's not even counting the daily fear of retaliation or imprisonment in our job." At a fever pitch, she finished by saying, "So do I know a thing or two about fear? You bet your ass I do." Michelle leaned back. The tirade had been draining.

Anna was stunned. She asked weakly, "How do you remain so strong?"

Michelle snickered at the ludicrous question. "I assure you, I'm not. There have been countless days I've been far worse than you."

Anna seemed lost for words. "I'm sorry."

"For what? None of this is your fault. You're just a victim in all of this."

Anna sat closer to the edge of the couch and secured the robe again. "But why is Chris doing this for me? If he thinks I'm going to love him someday for saving my life, he's crazy."

"That's not it at all," Michelle said while pushing a strand of sandy-blond hair behind her ear. "He knows you have no future together. There's absolutely no expectation on his part."

"Then why?"

"I've repeatedly asked the dumbass the same thing." That made Anna snicker. "Part of it is he wants to end this crappy way of life. We both hate what we're doing. Hell, we hate ourselves. We desperately want it to stop. And you happened to be the spark to make Chris finally rebel. An equal part is he admires you. He keeps telling me that you're smart, humble, passionate about curing cancer, and worth having a future so you can fulfill your dream."

"What's that supposed to mean?"

"Didn't he tell you what he did for Longfellow BioSciences?"

"No," Anna said, looking confused.

"Of course he didn't. So here's the scoop. While Chris was researching your company, he learned the president of some big pharma company – I think the guy's name is Robert Nole – had agreed to acquire your failing biotech while secretly stalling the deal until it went bankrupt. So Chris blackmailed this Robert Nole guy into fulfilling his promise to buy Longfellow so you and your friend – what's her name?"

"You mean Liz Walker, our chief science officer?"

"Yeah, that's her." Michelle suddenly remembered that discussing how Liz was coerced into having sex with the pharma president in a desperate move to save Longfellow was on Chris's list of truths never to disclose. "Anyway, Chris wanted the two of you to cure cancer, save millions of lives, and do it in memory of your little brother who died from that god-awful disease."

"I can't believe he did that," Anna said with amazement.

"Yeah, he did. Then he went ballistic after the acquisition went through and he learned the cancer technology was going to be buried and you were fired. It wouldn't surprise me if Chris retaliates against that pharma asshole someday."

"Why didn't Chris say something to me about it?"

"Because that's the way he is. He's willing to do anything for you and wants nothing in return. Believe me when I say the Chris you admired during the last few weeks was the real Chris. And in a way I'm jealous. I've never had to share him before. But I'm equally pissed because he jeopardized my life to save yours. So you're not expected to forgive him. I'm not sure I will either. All I know is he's willing to risk everything to keep you alive, but only if you let him."

"But how can I trust him?" Anna exclaimed. "All he's ever done is lie to me."

"Of course he has. That was his job. But I'm telling you, his feelings never lied. And now he's committed to telling you the truth. So cut him some slack."

Anna seemed doubtful. She finally said, "I don't know."

"Just think about it," Michelle said. "And if you want my help, great. I'd be happy to do it. If you prefer to drown in self-pity in this cave, that's okay, too. Either way, just let me know."

Anna fidgeted with fingernail stubs. "Yeah, okay, I'll think about it."

"Good," Michelle said. "And oh, by the way, you look like shit."

Anna snapped back to attention. Michelle gave an impish grin. Anna laughed. "I'm surprised I look that good."

"I'll tell you what," Michelle said. "Let's stop feeling sorry for ourselves. Why don't you get cleaned up, burn that hideous robe, and I'll take you shopping for some clothes using my alias credit card. I heard your clothes were abandoned in Québec City."

"That's nice, but Chris offered to do that for me."

"Really? And who would you guess has a better fashion sense? Me or him?"

Anna emitted a weak chuckle before looking worried again. "But I thought we weren't supposed to go outside."

"We're not. But I have some disguises in my room. While you're getting ready, I'll get them and be back in a few. And while we're gone, we'll have room service disinfect this pigsty. Sound like a plan?"

For the first time, Anna smiled.

Michelle suddenly understood why Chris was infatuated with this woman. She liked Anna, too.

TWELVE

Sunday

When Chris heard a gentle knock on the connecting door, he invited Anna into his hotel room and was immediately bowled over. She was unrecognizable beneath the wavy blond wig, green contact lenses and dark tan makeup concealing her olive complexion. She wore a white Panama hat, dangling hoop earrings and a blue-and-white striped sleeveless dress with two-inch heels. The ensemble had a fashionable flair, a sharp contrast to her normal attire. After spending nearly forty-eight hours wrapped in a robe, the transformation was remarkable.

Chris stuttered, "Wow. You look, uh, great."

"Proving the adage that looks can be deceiving, huh?" Anna snapped back. "But on the inside, I still feel like crap. And you look like a dork," she added with a frown of disapproval at his Ted Collins disguise. "I feel like we're going to a bad Halloween party."

Chris was at a loss for how to temper her snarly attitude.

"I'm sorry, Chris. I'm kind of suffocating here. Can we skip having cocktails in your room and walk to the restaurant instead?"

Doing anything to improve Anna's spirits was worth a try, even risking being out in public. Hours earlier, Michelle had suggested the foursome have dinner together. She contended the social time might soothe everyone's jittery nerves and begin building a positive connection.

Before leaving the room, Chris stuffed a pistol behind his back and covered it with a windbreaker.

Anna flinched. "Is that necessary?" she asked but already knew the answer.

Their slow pace through the Old Port of Montreal was mostly an awkward quiet. Anna's normal confident stride was gone. With head down and slumped shoulders, she acted exhausted and aloof. To try lightening the mood, Chris pointed out the Clock Tower[29] lighthouse at the end of a harbor, then explained the history of Notre-Dame-de-Bon-Secours Chapel.[30] She barely acknowledged him.

With unabated enthusiasm, he suggested they ride the Ferris wheel at Bonsecours Basin.[31] "No," was her flat response. Nor did any of the quaint shops inside Bonsecours Market[32] – a former custom house and farmers' market – spark any interest. Finally, in exasperation, he asked, "Anna, is there anything I can do or say to make things better?"

She looked up for the first time. Staring into her fake green eyes was unsettling. "Nothing," she said with dejection, "except put an end to this nightmare."

They trudged the rest of the way to the restaurant in silence.

When they reached Place Jacques-Cartier[33] – a popular public square that was the private garden of the governor-general of New France during the eighteenth century – they found Michelle and Ansel seated at an outside table. Ansel wore a sport coat and was drinking a neat bourbon or scotch. Michelle had on a lavender, ruffle-trim cocktail dress while nursing a cosmopolitan. Neither wore disguises. Chris was obviously underdressed, overcautious and at least one drink behind. Not an auspicious start.

Ansel jumped up and flashed his signature charm while holding out Anna's chair. The suck-up avoided eye contact with Chris. Michelle chimed in. "Okay, kids, listen up," she said, imitating a demanding housemother. "Here're the ground rules for tonight.

Park your troubles at the curb, put on your best Mr. Rogers happy faces, eat and drink too much, and have fun, damn it, or I'll kick your butt. Any questions?"

Ansel and Anna emitted a quick laugh. Trying to get into the spirit, Chris raised a hand like a school kid. "Yes, I have one. What kind of wine would everyone like? I was thinking of a bottle of Bordeaux, my treat."

Michelle accepted, yet Ansel declined, claiming the tannins gave him terrible headaches. Anna only wanted a Coke but begrudgingly agreed to a few sips. This was surprising. She and Chris had drunk lots of bold red wines almost every night during happier times. Michelle suggested, "Chris, why not just order by the glass?"

While trying to send his sister the telepathic message not to manage him in front of the others, Chris said, "A bottle's fine. I'll bring the rest back to the room." When the waiter arrived, Chris pointed to his selection while saying in French, "Je voudrais commander le Saint-Émilion pour la table aux quatre verres, s'il vous plaît. J'aurai aussi un Coke pour la dame."

"Oui, monsieur. Rien d'autre?"

Ansel ordered another double, as if hoping alcohol would calm some hidden guilt.

Michelle began to babble about their shopping excursion. No one cared about the details – least of all Michelle, who abhorred shopping – but the topic was noncontentious. Chris listened and sulked.

Soon the waiter returned with the wine. He showed Chris the label and waited for a nod before slicing away the seal and extracting the cork. When he offered it to Chris, he pointed toward Anna. Their ritual had always been for her to inspect the cork. Chris watched as a tasting amount was poured. Then he swirled his glass, savored the bouquet, and was about to sip when distracted by Anna frantically showing the cork to Michelle. His sister's head snapped up with wild-eyed alarm. "Chris!"

The warning was muted as a stumbling drunk slammed into Chris. Crimson splashed across his lap. The glass smashed. The drunk stabilized himself by grabbing Chris's shoulder, then whispered, "Redhead on bench. Poisoned wine."

The man was the freed assassin from Québec City. Ignoring the clamor at the table, Chris spotted a dowdy woman sitting in the square facing away from the restaurant, yet her phone was in selfie mode. She was watching intently. Chris asked, "Are there others?"

"Don't know," the man said as the waiter apologetically pulled him off Chris.

Not wanting to cause a panic, Chris was about to loudly complain about the service as an excuse for a hasty exit. A flowerpot exploded next to Anna's head. Pottery shrapnel rocketed in every direction. A second bullet shattered a picture window. A roar of glass crashed to the floor. The third and fourth shots were deafened by screams from the surrounding diners. The woman was charging their table, shooting indiscriminately.

The Québec City assassin was the first to draw his weapon. He dropped to one knee and squeezed the trigger. The redhead clutched her chest and staggered. The next slug pierced her throat, causing random firing as she spun wildly and collapsed. The third round was a kill shot to the head. Splatters of blood outlined a fixed stare.

"Go. Get outta here," the assassin said breathlessly. "I'll cover you. And oh, by the way," he added with a toothy smile, "we're even."

"That's for sure. Thank you," Chris said while stripping off his windbreaker and using it to conceal his SIG P229. Ansel brandished a Glock 17 while hotly searching for another threat. "Goddamn it," Chris screamed at Ansel. "Hide that thing, will you? Security cameras are everywhere."

Most patrons wailed, screeched or prayed while cowering on the ground, covering their heads, or clutching together in terror. Others desperately crawled into the restaurant. One man was unconscious with jagged glass shards protruding from his chest. A woman was missing part of an ear. The macabre sounds of rampant horror were grisly.

Michelle shielded Anna, who was trembling beneath the table. "Let's go," Chris said while extending his hand. Anna vehemently refused. Michelle muttered some words of encouragement, then they helped her stand. She wobbled and grabbed a chair for support.

"Are we clear?" Chris asked the men on lookout. After two affirmatives, he leaped over the terrace fencing, waited for Michelle to do the same, and together they guided Anna into the square. Ansel quickly followed.

Chris and Ansel hid their weapons beneath their coats as the four of them began running through a scattering crowd. Ansel led the way. Chris took up the rear. The two women were side-by-side until Anna's high heel wedged into a street paver. Her ankle buckled. She tried bracing for impact while plummeting to the ground. Her hat flew off. She skidded hard. Skin peeled away from both palms. Blood seeped across imbedded pebbles in a kneecap. Anna winced while cradling her leg. The twisted wig obscured her view.

Michelle bent over and asked with concern, "Are you okay?"

With tears in her eyes and a pained expression, Anna managed to nod.

"Can you move?" Chris asked. "We've got to keep moving."

Anna didn't answer but raised an arm signaling to be helped up. Michelle and Chris got her standing. After kicking off her shoes and bracing against Michelle, she resumed running with a limp. Every step seemed agonizing.

As they approached Château Ramezay,[34] the former residence of an early eighteenth-century governor, Chris shouted ahead to Ansel, "Turn right. Turn right." That was when another threat was spotted.

A mid-thirties woman was walking a dog on a lawn adjacent to the historic mansion. She seemed suspiciously unaffected by the chaos while watching her sniffing poodle. Something was wrong with her demeanor. Chris sensed she was poised to strike after they passed. He studied her face, her hands and her stance. There were no telltale signs of hostility, yet his radar screamed danger.

The foursome raced down Notre-Dame Street East. Ansel was hypervigilant as the point man. Chris monitored the rear. The women struggled to keep pace while clutching each other. No doubt raging adrenaline propelled them.

This is your fault. All of it. You should've never left the hotel, but you wanted to be nice to Anna. Agreeing to the dinner was idiotic, but you kowtowed to Michelle. Then you didn't object when Ansel and Michelle were sitting undisguised in the open. Hell, it was a perfect kill zone. And if you hadn't been distracted by Ansel, you would've seen that redhead. We should be dead.

Chris glanced back. No one was in pursuit. He watched forward. The pads of Anna's feet were raw as she struggled to maintain the pace.

Sloppy! Careless! No, stupid *is the right word. Get your damn act together. Your only job is to keep everyone alive until Irene is dead. So stop being talked out of your instincts. Who cares if you hurt someone's feelings? This is war. Act like it. Take charge. Be the leader.*

✦✦✦

Winded and thankful to have escaped, the foursome piled into Chris's 2000 Ford Explorer. The women sat in back and Ansel took shotgun with Chris behind the wheel. No sooner were the doors closed than a heated debate flared over where to go and how to get there.

"Shut up!" Chris screamed while pounding the steering wheel. "Just let me concentrate." After the outburst, the only sounds while driving across the Island of Montreal were Anna's muffled whimpers of pain.

An hour later, the sun was down, the car was dark, and Chris was confident they were not being followed. Michelle dared to speak. "Chris, can I ask a question?"

"Sure," he acquiesced.

"Who was that guy at the restaurant?"

"One of Irene's assassins," Chris said. "I spared his life at Québec City."

Ansel asked with a sardonic bite, "What? You let the guy go?"

"Why not? After he dropped his gun, what was I supposed to do, kill him in cold blood?"

"I would've shot him before he surrendered," Ansel contended.

Chris said with rising intensity, "Well, maybe that's the difference between us. I don't just kill for the sake of killing."

"Hell, it would've been self-preservation. He could've easily come back to kill us all."

"But he didn't, did he? Instead, I would've drank the wine without his warning."

Michelle spoke up. "That's not totally right."

Chris leaned back to shout, "What?"

"Anna spotted a needle mark running down the side of the cork," Michelle explained. "I was trying to warn you when that guy showed up."

Chris bristled while demanding, "Why didn't you say something?"

"Because maybe," Michelle said with resentment, "the damn gunfire was too loud."

"Either way," Chris said, "there's no question the guy saved us. But the big mystery is why Ansel declined the wine in the first place?"

"I told you," Ansel answered, "wine gives me headaches."

"You mean to tell me a big drinker like you never has wine?"

"An occasional white, sure," Ansel said. "But you never asked for anyone's preference. You just ordered whatever the hell you wanted."

"What difference did it make? You probably would've declined a white too."

Ansel shuffled in the seat to confront his accuser. "What are you saying?"

"What I'm saying is how the hell did that redhead find us in

Montreal, at that restaurant, then tamper with a wine only three of us were going to drink?"

Ansel became outraged. "You think I set you up?"

Michelle entered the fray. "Chris, how can you accuse Ansel? He's warned you twice about pending ambushes."

"Sure he did, but only seconds before they happened. Don't you see? He and Irene never expected me to survive those attacks. So his so-called warnings were just a ploy to build your trust in him."

"That's ridiculous," his sister protested.

With a dismissive hand toward the backseat, Chris said, "Michelle, just let me finish." Then he redirected his ire toward Ansel. "When Québec City failed, you came to Montreal ..."

Ansel interrupted, "I came because you invited us."

"No, I invited Michelle, not you. But you came anyway, told Irene, planned dinner outside and didn't wear a disguise so Miss Redhead could identify us."

"Are you fucking kidding me? What's so special about your clown mask? Did you wear it when working for Irene? Sure you did, probably lots of times. I'll bet she has all your ratty getups on wanted posters."

"But that's not the real issue, is it?" Chris reached for the gun wedged at the side of the car seat. "The real issue is you're Irene's puppet and have been since day one. Isn't that right? That's how she found us. What else could it be?"

"Stop it!" Anna bellowed. "Just stop bickering."

"But I'm trying to learn if he's a traitor," Chris protested.

"Maybe he is, maybe he isn't. I don't know," Anna said, then lowered her voice. "But it could also be, uh ... it could be my fault."

"What are you saying?"

Anna hesitated, followed by a deep exhale. "Could Irene trace a call from a hotel phone?"

"Absolutely," Ansel said with disgust.

Chris stared into the backseat. "What did you do?"

"I called my mom," Anna confessed, on the brink of tears. "It was only for about five minutes. Maybe less."

"Why the hell did you do that?" Ansel demanded.

"Because I'm scared. Absolutely terrified. I needed to talk with someone I love. But believe me, I didn't tell her where I was or who I was with. I just wanted to hear her voice. So if it's my fault, I'm sorry. Really sorry. Just drop me off at the next gas station."

"But they'll find and kill you without our protection," Chris objected.

"You keep saying that, but they keep shooting at us anyway. So if I have to die, I'd rather die at home. And at the rate you people are going, Irene has nothing to worry about. You'll probably kill each other soon."

Chapter Twelve: Montreal, Canada

Photos 29–34

THIRTEEN

PHILADELPHIA, PENNSYLVANIA
Monday

Irene Shaw dreaded early Monday mornings, the start of another endless workweek. She stared out of her law office window located at the peak of an architectural chevron at One Liberty Place.[35] The skyscraper in downtown Philadelphia was jammed with prestigious law firms. For her, being a prestigious defense attorney was a license to steal from successful criminals. They did the crimes, she got the spoils. A perfect arrangement.

A knock at the door distracted her thoughts. "Ms. Shaw," her gray-haired executive assistant inquired, "are you ready for your week in review?" The perfectly groomed man held a pile of case files and an updated day planner. Every hour of her week was undoubtedly scheduled. Regardless of how much she delegated to the partners and nearly one hundred associates, her workload was always arduous. At seventy-two, she was uncertain how much more of this shit she could tolerate.

With routine disdain, she said, "Place the stack on my desk, will you, dear? I'll call you if I need something."

"Yes, Ms. Shaw," he said. Then he added, "By the way, Mr. Wolfgang König asked for a few minutes of screentime to discuss an urgent matter. Do you wish to speak to him?"

Irene sighed. This better be good news, but probably wasn't. "Yes, please patch him through."

"As you wish."

She sat down in her chair, stared at the oversized monitor on the desk and critiqued her appearance in the screen's reflection. Age was taking its toll. That constant realization was disheartening.

A video conference invitation popped up on the screen. Irene positioned the cursor and clicked. Wolfgang König, the leader of the Thanatos division, appeared from his office at the Amish farm. His deep-set eyes were downcast. His jaw was rigid, his lips were pursed, and apprehension drained his complexion. This was definitely going to be bad news.

"What's wrong?" she bellowed.

He gathered his courage before saying apologetically, "Two things."

"Goddamn it," was her instinctive response. "Let's hear them."

"Well, first, in Montreal ..."

She cut him off by slamming her fist on the desk. "Don't you dare tell me they're still alive."

With a sigh of despair, he said, "I'm sorry to report this, but ... yes, they are."

"How the hell did that happen?"

"Frankly, I'm still investigating," the former mercenary said. "But from what I've uncovered so far, everything was initially going as planned. The foursome were seated outside the restaurant exactly as Ansel promised. And Chris ordered a bottle of wine just like you said he would."

"Of course he did." Irene laughed with smug self-satisfaction. "How many times was that boy warned that being predictable in this business is a death knell? So how could your people miss sitting ducks?"

"Well, our asset was able to inject the wine bottle with thallium, and then she got into a safe surveillance position. But when the waiter began pouring at the table, that's when all hell broke loose."

"That's not very specific, Mr. König," she said, hoping he noticed the ominous formality of his last name. "Exactly what does that mean?"

He cleared his throat, an obvious stall tactic. "From what I observed from our asset's phone and bodycam videos, a man stumbled into Chris, causing him to drop his wineglass. Unfortunately, our asset panicked and started shooting. She got off about three or four rounds before the man drew a gun and killed her."

"That's outrageous! Who was this damn mystery man?"

"From what I've been told, mind you the videos were jumpy and blurry ..."

"Spit it out!"

"It looked like Sam Lincoln," he said.

That name meant nothing. "Who's that?"

"He's from the Phonoi group. I don't personally know him, but apparently he's the one who surrendered to Chris in Québec City."

"Unbelievable!" Irene leaned back in stunned disbelief. It was inconceivable that fat ass went from a quivering coward to a cowboy hero. "How did he show up in the nick of time? Did he and Chris become pen pals after the Québec debacle?"

"That's unknown. Like I said, I'm still investigating. I'll update you as I learn more."

Total bullshit. Why is Chris so damn difficult to kill? The body count is now at six. When are he and his insufferable girlfriend going to stop breathing? And the client who ordered her hit is increasingly irate. Irene demanded, "Where are they now?"

"According to Ansel, they've arrived in Niagara-on-the-Lake. We won't have time to stage another attack before they leave again. He'll keep us posted on their travel plans."

"Did you consider telling Ansel to just shoot Chris and Anna and get this over with?"

"We can do that if you wish," Wolfgang said. "But that would jeopardize your goal of building Michelle's trust in him and possibly restoring her loyalty as an asset."

Irene still clung to that possible outcome. Michelle could be a critical factor to a successful succession. No one else since Dr. Yasin had her talent. "No, that directive remains unchanged," Irene said, then went back to hurtling accusations. "But why weren't you managing this shitshow? You know how critical it is."

Wolfgang stroked his protruding jaw. His Adam's apple lurched. He appeared tormented.

"I hate waiting, Mr. König," she scolded him. "Tell me."

"I was, uh, busy doing damage control on your other number one priority." He looked at his watch, then folded his massive arms across his chest. "Any minute now, you're going to get a call from Mr. Zola," a pseudonym for Irene's largest silentcide client ever. "He's not happy with yesterday's performance."

"You buried that headline!" Irene yelled. "Jesus! A debrief would've been nice before falling into that snake pit." A message popped up on her screen. Mr. Zola was waiting on phone extension number five. "He's calling now. Give me the abridged version."

"Apparently, our silentcide asset miscalculated the pharmaceuticals needed to be fatal, resulting in a hemorrhagic stroke, which means …"

"I know what that means," she said, shaking her head in disgust. "What's the prognosis?"

"For now, Senator Nisor is in a coma. I've been told this can last weeks or even years. Until he wakes up – assuming that he does – the extent of brain damage is unknown."

"So he's a vegetable," Irene concluded.

"Yes, with a fifty percent chance he'll stay that way for a long time, if not forever."

"Mr. König, we are not done with this discussion," she threatened, then abruptly exited the video conference. No doubt Wolfgang was now very worried about his future, especially after witnessing what happened to his counterpart for similar failures. Let him stew about getting a bullet in the head. Being terrified was a good motivator for improving performance.

Irene buried her face in her hands. Ever since Lionel was incapacitated and Dr. Yasin retired, everything had gone to hell. One fuckup after another. She was surrounded by incompetence. Maybe this enormous commission should be the last hurrah. It had been a great ride, but all good things come to an end.

She pushed the blinking button for line five. "Mr. Zola," she said with saccharine cheerfulness. "How are you doing on this lovely Monday morning?"

"Pissed as hell," he spat with anger.

"So sorry to hear that." Her tone remained condescending. "How can I brighten your mood?"

"You obviously have no idea what happened yesterday, do you?"

Acting ingenuous, Irene asked, "Are you referring to Senator Nisor? Tragic, isn't it?"

"Not tragic enough," Mr. Zola snapped back. "He's still alive."

"That's true. But from my understanding, he's not in full possession of his faculties."

"For Christ's sake, he was supposed to be dead. That was our agreement."

This conversation was deteriorating. Mr. Zola was combative, inflexible and unreasonable. It was time to gain the upper hand by changing his perception. She calmly said, "Let's look at the bright side, shall we? If there were two dead senators within a week – who both passed away unexpectedly – people might start talking. You know how people love to gossip. But this way your client can slowly manage the public conversation until orchestrating the crescendo."

Unimpressed with Irene's logic, he countered, "My client won't see it that way."

Struggling to control her temper, she said, "I'm sure your silver tongue can be very persuasive, Mr. Zola. Simply inform your client that plans have changed. You know how that happens sometimes in politics."

"I sure do. And we're planning on not paying you for this one," he said in defiance.

Her voice became dark. "Now *that* would be tragic."

"Are you threatening me?"

"Golly, I guess I am. Let me put it this way. I control an international network of people who specialize in solving problems permanently. After all, that's why you hired us. So I strongly suggest you deposit the full amount of bitcoin by the end of business today so you, your not-so-anonymous client and your two lovely daughters can rest easy while we implement the next phase. Frankly, you have no other choice if your client wants to maintain the original timetable." Becoming patronizing again, she added, "As an extra incentive, if the cryptocurrency is received by noon Eastern Time, you'll receive a free stadium blanket. Wouldn't that be fun? Have a nice day, Mr. Zola."

She disconnected.

Chapter Thirteen: Philadelphia, Pennsylvania

Photo 35

FOURTEEN

Niagara-on-the-Lake, Canada

Monday

A nna woke from a restless sleep and was plunged back into the nightmare of reality. A list of anxieties competed for attention. Collectively, they were numbing. A blazing hot flash. Racing heart. Stomach churning. Salvia flooded her tongue. She was going to be sick.

Throwing back the covers, Anna raced to the bathroom, slammed the door, yanked up the toilet seat and knelt on the floor. Pain shot up her leg. She wedged a bathmat below her skinned knee, winced again, bowed, waited, waited, waited, gagged, then vomited. The stench was repulsive. There was only time to flush and wipe away the drool before the second bout sent a crippling bolt through her lower back. She trembled and sobbed.

"Are you all right in there?" Michelle asked while knocking.

Throwing up was bad enough. Having someone hovering outside the door – especially someone you barely knew or trusted – made it worse. "Yeah, I'm okay," Anna managed to say. "I'll be out in a minute."

The foursome had spent over nine hours driving a circuitous route from Montreal to Niagara-on-the-Lake. After arriving in the small tourist town before sunrise, they were lucky to snare two hotel rooms,[36] which they shared by gender. Michelle had graciously taken the couch. Only three hours of sanctuary had passed before being sucked into another day of hell.

Anna struggled to stand, took a bathrobe from the hook, cringed at her raw palms while washing her face, and gargled with tap water. Again, she had no toothpaste. "I swear to god," she mumbled, "next time I buy a tube, I'm going to carry the damn thing everywhere like the guys carry their guns." After a deep sigh of resolve, she entered the bedroom.

Michelle asked with genuine concern, "Going back to bed?"

"No, I'm afraid lying down will make me nauseous again."

"Want to sit?" Michelle asked while jumping up to pull the extra blanket off the couch. She patted the seat cushion.

"If you don't mind, that would be great. Thanks."

"No problem," Michelle said. "I'll be right back." She returned with a wet washcloth. "Here, see if this helps."

The cold was refreshing across Anna's forehead. A water droplet rolled down her cheek. She sopped it up with the bathrobe sleeve, then shuffled to get comfortable. Her back spasmed. She flinched, then sucked in a breath to endure the pain until it subsided.

Michelle plopped down at the end of the bed, tightened her robe and said with worried kindness, "Is there anything else I can do to make you feel better?"

"No," Anna sighed. "Regardless of what you do, nothing's going to fix this."

Michelle looked perplexed but, to her credit, didn't pry. With hands folded in her lap, she remained silent.

Anna squeezed her eyes, contemplated, struggled for the little inner strength remaining and decided to proceed. Vocalizing the horrible truth would make it real. "I'm pregnant."

"Oh my god," Michelle said in shocked disbelief. "Are you sure?"

"Well, I haven't taken a test." Anna added with a weak smile, "I've been kind of busy the last few days." Her seriousness returned. "But

I was supposed to have my period during the cruise. When it didn't happen, I blamed it on my problems at work, with George, and then Jessica's death. But after being almost three weeks late and having morning sickness the last three days … well, yeah, I'm pretty sure."

With apprehension, Michelle asked, "Do you know what you're going to do?"

"I have no idea," Anna said while closing her eyes. "I'm still in serious denial."

Michelle hesitated before probing. "What about the father?"

"Well, it's not Chris, if that's what you're wondering."

"I know," Michelle said with certainty. "Irene saw to that."

"Say what?"

"Yeah, Irene had him fixed as a kid."

Still perplexed, Anna said, "Chris told me his ED was from the mumps."

"Nope, Irene's to blame," Michelle explained. "And believe it or not, she also had my tubes tied as I entered puberty."

"That's insane. Why would she do such a heinous thing?"

"So we couldn't have kids. She called them, and I quote" – Michelle used her fingers to flash quotation marks – "'a distraction.' But as you can probably imagine, I've often dreamed of having a family."

"Me too," Anna said. "But when I was married, Paul and I delayed having kids because we were broke. And I mean flat broke. Then our careers got in the way. Just before our divorce, my consolation prize was a dog. And now, at forty-one, this might be my last chance to be a mom." That was a stark realization. Her biological clock may never provide another opportunity.

Michelle flipped a long lock of hair behind her ear – a nervous habit Anna had observed before – then asked, "What do you think the father will say?"

"Nothing," Anna said definitively. "Your brother shot him."

"What? Are you saying George Henniker was the father?"

"Without question. We only had sex once. And despite all his bravado, George was terrible in bed. And I mean terrible." They shared a snicker, then Anna got upset at herself. "I can't believe I let that happen in the first place, let alone that the pill failed me. Just think about it. A couple of minutes enduring his crude grunts and groans will change my life forever."

Anna stopped talking as the devastating truth sank in. One mistake had changed everything. With exasperation, she said, "Michelle, I've tried really hard to do everything right in life. Heck, my brothers call me Saint Anna. So how the hell did I end up in this hotel room, hunted by assassins and pregnant?" Anna didn't expect an answer to the rhetorical question. Nothing about this quagmire made sense. "Would you mind giving me a minute?"

"No problem." As Michelle stood, she looked at her watch. "I have to meet with Chris in a few minutes, so take all the time you need." She lightly patted Anna's shoulder and gave her a sympathetic nod as she walked by.

While Michelle dressed in the bathroom, a whirlwind of options swirled through Anna's mind. None were good. She could keep the baby. But what would her parents and friends say? Would George's family get involved? Then imagine the struggles and sacrifices of being a single mom. And could she ever look at the child without being reminded the father had hired an assassin to kill her? Could his amoral genes be transferred to the child? Maybe adoption? But how could she possibly give up a child? An abortion would be a quick fix. But for her, it was morally wrong, at least that was what she had always believed, until now, when it was personal. But that decision would probably plague her conscience for life. When Anna realized her hands were cradling her stomach, she started to cry. The sorrow was all-consuming.

A few minutes later, Michelle emerged from the bathroom wearing the lavender cocktail dress from the night before. Surprisingly, it made Anna laugh as she wiped away a lingering tear. "Isn't that a bit fancy for a Monday morning?"

"You think?" Michelle quipped with a curtsey, then said, "I was hoping to buy something more appropriate after meeting with Chris. Can I get you some clothes too?"

Struggling to make light of a terrible situation, Anna joked, "Yes, something with an expandable waist."

Flashing an endearing smile, Michelle said, "You've got it." She grabbed her wallet and room key and was about to leave.

"Hey, Michelle," Anna asked while standing. "I have a favor to ask."

"Sure, what is it?"

"Would you please not tell Chris I'm pregnant?"

"Absolutely," Michelle assured her. "It's our secret."

"Thanks. And another thing …" Anna stopped. Completing the question might mean an admission of intent, and she was far from making any decisions regarding the baby.

Michelle waited, then asked, "What is it?"

"You're a pharmacist, right?"

"I've trained as one," Michelle explained, "but not actually licensed. Why?"

Anna hesitated again before blurting out, "Do you have access to abortion pills?"

Michelle slowly sat on the edge of the bed again. "Are you thinking about going that route?"

"I don't know," Anna said, avoiding eye contact. "Probably not. I just thought I'd, you know, ask in case I change my mind."

"I understand. My advice is to give it time. You have a few weeks left to think about it. But I'll get them for you so they're handy if that's what you later decide."

Relieved, Anna said, "Thanks again." With an apologetic tone, she added, "Hey, I'm sorry if I always come across as needy and whining. I know you have your problems too."

"That's okay. I hear listening is what friends do." A sadness swept across Michelle's face. "But then I wouldn't know. Other than Chris, I've never had a friend before."

"Now that's an area where I've been blessed," Anna said. "I'd be happy to show you how it works."

Chapter Fourteen: Niagara-on-the-Lake, Canada

Photo 36

FIFTEEN

Niagara-on-the-Lake, Canada
Monday

Chris stared absently at the Memorial Clock Tower[37] in the center median of Queen Street. On the cenotaph's plaque were the names of local soldiers who fell during World Wars I and II. Their ultimate sacrifice was honorable.

In contrast, his death would be meaningless, simply the end of a despicable life spent killing people to save his own. That stark reality was haunting. The struggle to stay alive was debilitating. Was the fight against Irene winnable or folly? Odds suggested survival was unlikely. Dying felt probable. The remorse hurt. Chris was despondent.

"Hey, donkey breath," Michelle yelled from the sidewalk. His sister's familiar childhood tease – delivered with a broad smile and mischievous blue eyes – was immediately uplifting.

Chris grabbed two coffee cups from the base of the monument, waited for a passing car, then dashed across the street to greet her. This was the first time they'd been alone in eight days. He had never fully appreciated their mutual dependence until he thought she was dead. Michelle was his rock. Together they were confident and strong.

"Here," he said while offering her favorite, an iced white chocolate mocha. They exchanged a lingering hug. The fleeting seconds soothed their shared angst. "How are you holding up?" he asked.

"Okay, I guess," she said bravely, obviously trying to hide her distress. "And you?"

He sidestepped an honest answer by joking, "Feeling underdressed compared to your pretty party duds." They shared a quick laugh. Keeping things lighthearted might help her cope. He needed to display a courageous calm in order to ease her worries. That was his role as a big brother.

Michelle said, "Yeah, I have some shopping to do after we're done talking. I'm also going to buy some clothes for Anna."

"That's nice of you. Thanks." Chris paused before asking with apprehensive concern, "How's she doing?"

"She's petrified. And it's not helping that you're withdrawn from her."

He protested, "I'm just honoring her request to be alone."

"That's not entirely true, is it?"

"What's that supposed to mean?"

"It means after your big confession to her in Québec City, you've just shut down." Michelle had always been keenly perceptive of his emotions. That trait was annoying at times. This was one of those times.

"Okay, of course I shut down," he begrudgingly admitted, "because I'm one hundred precent certain she resents everything about me. And justifiably so. What else am I supposed to do?"

"Have you tried being yourself? She liked that side of you before. So spend time with her. Talk to her. Better yet, get her talking and then listen. That's what you do best."

In frustration, Chris said, "I tried that last night during our walk before dinner. All I got was the silent treatment."

"Then keep trying, but don't force things. Just be yourself. Eventually she'll open up." That seemed like a reasonable suggestion until Michelle added, "And the same advice goes for Ansel."

Chris tensed. "Why should I worry about what he thinks?" he asked as resentment surged. "He challenges everything I say. I don't know what his problem is."

"That's easy. You're the problem." Before Chris could rebut, she held up a hand to silence him. "Before you say anything, just hear me out, okay? You're not going to like this, but you need to hear the truth." Michelle gnawed her lower lip as if struggling over how to phrase an unsavory message. "Ever since Ansel arrived, you've been nothing but suspicious and angry."

"I have not," he said defiantly to the insulting accusation.

"What do you call sucker-punching him and then calling him a traitor? And when you learned he wasn't, you didn't bother to apologize."

In Chris's mind, those actions were justified, yet he'd never convince her. He said instead, "Listen, Michelle, I'm just trying to keep us alive, while he's making one sloppy move after another."

"Like what?"

"Like not wearing a disguise, for one. Then eating dinner outdoors in a perfect kill zone. That's totally unprofessional. I noticed them at the time but said nothing because I wanted to play nice. Well, that's over. I've got to start listening to my instincts, make decisions and take charge. So if Anna, or Ansel, or even you for that matter, don't like it, that's too bad."

"You can't just declare yourself the leader and expect us to follow."

"If that's what it takes to stay alive, then yes I can." He assumed she would agree with his reasoning and be appreciative. Instead, she was acting blindly naive.

"Let me ask you this," Michelle said. "Were you the leader when it was just the two of us?"

"Well, no," he said with hesitation. "We've always been a team."

"That's right. Now that team has doubled. So start acting like you always did with me."

In defiance, Chris said, "I hope you plan on giving Ansel the same speech. He needs to hear it more than I do."

Michelle studied him. He took offense to being under her microscope. "What's really bugging you about Ansel?"

"I've told you. I don't trust the guy."

"I sense that's not the entire problem, is it?"

This interrogation was irritating. "What are you driving at?"

"You tell me."

Chris decided if she was going to confront him, then he would do the same. For dramatic effect, he threw the coffee cup into a trash container. "Okay, I'm not blind. I see the way he looks at you. It's not very – how should I put this delicately? – brotherly."

"If you're asking if something is going on between us, the answer is no."

"Good," Chris said with relief.

"But I make no promises about the future."

Outraged, he shouted, "I forbid it!" as spittle flew from his mouth. His anger was ablaze.

Intense and indignant, she said, "Chris Davis, you have no right to forbid it. It's my choice. I trust Ansel. He's been there for me several times when I needed it most and you were AWOL. He's also the first person other than you who accepts me for who I am."

"That's fine," Chris said, but meant the opposite. "That's still no reason to get romantic."

"Even if he makes me happy? You'd deny me that?"

Chris stewed but said nothing. How could he argue in favor of making his sister miserable? Yet somehow, he had to protect her from getting hurt. That goal had been his lifelong obligation.

Michelle said tenderly, "Listen, regardless of what happens, and I'm not saying something will, Ansel will never, ever replace you. Got that?"

Rather than comprehend what she meant, his brain flooded with fury. "You're making a huge mistake."

"Let me be the judge of that," she said boldly, as if the topic was permanently closed.

Disturbing silence. They had reached a stalemate. She was being gullible and stubborn. How could he make her understand?

Michelle filled the awkward gap. The edge in her voice was gone. "Remember about a week ago when I said I was going to be more independent? Well, making decisions like this one with Ansel is what independence looks like. Sometimes I'll be right. Sometimes I'll be wrong. It's okay to express your opinion if I ask for it, then be non-judgmental and supportive of my decisions. Otherwise" – a sudden sadness swept over her – "you'll push me away."

In shocked disbelief, Chris sensed her warning wasn't a threat or an ultimatum. It was a statement of fact. Losing Michelle was incomprehensible. Devastating. He hesitated to ask, "You mean that, don't you?"

"Unfortunately, yes," she said, nodding with conviction.

"So you're saying I'm alienating everyone? Including you?"

"Yes," was the blunt answer.

"And I suppose everything bad that's happening is also my fault."

"The harsh reality is … yes, it is."

Chris froze for a second to absorb the condemnation. Then he turned to leave, feeling rejected and ostracized.

She grabbed his shoulder, turned him around, stepped into his space and said, "Before you start feeling sorry for yourself, look at it this way. You made the right decision to rebel against Irene. I would've never had your courage. If you hadn't gone rogue, then Anna would be dead, Ansel would've never come back, and you and I would've been stuck in our old life forever. So, because of your boldness, the three of us are here and totally behind your mission."

This was the first positive thing she or anyone else had said about his actions since the debacle started. Hearing her unequivocal support made him proud.

Michelle continued, "But we're going to have to work together to succeed. So get your shit together and your head in the game. We need you if we're going to get Irene before she gets us. Can you do that?"

Before Chris could answer, a horse-drawn carriage[38] approached, carrying a young couple on a sightseeing tour of Old Town. Clip-clop. Clip-clop.

Michelle asked, "Does that sound remind you of the horse and buggy Lionel used to drive on the Amish farm?"

"Yup," Chris said. "But that Clydesdale is magnificent compared to the old workhorses we cared for as kids."

"We lost our futures at that farm," Michelle said. "Now's the time to get those futures back. The four of us. Agreed?"

With a broad grin and a high five, Chris said, "Agreed."

◆◆◆

Chris and Michelle spent the next hour planning how and where to get revenge on Irene. Their give-and-take of ideas was as free flowing and natural as always. The strategizing was invigorating. Later, during the southernly drive along Niagara River Parkway, Ansel offered his suggestions. They were surprisingly good.

Once the plan and a contingency were final, they created a tactical list. After entering the US, they would drive to Buffalo, New York, where Ansel would contact a trusted resource. His tasks were to purchase weapons and new disguises. He would also secure for Anna a new persona, including a driver's license and two credit cards, plus a minimal internet presence. Meanwhile, Chris and Michelle would make a day trip to the Twin Cities to get the special supplies they needed. It felt great to finally be all in agreement and going on the offense.

About midway through the drive, they made a pit stop beneath a canopy of trees at Brock's Monument[39] – a tall limestone tribute to a British officer who died defending an American attack during the War of 1812. Out of the watchful eye of security cameras, Chris wrapped incriminating evidence in plastic and stored the cache in the side panels of his Ford Explorer in preparation for the customs border.

As Chris drove the SUV across the Rainbow Bridge[40] toward the United States, Ansel began singing, "Somewhere Over the Rainbow." Michelle unexpectedly quipped from the backseat, "Hey, Ansel. Stop already. Your singing sucks."

Chapter Fifteen: Niagara-on-the-Lake, Canada

Photos 37–40

SIXTEEN

Elkins Park, Pennsylvania
Twenty-Eight Years Ago

Irene Shaw was hyped while bustling into her mansion two hours before sunrise. She kicked off her heels, briefly nursed a swelling bunion, then urgently pushed the intercom button for the guest house. "Come on, damn it," she said, cursing the need to wait.

Sounding disoriented, Lionel Jørgensen finally answered, "Hello?"

"What are you doing?" she impatiently asked her ex-husband.

"Sleeping."

"Not anymore. Get your ass over here. Now. And bring Nathan."

Irene flung her black blazer on the kitchen table, loosened the French bun, fluffed the tresses of dyed brown hair into a casual disheveled look, reapplied red lipstick and mixed a strong bloody mary while plotting a lucrative future. Her thoughts raced with possibilities.

About ten minutes later, the two men walked into the parlor. The ornate sitting room was decorated with antique Queen Anne furniture. Lionel looked half asleep yet always rugged in tight jeans and a black T-shirt. Nearly a foot shorter and one hundred pounds lighter, Nathan Yasin wore black dress pants, a starched checkered shirt and a worried expression. The fifty-year-old's trifocals enhanced the intellectual intensity of his eyes at the center of a receding hairline, pronounced nose and tight thin lips. He was six years older than Irene yet dutifully subservient.

"Sit, gentlemen," she said, pointing to an identical wingback couch across from her.

Lionel glanced at the cocktail Irene was absently stirring with a polished index finger and quipped, "Having some hair of the dog that bit you?"

"Hardly," Irene sneered. "More of a nightcap. It's been a busy evening. Want one?"

"No thanks. It's a little early for an eye-opener."

Irene didn't bother offering a drink to Nathan. Dr. Yasin had been substance-free since rehab after she got his conviction overturned for illegally selling pharmaceuticals. Staying sober had been one of Irene's conditions for employment after his stellar assistance with the demise of Cardinal McPherson in Chicago eight years earlier.

Now that she had their attention, Irene needed to demonstrate her control. She slowly set the glass on a coaster, reached for a gold cigarette case on the coffee table, tapped the filter to pack the tobacco, lit the tip with a diamond-encrusted butane lighter, savored the inhale, and began to talk only after the smoke drifted from her lips. "Who can tell me why Henry Ford is famous?"

A bit irritated by the inane question, Lionel said, "He invented the car."

"Actually," Nathan jumped in, "that distinction goes to Carl Benz in the late nineteenth century. About twenty years later, Ford introduced the Model T, the first mass-produced car. That's what made him rich."

"Exactly," she said, pointing the cigarette toward Nathan. "That man wins a Kewpie doll."

"Come on, Irene," Lionel said with exasperation. "I'm tired here. Can we get to the point so I can go back to bed?"

Irene was too energized to get irritated by Lionel's insubordination. "I had an epiphany this evening, gentlemen, a brilliant insight that will accelerate our financial trajectory."

"What's that?" Lionel asked, suddenly sounding interested.

"Do you remember Frank Ritchie?" she asked.

"You mean Shoot 'Em Up Frank? Sure, what about him?"

Irene quickly explained to Nathan, "He was a hitman for the Philly mob. A real goon." Turning back to Lionel, she said, "Notice I'm referring to him in the past tense? He was murdered last night."

"Huh," Lionel laughed. "Who finally got the ugly son of a bitch?"

"His stepkids."

"What?" Lionel said in disbelief.

"Yeah, his eight-year-old daughter and ten-year-old son. They beat him with a baseball bat and then stabbed him to death. I just spent the last several hours holding their bloody little hands at the police station."

"Okay, that's interesting," Lionel said while leaning back again. "But couldn't that news have waited until breakfast?"

"No, and here's why. I need a new revenue stream. A huge one. You see, my law firm had a big boom in defense retainers during the FBI's takedown of boss 'Little Nicky' and most of the Scarfo crime family. But now that cash cow is teats up, and New Yorkers are moving in to take over Philly."

"That might be good for our silentcide business," Lionel suggested, "especially with Ritchie out of the way. Scarfo was a bloody cowboy when it came to hits. Always gruesome, headliner murders. Maybe the New Yorkers would like our help in quietly cleaning up any resistance."

"Maybe, but that's chump change. No, it's time to take a lesson from Henry Ford and begin mass-producing our specialty."

"What's that supposed to mean?" Lionel asked.

Irene delayed an answer. To build suspense for the big reveal, she took a drag and flicked a dangling ash. With a smug smile, she said, "We're going to leverage the lucrative little business you boys helped create into an international enterprise."

Nathan asked with hesitation, "You mean mass-produce killing, like Murder, Inc.? If so, that ended poorly."

"Exactly," Irene said. "And why? I'll tell you why. It was founded by thugs like Bugsy Siegel. They recruited poor Jewish and Italian thugs to kill mostly mob wiseguys with guns and ice picks. What could possibly go wrong with that business model? The answer: everything."

"What are you thinking?" Lionel asked.

"Here's the plan," Irene said with zeal. "We find young orphans like the Ritchie kids who show a propensity for violence. Then we intensely train them to become disciplined, loyal and elite assassins. I mean the best the world has ever seen. Meanwhile, we create a network of resources – you know, like pharmacists, arms dealers, researchers, facilitators – to support them. Then we market our services not just to criminals but governments, corporations, and the wealthy … desperate people with deep pockets." Hearing the dream vocalized was infinitely more exciting than thinking about it. Irene reached a crescendo. "There's a big – and I mean really, really big – untapped opportunity for what we do. Now's the time to seize it."

"I don't know," Lionel said while folding his arms across his chest. "We've got a proven formula with just the three of us. Why screw that up? Besides, what you're proposing could take a decade or more. In the meantime, do we really want to wipe little butts until they're productive?"

"I grant you this is a long game," Irene admitted. "And we'll probably have to also recruit teenagers and twenty-somethings to accelerate the timeframe. But they have to be young and pliable enough so we can reshape their bad habits and assert total control." Shuffling to the edge of the couch cushion, she added, "But this is doable. Trust me. I feel it in my bones. What do you think?"

The room fell quiet enough to hear the grandfather clock ticking. Irene got pissed. Her idea should've received universal admiration, not festering doubts. These guys were complacent, short-sighted cowards. Her temper flared. "Damn it, Lionel, tell me what you think."

"I thought I did," he said, throwing up his hands. "Is there a market for it? Sure. Would the profits be huge if we pulled it off? No question. But it'll also be time consuming, expensive and risky. So, if you want us to gradually ramp up what we're doing today, then no problem. But what you're proposing ..." He shook his head with disapproval. "Well, I don't think it's doable."

"I do," Nathan said with confidence. "We can make this happen."

"Are you kidding me?" Lionel protested.

"Not at all," Nathan said. "We're smart enough to pull this off. All we have to do is structure and manage it like a successful big business."

Irene clapped her hands with glee. "There, that's the spirit."

Lionel intervened by standing up and towering over Nathan. "What the hell do you know about running a business? You screwed up yours so bad you almost landed in prison."

"I never claimed to be a business expert. That's Irene's domain. But I'm a damn good pharmacist and have proven myself essential for silentcides. I'm confident I can also teach others to do the same." Nathan rose to confront Lionel. Their mismatched size was comical. "I also have no doubt you can create, staff and run assassin boot camps. What sniveling little shit isn't going to do exactly what you tell them?"

"That's probably true," Lionel said while relaxing his shoulders and stuffing those enormous hands into his back pockets.

Nathan next faced off to Irene. "And I'm assuming this new business will be a three-way partnership."

"Hardly!" She bristled at the ludicrous suggestion. "It's my concept and my funding."

"You made that abundantly clear," Nathan countered. "But it's also a pipe dream without Lionel and me."

She suddenly admired the scrawny little doctor. He had finally grown a pair. She didn't dare admit it, but he was right.

Irene finished the bloody mary and crushed the cigarette into an ashtray. She gave them an icy stare. Neither of them would ever have a better opportunity. Hopefully, they recognized that fact. Nathan clearly did. Did Lionel?

She began her ultimatum like a closing argument in a courtroom. "Gentlemen, here's my final, nonnegotiable offer. I maintain full control and fifty-one percent of the profits. You two split the rest while building the business to my exact specifications. If you take the deal, great, start planning immediately. If you don't, that's okay too, but then get out. You're replaceable."

Nathan said with a smile, "I'm in."

Lionel walked toward the kitchen.

"Where the hell are you going?" Irene asked.

"To mix myself a drink so we can celebrate the new business. Want a refill?"

SEVENTEEN

A fter flying from Buffalo to the Twin Cities the day before, Michelle and Chris started Wednesday morning collecting supplies from his storage locker in a Saint Paul suburb. Then, despite her advice to resist the temptation, Chris drove their rental car to his former home in the Highland Park neighborhood. What an emotional mistake.

The rambler was in ruins from the gunfight two weeks ago. The windows were boarded. Bullet holes marred the siding. The collapsed front door was charred from the explosion that killed one of Irene's assassins. Drooping yellow tape encircled the lawn trampled by police and the curious. A huge sign read, "Condemned."

Chris was grave as he no doubt relived his brush with death. There was nothing she could say to ease his troubled memories. He loved that house. It had been his only sanctuary of normalcy. Now it was gone.

They rode in unsettling silence to her appointment in Como Park, a popular 760-acre recreation area. After turning off the engine, Chris spoke for the first time in a half hour. "You still want to do this?"

"Yes," she said while removing the seat belt.

His last words of caution were, "Then at least wear your disguise."

"Look, if I'm walking into a trap, what good is a disguise going to do me?" The conversation ended with the slamming car door.

Michelle felt her brother's watchful eye as she walked toward the inviting carousel music. Parents with children and grandparents with grandkids all seemed delighted as the dazzling wooden horses flashed by on the antique merry-go-round.[41] Michelle was jealous of their happiness.

"Want to go for a spin?" came a familiar gravelly voice.

Michelle turned to face her former mentor. Everything about Dr. Nathan Yasin looked old, except his intelligent eyes. His skin was pale and wrinkled. Liver spots and blotches of red dotted his bald head. The trifocals were thick. He had always been short, yet the spine curvature forced him to look up while talking.

Despite the physical frailty, he was still the smartest person Michelle knew. She had always admired him and aspired to be his equal. He had been a father figure while teaching her medicine and pharmaceutical science on the Amish farm, then her advisor as a silentcide assassin. She trusted his counsel implicitly.

They exchanged a hug. "Thanks for seeing me," she said in his ear.

"You know I always have time for my favorite protégé." Pointing toward the large, domed greenhouse,[42] he asked, "Would you like to tour the conservatory as we talk? The sunken garden has always been my happy place for tranquility."

"I'd love to," she said, "but I promised Chris I'd stay visible. He's watching from the car."

With a sigh of disapproval, Dr. Yasin said, "He's never been the trusting sort, has he?"

"It's not that," Michelle said in defense of her brother. "Just a bit overprotective."

"That's fair. Let's at least get away from this carousel music." After walking a few yards, he said, "So I was a bit surprised you wanted to get together again so soon. I assume you want to talk about Irene's offer?"

"What's that supposed to mean?" Michelle asked.

The creases in his brow deepened. He seemed equally perplexed. "Well, two weeks ago, after you asked for my advice on roles you might get in Irene's organization to replace your current one, I took the liberty of reaching out to her. She liked your ideas a lot. In fact, she asked me if I thought you were qualified to have my old job."

Michelle was taken aback. "What exactly would that entail?"

"Like managing the international network of approved pharmacists, teaching at the farms and being a pharmaceutical counselor for challenging silentcides. Frankly, it was just about everything you asked for."

Michelle thought about the pain and death that could have been avoided had Irene made that offer two weeks ago. Not now. Far too late. "That's not going to happen," she said.

"Don't sell yourself short. You deserve this. In fact, when I talked with Irene yesterday, she was still hopeful this could happen."

After a mocking laugh, she said, "She's either delusional, or lying, or both. She obviously hasn't told you what's been happening." Michelle proceeded to explain about the attempts on their lives. No gory detail was spared. As she talked, she monitored his expressions, trying to detect if he was surprised or already in the know. He was aware of the shootout at Chris's home. Apparently, the sensational violence dominated the local media for days. He also warned her about a massive police manhunt for Chris. Otherwise, Dr. Yasin seemed genuinely appalled by the other events she described. So what he suggested next was startling.

"I agree that's deplorable," he said. "But maybe if you ask for forgiveness, the role can still be yours. Irene might even be willing to make a peace offering to Chris."

"That's ridiculous!" Michelle exclaimed. "After all I've told you, how could you possibly reach that conclusion?"

"Because I think Irene is desperate. In fact, I know she is. In the past, I've seen her forgive and forget while making deals that serve her best interests."

"Seriously? What's she desperate about?"

"Her succession. She's proud of the network. And frankly, she's motivated more by pride and ego than money. But ever since Lionel got sick, and then I retired a few years later, she brought in the wrong leaders to accelerate the business. They recruited mercenaries, ex-military and criminals. Now, all Irene does is rant and rave about their incompetence. What I'm saying is, I think you and Chris could negotiate a package deal to be her successors."

Michelle was flabbergasted. "Would you honestly trust a deal like that?"

"Sure, if she needed you bad enough."

"And then, like a scorpion, she'd kill us as soon as that need was over."

"Not necessarily," he said, sounding a bit desperate.

His reasoning was illogical, actually ludicrous. She suddenly wondered if age was robbing his cognitive ability. Michelle said emphatically, "Yes, she would absolutely kill us down the road, just like she did to Preceptor."

"What?" he wailed in disbelief. "She killed Lionel?"

"Yes, a bullet to the back of the head. Chris watched it happen. She didn't tell you that?"

"No." His face distorted with grief. Eyes watered. Lips quivered. He began to tremble.

Worried he was going to faint, Michelle ushered him onto a park bench. "Here, sit down," she said with compassion, then placed a comforting hand on his skeletal shoulder. She watched as he struggled to compose himself. "Are you going to be okay?"

"Yes, just give me a minute." While rubbing the top of his head in anguish, he mumbled, "I can't believe it. I just can't believe it."

Michelle was surprised by the depth of Dr. Yasin's bereavement. "I wasn't aware you two were that close."

"You mean me and Lionel? Absolutely," he said with a sniffle.

"But you just worked together occasionally at the farm for a few years, right?"

"Heavens no. We've known each other – heck, let me think – at least thirty-six years."

"Oh, wow," she said, realizing that was her entire lifetime.

"Yes, in fact – maybe I shouldn't be telling you this – we created this whole network together. It was our baby."

"I had no idea," she said, then dared to probe, "Can I ask why you did it?"

"That's a long, sordid story, Michelle." He looked ashamed. "Let's just say I was at the crossroads of desperate and greedy … a really bad combination."

Sensing his need for contrition, she asked, "Do you regret it?"

"Not at the time, no. In fact, I was proud of it. We both were." He turned pensive. "But a funny thing happens when you get old. You start taking stock of your life, what you did and your poor de-cisions. And believe me, I made plenty of bad decisions." The pause was abrupt. Dr. Yasin took a troubled breath. His eye contact was direct. "Just like the bad decision I'm making right now. I am sorry, Michelle. I'm so, so sorry."

"For what?" she asked while studying his tormented face.

"For feeding you this line of crap about making a deal. I told Irene you'd never buy it. But she forced me to convince you."

"She forced you? How?"

Dr. Yasin took a handkerchief from his back pocket, dabbed his eyes, blew his nose, then struggled to explain. "Yesterday she called demanding I help with a huge silentcide commission. She said it was critical, the largest one ever. When I refused, she threatened my grandkids."

"Oh my god," Michelle gasped. "That's a new low, even for Irene."

"I know. I couldn't live with myself if something happened to the twins. Want to see them?" he asked. He pulled two worn school photos from his wallet. They were adorable boys, maybe ten or eleven. Dr. Yasin's eyes were loving and distraught. "I have no doubt Irene would have them maimed or killed. But I also know, once she has her claws in me again, she'll never let go. So, on an impulse, I told her I was meeting with you and reiterated my belief that you'd be a great long-term resource. She said if I could make that happen, she'd never call me again."

"I don't blame you." Michelle patted the top of his bony hand. "This big commission must be really important if she's making this kind of threat. Can you tell me what it is?"

"I would if I could," Dr. Yasin said, "but I don't know the details. She's being unusually guarded. She said I'd get my first assignment tomorrow."

"So what are you going to do?"

"What choice do I have? I have to do what she wants."

"Maybe …" Michelle said, then stopped. She was about to enter dangerous territory. One step forward was a point of no return. The downside could be catastrophic.

His head cocked with curiosity. "What were you going to say?"

Michelle weighed the risks, assessed his sincerity and decided to proceed. "What I was about to say is, maybe your way out is our way out." She spent the next couple of minutes discussing the plan for killing Irene.

He listened intently until she finished. "That might work," he said. "But instead of sarin gas, I suggest using VX. It's tasteless, odorless, not a lasting vapor hazard, and as little as one drop on the skin can be fatal."

"Do you have access to any?"

"Well, nerve agents have been outlawed since 1993. They're expensive and very hard to come by. But I can check with one of my cronies. With any luck, I might get a tiny amount by the end of the day."

Michelle was thrilled. "Thank you. That's all we'd need." Her enthusiasm then melted into concern for Dr. Yasin. "So, what are you going to do in the meantime with Irene?"

"I don't have a choice. I have to follow her demands. But what I can do, if you think it makes sense, is tell her we talked and that you're considering the leadership role. Maybe that'll stop the attacks for a while. How's that sound?"

As Michelle returned to the car, she worried if this had been a ruse orchestrated by Irene to learn their plans. The odds of that seemed remote, but it was a possibility.

Chapter Seventeen: Saint Paul, Minnesota

Photos 41–42

EIGHTEEN

Lancaster County, Pennsylvania
Thursday – Friday

Securing the nerve gas was successful. The trip back to Buffalo required two flights with a long layover. Chris and Michelle reunited with Ansel and Anna late on Wednesday night. They collectively decided to get an early start the next morning for the seven-hour drive to Philadelphia. When they climbed into Chris's late-model Ford Explorer – retrofitted with a high-performance engine plus ballistic glass and armoring – Michelle sensed an unspoken worry. Tension was thick and unsettling. They were finally on the offensive against Irene, yet the potential dangers were ominous. Everyone seemed anxious about their "do or die trying" plan.

As they traveled south along the Pennsylvania Turnpike, Chris looked hypnotized behind the wheel. Ansel and Anna slept in the backseat. Michelle was conflicted. Her heart knew the right thing to do, but she doubted the others would agree. The internal debate gnawed on her until reaching Allentown. The GPS on the burner phone indicated it was now or never.

"Turn right," she told Chris, shattering the silence.

"Why?" he asked. "That's the wrong way."

"Just turn off at Exit 56. Do it."

He did, but as the SUV slowed to get in line at the tollbooth, he questioned his sister. "What's going on?"

"We're going to the Amish farm," she declared.

"What the hell for?"

"To rescue Rachel Phillips."

Ansel leaned up toward the front seats. "Who's Rachel?"

"She's an orphan – I'd guess about fifteen. We met at the farm a couple weeks ago when Irene threatened to kill us both, then had Lionel shot. This is our chance to set her free."

"Okay, but why should we risk rescuing her?" Ansel asked.

"Because, among other things, she refused Irene's direct order to pull the trigger on me. That means she's not a hardened assassin yet. Don't you get it? She's just a scared and trapped teenager like we used to be."

Chris chimed in, "Assuming we rescue her – which I think is a really bad idea – what are we going to do with her?"

Impulsively, Michelle said, "Let's keep her."

Ansel scoffed, "She's not a puppy, for god's sake."

"But maybe we could use her as an asset."

"Not a chance," Ansel countered. "At best she'd be a liability."

"Then I don't know," Michelle said, flustered but resolute. "We'll drop her off at a church or a shelter … What difference does it make?"

"A big difference," Ansel said. "She'd expose us to the police."

Chris added, "And we'd broadcast to Irene that we're in the area."

Ignoring their logic, Michelle persisted. "But Rachel deserves freedom from that oppressive training camp, doesn't she?" She searched the faces of the two men. "Well, doesn't she?" They remained unconvinced. With an emotional plea, Michelle said, "Look, if someone had rescued us at her age, imagine how different our lives would be. We can give her the normal future we never had. Isn't that worth doing?"

Unexpectedly, Anna was the first to respond. "Personally, I think it's a great idea. I'm surprised you don't, given the hellish lives you've had."

The men looked at her, then each other, and finally agreed.

Ninety minutes later, they arrived at a two-star motel in the city of Lancaster, the core of Pennsylvania Dutch Country. Chris again suggested they rent two rooms to be shared by gender. He claimed the arrangement saved money. The obvious ploy was to prevent a late-night rendezvous between Ansel and her. Michelle was secretly glad to avoid the temptation.

Before leaving the motel, Chris made a needless speech to Anna about how he had promised not to involve her in dangerous missions, so she should stay behind. The pontification was humorous because Anna had no intention of going.

The three of them rode within blocks of the Amish farm where the siblings had spent ten years learning to be assassins. Chris turned down a deserted dirt road and cautiously navigated the ruts, rocks and overhanging branches until reaching a dead end. He pulled up the driver's side floor mat opened a concealed compartment, and pulled out three handguns. Ansel grabbed his Glock 17. Michelle got the SIG P229 Chris had confiscated in Québec City. Chris took the Glock 19 Ansel had purchased for him in Buffalo. In a well-practiced routine, each of them snapped in their magazines and chambered a 9mm round.

The walk through the woods was hindered by thistle bushes, blowdowns, thick undergrowth and hidden boulders. After Michelle's tennis shoe got stuck in a muck hole, it squished with every other labored step. The summer heat was oppressive. Sweat dampened their clothes. The mosquitoes, gnats and horseflies were ravenous. Red scratches soon crisscrossed their hands and arms while pushing forward. They were miserable but determined.

When they neared the tree line, Chris raised a fist, signaling to freeze, then retreated fifteen feet. "Okay," he said. "Michelle, you remain here. Ansel, you take the northern edge and I'll post the east. We'll rally back here a half hour before sunset. Take plenty of photos. Avoid engagement. If there's any trouble, then text. Otherwise, maintain silence. Questions?" There were none. Everyone had been similarly trained in surveillance techniques.

Michelle watched as Chris and Ansel disappeared into the woods. She slithered to the edge of the trees, wedged beneath a dense thicket and cleared the groundcover. From experience, she knew the hours of recon would pass slowly, leaving too much time for random thoughts.

From her position, she saw the backside of the barn[43] and stables. Within sixty minutes, Mamm came out struggling with a laundry basket. The woman wore a similar outfit – white bonnet, bland gray dress and dusty black shoes – as when she was the siblings' foster mother for a decade. Mamm, meaning "mom" in Amish, had aged considerably in the last sixteen years. She was frail and wrinkled.

"Rachel!" Mamm screamed through the screen. "Get out here. Now."

Rachel Phillips burst through the door, grabbed the basket and hurried down the rickety steps. Together they hung wet laundry on a pulley clothesline.[44] The teenager's denim-colored dress and untied bonnet flapped in the wind. She performed the task in efficient servitude.

Next, Rachel weeded the vegetable garden with a hand hoe and then picked a bucket of tomatoes. Michelle fondly recalled Mamm's spaghetti sauce and lasagna, especially the lasagna. She could almost taste the layers of venison sausage with homemade egg noodles and cheeses.

An hour later, Rachel disappeared into the barn, no doubt to tend to the horses and cows. Michelle remembered doing all of these laborious chores when she was Rachel's age. Mamm had always been a taskmaster.

As the surveillance dragged on, Michelle was surprised there was no sighting of Wolfgang König, the current leader of the Thanatos division. He had also been named Preceptor after Lionel Jørgensen was incapacitated eight years ago. Nor was Jacob Conners around. He was the self-confident and arrogant eighteen-year-old orphan who also lived on the farm. Jacob had shot Lionel in the head. They were an evil pair.

A twig snapped. Michelle whirled. The pistol was outstretched. Her finger hovered over the trigger guard, ready to shoot. She relaxed when seeing her brother's cheesy smile. Ansel arrived five minutes later. Within a half hour, they were back at the motel. The rest of the evening was spent comparing notes and planning. They worked together surprisingly well.

◆◆◆

When they awoke at four a.m., Anna kept apologizing to Michelle for vomiting again. To her credit, she pulled herself together to leave the motel room and be at the car on time. Chris and Ansel were already in the SUV.

They rode without talking. Anna's face was lit up as she stared at the GPS map on her phone, watching as the green arrow approached the Amish farm.[45] Chris slowed down. He pointed to the driveway, barn and house. Anna studied the scene. Then he sped up, U-turned, and drove back to the deserted road where the three of them exited the car. Anna drove off.

Walking down the dirt road was relatively easy in the moonless predawn. Trudging through the dark woods was nearly impossible. They broke through the thick trees near where Michelle had been stationed the day before. They shuffled down until reaching an unobstructed view of the property.

Without a word, Ansel pulled off a backpack and began assembling the sniper rifle he'd bought in Buffalo. His fingers were a fluid motion as he extracted the components, locked them together, screwed on the suppressor and adjusted the bipod. "Ready," he whispered. "Good luck."

Michelle and Chris crouched through the woods for about thirty yards so they could approach the backside of the barn. In unison, they crawled through the cow pasture, mindful to stay in the blind spot of the security cameras. The grass was wet with dew. Manure piles were putrid and infested with flies. Rocks and clumps of dirt pained their elbows and knees. Michelle worried about undetected sensors or booby traps leading up to the target. She mentally pictured Wolfgang and Jacob charging out with blazing guns. The unexpected crow of a rooster made her flinch.

Their assumption was that the daily chores on the farm hadn't changed since they were kids. They hoped Rachel would be in the barn at sunrise to milk the cows, feed and water the horses and collect eggs. The plan depended on the familiar routine.

The morning quiet was shattered when a screen door creaked and then slammed shut. Footsteps pattered down the porch steps. Sounds of excited animals came to life as the heavy barn door banged open.

Rachel was early, or they were late. Regardless of the reason, Michelle and Chris were not in position. They accelerated their pace until they reached the barn, stood up and pressed against the rotting wood siding. They paused. Michelle closed her eyes, slowed her pulse and breathing, and entered the zone. A glance at Chris confirmed he was also prepared. He mouthed the words, *Let's go*. She nodded.

With their handguns ready for combat, Chris slid against the barn. She watched him turn the corner. He would stop on the other side to guard the gap between the barn and the house. When she finished counting sixty seconds, Michelle inched toward the barn's service door. The latch was stuck from rust. Extra pressure wedged it free. The hinges squeaked, causing her to gasp. She pried open the door. The four-inch barrel of the SIG P229 was the first thing inside.

Michelle's irises struggled to adjust to the subdued light, but her nose triggered flashbacks at the smells of the hay, manure and animal musk.[46] Not much had changed. Rustic farm implements hung from the walls. The workbench was cluttered with tools. Animal stalls badly needed paint. Rachel was squatting on a stool, squeezing the teats of a cow. Streams of milk squirted into a steel pail with every tug.

A horse whinnied, sounding an alarm. Rachel jumped up in a panic. Terror swept across her fresh young face. She threw up her arms in surrender and began to cry. Watching the traumatized teenager was heartbreaking. Michelle saw herself twenty years earlier.

While lowering her weapon and signaling the girl to drop her arms, Michelle calmly said, "Hi, I'm Michelle Barton. We met ..."

"I know who you are," Rachel said with a shaky voice yet with a hint of defiance. "What are you doing here?"

"I – or I should say we – have come to get you out of here."

Suspicion registered in the teenager's dark brown eyes. "Why? Is this some kind of test?"

"No, nothing like that," Michelle tried reassuring her. "We honestly want to rescue you from this life."

"What do you get out of it?" Rachel asked, having been taught that anything good comes with a heavy price.

"Nothing, except the chance to give you a future my brother and I never had."

After a moment of contemplation, Rachel's round cheeks flushed with fear. "No, no, no, I can't leave. Wolfgang will track me down and kill me. Just go away and leave me alone. Please."

Michelle understood the girl's chronic struggle for self-preservation. They shared much in common. "Listen, you'll be safe. Soon Wolfgang, Irene Shaw, and her entire network will be gone. That's our mission. So this is your chance – probably your only chance – for a fresh start."

The girl hesitated. Her nostrils flared. Tears rolled. She bounced back and forth with anxious indecision. She finally spoke. "You promise?"

"Yes, I promise," Michelle said. "But we've got to go. Right now. Are you ready?"

"I think so."

"Good." Michelle pulled a phone from her pocket and announced, "Now!"

"Ninety seconds out," Anna responded.

Michelle looked back at Rachel. "Okay, so here's what's going to happen. A friend of mine is going to be here in ninety seconds. When she comes down the driveway, you'll run to the car and stop for nothing, hear me?"

Rachel nodded while wiping away the tears.

Michelle continued, "My brother Chris – you also met him a couple weeks ago – will be guarding our exit. When we're in the car, he'll join us. Then you'll finally be safe. Any questions?"

"No," she said. While they waited, Rachel pulled off the bonnet, loosened her long brown hair and shook it free. She was already anticipating a new life.

Michelle watched out the barn door. The seconds passed slowly. Too slowly. In a cloud of trailing dust, Anna sped down the driveway and came to an abrupt stop. Michelle told the teenager, "Okay, this is it." Into the phone she announced, "Coming out." Back to Rachel, she commanded, "Go! Run!"

Rachel was athletic. Her long legs sprinted toward the SUV. Michelle was close behind. The screen door burst open.[47] Mamm emerged, holding a double-barreled shotgun. She screamed, "Stop! Now!"

The teenager froze. Michelle was out of position to aim the pistol. She'd be dead before spinning around. Anna looked horrified from the driver's seat. Chris yelled, "Drop the gun, Mamm." He pointed the Glock 19 through the wooden slats of the porch.

"My, my, my," the old woman said, "isn't this just something else. I am sooo disappointed in you two. You were my favorites. Thank heavens Preceptor isn't alive to see this. After all we've done for you, you have the audacity to come back and pull something like this."

Chris was unaffected. "I said, drop the gun or I'll shoot."

Mamm shook her head in disbelief. "You used to be such a sweet boy, Chris Davis. I can't imagine you'd shoot me."

"Yes, I would, in a heartbeat. And it'll be your last one if you don't drop the weapon and let them go."

The showdown appeared to be a stalemate. Nobody seemed willing to concede, yet nobody was pulling a trigger. Rachel's eyes darted in terrified bewilderment. Mamm's eyes were fixed and unflinching. Chris edged toward the stairs, hoping to disarm Mamm peacefully. Michelle contemplated raising her pistol.

Rachel panicked. She bolted toward the Ford Explorer. Mamm swung the shotgun. The blast was deafening as Rachel slammed into the car. Almost instantaneously, Ansel's sniper bullet struck Mamm in the chest. The old woman's body ricocheted against the house before collapsing on the porch. Rachel's fingernails clawed at the car door handle. She was desperate, scratching frantically until slumping to the ground.

Michelle dropped to her knees in sorrow and grief. Attempting to rescue the teenager had been foolhardy. The rash decision was all her fault. Instead of giving Rachel a future of freedom, she got her killed. The girl would have been better alive and trapped than dead. The guilt was overwhelming.

Chapter Eighteen: Lancaster County, Pennsylvania

Photos 43–47

NINETEEN

Friday

Anna sat in terrified paralysis behind the wheel of the SUV. A growing circle of crimson seeped across the gray dress of the crumpled old woman. Her legs were askew, her bony fingers still clutched the shotgun, and her mouth was agape in death. The teenager lay face up in the dusty driveway. Horror and shock distorted her young face. Michelle knelt in devastation, sobbing.

Anna watched as Chris approached his sister. After shoving his pistol behind his back, he tenderly held Michelle's shoulder, touched his forehead against her temple, and whispered something. She nodded through her tears. They shared a moment of grief. Then he took her gun, helped her stand and ushered her to the other side of the car. After getting her seated in the back and assisting with the safety belt, he kissed her on the side of the head. She rubbed away some tears, managed an appreciative smile, and uttered, "I'm okay," but clearly, she wasn't. With empathy, he patted her knee before closing the door.

Chris returned to the driver's side. Rachel's body blocked the access. He grabbed the teenager's legs and dragged her fifteen feet. A trail of blood followed in the wake. He seemed remorseful while straightening the girl's denim dress. The gesture was clearly meant to offer Rachel some dignity in death. Then he opened the driver's door.

Anna wanted to scream, to damn him for the incessant exposure to violence and death. Repeatedly, Chris had violated his promise to keep her safe. But he did the unexpected. Chris hugged her. The warm embrace seemed mutually soothing. With a quiver in his voice, he said, "Thank god you're okay too." The plural suggested he was equally grateful she and Michelle were unharmed.

Without letting go, he pulled back a few inches. There was something baffling about his expression. His skin was blanched. Those blue-green eyes were troubled. He was struggling to stay strong yet appeared painfully vulnerable. Or was it a repentant mourning? Perhaps a hopeless resignation? With unsteady fingers, he touched Anna's brow, then her cheek. The gesture spoke volumes about his compassion. But rather than share his feelings, he spoke with controlled and patient professionalism, "I should probably drive. If you can hop in back, I'll return in a minute."

"Where're you going?" Anna asked.

"To retrieve the surveillance videos. Hopefully they're stored here and not in the cloud."

As he dashed off, Anna suddenly realized this failed rescue was not his fault. Maybe none of the atrocities had been his fault. Just like Rachel, he and Michelle were lifelong victims trying to escape tyranny or die trying. Maybe they really were inherently good people forced to lead terrible lives. Their degeneracy had started at this hellish farm. Now two of their childhood captors – Lionel and Mamm – had died on this farm. With any luck, no orphan would ever be abused here again. At least they had accomplished something good.

Anna stepped out, opened the back door, slid across the seat and wrapped her arm around her friend. Michelle accepted the comfort by burrowing her head into Anna's shoulder. There was nothing appropriate to say.

Anna then came to another realization. It was time to stop solely thinking about herself. Chris and Michelle were hurting just as badly … maybe worse. They owed her nothing yet were willing to sacrifice everything. So, rather than expect their protection, Anna also needed to be grateful and start helping if she could. Too bad a precious young girl had to die before they coalesced as a team.

TWENTY

Elkins Park, Pennsylvania
Friday – Saturday

C hris was despondent. If he had shot Mamm when given the chance, then Rachel would be alive. He was also determined. Another failure was not an option. The best remedy for both was getting immersed in the minute details of how to kill Irene.

His disposition improved the moment he opened the laptop he'd retrieved in Saint Paul. While Michelle, Anna and Ansel ate lunch at the hotel restaurant, Chris sequestered himself in the room he shared with Ansel. The target was Irene Shaw's mansion in Elkins Park, a prestigious suburb ten miles north of downtown Philadelphia. The community of seven thousand residents had been an epicenter of business elite dating back to the late nineteenth century.

Step one was to learn everything about her estate. The fourteen-thousand-square-foot mansion[48] was designed for a railroad magnate in 1896 by Horace Trumbauer, a famous architect of extravagant Gilded Age manors. The ornate, white marble façade featured a sweeping double staircase, Corinthian columns and a grand crescent-shaped balcony. In the center was a spacious courtyard. Also on the twenty-acre property were a sizable guesthouse, a six-car detached garage, four sentry posts, a gatehouse and an elaborate garden.

It seemed fitting the original owner was a robber baron whose wealth was created by exploitative business practices. When he was forced into bankruptcy after the 1929 crash, the estate was sold for pennies on the dollar to his attorney, Gilbert Maynard Shaw, Sr. Irene was third generation. Soon, the Shaw legacy would end with her death.

Chris studied everything he could find about Irene's property. He also analyzed access roads, neighboring homes and nearby parks, plus Saturday's weather forecast. After a late-afternoon scouting drive through the neighborhood, he reviewed the findings with Michelle and Ansel. Together they considered the options and selected the best approach. Chris wasn't satisfied. He was rarely content until he repeatedly considered every nuance and committed the details to memory.

To his credit, Ansel kept asking how he could help. The best way to help was to give Chris solitude. The only irritation was when Ansel returned to the room shortly before nine o'clock. Booze breath. Chris had a strict policy of never drinking the night before a mission.

◆◆◆

At five thirty Saturday morning, Chris and Ansel left the hotel parking lot. Having his former foster brother in the passenger seat was unsettling. Chris had always partnered with Michelle. The siblings were a well-orchestrated pair. In contrast, he knew nothing about Ansel's habits in the field. However, the unfamiliarity posed minimal risk because today's plan could be implemented by one person. That was why Chris had suggested Michelle and Anna spend their day recovering from the disaster at the farm. They needed a stress-free rest.

Almost immediately, Chris began worrying he'd made the wrong decision. But then, he worried about everything on game day, especially a day as important as this one.

At sunrise, they arrived at a dog park.[49] The grassy area was already filling up with a mix of purebreds and mutts at play. The site was chosen for several reasons. People were distracted by their dogs or chitchatting with neighbors. Few probably stayed at the park for more than fifteen minutes, a half hour tops. Nearby was an open field[50] surrounded by trees. These were perfect conditions for anonymity. Best of all, the location was about ten blocks from Irene's mansion with no houses in between.

Chris extracted a small aluminum case from the back of the Ford Explorer. Ansel grabbed a blanket and a paper sack filled with deli food and refreshments. They nonchalantly walked toward the field until finding an isolated spot. After spreading things out to simulate a picnic, Chris asked, "Are you ready to see this?"

"Yup," Ansel said with excited anticipation.

"Ta-dah." Chris unveiled a handheld controller and a mini drone wedged into foam.

"Wow, that's cool," Ansel said as he admired the hummingbird-shaped drone. It was painted iridescent green, black, red and white to simulate a male ruby-throated hummingbird, the only species that nests in Philadelphia. "I've never seen a hummer up close, but it seems bigger than I imagined."

"It is," Chris admitted, "but not by much. Its six-inch wingspan is about fifty percent bigger. And, almost like the real bird, those paper-thin wings can fly vertically, horizontally, and diagonally. It even hovers."

"That's amazing." Ansel seemed genuinely impressed. "But couldn't a guard still detect it as a drone?"

"Unlikely," Chris said with confidence. "At high altitudes, it's hard to perceive a size difference. Near ground level, I make sure something like background foliage provides camouflage. It's also remarkably quiet."

Ansel nodded his understanding, then pointed at a tiny opening in the bird's belly. "Is that the spray nozzle you were talking about?"

"Don't touch," Chris warned. "It's extremely toxic." After Ansel pulled back his finger, Chris continued, "Yes, inside that tube is the VX nerve agent."

SILENTCIDE 2: VENGEANCE   139

"The volume must be infinitesimal," Ansel said. "You sure it's enough?"

"Plenty. The fatal dose for inhalation or skin contact is about half the size of a drop of water. All I have to do is maneuver Walela within thirty feet overhead."

With a questioning expression, Ansel asked, "What did you just call it?"

"Walela. That's a woman's name in Cherokee meaning hummingbird. Ready to launch this little girl?"

Chris carefully removed the drone from the case, stomped down grass to create a launch pad, and placed the small bird on its four wire feet. Then he lifted the controller, extended the antenna and turned it on. The video screen flickered before showing an image. Chris pushed Start and gripped the joystick. Walela fluttered, lifted, hovered, then darted toward Irene's mansion. Chris asked, "Did you start the timer?"

"Oh, yeah, sorry," Ansel said while pulling out his cell phone. "That was twelve minutes, right?"

"That's the max flight time, so set it for ten to allow a couple of minutes for the return trip. That should be plenty."

The two men focused on the screen as the hummingbird reached the property line surrounded by a tall wall. Phase one was strictly reconnaissance. Chris maneuvered the drone to inspect areas unavailable by satellite view. As he identified points of interest – guards, cameras, windows and doors, the front portico, the inner courtyard, balconies, HVAC intakes on the roof – Ansel annotated the hand-drawn map of the compound.

The cell phone timer beeped, indicating time was up. Chris reversed course on Walela and expected it to land in about sixty seconds. A fifteen-to-twenty-minute recharge would be required before the next flight.

Ansel's voice filled the wait. "That thing really is cool. Do I remember you saying you stole this baby from the Defense Department?"

Chris looked up and laughed. "Not exactly. My Thanatos facilitator secured it for a past silentcide commission. But yes, it's a third-generation Defense Department prototype."

"What's something like that cost?"

"From what I've read, the R&D on this unit was about four million bucks."

Ansel whistled at the price tag. "That's a bit out of my budget."

Chris bantered back. "Mine too. Heck, with my paycheck, I can barely afford a kite." When Chris looked back at the controller screen, he panicked. "No, no, no, no, no," he said while trying to determine why the video was black.

"What's wrong?" Ansel asked, sharing the distress.

"Not sure. The controller seems fine. I'm guessing Walela crashed."

"Shit. How'd that happen?"

"Any number of reasons," Chris said. "I'm guessing a gust of wind knocked her down, or maybe the battery died."

"So now what?"

"Luckily it has a GPS, but it's only good within ten to fifteen feet. So we go looking for her. My guess is it's in the middle of that field someplace." Neither of them wanted to speculate if the drone was broken.

As they started walking, Chris cursed his sloppiness. He should have never relaxed and taken his eyes off the screen. Total stupidity. But being around Ansel always knocked him off his game. It was as if there was a childlike need to impress his older foster brother. He chastised himself. *Stop being emotional. Start being professional. Assess the risks. Take action.*

"Listen," Chris said. "I didn't see a guard on Irene's roof. But if one is there and he's scoping the area, we'd be easy to see. So here's what I'd suggest. When I tell you, don't freak out."

"I'm listening," Ansel said with apprehension.

"We're going to casually stroll, hold hands …"

"What?" Ansel barked.

"Yeah, no one is going to question seeing a romantic date on a Saturday morning."

"Hell, I'm questioning it. Big-time."

"Just do it," Chris asked as he grabbed Ansel's hand.

"You realize this is really creepy, right?"

With a deadpan expression, Chris responded, "You realize your palm is really sweaty, right?"

Ansel burst out laughing, began skipping and singing "Zip-a-Dee-Doo-Dah" toward the GPS marker. They searched the tall grass for nearly an hour before finding the hummingbird drone. Fortunately, Walela seemed unscathed except for a bent antenna. The real test had to wait until after the recharge. Neither of them breathed when Chris turned the unit on. With trepidation, he nudged the joystick. Walela sprung up, twisted in the air, then flew back toward Irene's mansion.

Five hours passed, consisting of ten flights and ten recharges. Several times, Chris tried extending the battery life by perching Walela in a tree. Moving around the mansion exterior and over the Islamic-style courtyard were essential if they hoped to catch Irene walking her beloved dog, entering a car, or opening a door or window.

The ugly truth was she was probably on high alert with no intention of exposing herself. Or they could have missed an opportunity during a recharge period. Irene might not even be home. Chris was increasingly discouraged yet resolute. He'd stay until sunset and return the next day if needed. And the next day. His vengeance would not be denied.

Ansel's cell phone timer started beeping when it finally happened. Walela was hovering over the courtyard when Irene stepped out with an Afghan hound. She was wonderfully predictable in allowing no one but herself to care for that mutt. She had repeatedly warned the siblings that predictability was an Achilles' heel. Thankfully, the phrase "Do as I say, not as I do" would be her undoing.

Chris throttled Walela into a nosedive as the dog lifted his leg on a marble fountain suspended by white lion sculptures.[51] Irene was prepared to throw a tennis ball as Chris fixated on her tight French bun. His finger slid over the nerve agent trigger. He calculated the optimal height for the spray. His heart raced. Sixty feet. The hummingbird kept plummeting. Fifty feet. He pictured her nerves misfiring, muscle paralysis and asphyxiation. A painful, terrifying death. Forty feet. The controller screen went haywire.

"Shit! Shit! Shit!" Chris screamed as the video gyrated wildly. The drone hadn't crashed. It was gaining altitude and moving fast. He maneuvered the joystick in every direction. No response. He banged the side of the control box. Nothing. The tops of buildings and homes flashed by. The cars on the streets seemed smaller with every passing second.

"What's wrong?" Ansel kept asking.

"I don't fucking know," Chris said in a panic while struggling to regain control.

A water tower[52] appeared on the screen. Walela was on a collision course. Within seconds, the hummingbird would smash into pieces.

The drone abruptly stopped. A giant black eye encircled with a yellow ring appeared as a gray hooked beak shattered the camera.

"What happened?" Ansel yelled.

Chris lowered his head. Completely demoralized. Barely above a whisper, he said, "Walela was attacked by a peregrine falcon."

At first, Ansel was in stunned disbelief. Then he started to laugh. It wasn't funny.

Chapter Twenty: Elkins Park, Pennsylvania

Photos 48–52

TWENTY-ONE

ELKINS PARK, PENNSYLVANIA
Saturday – Monday

Chris slumped in the corner of the dark hotel room with his face buried between his knees, drowning in morose thoughts. For nearly twenty-eight years, he had dreamed of ending Irene Shaw's tyranny. Since rebelling three and a half weeks ago, countless people had died while he'd jeopardized the people he cherished. He had one chance to stop the torment but had failed. No one was to blame but himself.

There was a knock at the door. "Chris," Michelle called out tentatively. "May I come in?"

He resented the intrusion and didn't respond.

"Come on. You've been in there for hours. Let's talk about this. Please."

He ignored her pleas until she went away.

Fifteen minutes later, Ansel burst into the room carrying a pint of bourbon. He flipped on the lights, pulled back the curtain, retrieved two glasses from the bathroom and poured a double into each of them. "Drink this," he bellowed.

"Go away," Chris demanded, refusing to take orders from a suspected drunk.

"I'm not going away, and I've been able to kick your ass since you were ten. So, suck this down, then suck up your woe-is-me bullshit."

Ansel's stance was commanding. He wasn't going to back down and Chris didn't have the fortitude to argue. He took a sip.

Ansel got belligerent. "Stop being such a wuss. Chug it."

Chris cringed as the alcohol scorched his throat. Fire erupted in his stomach. After a coughing fit, his eyes watered. The demeaning ordeal was reminiscent of when Ansel bullied him into smoking a cigarette at age twelve.

Ansel gulped his bourbon as if it were water, then slammed the glass down on the windowsill. His tone was suddenly conciliatory. "Look, your plan was brilliant – much better than anything I could've come up with. I mean that. I was really impressed. And it almost worked, except for that fucking falcon."

Chris stared at his former foster brother, trying to read his sincerity. Ansel didn't seem patronizing. His praise sounded genuine.

Ansel squatted to Chris's eye level before saying, "Now I have one question, and I want you to think about your answer very carefully. Do you want to be the sniper or spotter?"

Ansel was obviously proposing Plan B consistent with his training as a violent assassin. Chris said, "You're the more experienced sniper – by far – so logically you should be the spotter and take command."

"You're right. That also lets you pull the trigger on Irene. So it's settled."

"Not really," Chris said with self-doubt. "I might freeze when it comes to the kill shot."

"That's a load of crap," Ansel said. "From what you told me about how you handled Québec City, you'll do just fine on the trigger."

"That was all adrenaline to stay alive," Chris rationalized. "This type of shooting requires total body and mind control. I'm not sure I've got that in me anymore."

"I know you do," Ansel said with confidence, "but suit yourself. You're officially the spotter." He reached out his hand. "Now get your lazy ass off the floor and let's go to work."

Chris contemplated the proposal. It might work. It had to work. Not trying again was unacceptable. But the next attempt must be flawlessly implemented. There might never be a third chance. He said, "Before I agree, do me one favor."

"What's that?"

"Stop drinking, at least for tonight," Chris said, trying not to sound judgmental. "We both have to be stone-cold sober tomorrow."

Ansel rubbed his chin stubble while contemplating the request, seemed prepared to act offended, then nodded. He took a long swig on the way to the bathroom, poured the rest of the pint into the sink and dramatically dropped the bottle into the wastebasket. When returning to the bedroom, he said with a charismatic smile, "Okay, let's rock and roll."

They first reviewed Chris's hand drawings of the property, the hummingbird surveillance videos, satellite views and topo maps. They decided there was only one feasible location for a sniper's nest. The conclusion worried Chris. "If we figured out the perfect location so quickly, wouldn't Irene's security have done the same thing and created countermeasures?"

Ansel's answer was ominous. "Absolutely."

They spent several hours reviewing the sniper rifle and spotting equipment, selecting units of measure such as MOA versus mils, and meters versus yards, plus agreeing to field communication terms, signals and protocols. Getting in sync was relatively easy when realizing they shared weapons instructors at their respective farms.

As the discussion progressed, Chris was inspired by Ansel's transformation. He was a seasoned pro who painstakingly considered every detail and alternative. They shared a passion for microanalysis. Ansel was also comfortable and confident on his own turf yet was treating Chris as a respected equal. Chris realized he had to stop suspecting Ansel and start respecting him if this mission was going to succeed.

After making a list of needed supplies, the foursome drove twenty miles away. They took turns shopping at different places to minimize the chance of being identified on in-store cameras if something went wrong. Big-box and sporting goods retailers were avoided in favor of small, local shops. Then they huddled in the hotel room, made preparations and reviewed the plan until nine o'clock. When the lights went out, Chris stared at the ceiling and worried. Ansel snored.

+++

Chris slapped the top of the clock radio before the alarm went off at three thirty. Within forty-five minutes, Michelle stopped the Ford Explorer along a service road near the dog park. The men jumped out at the tree line. Her role was to leave the car at a nearby crowded apartment lot, double back, retrieve their backpacks and act as overwatch. The foster brothers were confident she could secure and defend their position, as well as warn them of potential threats.

Under the concealment of heavy brush, Chris and Ansel removed their jogging suits, revealing black jeans and sweatshirts that had been spraypainted to replicate the surroundings. Black hockey tape was used to secure minimal snacks, water and supplies to their upper arms. The Glocks were shoved behind their backs. On the bottom of their homemade ghillie suits were heavy tent canvasses to protect their chest and legs. The upper layers were black mosquito netting covered with multicolored yarn and twine. After wiggling into the makeshift cloaks, they attached an abundance of foliage.

They also had to improvise when camouflaging their faces. Using the buddy method, they took turns applying layers of brown makeup concealer. Next, with face paints intended for kids' parties, they created random patterns and blended them together. Finally, they attached leaves to their spraypainted gear, boonie hats and bandanas before slipping on heavy-duty gardening gloves. When finished, they were confident they could go undetected within two yards.

The plan was simple. Implementation would be arduous. Twenty hours were allocated to crawl a half mile. That allowed an additional four hours to prepare the sniper's nest before dawn on Monday morning. If needed, they had agreed to lie in wait until sunset Tuesday. The maximum time of the mission could be seventy-two hours. Hopefully, Irene would be dead long before then.

With two thumbs-ups, they got on their bellies. Ansel cradled the collapsed Nemesis Valkyrie takedown rifle in the crooks of his arms. Chris clutched the spotter's scope. The gear was encased in plastic but was hardly waterproof. Using their elbows and knees, they began inching forward.

The first leg of the journey was relatively easy. The temps were cool, the morning dew acted as a sound suppressor, the terrain was mildly cluttered, and the lush foliage offered optimal concealment. Best of all, this stretch of woods was not in the mansion's line of sight. They covered four hundred yards in five hours.

The advance got more challenging at the base of a tall retaining wall. Above them was an empty parking lot of the only commercial building in the area. Below them was a marsh filled with a foot of muck and water saturated with green algae. The wetland was choked with sawgrass, reeds, tangled shrubs, rotting blowdowns and discarded trash. They used handfuls of vegetation to change their camouflage before proceeding. The hovering horseflies were unrelenting, causing painful welts. The afternoon heat intensified the stench. Rolling sweat stung the eyes. Their arms ached from holding the sniper equipment above the waterline during the five hours they moved 180 yards.

At three o'clock, when they emerged from the slough, they rested for a few minutes, nibbled on an energy bar, picked at caked mud and shared anxious glances. The last 290 yards had the greatest potential to be treacherous. Irene was always paranoid. Having security measures only on her property would be insufficient. She would naturally insist on a wider perimeter of defense. They were about to enter that zone. One wrong move could trigger an alarm, or worse, trigger a death trap.

Their pace started at three yards an hour. The first obstacle was a rusted barbwire fence. It seemed innocuous, but cutting or climbing could signal an intruder. Digging a channel took an hour. Fortunately, the water level of the nearby swamp was a foot below the topsoil.

During their granular advance, Chris used a palm-sized pinpointer metal detector to sweep the ground ahead. Each vibration made him flinch. Most were false positives, such as buried beer cans, a hubcap, appliances and utility lines. However, he did uncover what appeared to be a pressure plate and later a booby trap. They circumvented the threats.

One security camera was spotted. If there was one, there were more. As it got dark, Chris worried the cameras could be infrared, capable of detecting body heat. The only consolation was the abundance of deer scat suggesting a herd of whitetails lived in the woods. But with a superior night camera, a vigilant guard could detect the difference between Bambi and a bad guy. They could be screwed.

By midnight, their forward progress was less than two yards per hour. When they arrived, they spent sixty minutes searching for an ideal location for the sniper's nest. There wasn't one. According to the topographic map, the knoll leading up to the commercial building should have provided sufficient elevation to see over the mansion's boundary wall from a prone shooting position. But even a kneeling position wouldn't provide an unobstructed view. They'd have to risk detection and an unstable shot by standing. Equally bad, trees on Irene's property might block clear scope visibility, especially in a high wind. The conditions were deplorable.

They retreated a few yards before painstakingly stripping and attaching bark, limbs, branches and leaves to the ghillie suits. Their face camouflage was darkened and then concealed by bandanas until only their eyes were exposed. Ansel extended the rifle stock,

removed the thread protector, and screwed on a suppressor to re-
duce the muzzle blast and flash. Then they advanced into position
before bracing the sniper rifle and spotting scope into crooks of
trees for stability.[53]

Ansel pulled back the bolt, placed a 7.62x51mm cartridge into
the chamber, and locked it in. The .308 Winchester Magnum would
travel at supersonic speed over a half mile in a second. At the estimated target range of 490 meters, the impact assured one shot, one
kill. Chris smiled. He had etched Irene's name on the shell casing.

Chapter Twenty-One: Elkins Park, Pennsylvania

Photo 53

TWENTY-TWO

Monday

For two hours, they stood motionless in the dark. Chris battled exhaustion by controlling adrenaline flow to stay awake without elevating his pulse. He estimated the effects of temperature and air pressure on the bullet's velocity. Twice he calculated the bullet drop based on the target range. He tried ignoring the blisters inside wet socks and cramping calves from dehydration. The head fog was increasing from a lack of food. As the wind picked up, he repeatedly determined the bullet drift in mils. A few cars had already arrived in the parking lot above their left shoulders. The sound of songbirds at first light was welcoming. While taking another reading, Chris's concentration was shattered.

Someone was running toward their position from down below. His hand slid beneath the camouflage. Footsteps pounded the asphalt of the neighborhood road while approaching the base of the knoll. Only one assailant could be heard. He began extracting the Glock 19.

A young woman – perhaps mid-twenties – jogged past them. Her ponytail flopped back and forth with a stride like Anna's. Once she was out of sight, Chris relaxed and resecured the weapon. Blood pressure slowly returned to normal.

As the sun began rising, the target zone was finally illuminated. He looked through the eyepiece, zoomed to six power, adjusted the

focus and groaned with disgust. The angle was worse than imagined. Assuming there was a chance to take a shot – the odds were
no better than ten percent – accuracy would be extremely difficult,
bordering on impossible.

During planning, he and Ansel had agreed the ideal way to kill
Irene would be straight on as she stepped out the front door and
into her chauffeur-driven car, yet there was no safe cover at the end
of the long driveway. That forced them to select an inferior alternative: a side shot. But the space between the front door, where a
car would park, and the roof of the overhanging portico was much
smaller than they calculated. "Shit," he heard Ansel whisper as he
came to the same conclusion.

They waited and watched. The sun climbed above the trees,
causing whiteouts and nasty shadows. The wind became variable
with unpredictable gusts up to twenty miles per hour. Chris kept
telling Ansel how to adjust his rifle, but the crosswinds were becoming unpredictable. Prudence suggested to abort.

Then it happened. This could be it. After twenty-five hours of
anticipation since entering the woods, a man came out of the mansion. Chris zoomed to ten power. Wearing a black suit was John,
Irene's longtime driver. He always accompanied her. As he walked
toward the six-car detached garage, Chris pushed the fob-shaped
transmitter attached to the scope, signaling Michelle the ambush
was imminent. John entered the side entrance.

The foster brothers began whispering their communication
sequence.

Chris: "Target, mansion front door."

Ansel: "Contact."

Chris: "Distance reading?"

Ansel: "Two-point-one."

The main garage door opened.

Chris: "Up three-point-zero-four from one-hundred-yard zero."

Ansel: "Up three-point-zero-four."

A black, midsize Rolls-Royce Phantom drove out of the garage.

Chris mentally cursed the strong wind gusting from left to right. "Dial in left one-point-four."

A miniature French poodle started yipping. Chris dared to look down. The perfectly groomed dog was looking up from the base of the hill, pulling wildly on the leash.

"What do you see, Buttons?" an old woman asked while searching the tree line and struggling to control the pet.

The bark was incessant as the limousine made a circular turn and pulled beneath the portico, stopping at the front entrance.

The woman was becoming frantic. "Be a good boy. Heel, Buttons. Heel!"

John opened the driver's door.

With a yank of the leash, the dog tumbled backward, then clawed and scratched to return.

John opened the back passenger door.

She shouted, "We're going home. Now!" then began dragging the animal down the street while John casually leaned against the limo.

Chris struggled to regain his composure. He focused on the gap between the mansion entrance and the limo door. It would take Irene one second to approach the car, perhaps another if she was ladylike getting in. That was barely enough time to confirm the target, issue the command to shoot, for Ansel to pull the trigger and the bullet to end her life.

There had to be a way to give Ansel at least two more seconds to control his breathing and heartbeat, or his accuracy would be jeopardized. Missing the kill would be catastrophic.

John shuffled his feet, looked at his watch, appeared irritated, then folded his arms.

The delay lasted eight long minutes. The wait was insufferable.

John was scrolling on his phone when he snapped to attention.

In the reflection of the car door, Chris saw something white moving. Assuming it was Irene's gray hair, he whispered, "Tally."

Ansel groaned, "Ready," on his exhale.

"Send it," Chris commanded before Irene emerged in the open.

The next second seemed like an eternity before the blast. Chris watched the thermal pattern of the bullet in flight. Irene appeared. The impact was gruesome. A direct hit to the chest. Red spray exploded as she slammed against the limo door. Her lifeless body collapsed.

TWENTY-THREE

Michelle's knee bounced with anxious anticipation. Fingers tapped on the steering wheel inside the stolen Mazda at the end of the commercial building's parking lot. Her other hand held a cell phone as a prop, pretending to talk. Every employee arriving for work could be a potential witness. Looking natural was the best way to go undetected or unremembered.

She pulled the brim of the baseball cap tighter over her long black wig and sunglasses while glancing to the right at the building's windows. Hopefully no one was becoming curious about the idling white car. She glanced left at the trees along the grassy knoll. Chris and Ansel were hiding there someplace. Straight ahead, two people were smoking near the employee entrance. Michelle had only been parked for two minutes. Yet each passing second at the rendezvous point was elevating her pulse. Countless things could go wrong. Any one of them could be disastrous.

The muffled sound of a high-powered rifle made her flinch. *Oh my god. Did they shoot Irene?* Whiplashing her attention toward the corner of the retaining wall, her eyes riveted on the planned spot for their extraction. Thirty seconds ticked off. Sixty. Ninety. "Come on, come on, come on, come on," she whispered frantically.

One gloved hand appeared at the top of the retaining wall. Then another. As Ansel's face appeared – struggling to pull himself up and over – there was a massive explosion. The car shook as the ridgeline disintegrated in an inferno. The wildfire engulfed twenty yards into the woods. Trees and brush were consumed by crackling flames. Billowing smoke swirled around the destruction, blocking her visibility. Red-hot ash rained on the windshield and hood. Michelle was helpless. Frenzied. Panicky.

She shrieked when the back door swung open. A black cloud of blistering heat swept in as Ansel jumped into the seat and dropped the rifle in the cargo space of the hatchback. Chris stumbled, grabbed Ansel's hand, crawled in, and placed the sniper's scope on the floor. Dark soot covered their camouflaged faces.

"Go, go, go," Chris shouted in a raspy voice as the men slumped down so they couldn't be seen from outside. His coughing and wheezing were dreadful.

Michelle struggled to get the gear shift into drive. Her foot twitched before pressing the accelerator. She proceeded cautiously until clearing the smoke and ignored the rubberneckers by staring straight ahead through the parking lot. After turning onto a two-lane road and checking the rearview mirror to see if they were being followed, Michelle asked, "Are you guys okay?"

"What?" Ansel yelled back.

With increased volume, Michelle repeated the question.

"Yeah, I think so," Ansel said, "except for the ringing in my ears."

"How's Chris?"

There was a brief silence before Ansel answered. "He just gave me a thumbs-up, so I think he's going to be fine. I suspect he got a chest full of smoke."

"What happened back there?" Michelle asked. "Did they shoot an assault missile or something at you?"

"I don't think so," Ansel said. "The explosion seemed to come from underground."

Chris managed to clear his throat before saying, "I think the fire was Irene's soul going to hell." His laugh was interrupted by another coughing fit.

Michelle smirked. Her brother's lame joke was a great indication he was going to recover. "So does that mean Irene is dead?" she asked with elevated expectations.

They waited for Chris to respond. Verifying a kill was a critical role of the spotter because the rifle recoil typically prevented the sniper from seeing a bullet's impact. As Chris struggled to breathe, Ansel said, "I feel good about the shot." That was hardly a confirmation. He added, "Chris is nodding back here."

Michelle asked, "And he's sure it was her?"

"Yeah, I'm pretty sure," Chris weakly answered.

Ansel got angry. "You're either sure or you're not. Which is it?"

After a pause, Chris said, "Yeah, it was her. It was definitely her."

Ansel whooped. "Fantastic! Then the wicked witch is dead." He began singing with a loud munchkin voice.

Michelle joined the chorus. Chris sang the best he could before hacking again.

The return trip to the apartment building was short, yet tensions remained high. They couldn't relax until their escape was assured. She heard Chris and Ansel stuffing sniper equipment into their backpacks, putting on jogging suits over their camouflaged jeans and sweatshirts, using baby wipes to remove face makeup and paint, and rubbing leaves and dirt from their hair. Their physical transformation wouldn't be perfect but good enough to be unremarkable from a distant glare.

The original plan was to return the stolen Mazda unscathed. That objective failed. The interior reeked of smoke and the exterior was charred by flying embers. Michelle dropped them off at the Ford Explorer near the dog park, found an empty space at the apartment complex out of sight of security cameras, wiped fingerprints off the steering wheel and searched for incriminating evidence left behind.

Michelle had wanted to hustle back to the SUV but couldn't risk being noticed by the clusters of people watching thick black smoke in the distant sky. Sirens from racing emergency vehicles seemed to be converging on the fire from every direction. She pretended to gawk while meandering toward the car, then hopped in. Ansel was impatient and edgy behind the wheel. Chris was slouched in the front passenger seat. His skin was ashen and sweaty. His eyes were red, raw and watering. At least the coughing had subsided.

As if sensing her concern, Chris said, "I'm fine, Michelle. Believe me, I'm fine."

She hoped that was true.

During the twenty-minute drive to the hotel, unbridled exuberance melted into sheer exhaustion. The twenty-six-hour mission without sleep had been draining despite the successful outcome. The three of them agreed to reconvene for cocktail hour before traipsing to their rooms. Michelle used the prearranged knock and leaned against the doorframe until the lock was undone from inside.

Anna's expression registered nervous optimism. "Is everything okay?"

Michelle remained straight-faced while throwing the wig and sunglasses on one of the twin beds. She solemnly walked up to Anna, held her shoulders at arm's length, and feigned a sigh of gloom. An enormous smile followed as she declared with excitement, "We did it!"

"Did what?" Anna asked, as if hesitant to jump to a conclusion.

"I should say the boys did it. They shot Irene."

Still doubting the news, Anna asked, "You mean she's dead?"

"Yes indeedy!" Michelle gushed. "Dead as dead gets."

"Oh my god," Anna squealed with happiness while jumping up and down. "That's awesome. Really, really awesome. And the boys are safe?"

"Chris got a snoot full of smoke, and they're exhausted, but otherwise they're fine."

"Thank god," Anna said, rushing in for a hug.

Michelle returned the affection. They shared joyful tears of relief. For Michelle, crying seemed to release decades of fear and oppression. Suddenly, the implications of this dream come true became real. They were all safe to start new lives. The realization was difficult, almost impossible, to fathom. A wonderful future lay ahead. Liberation was exhilarating.

After spending a few minutes describing what happened, Michelle said, "I'm sorry but I really need some sleep. Besides, Chris and Ansel can do a better job of explaining everything. Wake me about four o'clock, will you?"

"Sure," Anna said. "In the meantime, I'll use my iPad to monitor online news about the fire and shooting. Is there anything I can do for you?"

"Just give me dark and quiet. That's all I need." She crawled into bed without undressing. The sounds of Anna pulling the curtains and turning off the lights were the last things Michelle heard.

TWENTY-FOUR

ELKINS PARK, PENNSYLVANIA

Monday

It was amazing what seven hours of sleep and a long hot shower could do for one's vitality. Michelle and Anna took turns in the bathroom getting ready to celebrate. Wearing the same dresses from the disastrous dinner in Montreal was initially disconcerting, but they refused to let those memories ruin the evening. Michelle let Anna wear her high heels to replace those that had broken during the shootout escape eight days earlier. Dirty tennis shoes hardly matched Michelle's lavender cocktail dress, but what difference did it make?

When they met Chris and Ansel in the lobby, Anna volunteered to be the designated driver, a clever way to conceal her pregnancy. During the drive to the restaurant, the men took turns describing the mission details. They were justifiably proud of what they had accomplished. They also showered Michelle with praise for her role. Ansel ended by paraphrasing a movie line, "Wherever there is injustice, suffering, or liberty is threatened, you will find ..."

"The Three Amigos," the foster siblings proclaimed together.

"Who will you find?" he asked again as a rallying call.

"The Three Amigos!" they shouted in unison, pretended to ride horses, and laughed hysterically. Their childhood bond had been reestablished. The evening was going to be spectacular.

The aromas inside the steakhouse were heavenly, especially on an empty stomach. Fresh-baked bread. Meat flaming on an open grill. Garlic. Without reservations, they were required to wait in the bar. The piano player's classical music was barely audible over the crowd noise. Chris and Ansel downed several shots of high-priced tequila. Michelle joined for the first one, then sipped a cosmopolitan. Anna drank a Coke while listening to them reminisce about the good times they'd shared in the foster home. The banter and razzing were filled with laughter.

Ninety minutes later, when their table was finally ready, Chris ordered a bottle of Dom Pérignon. The sommelier professionally displayed the label, cut the foil, placed a linen napkin over the wire gage and cork, gingerly wedged them free, poured four glasses, and placed the bottle in an ice bucket.

As Chris prepared a toast, Anna interrupted, "Can I have the honors?"

He nodded.

"I just wanted to say thank you, to all of you, especially Chris, for keeping your promise. The last eleven days have been, uh, what should I call them?"

"Hell," Chris quipped.

"Yeah, that's a really big understatement. Anyway, you all promised to keep me safe, and you jeopardized yourselves doing it. And although I had my doubts along the way," she added with a snicker, "you did exactly what you said. So thanks again." Anna looked fondly at each of them before continuing the heartfelt tone. "I'm also thrilled all of you are finally free. May the rest of your lives be everything you hope for and deserve. Cheers."

Chris was misty eyed. Michelle dashed over and gave Anna a warm embrace. Ansel echoed the sentiment. "To us, to all of us, and our futures. Cheers."

Dinner was gluttonous. Course after course of oversized popovers, soup, salads, sides, and gargantuan slabs of sizzling beef cooked to perfection. Even the sampler dessert tray was enormous.

Michelle was stuffed and ready to leave when the boys suggested a nightcap. Three of them were reseated at the bar. Ansel excused himself and walked unevenly toward the restroom.

A few minutes later, Michelle heard someone playing off-key with one finger on the baby grand piano. Ansel's voice was immediately recognizable as he bellowed the opening lyrics of "Yankee Doodle Dandy."

"Oh my god," she exclaimed while pointing. "Ansel's making an ass out of himself."

She leaped up from the table. Anna followed behind to offer support. Ansel pretended to flip tails on the backside of an imaginary tuxedo before sitting on the piano bench and flashing a "catch me if you can" smile. He bent over the keyboard, positioned his hands and began playing an improv boogie-woogie. The music was magical.

Michelle stopped in amazement, listened and watched as his left hand bashed out a repetitive bass beat. His right fingers fluttered frantically over the upper keys in a counter rhythm. The driving tune was wild and infectious.

Anna leaned toward Michelle's ear and said, "I'll take care of this."

"No, let him play," Michelle responded. "He's good."

"It's embarrassing. Let me handle it." Anna walked up to the piano, stared at Ansel with disapproval, gave him a playful nudge on the shoulder, and sat down beside him. With a delightful grin, she joined as a duet.

Anna's feet were tapping as Ansel increased the dizzying pace. "Faster. Faster." They were all giggles and smiles as their hands pounded out the syncopated melody. "That's it. That's it." Heads bounced. Bodies gyrated. Fingers flew. Their fun was a blur of musical motion. "Yeehaw!"

People started clapping in time with the rapturous beat. A few recorded the performance on cell phones. One man tapped forks on the tabletop like a snare drum. Another clinked water glasses. The crowd was loving it.

"Wanna swing dance?" Chris yelled from behind Michelle.

"Absolutely!" she said.

Chris grabbed her hand, pulled her close and spun her free. They were in perfect sync with wild steps, high kicks, and jockeying side by side. Left foot, right foot, joining arms, backward, forward, turn and swing. Every move was electrifying.

As the foursome returned to the table among roaring applause, Michelle concluded this had been the best day of her life and the start of a promising new one.

The car ride to the hotel was quiet. At eleven thirty, three of them were drunk and exhausted. Anna drove cautiously. Chris was napping or passed out; it was hard to tell the difference.

Ansel unexpectedly leaned against Michelle in the backseat. Initially startled and surprised, she sensed a romantic intent. His breathing changed. Her chest fluttered. With an index finger, he touched her chin, drawing them closer. The shadows heightened the sensuality. She closed her eyes and tilted her head.

Their first kiss was gentle and exciting beyond expectation. The warm rush of affection was arousing. They pressed together. Their kisses lingered and explored. The passion was shattered as Anna turned onto a frontage road leading to the hotel.

Ansel pressed a plastic card into Michelle's hand and whispered, "I rented a room for us. Please join me in 419 when Anna goes to sleep." He sealed the invitation with another quick kiss as Chris stirred and awoke.

Michelle was ecstatic and couldn't wait to tell Anna when they entered their room. Then, with self-doubt, she said, "I know what you're thinking. Chris will probably get pissed, right?"

"So what?" Anna said with conviction. "You deserve to be happy. Just do it."

"You think so?" Michelle asked to build her confidence.

"I know so. Go. Have fun. That's an order."

"Alrighty then," she said with nervous glee.

Michelle rushed into the bathroom, brushed her sandy-blond hair and was reapplying makeup when Anna entered. "Seriously? You're wasting time in here getting all dolled up? You realize Ansel couldn't care less at this hour, right? Get going. Now!"

Michelle twirled with excitement, started leaving, returned for the key, mentally verified the room number, dashed out, coaxed the elevator to hurry, checked her reflection in the mirror after pressing the floor button, tried calmly walking down the hall, stood at the door, took a deep breath, then another, and inserted the key.

The room was dark. Thinking he was already in bed, she allowed her eyes to adjust before groping forward. "Ansel?" There was no answer. She flicked on the nightstand light and sat down. Two hours later, she realized he wasn't coming.

TWENTY-FIVE

SEVILLE, SPAIN
Tuesday

Irene rolled over and relished the warm towel being draped across her body while she admired the gold mirrored dome above her living room. Gifted artisans had lovingly recreated the Hall of Ambassadors' ceiling. Each of the four walls featured triple arches of exquisite ceramic tiles and plasterwork. The Mudéjar style, a blend of Muslim and Christian architecture, was showcased throughout Real Alcázar.[54] Europe's oldest palace still used by monarchs was located four hundred feet from her penthouse apartment in Seville, Spain. She envied the royal family. She deserved to emulate their opulent lifestyle.

A debonair shirtless man with bronze skin, an ink-black beard, plus curly hair leaned down within inches and asked in a sultry voice, "May I, Ms. Shaw?" She blinked. With unhurried efficiency, Alejandro removed a dozen bobby pins from the French bun, brushed out the long gray hair and caressed her scalp. The relaxation was decadent.

The masseur's gifted fingers proceeded to release the tension from her temples, then stroked her cheeks and chin. Every touch was pure bliss. After applying heated oil to his palms, he coddled her throat. The movement of flabby skin was distracting and spoiling the mood until his sensuous advance toward her chest.

The carnal aura was shattered by a knock on the door. "God-damn it," she muttered before screaming, "I explicitly told you not to disturb me."

"I realize that," her manservant said in an apologetic voice, "and I'm very sorry."

"What is it?" she demanded to know.

Pierre answered, "Mr. Wolfgang König is requesting a video conference."

"At six o'clock at night? Screw that. Tell him to call me in the morning."

"I suggested that, Ms. Shaw. But he claims to have important information you'll want as soon as possible."

Irene sighed with disgust and mumbled, "Everything is always urgent with that man." Then she yelled to Pierre, "Have him call in a half hour. Then go to my dressing room."

There was a forlorn expression on Alejandro's handsome face as he asked, "I assume our session is over?"

"I'm afraid so, dear. A woman's work is never done." She extended her hand. The towel fell to the floor as he helped her off the massage table. Like a true gentleman and professional, he didn't gawk while holding the Pima cotton robe.

Pierre could only do so much to get her ready in thirty minutes. He coiffed her hair and reapplied makeup. There was no time to get dressed. She settled for red silk pajamas. The outfit was a bit suggestive, but it would give Wolfgang something to fantasize about.

When Irene sat down in the study, the invitation to join an en-crypted video conference was already flashing on the thirty-four-inch computer monitor. Wolfgang König looked grim, as if consumed by stress. His short hair was messy, he hadn't shaved in days, and his clothes were disheveled. But those inset black eyes were still intense.

Too bad. Stress comes with the job. There's no sympathy at the top. Irene's opening salvo was, "What's so damn important?"

"I have good news, bad news and an update. If you're pressed for time, I can deliver only the two pieces of bad news," he said in a monotone, as if too exhausted to be worried about her shooting the messenger.

"Oh, goodie," she said sarcastically. "This sounds like a delightful agenda. Let's start with the sugarcoating."

"I just sent you last week's P&L report for both divisions," Wolfgang began. "The highlight is that Thanatos sales are up significantly, especially in Europe, and all account payables are current. Unfortunately, Phonoi revenue is down twelve percent, and that's before the write-offs I discovered that were never reported. Frankly, I suspect Jürgen withheld information from you for years."

"Point of clarification, dear. Have you already switched to the bad news?"

"No, Ms. Shaw. The good news here is the Phonoi books are now clean. And as you requested, I've verified all commissions are on track and client satisfaction remains high."

Irene was impressed. Wolfgang had done a lot of housekeeping since the demise of Jürgen van Oorschot ten days ago. But she had to keep him on his toes. "That's fine, dear. But I expected those reports yesterday. That's why they're called Monday reports. Why the delay?"

"That leads me to the bad news," he said as his nostrils flared. Those nose hairs really needed grooming. "And before you ask me why this information is also delayed, I wanted to get all the facts first so I could answer your inevitable questions."

"This sounds ominous. Okay, so what are the facts?"

"First, Farm One was attacked Friday morning. It wasn't discovered until Jacob returned from an assignment early Saturday afternoon."

"Jacob?" she asked while trying to place the name.

"Yes, Jacob Conners. He's the teenage orphan who lives there.

Anyway, Mamm and Rachel were killed in the attack led by Chris and Michelle. Anna was the driver. And I suspect Ansel was the sniper but that can't be confirmed."

"Goddamn it!" she screamed. "Was that some kind of revenge against me?"

"Perhaps, but it appeared they were trying to kidnap Rachel."

"Why on earth would they want that brat? They couldn't possibly think I'd pay more than a nickel in ransom."

"Their motives are not clear, but I did retrieve from the cloud a security video of the shootings. Would you like to review it?"

"Heavens no. Why take time watching a movie when I know the ending? So what've you done about this unfortunate mess?"

"We discreetly cleaned it up. Their bodies were entombed in concrete and buried next to Lionel's deep in the woods. And all evidence of our operations was scrubbed from the property. I'm confident there will not be police repercussions. In an abundance of caution, I also closed neighboring Farm Two. Our European, Asian and Middle East facilities seem secure for now, but we've heightened security."

Irene got irate. "That's a stopgap at best, Mr. König, and you know it. Those domestic training facilities are vital to our business model. You must establish new sites as soon as possible. Do you understand?"

"Of course," was his less than satisfactory answer.

Irene pressed for a specific deadline. "By when?"

"Give me ninety days."

"You have thirty. Understood?" She didn't wait for a response. "If we're done with this distasteful topic, let's move on to your second piece of bad news." Wolfgang was about to speak when there was a knock on Irene's study door. "Hold that thought," she said to Wolfgang with a raised index finger, then yelled out, "Come in."

Pierre walked in pushing an antique tea cart. "Excuse the interruption, Ms. Shaw, but I thought you might be hungry."

"Aren't you an absolute sweetheart."

The manservant placed two platters on the desk. One was a selection of cheese and crackers. On the other were different finger sandwiches containing Nova Scotia lox, Spanish Iberian ham and Russian Osetra caviar. Pierre also set down a Baccarat brandy snifter suspended in a sterling glass warmer. With his normal aplomb, he lit the candle wick then stepped back. "The Louis XIII cognac should reach the proper temperature shortly. Enjoy."

Oh my god. That boy deserves a raise. While nibbling a triangular delicacy, she looked back at Wolfgang. He was still standing at attention. She said, "Okay now, where were we?"

"At the second piece of bad news."

"That's right. Proceed." Irene swallowed. "Oh, it's such a shame you're not here to taste this caviar. It's marvelous."

Wolfgang took a pained breath. His jaw twitched. "There was also a shooting at your estate yesterday morning."

Now that was alarming. "Was anybody hurt?" she asked with concern.

"Yes, unfortunately your body double was killed."

That was unfortunate – the old coot had served Irene for eight years – but it was the cost of doing business. "Please tell me Brutus is okay."

"Your dog is fine, Ms. Shaw, but he misses you."

Relieved, she said, "Please send him my love. And up his anti-anxiety meds, will you?"

"Of course."

She sipped the cognac. The taste was tainted by this repugnant conversation. What a waste! "Last week you warned of a high risk at the estate and suggested I go to Spain. Your job was to monitor the situation on site. Why didn't you stop it?"

His stoic stare was betrayed by a pinched brow. "Because I was managing the cleanup at the farms."

"So their motive for the farm shooting was a diversion. And it worked. Goddamn it, Mr. König, if I've told you once, I've told you a thousand times. Delegate. Delegate. Delegate. Where the hell are your priorities?"

Wolfgang became brazen. "With all due respect, Ms. Shaw, the people at your estate are expendable. My priority was to protect your training operations from being uncovered by the police. Exposing them could've unraveled everything. So I stayed at the farm but immediately put your estate guards on high alert. They didn't detect any threats on Saturday or Sunday, but I knew Chris and the others were out there someplace. So, on Monday morning, I told them to deploy a decoy with the hopes of flushing them out."

She didn't approve of his tone, but Wolfgang had made excellent decisions. Perhaps he had the brains and balls to succeed her someday. "What happened exactly?"

"Your double was shot leaving the front door to get into John's limo."

"From a position at the end of the driveway?"

"No, from the hill about five hundred yards northwest of the property."

Irene pictured the location, considered the angle, calculated the exposure time, and said, "That was a hell of a shot. Sounds like Ansel's handiwork. Did your people take countermeasures?"

"Of course. Within ninety seconds, they triggered the incendiary. Unfortunately, no bodies were found in the rubble. But as planned, the authorities are calling the explosion a ruptured natural gas line. The local utility company has already made a public mea culpa and has agreed to pay for all damages. In short, we're in the clear."

"Hardly. We still have that troublesome foursome running around. Please take careful note of the number four. Ansel and Michelle are no longer considered assets and should be permanently removed from the payroll. Understood?"

"I reached the same conclusion. We now have the advantage because they've let their guard down. I presume they think you're dead. Ending this soon should not be a problem."

"It's an absolute problem," she countered. "It'll be a lot harder finding them without Ansel's support."

"Not true. In fact, it's become easier and more reliable to track them."

"How so?" she asked while deciding to sample the lox.

"As per standard protocol, we've been running three AI-enhanced facial recognition programs on all posts where we have data share contracts with the major social media platforms. Last night, we got two hits – one on Facebook, the other on TikTok – showing Ansel and Anna playing boogie-woogie on a piano."

"I love that kind of music," she proclaimed.

"Want to see the clip?"

"Sure." She tapped her finger on the crystal glass while watching. "I had no idea Ansel played." She cackled. "He's good, but also looks drunk as a skunk."

"He was. Otherwise he would've never allowed someone to record his public spectacle."

"So other than providing some amusement, how does this help us?"

"Well, the GPS coordinates on the video's metadata identified the location as a steakhouse. I immediately instructed one of the Philly cops on our payroll to secure a warrant for the pursuit of persons of interest in the firestorm near your mansion."

Irene interrupted. "I hope to God you're using Seargeant Joey. He's the best for tasks like this."

"Of course, Ms. Shaw."

She nodded her approval.

"Anyway," Wolfgang continued, "Joey searched the restaurant's reservation system and paper credit card receipts. Then we conducted a background screen of the customers. Only one had a spotty internet presence. Using that name and the warrant, Joey secured the card association company's cooperation. He learned the prepaid card was purchased a couple years ago yet was first activated two weeks ago. History showed purchases stretching from Saint Paul to Québec City and down to Pennsylvania. In short, this card belongs to Chris Davis. Joey will be notified on future card activity and, of course, discreetly pass the details along to us. So, assuming Chris keeps using it, he and the others will be easy to find until we can plan the best time and place to strike."

"Terrific." The compliment just slipped out. It would be rude to retract it. "Let's get that done tout de suite and notify me the minute it happens. Does that conclude today's bad news?"

"Almost," Wolfgang said. "There's one minor issue where your opinion would be valuable."

These endless administrative issues were tiring. In order to stretch her legs, she got up and stared out the window. While watching throngs of tourists in Plaza del Triunfo, the epicenter of Old Town Seville, she said, "Okay, but let's pick up the pace. I'm busy."

In his continuous dry, unflappable style, Wolfgang said, "The matter concerns the client who ordered the commission on Monteiro."

"What about him?" she asked with contempt, then took a gulp of the cognac.

"He's furious about the missed deadlines, wants a deeper discount and demands results before the end of the month because he has a critical deadline."

Irene had a hot flash of anger. "Does that son of a bitch have any idea what this commission has cost me in time, money and people's lives? And he has the audacity to make demands? Tell you what. Let's cut our losses. Just silence the bastard and end the distraction. Understood?"

"Does that mean you've changed your mind about having Anna killed?"

"Heavens no. She still deserves it for all the trouble she's caused."

"We are in total harmony on the matter. Consider it done. In conclusion, here's an update on your number one priority."

If he knew it was her number one priority, why did Wolfgang always discuss it last? "Proceed." She sat down and listened intently.

"The highlights are Senator Nisor remains in a coma. Dr. Yasin has delivered his magic potion for the next senator on the list. And our silentcide asset has begun reporting the results of her surveillance. Based on the senator's debauched secret life, there should be plenty of opportunities soon. Of course, I will continue to manage every facet of the operation. I'm confident this next senator's death should really get tongues wagging."

"And that crybaby Mr. Zola remains happy?"

"Other than his incessant crankiness, yes, he's fine."

Irene leaned back in the chair, considered all she had heard, and said, "Excellent work, Wolfgang. Really excellent."

For the first time in the eleven years she had known him, he smiled. "Thank you, Ms. Shaw." His teeth were a dingy yellow.

She couldn't resist adding, "Now my advice is to take a shower, change those wrinkled clothes and for god's sake clip those nose hairs."

Chapter Twenty-Five: Seville, Spain

Photo 54

TWENTY-SIX

For Anna, waking up the next morning was a weird yet wonderful sensation. The fear was gone. No more threats. Even the daily routine of vomiting was missing. The big unknown was what the future held once getting home without a job and with a baby.

The ringing phone jostled Michelle awake in the adjacent bed. Ansel profusely apologized for passing out and standing her up. He begged for forgiveness and the chance to talk. She acquiesced. When the foursome got together for breakfast, Michelle announced she and Ansel were flying back to Minnesota to spend a week camping in the northern woods.

Chris was livid but struggled to contain himself. His eyes expressed disgust and betrayal at Ansel. He locked onto his sister with disapproval. Michelle's nonverbal communication was to accept it and don't make a scene. Rather than express his anger, Chris offered to drive Anna back to Boston. It came across more as a "two can play that game" than a courteous gesture. Anna was not sure why her impromptu answer was, "Yes." Maybe her response helped Chris save face. Maybe there was no reason to hurry back to an empty house filled with unresolved problems.

The departure of the two couples in the hotel parking lot was bittersweet. Sure, there were lots of hugs, a misty eye or two, and plenty of remarks such as, "Thanks for everything," "Let's stay in touch," and the whisper in Michelle's ear, "Have fun." But it was clear to everyone that Anna had been thrust into their world, didn't belong there and would never return.

Anna drove for ninety minutes while Chris slept in the passenger seat. When she stopped for gas, he woke up, gave her his credit card so she could pay the pump attendant, and went inside to use the bathroom. When he returned, she handed back his card. "It was rejected," she announced with a hint of judgment.

"No problem," he said while extracting another from his wallet. "All of my alias cards are prepaid. That one must have hit the limit."

"Put it away," she said. "I already paid the guy for the gas. Let's go."

His accusatory temper flared. "You didn't use your credit card again, did you?"

"Give me a break. No, I used one of the cards Ansel got for me in Buffalo. He also set up a direct payment plan so, unlike somebody I know, it won't hit a spending limit."

"Oh, okay, thanks," he said apologetically, paused, then tried changing the subject. "Where are we?"

"Someplace in New Jersey."

Naturally, that answer wasn't good enough. Chris found their location on the phone's GPS and said, "Hey, we're not far from the Big Apple. Wanna go? I've never been there."

"Seriously? The world traveler has never been to New York City?"

"Nope, and it's always been on my bucket list. Come on, let's do it," he said before climbing into the driver's seat.

As the mile markers flew by, Chris's mood behind the wheel transitioned from enthusiastic to contemplative, perhaps sullen. Anna broke the silence. "What's wrong?"

He hesitated before muttering, "Michelle and Ansel."

"What about them?" she asked, but already understood his problem.

"It doesn't seem right," he said while tightening the grip on the steering wheel.

"Why not? Because she's your sister?"

"Yeah, and he's our foster brother."

"Was your foster brother, Chris. Was. That was over twenty-five years ago. They're adults now. Don't they deserve to be happy?"

With a glance toward Anna, he said, "Now you're sounding like Michelle. She said almost the exact same thing about a week ago."

"Well, she's right."

His expression pinched with condemnation. "But what if they're sleeping together?"

"So what? Have you forgotten how exciting that early infatuation phase is?"

"You mean like we had?"

"Oh, sure," she said with an unintended scoff. "How long did that last? About four days? No, I mean that ecstatic feeling of falling in love."

Sadly, he said, "No, I've never had that. I assume you have?"

"Yes, but only once when I met Paul in grad school. I quickly knew he was the one and that someday we'd get married and have a family. You know how that story ended." With a pensive sadness, she said, "Frankly, it took years to get over Paul's cheating on me, especially when he left me for a man. I questioned everything about myself while sinking into a deep, dark hole. I only recovered after building a wall around myself. Since then, I've been resigned to live alone. It's easier, and I don't get hurt."

"You mean like I hurt you?" Chris asked with a forlorn expression.

"Exactly." The single word sounded harsh but summed up her feelings. Chris had traumatized her beyond what she thought possible.

"I'm sorry about that, Anna. I really am. I hope someday you can forgive me."

"Chris, I understand why things happened the way they did. I wish they had been different. I really do. But as far as forgiving and forgetting is concerned, I'm not sure that's in the cards. All this experience has done is reinforce why I'm safer behind my wall."

Hearing herself reach that conclusion was depressing. Maybe keeping the baby was the only way to have a lifetime of love with someone else.

◆◆◆

After checking into adjoining rooms at a Manhattan hotel, they hired lots of cabs to follow Chris's sightseeing itinerary. Among the highlights were the Statue of Liberty,[55] the observation deck on the Empire State Building,[56] and a hot dog vendor on the perimeter of Central Park.[57]

Throughout the day, the heat and their feverish pace were making Anna increasingly lightheaded. She drank plenty of fluids to restore electrolytes and avoid dehydration. Nothing seemed to help. As they were walking through Times Square,[58] Chris suggested getting dinner followed by a Broadway musical.

"That sounds nice," she said. "But I think I'll pass."

With a look of concern, he asked, "Are you feeling all right?"

"Yeah, just kinda tired. It's been a long day. Let's go back to the hotel, okay?"

While waiting alone for room service, Anna started feeling crampy. She turned on the TV, hoping a good program would be distracting. The cramps worsened. She held her belly and felt weak. After running to the bathroom, she sat down and discovered the brownish discharge with bright red clots.

"No, no, no, no," she wailed among a torrent of tears. She suffered in pain and grief for about an hour. The loss was heart-wrenching.

There had been so many deaths during the last three weeks. This was the worst of them all.

The bleeding worsened. She got scared. She didn't want to overreact but sensed the need for medical help. Waiting could be a mistake. Calling for an ambulance seemed melodramatic. Going alone could be dangerous. Involving Chris would reveal her guilty secret. The sudden back spasm made the decision.

"Chris?" she called out while knocking on the connecting door.

His face blanched upon seeing her. "What's wrong?"

She admitted softly, "I'm, uh, having a miscarriage."

"Oh my god." He gently ushered her to a chair, then froze. He looked scared too. To his credit, he didn't ask any personal questions, only ones of concern. "How can I help?"

"I think I need to go to a hospital."

After a five-minute cab ride and a two-hour wait in the emergency room, Anna was finally assigned to a cocky hurried resident. Her vitals were taken, a litany of embarrassing questions was asked, a pelvic exam was conducted, blood was drawn, an ultrasound was given, and she endured a suction aspiration. Each procedure was more invasive and frightening.

Near the conclusion, the doctor burst into the recovery room. Anna was stunned when he said in a clinical and dispassionate way, "The vacuum procedure removed the bad tissue but may cause cramping and bleeding. That unsavory process should end in about twenty-four hours."

The insensitive bastard! That "bad tissue" was my baby. My dead baby. Mourning the loss will not end in twenty-four hours.

During the cab ride back to the hotel, Chris held Anna's hand in silence. When they returned to her room, he asked, "Is there anything else you need?"

"No, I appreciate your going along. Thank you."

"It was the least I could do. I feel terrible for you." He hesitated, as if struggling for anything comforting to say. There was nothing to be said. With a despondent look on his face, he whispered, "Good night," then closed the door.

Being alone again opened the floodgate of emotions. Anger. Denial. Fear. The cramps worsened. The bleeding persisted. The grief was crushing. While splashing cold water on her face, she remembered the abortion pills Michelle had given her. They went down the toilet. Fate had made the decision about the baby that she was unwilling to make.

She knocked on Chris's door.

"Are you all right?" he asked with worry.

"No," she said with a quivering voice. "I can't be alone right now. Can I stay with you?"

"Absolutely." He turned down the bed, covered her up and sat alongside.

"I owe you an explanation," she said with her head down.

"No, you don't. It's none of my business."

She felt compelled to get the confession over with as quickly as possible. "The father was George. We only had sex once. Just once. I knew at the time it was a mistake. I had no idea how big of a mistake it was."

"None of that matters," he said with empathy. "Just rest. You've been through hell. I'm so sorry for your loss, and everything else you've been through. You didn't deserve any of this." His eyes expressed genuine sorrow.

She tried sleeping. He remained seated beside her. After about fifteen minutes, she said, "Chris, thanks for your compassion. I've seen it many times during the last few weeks. Deep down, you're a good man. I only wish you were the person I thought you were."

"I could have been," he said with torment, "if it hadn't been for Irene."

Chapter Twenty-Six: Philadelphia, Pennsylvania to New York City, New York

Photos 55–58

TWENTY-SEVEN

Cambridge, Massachusetts
Wednesday

During the five-hour drive from New York City to Cambridge, Anna was slumped in the front seat, often pretending to nap. Her complexion was white. Her eyes were dull. She seemed broken. Whenever she shuffled uncomfortably while cradling her abdomen, he wanted to ask if she was all right. He resisted. Of course she wasn't all right. He was at a total loss for what to say to make things better. The conclusion: don't try. He only ran the risk of making things worse.

Chris grasped onto one positive aspect of Anna's hellacious miscarriage. If she had not gotten pregnant, she would have had her period during the cruise and maybe taken the poisoned Midol. Then she'd be dead. Instead, fate took the life of her friend Jessica and now her unborn baby. Anna didn't deserve being surrounded by so much personal and random death. He blamed himself. Guilt and remorse assaulted his gut.

After turning onto Memorial Drive[59] running parallel to the Charles River and approaching the MIT campus, Chris said, "We'll be there in a couple of minutes."

Anna sat up, turned down the visor, inspected her reflection, fluffed up the black pixie haircut, wiped away a smudge under an eye, snapped the visor back and folded her arms in disgust. She looked as traumatized as she felt.

They parked near Longfellow BioSciences.[60] Anna had been the vice president of marketing at the start-up biotech firm for five years. Six weeks ago, sixty percent of the employees were laid off when disappointing clinical trials and a wrongful death lawsuit forced the company toward bankruptcy. Seventeen days ago, after a last-minute acquisition by Fármaco – a pharmaceutical company with twelve billion in annual oncology drug sales – Anna was declared redundant and fired. That day, she flew to Québec City to join Chris. He winced at all the violence that had happened since.

Anna was surprised then frustrated when the office building was locked. She knocked repeatedly until an elderly woman opened the door. There was a commercial cleaning logo on her shirt. "May I help you?" she asked.

"Hi, my name is Anna Monteiro. I used to work here. We've just stopped by to pick up some luggage that was shipped from Québec City."

The woman said suspiciously, "This place is closed, hun. Only a few people left. I don't know who you should talk to."

Anna asked, "By chance is Liz Walker here?" The woman tilted her head with confusion. "She's the chief science officer." The woman was clueless. "She's about five-nine, green eyes, freckles, with curly red hair and bangs."

The woman's face lit up. "Oh, sure. She was there a minute ago. Go on up."

Anna was sullen as they walked toward executive row. The empty cubicles were all that was left of the vision to cure cancer with Liz's neoantigen immunotherapy technology.

Liz seemed exhausted while sitting at her desk. After hearing the knock on the office door, a huge smile brightened her face. She rushed to greet her best friend since high school. They shared a long, endearing hug. Liz was misty-eyed. "Oh my god. I can't believe it.

This is so awesome. I never thought I'd see you again after I fired you."

"It's not your fault," Anna assured her. "You were just doing what you were told."

"I know, but I felt awful. I tried calling to apologize, but your phone was disconnected. I sent several texts and emails, but no reply. I was sure you never wanted to talk to me again."

"It's nothing like that. I've got a new phone number and email address. Here, let me write them down for you," Anna said while grabbing a Post-it® Note and pen from the desk.

"Why all the changes?"

Anna couldn't begin to explain all the reasons, so she said, "It's part of my fresh start initiative. Out with the old, in with the new life for Anna Monteiro."

As Anna was writing, Liz acknowledged Chris standing against the wall. She warmly extended her hand and said, "And you must be Chris Davis."

He snickered. "Yes, I am. How did you know?"

"Because Anna described you to a tee while telling me how you both enjoyed the cruise."

Liz's eyes twinkled as if knowing intimate details about their whirlwind romance. Hopefully, Anna wouldn't provide an updated assessment of him. The new description would be far less favorable. He played it safe by saying, "That was a fun trip."

Liz asked with a wink, "And have you been having fun ever since?"

Wow, that was a loaded question. Chris hesitated. Anna jumped in. "We sure have. We've been road-tripping through Canada. Which is kinda why we're here. Have you seen two suitcases that were shipped here?"

Liz walked over to the closet and waved her arm like a gameshow hostess. "You mean these? Why did you send them here?"

"What a mess," Anna said as a prelude to a fabrication. "They were stored with a bell captain when they apparently were loaded onto a tour bus. So I thought they'd be safer here than outside my house for a couple weeks. Hope that wasn't a problem."

"No problem at all," Liz said, then studied her friend with concern. "Hey, are you okay? You look peaked."

Anna feigned a laugh. "I don't doubt it. We were up late last night having dinner, a Broadway show, then cocktails overlooking New York. We just drove back."

Chris was impressed at how proficient Anna had become at lying. She was very convincing, especially considering the torment she endured last night.

Liz said, "I'm jealous. Sounds like being unemployed agrees with you."

"Speaking of which," Anna said, "what's happening around here? It's a ghost town."

Liz's head tilted back. Her eyes narrowed. Her jovial expression turned gloomy. "Yeah, it's gone from worse to hell since you left. I told you how Fármaco bought us with the goal to kill our cancer technology within six months to protect their oncology drug sales. Well, after a firestorm of bad press, participants backed out of our clinical trials in droves. I swear, Fármaco was fueling the flames. So on Monday, they'll cancel the remaining trials and let the support staff go. After that, the only ones left will be two other senior executives, one assistant, and a cleaning lady. And frankly, she's the most productive of all of us."

Anna's shoulders slumped. "God, that's terrible," she moaned. "I can't believe it's gotten that bad. Does this mean you'll also be gone soon?"

"No, I'm still slated to run Fármaco's new Women's Dignity Foundation – that's what they named it. But I'm telling you, Anna, my heart really isn't into it."

"I've asked you this before, but why not just take your buyout money and run?"

Liz's cheeks flushed while struggling to talk. "Because as soon as I do that …" She stopped. Her chest heaved with a pained sigh. "If I give up, it means our technology is buried forever. Then millions of people will needlessly die from cancer. So, as long as there is a pulse – and I mean even a faint pulse – I'm not declaring the dream to be dead. Our dream, Anna." Tears overwhelmed Liz. "There's got to be hope. There just has to be."

He watched as the women consoled each other. Their shared bereavement was gut-wrenching. He was also envious of their deep friendship.

After a couple of minutes, Liz wiped the sorrow from her face and said to Chris, "I apologize. You didn't need to hear all of this." She tried sounding upbeat again by changing the subject. "Where are you guys going next?"

Chris said, "I'm dropping Anna home, then going back to Minnesota. Time to be a responsible adult again."

"Don't you hate when that happens? Well, I hope to see you again under better circumstances the next time you're in Boston."

"I'd like that," Chris said and meant it, but knew it would never happen.

Liz's cell phone rang. She looked at the caller ID. "Sorry, but I've got to take this. It's one of Fármaco's corporate attorneys … the bloodsuckers." Pointing toward Anna, she said, "Listen, give me a couple of weeks, then let's get together. I could really use a good binge." As they turned to leave, Liz added, "Oh, one more thing. Some detective from the San Francisco police called a couple of times looking for you."

Anna handled it like a pro. "Thanks, but I've already talked to him. He just had a few follow-up questions about my friend Jessica's death. Take care."

As the couple pulled their roller bags down the hall, Chris was concerned why the police would still be investigating Jessica's overdose caused by the poisoned Midol intended for Anna. He asked, "Do you think Jessica's ex-husband and parents are still implicating you in her death?"

Anna's tone was as stiff as her posture. "I have no idea, but I'll handle it." The abruptness ended that topic.

While they rode down the elevator, Chris said in an attempt to break the tension, "By the way, I really like Liz."

Anna said proudly, "Now you see why I'd do anything for her. She's a pioneer in the next generation of cancer treatment." Then her tone became somber. "Unfortunately, she's the last person standing. She's going to lose. But the real losers are people with cancer. They'll die so big pharma can get rich. It's so fucking unfair."

They got to the Ford Explorer. Chris started to load the luggage in back when Anna grabbed them. She opened the suitcases on the parking lot asphalt. "What are you doing?"

Without making eye contact, she said, "Whoever packed these at the hotel got our stuff all mixed up. I'm straightening things out."

"Don't you think it'd be better if we did this at your house?"

"No," was the emphatic answer. Her message was clear. This was a rejection of him. There was no way he was going to be invited inside her home.

A few minutes later, when he pulled the SUV up to her brownstone,[61] she hopped out, grabbed her suitcase and said without emotion, "Thanks for the ride. This is where it ends. I hope you have the life you want."

"That's it?"

"Yeah, Chris, that's it," she said coldly. "Please don't make this difficult. I've got to go."

He watched in disbelief as Anna dragged the suitcase up the stairs, opened the door and went inside without even looking back. It was over.

He drove a block, parked the car and put his head on the steering

wheel. Waves of sorrow swept over him. Anna had been so vivacious when they met. Now she was devastated. Recovery could
take months, maybe years if the anxiety evolved into PTSD. So of
course she would escape when finally given the chance. What did
he expect? He got what he deserved.

His thoughts shifted to Liz. He was impressed with her intelli-
gence, drive and passion. She was remarkable. Her goal was to save
millions in partnership with her best friend, compared to his fixation
to kill Irene and stop being an assassin. What a pathetic contrast.

Self-pity shifted to anger. Anna and Liz deserved another chance
to achieve their vision. There was only one way to make that happen:
target Robert Nole, the president of Fármaco.

Three weeks ago, Chris had hacked into Nole's laptop to watch
Liz's ill-fated negotiation to save Longfellow from being acquired by
the big oncology drug company. The pompous executive agreed on
one condition: Liz had to sleep with him. She complied. No sooner
had she left his hotel room – humiliated and disgraced – when Nole
reneged. He instructed his acquisition team to stall the purchase
until Longfellow was bankrupt.

In retaliation, Chris confronted Nole at O'Hare Airport. The
blackmail terms were either buy Longfellow and establish an anti-
harassment foundation, or Chris would release the video to the
media. Nole followed the terms but not the spirit of the agreement.
Within weeks, the greedy bastard was strangling the life out of
Longfellow in order to protect Fármaco's profits.

Obviously, Robert Nole needed more convincing to do the right
thing. The question was how to get close to him again. Corporate
headquarters was off-limits. Catching the president outside the
office might take days and, if Nole was smart, he'd now have a bodyguard. He could try hacking into Nole's computer again, but Nole
probably had the cybersecurity increased. Chris was stymied until
remembering a fundamental silentcide teaching: simple is often best.

Chris smiled. The idea was perfect. Using the laptop he'd retrieved at Longfellow, Chris began typing a letter to Robert Nole's wife.

Dear Mrs. Nole:

I have spoken to your husband about this issue, but apparently profit is more important than business ethics, women's dignity, curing cancer, and his vows to you. Enclosed is a video of him coercing a senior executive to have sex in exchange for buying her company, and emails of his plan to immediately renege on the deal.

Chris went into more details before concluding.

The choice is simple. By the end of business Monday, he can announce his full financial commitment to Longfellow's technology as Fármaco's promising cancer platform of the future, and offer all employees their jobs back, or the enclosed materials go public.

Mrs. Nole, I apologize for the predicament. I wouldn't make this request if I didn't believe this decision will save millions of people. If you don't believe me, ask Robert. If he's finally honest, he'll tell you personalized cancer treatments that optimize people's immune systems to fight cancer will initially augment and eventually replace the toxic drugs his company sells. And that's what he's afraid of. It's time for him to regain his moral compass and fulfill Fármaco's mission statement and slogan: "Saving lives through better oncology solutions."

Chris put on the Ted Collins disguise, then drove to a nearby FedEx office. He was downloading the incriminating video onto a thumb drive when his cell phone rang. Michelle was calling. No way did Chris want to hear about her budding romance. He printed the letter, inserted the materials into a shipping envelope, wrote Nole's home address on the label and wiped off fingerprints from all surfaces. While asking the clerk for next-day delivery, his phone rang again. He swiped reject.

When he got back into his car, turned the ignition and shifted into drive, Chris came to a realization. He had nowhere to go and no idea how to spend the rest of his life.

Chapter Twenty-Seven: Cambridge, Massachusetts

Photos 59–61

TWENTY-EIGHT

Michelle glanced at the hotel clock radio, then rolled back across the pillow. Ansel's pale blue eyes were inches away. They sparkled. His short, wavy black hair was tousled. She cherished how his arm embraced her bare shoulder, strong yet gentle. Being with him was comforting, warm and sensual. All she wanted was to keep snuggling. She whispered, "It's time to get up."

"Do we have to?" he asked with an exaggerated, little-boy whine.

"Yup, it's almost three o'clock."

"So?"

She laughed. "So we'll start getting bedsores soon."

"I'm okay with that." He flashed an endearing smile.

"Seriously, we've got to leave in about thirty minutes or we'll be late. Or at least I'll be late. You don't have to come with me."

"I said I'll be there for you, and I meant it."

She was appreciative of his support. "Okay then, get moving." She gave him a quick kiss, pulled back the comforter and started toward the bathroom.

He called out with a mischievous tone, "I don't see any bedsores on your back."

"Good to know," she said before closing the bathroom door. She couldn't remember being happier.

After walking through the elegant lobby of the historic Saint Paul Hotel,[62] they were greeted by a distinguished doorman wearing a tux and top hat. The parking valet took the claim ticket and dashed off for the rental car. Michelle filled the wait time by describing the Ordway Center,[63] James. J. Hill Library,[64] and the pink granite façade of the Landmark Center.[65] The distinctive buildings shared the edges of Rice Park in the center of downtown.

During most of the fifteen-minute drive, Ansel wanted to hold hands. The gesture was charming yet sophomoric. This six-foot, forty-year-old man seemed as smitten as a teen with a first crush. The feeling was mutual. As she turned off the freeway and steered toward the parking lot, he reached for the Glock 17 beneath the seat.

"Are you kidding me? Put that thing away. Irene's dead, for Christ's sake."

Ansel was equally intense. "True, but a cobra can bite long after being decapitated."

"Get serious," she admonished him. After dramatically releasing the seat belt, she turned to confront him. "I'm meeting with a seventy-eight-year-old man. What's he going to do?"

"He's still the same man who helped build Irene's assassin network. I'm not taking any chances. And neither should you."

"I trust him implicitly."

"That's fine, but I don't. I'll be watching the whole time."

Michelle left the car in a huff, walked a few yards to an observation platform and savored the puffy white clouds hovering over the Mississippi as the river flowed between Minneapolis and Saint Paul. According to oral tradition, the Dakota people considered this Bdote bluff[66] to be the center of the earth. The sacred ground seemed like an ideal place for a meeting.

"Beautiful, isn't it?" Dr. Yasin said in a frail voice while hobbling toward her.

"Incredible." She gave him a quick hug.

With an inquisitive stare through oversized trifocals, he asked, "Will your traveling companion mind if we walk through Fort Snelling?"[67]

She grinned. "How did you know?"

He returned a toothy grin. "I may be old, Michelle, but I'm not blind ... yet."

"That's Ansel Meehan," she said. "You might remember him. He grew up on the other farm in York County."

Dr. Yasin thought about it before saying, "Oh sure, I didn't teach him often because he was part of the Phonoi training program, but I remember him. That kid was always too handsome for my taste, and he knew it. And judging from what I just saw, he hasn't changed much ... except he needs a shave. Why's he your backup and not Chris?"

"My brother is in Boston."

"Well, okay, I assume your beau will follow along, which, at my speed, won't be difficult."

"Why did you call him my beau?"

A hearty chuckle was followed by, "As I said, I'm not blind. Let's go."

She stabilized him as they passed the visitor center and headed toward the Round Tower[68] of the citadel built in 1820. In an abundance of caution, Michelle suggested they talk on a grassy area away from the crowded main path.

When settled, Dr. Yasin said, "So tell me. The last time we met, you had grand plans to kill Irene. What happened?"

Michelle ignored the question while handing him a gift box in eager anticipation. "Here, I have a present for you. Open it."

Her former mentor struggled with the wrapping. After he looked inside, his brow pinched with confusion. She felt compelled to explain the bronze replica she had purchased in Philadelphia. "It's the Liberty Bell."

He closed the cover. "I don't mean to sound unappreciative, but what's this for?"

Clearly, he hadn't heard the great news. With unbridled excitement and pride, she blurted, "It symbolizes freedom. Our freedom. Irene's dead!"

Dr. Yasin scowled. "No, she's not, unless she died in the last few hours."

Michelle was stunned. "That's impossible. We killed her on Monday."

"Michelle, I'm not sure what you did, and Irene is capable of lots of things, but speaking from the grave is not one of them. I just talked to her."

In total disbelief, she asked, "Are you sure it was her?"

He looked offended. "I've known the woman for nearly four decades. So yes, I'm positive."

"Shit, shit, shit, shit," Michelle muttered, pacing in circles. A lifetime of fear and oppression came crashing back. "I've got to warn Chris," she said in a panic. Reaching for her phone, she waved frantically to Ansel, who was mingling among tourists. Repeatedly, she yelled at the phone, "Pick up, pick up, pick up." Chris didn't answer. Her voicemail was, "Call me. Now! Irene's alive." The same message was left as a text.

Ansel walked over with caution. The two men shook hands but obviously had a low opinion of each other. With nothing to say, they waited until Michelle pocketed the phone.

"What's going on?" Ansel asked.

Michelle pushed sandy-blond hair behind her ear. "It's about Irene. She's not dead."

"That's a load of crap," Ansel roared. "I shot her myself." With a threatening stance, he directed his outrage toward Yasin. "Are you telling me I missed?"

Despite being a fraction of Ansel's size, the doctor was not intimidated. He stared up at the towering man. "I'm not telling you any such thing, son, other than Irene's very much alive."

Ansel waved a hand in frustration. "I don't believe it."

Michelle intervened. "Calm down. Let's hear him out." She looked back at Dr. Yasin. "You said she called today. Was she asking if I was still considering the role as your successor?"

"She never brought that up," the doctor said, "which makes me believe that's off the table. No, she told me my first assignment was a success, and she had another one for me."

"Hey, wait," Ansel interrupted. "Back up a minute. What was the first assignment?"

Yasin hesitated, obviously being cautious. "I shouldn't tell you that."

"Why not?" Ansel was getting too pushy.

The doctor got defensive, borderline contentious. "Because Irene is threatening my grandkids, that's why."

Michelle said sympathetically, "Doctor, you and I both know she's going to keep threatening you until we stop her. And the only way we can do that is if you help us."

"Michelle, I don't care what happens to me. I'm old. My life is almost over. But before I say a thing, you have to promise you won't put the twin boys in further jeopardy."

"I promise."

"I believe you. You know that. But can you also promise to control Chris and him" – Yasin accented the word *him* with a cold glare – "so they don't go off half-cocked?"

Ansel stiffened at the insinuation he was incompetent. Michelle placed a palm on Ansel's chest. "Relax. Just relax." Turning back to Yasin, she said, "I have full confidence in them."

The doctor's last request was, "Don't make me regret this, Michelle," before he started explaining the first assignment. "About a week ago, Irene told me a critical silentcide had been botched and she only trusted me to get the next one right. She said it was mandatory that I specify a fatal compound to embed in one-hundred-milligram doses of sildenafil."

Michelle translated for Ansel, "That's the max dose of Viagra."

"So anyway," Yasin continued, "I prescribed two thousand nano-grams of botulinum toxin – twice the lethal dose – together with twenty milligrams of tizanidine, which is a fast-acting muscle re-laxant and sedative. Working together, they lead to rapid muscular paralysis followed by respiratory failure and an unpleasant death."

Michelle asked, "But couldn't those be detected in a post-mortem toxicology test?"

"Probably, if an ME knew what to look for. But Irene specifically wanted it that way."

"That's odd. Careless actually. Did she tell you who the target was?"

"No, that was very secretive. I also didn't get any medical records of the target, nor did I do the drug compounding. I was instructed to send the specifications to Wolfgang. As you know, all those things are against Thanatos protocol. But the biggest curiosity is Irene's involvement. To my knowledge, she's rarely gotten her hands dirty with a silentcide during the last decade or so. All that told me one thing: this is a very, very high-value commission."

"Any idea who?"

"Now that part was easy as of today. Turn on the news. You'll hear how Senator Classon was found dead in his intern's apartment last night with Viagra in his pocket. The media is having a field day calling it a scandalous love nest. But there's no doubt in my mind it's connected to Senator Tomlin's aneurysm and Senator Nisor's stroke."

Michelle asked with a hint of hope, "Is it possible the last senator was the end game?"

"Absolutely not. Irene requested another lethal compound for a hydrofluoroalkane version of albuterol."

Ansel blurted out, "Could you both talk in English please?"

Michelle explained, "It's a rescue inhaler for asthma in a spray canister."

After the interruption, the doctor continued, "I prescribed an aerosolized poison ivy resin called urushiol. It should cause an immediate bronchospasm."

Ansel said sarcastically, "How about skipping the shop talk and get to the point."

Dr. Yasin was becoming annoyed. "The point, son, is another senator is going to die soon unless Irene is stopped."

"So what? Why should we care about a few old political hacks dying?"

"Look, I have no love for politicians either," Yasin said, struggling to control his temper, "but this is going to keep escalating until it becomes a national crisis."

"That's not our problem," Ansel countered. "Irene is."

Dr. Yasin was becoming red-faced. "But think about it. There must be some powerful people behind this plot. If Irene fails, maybe they'll take care of her for us."

"That's a really big if," Ansel said, then demanded, "so just tell us where she is and we'll take care of her ourselves."

"Goddamn it, I don't know where she is," Yasin yelled, shaking with anger. "Don't you think I'd tell you if I did?"

"I'm not sure you would," Ansel said in defiance.

The confrontation was escalating out of control. Michelle intervened. "Ansel, listen. Why don't you go call Chris again and let me finish."

Ansel was unwavering.

"I'm serious. Go."

Yasin watched Ansel stomp off, then said to Michelle, "He doesn't look in control to me. In fact, he's a loose cannon. I'm not sure I want the fate of my grandsons in his hands."

"I promised I'll control him, and I will. But is there a chance Irene's making idle threats? I know she's despicable, but would she really hurt the grandkids after your decades of loyalty?"

"No question about it, especially if this is her swan song.

Whenever her master plan is done, I suspect she'll eliminate all evidence, which probably includes me and my family."

Michelle concluded, "Hell's too good for her." She switched into action mode. "All right, let me talk this over with Chris and Ansel and we'll come up with a game plan. In the meantime, do whatever she says and try to learn her location. Then let's keep in touch, okay?"

"That's not exactly reassuring, but I don't have another choice, do I?" He looked demoralized, as if all hope had been lost. "Here," he said, handing back the box with the Liberty Bell. "Keep this. Hopefully someday it will be apropos." Dr. Yasin shuffled off. His back was bent. The gait was unstable. The man seemed resigned to a heartbreaking fate.

Ansel was pacing with impatience. She motioned him over. As he approached, he said, "I don't like that guy."

She was livid. "And you were a horse's ass. Why did you have to be so combative?"

"Because he was rambling on and on with all that pharmacy crap yet holding back real information. You sure he's not setting us up?"

"Absolutely sure. He's always treated me like a daughter. In fact, he's the only decent father I ever had. He'd never betray me."

Four gunshots rang out. Ansel reached for the Glock behind his jacket.

She grabbed his hand before he retrieved the pistol. "Stop! We're not under attack. Those are muskets inside the fort.[69] They reenact a military drill every half hour."

Ansel gasped in relief. His fight-or-flight response was on overload. He tried relaxing but remained edgy. With a sigh, he said, "You know what? Maybe I was a horse's ass. But I'm pissed Irene's alive and that I missed the shot." He held her hand. "I'm sorry. Can you forgive me?"

"Maybe," she said in jest. "But the next time you piddle on the floor, I'm going to smack you on the nose with a rolled-up newspaper. Got it?"

"Got it. So now what?" he asked.

"Did you reach Chris?"

"No, he didn't answer."

Michelle suggested, "Let's try calling Anna. Maybe they're still together. Once we know they're safe, we can decide what to do next."

Chapter Twenty-Eight: Saint Paul, Minnesota

Photos 62–69

TWENTY-NINE

Anna sobbed softly in isolation while sitting on the gold-and-blue comforter atop the canopy bed. The enormous master bedroom of her parents' brownstone had been a peaceful haven for five years. Typically, pulling the curtains, dimming the lights and occasionally watching the flames flicker in the Victorian cast-iron fireplace created a comforting sanctuary.

Not now. For over a half hour, traumatic memories of the relentless ordeal clashed in a nightmarish loop. Although physically safe, Anna's emotions were raw.

While feverishly stripping the bedsheets where Chris had slept nearly a month ago, her cell phone rang. Caller ID showed it was Michelle. Anna hesitated. The phone kept ringing. She debated. On the fourth ring, she wiped away a tear and sat up straight. "Hello."

"Hi," Michelle said. "I have Ansel with me on speaker."

"Hi, Ansel," she said, trying to sound cheerful. "You guys having fun in the northern woods?"

Ansel was surprisingly quiet. Michelle said, "Well, we're in Minnesota but never made it to the woods." There was something unsettling about her tone.

"Why not?" Anna asked.

"Where are you right now?" Michelle's avoidance of the question confirmed there was a problem. It felt serious.

"At home. Why?"

In the background, Ansel whispered, "That's the first place they're going to look for her."

Michelle said, "Shush," then asked Anna, "Is Chris with you?"

Anna gnawed on a fingernail as apprehension surged. "No, he left about forty-five minutes ago. What's wrong?"

In a hushed voice, Ansel said, "He might not get back in time."

The sound of a hand briefly covering the microphone was followed by Michelle saying, "Well, we, uh … we have some bad news."

"Just tell me," Anna insisted. "What is it?"

Ansel blurted, "Irene's alive."

"Oh my god, no." Anna became frantic. "That can't be. Am I still in danger?"

"Maybe," Michelle said tentatively.

Ansel boldly said, "Yes, you are."

"What should I do? Should I call the police?"

Ansel responded rationally, "You could, but do you really want to explain everything that's happened?"

"Sure, if it means saving my life," Anna said in desperation.

He countered, "But you'd probably end up in prison if you confess. Do this instead. Can you go someplace safe where you can lock the door?"

"There's one on my bedroom door. And another on the bathroom."

"That's great. Do it."

Anna rushed across the room, turned the skeleton key beneath the crystal doorknob, pocketed the key, ran into the bathroom, locked that door, sat on the edge of the clawfoot tub and fought the urge to cry again. "Now what?" she managed to ask.

"Call Chris," he instructed. "Hopefully he answers, he's not too far away, and he can come back to get you."

"I can't do this again," she wailed. "I just can't."

"Anna, listen to me," Michelle intervened. "You must do this. Understand? I don't want anything to happen to you. So please, please, just call him. If he doesn't answer, call me back and we'll think of something else. Can you do that?"

"I think so."

Michelle persisted. "I need a definitive yes."

"Yes, okay, sure. I'll call him right now. I promise. Oh my god, I can't believe this is happening again."

THIRTY

A fter finishing at the FedEx office, and still wearing the Ted Collins disguise, Chris's Ford Explorer slowly emerged from a Back Bay parking garage. He cursed when the cell phone rang. He assumed Michelle or Ansel was badgering him again. Anna's name was on the screen. Perhaps she wanted to apologize for the abrupt departure or properly thank him for getting her home safely. Could she be inviting him back? He tapped the speaker button. "Hi," he said warmly while entering a side street clogged by a moving boom lift.

"Irene's alive!" she screeched.

"What?" Chris exclaimed in disbelief. "That's impossible."

"That's what Michelle told me. And Ansel thinks I'm in danger."

Ansel had a sixth sense for smelling threats. Anna was probably in deep shit. Chris tried regaining his composure so as not to further alarm her. "Where are you?"

"Locked in my bedroom bathroom."

"Good. Have you heard anything suspicious?"

The construction crew in front of the car was irritatingly slow while positioning the equipment. The bored flagman held a stop sign while smoking a cigarette.

"No, but I did see a Jeep pass slowly by the house a couple of times after you left."

"So …?"

"So, I think it was also parked near Longfellow."

With heightened concern, Chris asked, "You think or you know?"

"I know, because it had the same tinted windows and a huge dent on the side."

That was conclusive. Irene had Longfellow and Anna's house under surveillance. The brownstone was a perfect place for an assault.

Her voice quivered. "Can you come get me?"

"Absolutely." Chris honked twice and waved the flagman aside. The man flashed the finger and stood firm until Chris lurched forward. Then the SUV bolted onto Saint James Avenue at Trinity Church[70] and crossed three lanes before straddling a narrow bike path.

"Stay put," he told Anna. "I'll be there in three minutes."

"Hurry," she pleaded.

"I am." He maneuvered among people in the crosswalk, turned sharply onto Dartmouth Street and sped past Copley Square and Boston Library.[71] "Can you find some kind of a weapon?"

"I don't know." Her voice was jittery.

He ran an amber light at Boylston Street.[72] "Look for something, anything," he said while weaving between a double-parked delivery truck and a family on rented bikes.

As he approached Newbury Street, Anna said, "I found a scissors in the medicine cabinet." The light turned red. Pedestrians and opposing traffic started moving. He laid on the horn, winced and flew through the intersection.

"That's good." The Ford accelerated. "I'm almost there. Go to the front door now. If you hear anything, anything at all, run back to the bathroom."

"Do you think they're in the house?"

"No," he said with as much assurance as possible. "Oh, shit. Just a second."

"What is it?"

Cars were stopped at Commonwealth Avenue. After tapping the brakes, Chris yanked the steering wheel and struck a parked Acura. He floored the gas pedal. The tires squealed and smoked. The Acura slowly pushed aside. He drove up and over the curb, waited a downbeat for the oncoming traffic, then gunned it.

"What was all that noise?" she asked.

"Nothing but traffic," he said as the Ford careened in front of a bus, fishtailed, then raced down the other side of Commonwealth Avenue.

"Shouldn't I just wait here for you?"

If Chris entered the house, attackers would probably surround it, trapping them in an ambush. "No! Start moving. Please."

Anna sounded frenzied running through the house.

As rows of brownstones flashed by on his right and tourists gawked along a parklike median on the left, he mentally pictured the front of Anna's house. She'd make an easy target exiting from the elevated front door. "Change of plans," he said. "Can you get inside the lower apartment?"

"I can if my dad left the key to the back stairs where it's supposed to be."

"Try it."

Three cars idled for a red light ahead, blocking his path. The Ford Explorer catapulted onto the sidewalk. The speedometer reached fifty. Pedestrians jumped aside.

"I've got it," Anna declared.

"Go to the apartment front door but not outside. I'm fifteen seconds out." Chris gritted his teeth while launching into the intersection. A Honda Civic crashed into a tree. A van spun wildly after being rear-ended. Glass, steel and plastic scattered across the pavement.

Footsteps pounded down a staircase. "I'm scared, Chris. I'm really scared."

"I understand."

"I don't want to die."

He tried sounding calm but his heart was pounding. "You won't. Trust me."

Chris's eyes swiveled in every direction looking for assailants. "Ten seconds." Maybe this was a false alarm. Maybe not. Irene's assassins were all trained to blend in like chameleons until they pulled the trigger. "Five seconds." His instincts were ablaze.

Anna was hyperventilating.

Chris slammed on the brakes alongside parked cars in front of her house[73] and was unlocking the passenger door when a bullet ricocheted off the window next to his left ear. "Shit!"

"You okay?" Anna screamed.

The one-and-a-half-inch, bullet-resistant glass was designed to stop a 9mm, not a supersonic sniper bullet. The second round created another spiderweb of external cracks, yet the window didn't break. If it did, he'd die instantly.

Chris estimated the sniper's position. He had to be across the grassy median and low enough to shoot beneath the trees. "Anna, I'm here. I want you to crawl out the door and between the parked cars as fast as you can. Understand? Do not stand up. For any reason."

"I don't think I can."

"Just do it!" he demanded.

Another bullet smashed into the car's side panel and was absorbed by layers of ballistic nylon and Kevlar. The sniper was testing for a vulnerability in the armoring. A Jeep Cherokee quickly approached from behind. The apartment door swung open. Anna crawled out. The Jeep braked. A fourth bullet hit the driver's window. The glass bulged and would soon fail. Anna slithered toward the Ford. A man leaped from the Jeep with an AK-47. Chris stretched over the center console to open the passenger door. She grabbed the seat. A spray of slugs hammered the back window and hatchback. The assault was deafening. She climbed in. Chris started driving before the door closed. The side window imploded. Anna was hysterical.

The tachometer spiked as the retrofitted engine roared. At the end of the block, a woman stepped into the crosswalk along with her poodle on a leash. The Ford raced forward.

Anna yelled, "Chris, do you see her?"

"Yup," he said while gripping the steering wheel and accelerating.

Unfazed, the woman kept walking.

"You're going to hit her!" Anna shouted.

Chris made eye contact. A positive identification. She and her dog were at Château Ramezay during the assassination attempt in Montreal. The woman released the poodle, took a shooter's stance and fired the SIG P229 pistol into the windshield. Six 9mm rounds pounded the glass, creating clouds of dust and vicious cracks as the bullets bounced off. At the last second, she leaped and rolled to the left as Chris swerved to the right. The Ford destroyed a streetlight, dodged a bicyclist and skidded into a violent turn down Fairfield Street. The woman unloaded the remaining nine rounds into the back of the SUV before being picked up by the Jeep Cherokee.

The chase was on. Immediate evasion was essential.

Chris reached below the dashboard and pushed a button, releasing forty jack-shaped spikes. The sharp steel tacks scattered across the street. Tintinnabulation. As the Ford blew through a four-way stop, Chris watched in the rearview mirror. The driver braced himself as the Jeep bounced over the spikes, swayed, sideswiped a parked car, avoided a collision and kept coming. The assailant's car obviously had run-flat tires.

A pistol emerged from the Jeep's passenger window, then the woman's head and upper body. Rapid gunfire. Muzzle flashes and smoke. Flying shell casings. Each bullet striking the Ford made Anna scream. The onslaught was unrelenting.

The traffic signal in the intersection ahead was red. Chris scanned the oncoming, one-way traffic. An eighteen-wheeler and a Land Rover were speeding side by side, trying to beat the amber light.

"Don't do it," Anna warned. "You'll never make it."

Chris eased off the gas. The Ford slowed. The Jeep advanced. The pursuing car was dangerously close. Chris calculated the timing, stiffened, then rocketed into the intersection. The assailants followed.

The Land Rover veered wildly, screeching to a stop. The truck barreled ahead. The Ford Explorer escaped unscathed. The Jeep Cherokee did not. The semi-tractor broadsided the assassins' car, flipped it over and crushed the front end with two massive tires. The trailer swung out of control, disconnected, crashed into the Land Rover and heaved it forward before jackknifing on top of the Jeep. The twisted wreckage slid violently to the curb. A final glance in the mirror indicated they were finally safe.

A block later, they reached the end of Fairfield Street and the start of a pedestrian bridge over Storrow Drive.[74] The six-lane crosstown parkway was a fast route out of the city. "How do I get down there?" he asked in frustration while watching the speeding traffic.

"Make a right here on Back Street. An entrance is down five or six blocks."

At first, the Ford sprinted down the narrow alley behind garages and reserved parking spaces for apartments and row houses. Then Chris slowed to a crawl.

Confused by the abrupt change in speed, Anna asked, "Now what're you doing?"

"As much as I hate to say it – I love this car – we have to ditch it. Soon, every cop in Boston is going to be looking for it. And it's very easy to identify."

Twenty yards ahead, he spotted a Lexus RX 350 idling unattended at the side of a brick garage. Hardly a speedster but easy to hide in plain sight. A security camera was directly overhead. His Ted Collins disguise would provide some anonymity until police forensics finished their work in a day or two. He pulled up beside the Lexus.

"Stay here," he told Anna. "On my signal, cover your face with your blouse and run to the front seat. Got it?" He didn't wait for her answer.

The damaged back of the Ford was a challenge to open. He quickly removed what remained of his possessions: luggage, go-bag, duffel of guns and ammunition, and a satchel of money. He scanned for onlookers before testing the Lexus's liftgate, and almost finished loading the cargo space when he yelled to Anna, "Go now!"

He was a couple of steps behind her getting into the car. "Chris," she exclaimed, "there's a kid in the backseat."

"Oh, shit," he said while staring at the blond-haired, blue-eyed five-year-old. The boy looked confused and frightened.

"Don't swear in front of him," Anna admonished. "And don't even think about kidnapping him."

Chris jumped out, opened the side door, and struggled to extract the booster seat. "Any idea how to undo this thing?" he asked her.

"How should I know? I don't have kids."

"What the hell are you doing?" a bald, middle-aged man hollered as he ran breathless toward Chris.

"I'm stealing your car," Chris said matter-of-factly.

The man boldly declared, "Over my dead body."

Chris pointed at the bullet-ridden Ford and said, "Believe me when I say that can be easily arranged." The man stepped back in horror. "Listen, this is going to happen, but I don't want to take your son. Just tell me how to remove his car seat, and I'll be on my way."

Sheepishly, the man said, "Only my wife knows how to remove that contraption."

The little boy jumped out of the car, ran to his dad and hugged his leg.

"Problem solved," Chris said with a smile. "Now back away." He got into the driver's seat, threw it in reverse, did a half turn and drove off. A last glance revealed the man was already on his cell phone calling the police.

Ahead, the situation was dire. Four or five cars were logjammed and blocking their escape. Chris couldn't risk waiting. A gap in the retaining wall was crumbled hunks of concrete scattered among brush and overgrown grasses. He hoped to god there was enough clearance for the Lexus's undercarriage.

A hard left. A sickening thud. Loud scraping. Rocking suspension. More gas. Bouncing tires. Clear.

The Lexus lurched down the embankment, landing hard on the freeway and nearly T-boning a car. An angry horn from the driver's road rage. A hard right. Struggling for control. Straightening. Zero to sixty in seconds. Now to get the hell out of Boston.

"Are you hurt?" he asked with concern.

"Not hurt, but scared shitless." Anna was irate. "Where're we going next?"

"I don't know," he said with a quick look in her direction. "But the first thing we have to do is swap this car for one without GPS so the police can't track us."

"Then what?"

"I guess we find a place to hide, then make a new game plan with Michelle and Ansel."

She slammed a fist on the leather console. "I can't do this anymore, Chris. I absolutely refuse. I don't care what you do. Just drop me off at my parents' summer house at Cape Cod."

"Not smart," he countered. "Irene's people will find you there. You don't want to put them in danger too, do you?"

With a heavy sigh of exasperation, she asked, "What do you suggest?"

He gave it some thought. "How about Portland, Maine? It's only about two hours away."

"Do you really expect to find an available hotel on such short notice? Fat chance, especially at the height of tourism season."

"You're probably right. But go online anyway and see what you can find." She was really ticked off, so he added, "Please. Maybe we'll be lucky."

"Oh, sure," Anna said sarcastically, "as if you and I are always lucky together."

Twenty minutes later, as Chris drove around a suburban shopping mall in search of a replacement car, Anna dropped the cell phone in her lap and announced, "Got it."

"Got what?"

"Two rooms in downtown Portland overlooking the waterfront."

"Awesome," he said, leaning over to pull out his wallet.

She raised a palm to stop him. "Don't bother. I've already paid for them."

"Thanks, but you didn't have to do that."

"Sure I did. All I've paid for since I met you is one tank of gas. But if it makes you feel any better, when we get settled, you can buy me a toothbrush and toothpaste."

Chapter Thirty: Boston, Massachusetts

Photos 70–74

THIRTY-ONE

Wednesday

Irene Shaw was in repose in a king-size bed at her Seville apartment. Wearing a pink satin babydoll negligee, sipping Frangelico liqueur and occasionally nibbling on shortbread cookies from a silver tray, she was impatiently watching cable TV aired from the States.

After an endless string of insufferable commercials, the sixty-inch screen again showed the host of the popular pseudo-news program. The silver-haired fox wore an open white collar, an expensive black suit and a smug smirk.

"My next guest is no stranger to my loyal viewers," Lyle Mannity said. "Please give a warm welcome to straight-talking, hard-hitting, gets-things-done DC veteran and presidential hopeful, Republican US Senator Vickie McLoren."

The camera panned across the clapping audience, then switched to the senator, an entitled, overbearing woman. She was perfectly outfitted in a designer power dress accented with excessive, gaudy jewelry. The mid-fifties career politician could benefit from losing twenty pounds and using Irene's plastic surgeon.

Senator McLoren said, "Thanks for that wonderful introduction, Lyle, with one correction. I'm not a presidential hopeful. I will be the first female president of the United States."

With a shrug of his shoulders, he said, "That's very confident talk for someone who is second in delegates going into next month's Republican National Convention, isn't it?"

"You're right, I am confident, and that's what America needs: a confident, competent and unifying leader." She stared into the camera. "My unworthy party opponent may be ahead in the delegate count for now, but he's short of the needed majority. I will become the Republican presidential nominee after the second round of voting at the contested convention but…" With an impish grin, she added, "I'd settle for winning the nomination in the third round. Then I can focus on unseating our incapable, buffoonish and frankly dangerous incumbent president."

"His incompetence is terrifying." Lyle nodded in vigorous agreement. "And I'm concerned that North Korea knows it, Iran knows it, Russia knows it, China knows it, and so do our allies."

"Sure they do." Her diamond bracelet slid across her wrist during a dramatic hand gesture. "That's why Rocket Man keeps playing with his toys, Iran is enriching uranium, Russia is threatening to repatronize sovereign territories, China keeps stealing our trade and military secrets, and our leadership position on the world stage has eroded. And to make matters worse, he's pulling out of Afghanistan and declaring victory over ISIS. Totally irresponsible and perilous."

Lyle responded with seriousness, "It seems to me the only people who don't know the truth, because of their habitual lies, are the people at this week's Democratic Convention. Have you been watching that debacle?"

"Only when I can spare a few precious minutes from my important work for the nation's people. Lyle, I know you'll agree, the liberals' endless speeches are grandiose, pompous and" – she chuckled –"funnier than any *Saturday Night Live* sketch." Then the senator shook her index finger in anger. "They're a parody, a sham, and a lying disgrace. Fortunately, Americans are smart. They're not fooled by the empty rhetoric. In November, they will not give our commander-in-missteps another four years to destroy our country."

During the roaring audience applause, there was a knock on Irene's bedroom door. Using the TV remote, she clicked Mute and turned on the subtitles so she could monitor the interview, then said loudly, "Enter."

Before the door creaked open, a dog barked.

"Brutus!" she exclaimed with joy. The Afghan hound was at the end of a leash led by Wolfgang. "Come to Mama."

The fifty-five-pound purebred tugged at the restraint, yanked free, raced toward the bed and leaped into Irene's lap.

"Oh, my sweet baby," she cooed while stroking his head. "You look so jetlagged. Your trip must have been horrible, simply horrible. But you're finally here with me where you belong. Now all is right with the world. Such a good boy." The animal snuggled with contentment.

Irene made eye contact with Wolfgang. In a rare moment of gratitude that surprised even her, she managed to say, "Thank you, dear."

"You're welcome, Ms. Shaw," he said with a stoic expression. "I am delighted you're together again."

"Have a seat. You're just in time to see our client grandstanding with Lyle Mannity. The brazen hussy is really putting on a performance."

Wolfgang searched for a place to sit, but the two chairs were covered in clothes. The dog growled as if warning him the bed was his exclusive domain. The leader of Thanatos elected to lean against an antique armoire as Irene turned the television volume back on.

The news host said, "We only have a few more minutes of this segment. Before you go, Senator McLoren, I want to get your take on what the media is calling the Little Blue Pill Scandal."

"Oh, the media can be so cruel, can't they?" she said with disapproval. "Lyle, you know that Senator Classon and I had our differences across the aisle."

The host grinned. "That's putting it mildly. I've often called you the mongoose against the cobra."

"There may be some truth to that," she said with a laugh, then faked sincerity. "But outside the Senate chamber, I've always considered Senator Classon to be a good friend, a good man, and a good husband and father." She clutched her chest with a practiced forlorn expression. "My prayers and deepest, heartfelt sympathy go out to his devoted wife, Linda, and their two lovely daughters. Look, except to the tabloids and shameless gossipers, it's not important that an elderly statesman died in an intern's bed with a bottle of Viagra in his suit pocket. What's important is how he died."

"As you know," Lyle said, "the media is speculating the cause of death is – how should I discreetly phrase this on a family show? – from overexertion."

"Maybe, and I'm sure the coroner's report will reveal more details, assuming the Democrats don't suppress the truth. But I suggest the ME carefully check for a less obvious cause of death."

Lyle's brow raised above a wide-eyed stare. "What are you suggesting?"

"I'm not suggesting anything. I'm only asking. Is Senator Tomlin's aneurysm, Senator Nisor's stroke, and now Senator Classon's apparent heart attack – all within two weeks – more than a tragic coincidence among old men who had a chokehold on America's future?"

"Wow," he exclaimed, clapping his hands for emphasis. "Folks, you heard it here first on my show. Are you saying these were crimes, that maybe they were poisoned?"

"Lyle, you rascal, don't go putting words in my mouth. I'm only saying our enemies have a sordid history of attacking our democracy. Russia, for example, has never been discreet about silencing dissidents with poison. So, as our incompetent president spent lavishly on wasteful social programs while slashing our defense and anti-terrorism budgets, our enemies have flourished. These cancers were surgically reduced by the previous administration. But the current one has shamelessly allowed these malignancies to regrow and metastasize. It's imperative we stop them from becoming fatal. And who is that cancer patient? U! S! A!" She yelled to rally the crowd, "Who is it?"

The audience chanted in unison, "U! S! A! U! S! A! U! S! A!"

"That's right." The senator beamed with pride before continuing her self-righteous speech. "When I'm elected as your president, my primary goal will be to keep America safe. That's why I'm introducing my promise and new mantra on your show: Keep America Safe." The camera zoomed in for an extreme close-up. "It's a matter of saving our precious yet fragile freedom. I pledge to all of you, and your loved ones, I ... will ... keep ... America ... safe."

The audience wildly clapped and cheered. Even Lyle Mannity joined the applause before saying, "Unfortunately, time is up, so I have to end things here. But this interview has been very enlightening. Thanks for joining me today, Senator. I look forward to having you back soon to explore the latest Washington scandal and your exciting progress on the campaign trail."

Irene clicked off the TV in disgust, then asked Wolfgang, "That was one hell of an acting job, don't you think? Especially the way she planted that false flag."

His forehead creased below his misshapen black bangs. "From what you said before, I knew McLoren was going to light the flames about the three senators. But I had no idea she'd imply they were poisoned. That might significantly complicate our next commission."

"Don't worry about it, dear. I know your people are up for the challenge. But you've given me an excellent idea. I'll call Mr. Zola and demand a twenty percent increase for our next payment." Irene continued talking as if the previous topic was fait accompli. "I guess I don't need to ask, because you look like crap, but how was your flight?"

"It was fine," he said, "until I landed."

"What's that supposed to mean?" she asked while hugging Brutus.

"I got more bad news," he said while shifting his weight, "but it can wait until morning if you prefer."

The dog growled and Irene snarled as if neither of them wanted their tender reunion tarnished by harsh realities. "Tell me, goddamn it. You've already spoiled the mood."

"It concerns your four least favorite people," he explained. "It seems the Phonoi team lost their trail somewhere in New Jersey when Chris's credit card was rejected, so they hoped the foursome would reappear in Boston."

She interrupted the saga by demanding, "Skip the damn details about their continued incompetence and get to the bottom line."

Wolfgang's sigh bordered on insubordination, yet he maintained his professionalism. "A couple of hours ago, Chris and Monteiro were spotted at Longfellow BioSciences. Then he dropped her off at home and left before the team was in position. There was no sign of Michelle or Ansel. The team decided to at least take care of her when …"

"Please tell me Monteiro is dead."

"No, Ms. Shaw, she's not. According to the sniper, Chris came in hot and rescued her at the last minute. Countless bullets were fired at his car but bounced off with no effect."

Irene asked, "How the hell could Chris afford armoring his car using lunch money?" She turned the question into a self-serving compliment. "But I guess it attests to his excellent training. So what happened?"

Without flinching, Wolfgang said, "The bottom line is two more assets are dead and there is no trace of the foursome."

"What an unbelievable clusterfuck!" Irene screamed, causing Brutus to cower and tremble. Then she became contemplative before asking, "The sniper said Chris came in hot, as if he knew about the pending assault? How the hell could Chris know that?"

"I have no idea, Ms. Shaw."

She was in a froth. "Mr. König, it's your damn job to know."

His broad shoulders absorbed the verbal abuse. "I will find out, I promise. But I was thinking, you mentioned Michelle met with Yasin last week. Could he have said something to her in the last day or two?"

Irene contemplated the question, appalled that Yasin may have betrayed her. But it only confirmed she couldn't trust anyone. "Maybe," Irene finally said, unwilling to be definitive without proof. "If it's true, I'm very disappointed."

"Do you want me to retaliate?" he asked.

"No, not yet. All in due time, dear. Yasin can still be useful."

"I agree. In fact, I just received his compound specification for the next commission and will forward it to the sanctioned pharmacist in a few minutes. Plus, my silentcide asset is currently tracking the next senator."

Unimpressed and unappreciative, she demanded, "Give me one good reason why I should believe the asset can handle this commission after the miserable failure you just described."

"The Phonoi team that just failed were hired by Jürgen van Oorschot, and you justifiably fired him – literally – for his incompetence. I personally trained the silentcide asset I've assigned, so I can vouch for her abilities." Wolfgang's face was rigid. "If she fails, I will hand you my gun, kneel before you, and accept my fate."

Irene admired Wolfgang König. He did have the brains and balls to succeed her.

THIRTY-TWO

Michelle and Ansel were holding hands, sipping beers, and enjoying the passing scenery on the upper deck of a paddlewheel steamboat when her cell phone rang. She was delighted to see her brother's name on caller ID. "Hi," she said. "Just a sec. Let me put you on speaker. Okay, I have Ansel here with me. Are you guys all right?"

"Yeah. Where are you?" Chris asked. "There's lots of noise in the background."

There was a loud partying crowd encircling them. Everyone was enjoying a perfect summer evening. Michelle answered, "We're on the *Jonathan Padelford*."[75]

"How romantic," he said sarcastically. "You're floating down the Mississippi having cocktails while we're running for our lives?"

"What's that supposed to mean?" Michelle asked.

Then she heard Anna say in the background, "Drop the attitude, Chris."

After a frustrated sigh, he apologized. "I'm sorry, but we've been through hell and back."

"What happened?" Michelle asked while Ansel pressed closer to hear better. "Your text a couple hours ago only said you had serious trouble but were safe."

Chris asked, "Can you guys find someplace private to talk? Or call back later?"

Michelle repeatedly motioned her index finger straight down. Ansel nodded in agreement, then she said to Chris, "I think we can find a quiet spot on a lower deck. Let me call you right back."

When they reconnected, Ansel and Michelle huddled together to avoid using the phone speaker. She said to Chris, "Now we can talk. So tell us what happened."

Her brother described everything from when he received Anna's distress call until he stole the second car and drove to Maine. "Now we're standing along the waterfront in Portland,[76] and I promised Anna a lobster dinner when we're done talking."

"That sounds terrible," Michelle exclaimed. "Not about the lobster, but everything else. What a frightening ordeal. How are you doing, Anna?"

"*Numb* is the best word to describe it," she said with exhaustion. "But that's an improvement from being in shock."

"Hey, Ansel," Chris said. "Thanks for the warning. You've become our guardian angel."

"Don't thank me," Ansel replied. "It was Dr. Yasin who told us Irene was alive. I just assumed the wicked witch's people would go gunning for Anna at her house."

Sounding perplexed, perhaps ticked, Chris asked Michelle, "Why did you talk to Yasin again?"

"I wanted to celebrate Irene's death," Michelle explained. "When we learned the bad news, we tried calling you immediately."

Chris probed, "Did you tell him I was in Boston?"

After a pause with a twinge of guilt, Michelle said, "Yes, but –"

Ansel interrupted, "You didn't tell me that. How do we know that guy didn't give Chris and Anna up?"

Michelle stammered, "Well, uh, because he's loyal to me, that's why. And Irene's threatening his grandkids, so he's pissed at her."

Ansel continued the interrogation. "How do we know that grand-kid story isn't a lie?"

A hot flash of anger coursed through Michelle. "Listen, if Yasin was still loyal to Irene, we would've been killed at Fort Snelling. He is not the bad guy. Trust me for a change, will you?" Michelle gave Ansel a cold stare before continuing. "I'm guessing Irene's people had Longfellow and Anna's house under constant surveillance."

Anna piped in, "Would you all stop bickering? Please. Just let it go. It happened but we're safe. Now decide what to do so I can get my life back. And the sooner the better. I can't take much more of this crap."

There was a long silence. Michelle took the chastisement to heart. "Anna's right. So now what?"

"Before you go there," Ansel said, still on his high horse, "I want to know why Irene's still breathing. Chris, what exactly did you see in Elkins Park?"

Chris mumbled "shit" before admitting, "To be honest, I, uh, never saw Irene's face from the hummingbird drone, nor when she stepped toward the car. I do know your bullet was a direct hit. You killed somebody, at least somebody who looked like Irene."

Ansel exclaimed in disbelief, "You mean a body double?"

"Yeah, that's the only thing I can think of, assuming Yasin's telling the truth."

"Unbelievable," Ansel muttered in frustration.

Anna interjected again, "I guess we can all agree Irene is smarter than us, right? Great. Now can we please focus on what's important?"

Michelle admired her for always being the voice of reason despite being emotionally traumatized. "Anna, I agree with you, but is it okay if I first tell Chris about my meeting with Dr. Yasin?" Michelle proceeded to explain Yasin's theory about the three senators and Irene's demand for another lethal compound he assumed was going to be used on the fourth. She finished by saying, "Yasin thinks maybe these senator assassinations are Irene's big swan song before retiring."

"That's a crock," was Ansel's knee-jerk response. "She'll never retire."

Her brother's comeback was more thoughtful. "Why should we care about Irene's big payday? Anna's right, we should be focused on killing her."

"Hold on just a second," Anna injected with an uncharacteristic intensity. "We should absolutely care about the next senator. We can't just stand back and let another die. That's unconscionable. The least we can do is send an anonymous tip to the FBI or something."

Ansel was the first to disagree. "Way too dangerous. There is no such thing as anonymous with the FBI. A tip like that would come back to bite us."

Anna was becoming livid. "Well, then, Ansel, think of something better for a change rather than always criticizing everyone. All I know is you're all too callous about death. My dream was always to save millions. You people consider it an imposition to save even one."

A wave of remorse washed over Michelle. "Anna, that's not entirely true. Remember what happened when we tried saving Rachel?"

"Sure I do. Absolutely. You desperately wanted to save her from the hell you've been living through. I was all for it. But it went wrong. It's nobody's fault. That doesn't mean you try once, fail, and give up, does it?" Her tirade was intensifying. "Where's your humanity, for god's sake? You all say you want a better life. Then prove it. Earn it. Save someone else's life."

Nobody spoke. The uncomfortable stillness was deafening.

Ansel was the first to break the quiet. "That's not a good idea," he said slowly.

"Bullshit!" Michelle said with conviction. "Not only is it the humane thing to do like Anna said, but stopping more senators' deaths prevents a national crisis *and* puts the financial screws to Irene's swan song. Big-time! And Dr. Yasin worries if her plan succeeds, then she'll eliminate all the evidence, including killing him and his family."

"Yeah, but ..."

"Stop, Ansel. Let me finish." Michelle took a calming breath. "Yasin also thinks if we prevent another senator from dying, then the powerful people behind this plot might go gunning for her. Maybe they'd kill her first." Michelle then began an impassioned plea. "Look, I made a promise to help protect Yasin's grandkids. I'm not going to break that promise. So we're going to do this. At least I am. Chris, are you in?"

"Yup, assuming we can figure out who the next target is. That's not going to be easy."

Ansel shook his head but said nothing. His silence was a reluctant agreement to try saving the next senator.

The threesome spent the next fifteen minutes discussing how they could identify the correct senator. Then they divvied up the tasks and agreed to compare notes late Thursday morning. Before they disconnected, Michelle asked Anna, "What are you going to do? Take it easy, I hope. I hear Portland is a lovely city."

Anna replied, "I'll find something to keep myself busy."

After all of the goodbyes, Michelle pocketed the phone. Ansel took a sip of beer and started toward the stairs as if to resume the river cruise. Michelle called out, "Where're you going?"

"Upstairs, why?"

"Wait just a minute." She pushed some hair behind her ear, sighed, and said in controlled and firm way, "This isn't going to work."

"That's what I was trying to say, but no one would listen to me."

"No, I'm not referring to saving the senator. I mean us."

Ansel was startled, then rattled. His self-confidence slumped. His forehead wrinkled and his mouth tightened. "What? Why?"

Michelle decided to hold nothing back. "Because you get too snarly. Too judgmental. Too arrogant at times, as if you know more than anyone else. And you never listen to anyone's opinions, nor support mine."

He genuinely seemed hurt and lost for words. "Seriously?" he said in a conciliatory tone.

"Yes, and I don't know why. When it's just the two of us, everything's great, most of the time. But when you get around Chris and Anna, or we talk about Irene, you become a different person. And I don't care much for that person. So what's the problem?"

Ansel lowered his head, crossed his arms, and stared at the floor. Obviously, he heard the criticism and was doing some serious soul searching. She gave him all the time he needed.

When he finally looked up, he seemed worried and distressed. "First of all, let me say I don't mean to be that way. I'm really sorry and appreciate your being candid." He shifted uncomfortably. "Second, the only reason I can think of for my behavior – and this might sound strange – but I've always been alone. The job prevented me from having relationships, and I never had a family."

He stopped, took a deep breath, mumbled, "Jesus, this is hard," then continued. "And I've never been with a someone like you who I care about ... deeply. In short, I've survived by being alone. I obviously have no idea how to talk with people who I'm now close to. Does that make any sense?"

Michelle was surprised but convinced by his answer. She rushed to give him a long embrace. The big man melted in her arms. She understood his pain. Other than Chris, and maybe Dr. Yasin at times, she too had always felt alone.

He whispered in her ear, "Rather than dump me, would you give me a second chance? Then signal me when I'm being a jerk."

She pulled back, stared into his blue eyes, hesitated, then gave him a passionate kiss. Ansel was worth several second chances.

Chapter Thirty-Two: Saint Paul, Minnesota and Portland, Maine

Photos 75–76

THIRTY-THREE

PORTLAND, MAINE

Thursday

A nna reached the end of the two-mile Eastern Promenade[77] in Portland, did an abrupt U-turn, then reversed her mid-morning run along the shoreline of Casco Bay. Pounding feet. Pumping arms. Rhythmic breathing. Fluid stride. Surging endorphins soothing the stress.

She checked the fitness tracker on her watch. Averaging a nine-minute mile. Good, not great. Go faster. Push harder. Sudden cramping. Mild at first, then intense. Gritting teeth. Keep sprinting through the pain.

Crippling agony. Doubling over. Stumbling to a stop. Needed bathroom. Now. Bleeding. Clotting. She cursed herself for ignoring the New York City doctor's warning about strenuous exercise too soon. Worst of all were the morose feelings over losing the baby.

Anna slowly walked toward East End Beach,[78] sat on the sand, pulled up her legs, lowered her head and wanted to cry but couldn't. She was emotionally bankrupt. All she wanted was something, anything to be normal again. That wasn't happening soon. No matter how far she ran, she'd still be in peril.

She also worried about today's phone message and unopened email from Sergeant O'Neill. The Boston policewoman had investigated George Henniker's assault on Anna's home nearly seven weeks ago. The sergeant had obviously tracked down Anna's new contact information from Liz Walker. The email title read: "Questions about Yesterday's Shooting near Your Home." What did O'Neill suspect, what did she know, and who did she want to arrest? Anna contemplated calling the sergeant but feared her plight would worsen.

When Anna got back to the hotel room in the Old Port neighborhood, there was enough time for a quick shower and towel drying her black hair. The pixie cut resembled a Brillo pad. Her makeup-free face looked as bad, maybe worse, than she felt: peaked, haggard and distraught.

She grabbed Chris's extra laptop off the bed, walked down the hall and reconsidered before knocking on the door. Was she really up for this? Could she tolerate three quarreling assassins again? She respected Michelle, appreciated Chris and was losing patience with Ansel, but collectively they represented the only path back to normalcy. She was trapped with them until they found a way to set her free.

"Come in," Chris called out.

When she entered his room, Chris was hunched over his laptop. His eyes were red, he hadn't shaven, and empty coffee cups were stacked within arm's reach. "I had room service bring us some lunch," he said, pointing to trays on the unslept-in bed. "I'll be with you in a sec."

She lifted a plate cover, ate a few red grapes but didn't have the stomach for the soggy club sandwich. She sat down across the small table from Chris and waited. At two minutes before eleven, he finally looked up and asked the routine question, "How are you doing?" without really listening to her response. He grabbed his cell phone, pushed a button, set it on the table speaker side up and nibbled on potato chips during the ringing.

"Hello," Michelle answered.

"Hi," Chris said. "I have Anna here with me."

"Hi, Anna. Ansel's here too. Ready to discuss what we've learned about the next senator?"

"I guess so," Chris replied without conviction. "Do you want me to go first?"

"Sure, why not?"

"Okay. Well, as Michelle knows all too well and dislikes all too much," he said for a laugh but got none, "I started by playing the Name that Client game. I listed all the foreign entities that hate the US. It was a long list. For each one, I examined potential motives and possible gains. The most likely candidate is Russia. But why would they subcontract with Irene when they have vastly superior capabilities?" He clearly didn't expect an answer.

"Next, I examined several global radical groups. But again, they seem unlikely. None of these combative entities are ever subtle about their MOs. Typically, they also claim responsibility fast to boost their prowess, rally their supporters, increase recruitment and fan public fear. In conclusion, I'm guessing this isn't a foreign act of terror."

Chris kept rambling, "I did a similar analysis on domestic extremist groups and outspoken zealots. That list got more interesting."

Michelle interrupted, "Brother, we don't need a blow by blow. Just the facts, ma'am, only the facts."

"Sorry. Okay, I sent you both a spreadsheet of potential clients ranked by likelihood."

"Of course you did," she said with a chuckle. "And ..."

"And I'm sorry to say, no group jumped to the top of the leaderboard." He took an apologetic breath and kept going, as if describing his hard work would somehow produce positive results. "I also did a deep dive on the three senators." He began raising his fingers to count each criterion. "I looked at their demographics, voting history, committee involvement, special interests, political endorsements, known hate groups and enemies, who they're endorsing for president and a bunch of other factors. Then I tried identifying senators with similar characteristics and found five possible targets. I sent you that spreadsheet as well."

"Please," Michelle said with impatience. "Get to the point."

Chris rubbed his face with both hands, dropped his elbows on the table and held his head. "The point is … I have little confidence about any of it."

"That's discouraging," Ansel said with a surprising nonjudgmental tone.

"No shit," Chris responded. "The only thing I know for sure is social media is going viral with conspiracy rumors sparked by Senator McLoren on Lyle Mannity's show last night. She all but claimed the three senators were poisoned."

"We saw that too," Michelle blurted out.

"Incredible, right?" Chris asked rhetorically. "In my view, she's either Irene's client, grandstanding for her presidential bid or has a death wish to be the next target. Maybe all three. Regardless, I doubt Irene is very happy about the attention."

"Our take is she's a gossipmonger trying to create public panic so she can become America's savior. We definitely have to keep her loud mouth on our radar." Michelle then switched gears. "Ansel, do you want to explain what we tried?"

"Sure, but it didn't produce much. I reached out to Tonya, the Phonoi facilitator who I grew up with on the Amish farm. If you remember, she warned me about the attack in Québec City. Anyway, I was hoping she could track silentcide assets domestically. She can't. Then I asked if she could hack into senators' medical records in DC Health Nexus. That's the health insurance group covering Congress. She said maybe, given enough time. Unfortunately, she's too busy supporting a new, high-value commission in the Middle East to help with a fishing expedition. At best, she might handle a fast question. She did say there were rumors a black hat had breached the database. So I spent half my night – with Michelle's help – trying to find the data mole on the dark web, and the rest of the time trying to hack into DC Health Nexus. All I got was a big fat goose egg."

Michelle jumped in, "I didn't have luck either. I reached out to several sanctioned pharmacists who I have a good rapport with – and who hate Irene – to see if I could learn who filled Yasin's toxic asthma compound. Zip. Nada. Nothing. I also asked Dr. Yasin to make a few discreet calls to his old cronies. He said no, it was too much risk for a shot in the dark. In summary, we came up empty handed."

Chris slapped his thighs and sighed with resignation. "Well, I guess that's it." He pushed back his chair, stared apologetically at Anna, and said, "I'm sorry. It's a bust. We can keep trying, but I doubt we'll get better results finding the target senator."

Anna responded without fanfare, "Try Rosa Phillips."

"Who?" Michelle asked.

"A three-term Democratic senator from Colorado who has chronic asthma."

Chris's eyebrows raised. "How did you learn that?"

"Well," Anna said methodically, "I researched asthma demographics and learned African American women are three times more likely than white men to die from asthma. There's only one black female senator. A quick Google search revealed she was a former board member of the American Asthma Institute in Arlington, just across the Potomac from DC. Their website lists her as a prolific fundraiser. AAI also routinely invites other senators and house members with asthma as guest speakers. So I have six more senator names."

Anna passed the handwritten list to Chris. He immediately started typing into his laptop.

"That's impressive," Ansel said, the first time he had ever complimented her. "How did you do that so easily while we flailed around?"

She responded humbly, "Disease research was a big part of my marketing job at Longfellow." Anna didn't wait for accolades. They weren't needed. All she wanted was to help save a life. "Oh, Michelle, there's something else. You might want to watch Senator Phillips's speech at the Democratic Convention. See if her coughing and wheezing symptoms are consistent with the rescue inhaler Dr. Yasin described."

Michelle said, "Thanks, I'll do that."

Chris sat up, snapped his fingers, and exclaimed, "Guys, guys. Senator Phillips is ranked seventh on my spreadsheet of characteristics similar to the first three senators. This is huge."

"Awesome," Michelle said.

Anna ignored his excitement and nonchalantly asked, "Hey, Ansel, if your facilitator friend can only answer one question, can she learn if any T&E expenses are being incurred in Denver?"

"I can ask, but why?"

"According to Senator Phillips's press releases and website, she returned home yesterday and has a full schedule of events through the weekend. If an asset is following her, maybe there's a paper trail somewhere in or near Denver."

"Goddamn you're good at this!" Ansel proclaimed. "Really, really good."

Three hours later, the foursome reconvened on a call. Everyone was eager to share their good news.

Ansel said the facilitator had a backdoor into the main server containing the consolidated accounting records of both assassin divisions. Line items were cryptic; people and vendors weren't named. But the facilitator recognized the code for Colorado, and a trickle of expenses had begun three days before. The coding suggested only one asset was assigned.

Michelle's report was more exciting. She had brainstormed with Dr. Yasin. Together they created a simple yet effective ruse. He called the Denver sanctioned pharmacist under the pretense of confirming he had received and filled Wolfgang's compound. He was told the asset had already made the pickup. That verified Senator Phillips was the target.

"Outstanding!" Chris jumped up and did a happy dance. Anna laughed; she had never seen him so animated. His elation lasted only seconds before he sat down and got serious again. "Excellent job, everyone. Unfortunately, the asset is already one step ahead of us."

His sister said, "Yeah, let's hope we get there in time."

Without acknowledging the consequences if they were too late, Chris said, "Hey, Michelle, do you think Yasin can whip up two inhalers, one tainted and one not?"

"Sure, I suppose. Why?"

"I've been thinking," Chris said. "It's not good enough to stop the assassination attempt on the senator. Irene will keep trying until the job is done. I propose when we ID the asset, we discreetly kill him, then plant evidence like the poisoned inhaler and maybe a photo of the senator or something. The police will quickly sort out the pieces, then blanket Senator Phillips with protection."

Michelle said with concern, "Wouldn't that send a big red flag back to Irene? And possibly implicate Dr. Yasin?"

"Maybe, maybe not, depending how we do it. But here's the beauty of it. Today, only the top nine senators get government-paid security details. Once the media has a field day over the fourth targeted senator, I'll bet all one hundred senators get round-the-clock protection from the Capitol Police, local state police and the FBI. Let them do the work of stopping Irene's plans versus just the three of us."

Ansel said, "That makes perfect sense. But what do you want with the extra good inhaler?"

"Think of it as insurance," Chris answered. "See, I'm assuming we can't cover the senator every second. If we ever think the asset made the switch when we weren't watching, we exchange it with the good inhaler. That way the senator remains safe while we search for the asset who, as we all know, is required to keep tracking the mark until death is confirmed."

With angst in her voice, Michelle said, "All that sounds good, as long as you promise this doesn't backfire and endanger Dr. Yasin and his grandkids. I'm serious about that."

After giving his assurance, Chris explained he had started mapping the senator's announced activities, as well as routes from her office and home. He also promised to create a preliminary cat-and-mouse plan so they could monitor her twenty-four seven. He would include in the email a list of surveillance equipment and disguises Michelle should retrieve from his storage unit in Saint Paul.

Throughout their conversation, Anna listened intently but said nothing. She was confident the team would do everything they could after landing in Denver. Michelle then asked Anna, "Do you want to join us?"

"You're kidding, right? No way," Anna said. "I'm very content here. But I'll provide research support if needed."

After the call, Chris bounced up, smiled that once-endearing smile, and rushed forward for an impromptu congratulatory hug. Anna turned away. He was visibly hurt by the shun. He tried recovering by offering a nice dinner in appreciation for her contribution. He was disappointed when she declined that too.

"I'm sorry, Chris," Anna said with remorse. "I know you mean well, but you have lots of work to do, and I need to be alone. The best things you can do for me are to save that senator, kill Irene and give me my life back. I hope you understand."

He said nothing as she walked out the door. She wondered if she would ever see Chris again. She felt shitty about ending things so abruptly for the second time in twenty-four hours.

When she got back to the room, Anna stared at Sergeant O'Neill's unopened email. She also remembered her mom and Liz saying the San Francisco police wanted to talk with her about Jessica's death. She contemplated sending a warning about Senator Phillips to the FBI tip line.

Perhaps the only way to freedom was confessing everything to the authorities. Then maybe, just maybe, a good lawyer could prove her innocence. That meant burning Chris, Michelle and Ansel. But they were assassins, for Christ's sake, not friends.

Chapter Thirty-Three: Portland, Maine

Photos 77–78

THIRTY-FOUR

Denver and Boulder, Colorado
Friday – Sunday

Chris landed in Denver midmorning and was too early to check in to the downtown hotel, so he went directly to Michelle's room. When she let him in, the first thing he noticed was Ansel's open luggage at the side of the queen-size bed. That confirmed it. They were sleeping together.

"Let it go, Chris," Michelle said matter-of-factly while returning to the laptop on a table.

"How do you know what I was thinking?" he asked, feigning innocence, yet a bit pissed at her scolding mantra.

"The same way I know the sun rises in the east," she said without looking up. "So cool your jets and have a seat. We've got a lot to cover and not much time."

Michelle had that vibe, the intensity and laser focus she always had during a silentcide commission. She was on the hunt and refused to be distracted by superfluous issues. It was going to be wonderful working with his sister as a partner again. He missed their close relationship.

Sitting across from her, he said, "So fill me in."

"Okay, well, last night Ansel placed two microcameras facing the front and back yards of Senator Phillips's house. Their motion detectors will send us an alarm at any sign of an intruder. Then we took turns monitoring them in a car two blocks away. They also display here." She pointed at two video feeds on the laptop. "Early this morning, Ansel got the license plate of the senator's car when she drove off."

Chris asked in surprise, "The senator drives herself?"

"Yeah, we thought she'd have a driver, but clearly this is an independent woman. She's obviously not caught up with self-importance. Anyway, he texted it to Tonya and begged her to get GPS tracking of the car. Bless her heart, she came through, but said this was absolutely the last favor because she's really busy."

"We owe her big-time," Chris said.

"I agree. She's our kind of people. Meantime, I figured we needed the senator's full calendar, and not just the public events. I found the name of Phillips's executive assistant on LinkedIn, scanned her social media, and learned she's married with two small kids. One of the photos had the logo of a daycare center in the background. Hoping she'd drop them off, I staked out the center early this morning. Fortunately, she arrived. When she drove off, I followed her to a gas station and did a bluesnarfing hack of her cell phone through her car's Bluetooth connection. We now have all of her contacts' email addresses and phone numbers, and the senator's complete calendar."

"That's awesome," Chris said. "When I get the chance, I'll use my malware program to get access to the assistant's and senator's computers. Maybe the senator's phone too. Then I'll update the cat-and-mouse surveillance plan."

"I was hoping you'd say that." Michelle got distracted by something on the laptop.

"What is it?" Chris asked as he hurried to stand behind her.

She pointed to a third video feed. The picture was jumpy and out of focus. "That's Ansel walking into the reception area of the senator's downtown office. He's posing as a delivery guy with a package for the other US senator whose office is six blocks away.

Look, there, he's planted the camera," she said as the video stabilized, showing the reception room and doorway leading to Phillips's inner office complex.

The video did not have sound, but the gist of the conversation was obvious. Ansel presented the package, the young woman handed it back, shook her head, wrote something down for him, smiled and said goodbye. Fifteen seconds later, Ansel's voice boomed over the laptop speaker. "Michelle, you there?"

"Yup."

"Camera's in," Ansel said. "I'll monitor it from the parking lot next door as long as the senator is in her office."

"Great," she said. "Was there a bathroom down the hall? If so, should you plant a camera there too?"

"I suppose, but we're using them up pretty fast. We only had a six-pack of cameras."

"I know, but the bathroom would be a perfect place for the asset to make the inhaler exchange," she said, and Chris nodded in agreement.

"You got it. I'll find a way into the ladies' room. Anything else for now?"

Michelle looked back at her brother, gave him a big smile, and said, "Chris just got here."

"It's about time you showed up, you lazy lout," Ansel said in jest. "You've got to hit the pavement running, Jack. We need you."

"I love being needed," Chris said with a smirk before they signed off.

The lighthearted mood vanished as Michelle unzipped a pencil case next to her laptop. "Here are some things you'll need for your first assignment," she said. "More stuff from your storage unit is in my luggage." She handed him a two-way earbud.

"From what I just heard," Chris said, "I take it we're ignoring the standard Thanatos protocol of maintaining radio silence."

"Absolutely. It's a lot easier talking to each other than those ridiculous coded dings." Moving on, she said, "Here's your body-cam." The miniature camera resembled a shirt button. "And your *Washington Post* photographer press badge. I assume you brought your Nikon."

Chris gave her a look indicating the answer was obvious. When he stared at the ID photo of himself as the Benjamin "Sully" Williams alias, he said, "Oops, we've got a problem here. I threw my Sully disguise into the Charles River in Boston after shooting George Henniker."

Showing him no sympathy, Michelle said, "Well, you'd better find a fast way to suit up like Sully. You've got less than an hour. Ticktock."

The transformation into Sully only required a little of Michelle's makeup and a quick trip to a nearby costume shop. An eyeliner darkened his blond brows, and a layer of foundation gave his pale complexion a Mediterranean skin tone. A shaggy black wig, fake beard and mustache, plus aviator sunglasses completed the ensemble. It felt great to be dressed as his old buddy again.

Chris was standing at a balcony railing on the second floor of the Colorado State Capitol Building[79] when Ansel spoke in his earbud. "Phillips is entering through the Grand Street door. Tag, you're it. I'm headed back to take a nap."

A floor below, US Senator Rosa Phillips was a burst of energy while leading her entourage toward the governor's office for a scheduled meeting. Chris pretended to photograph the exquisite white-and-rose-colored marble interior, including the entrances to the senate and house chambers. He actually snapped photos of everyone walking the halls on three floors.

An hour later, the governor, Rosa Phillips, and the other Colorado US senator assembled in the rotunda[80] for a press conference. They represented the trifecta of the state's Democratic party. Each delivered a speech. There was no doubt who mesmerized the crowd.

Rosa Phillips was early sixties and slim with short, curly gray hair.

The senator wore tasteful pearl earrings and a red blazer matching her lipstick. Wisdom lines accented intense sparkling eyes and a never-ending smile. Her words sounded sincere, caring and pragmatic. Chris sensed she could be vivacious and engaging reading a grocery list.

He studied everyone's face in the audience using the zoom lens of the Nikon D850. He wasn't sure if the two uniformed Denver policemen were assigned to the capitol or were present only for this event. He also identified what he believed to be a plainclothes guard. There was no sign of anyone suspicious who could be the asset, but he photographed everyone nonetheless.

In the middle of her remarks, Senator Phillips stiffened, gasped for breath and started coughing. Chris winced when she weakly apologized before reaching into her purse and taking two deep shots from an inhaler. The crowd looked worried and sympathetic as the senator struggled to recover. A minute later, Phillips smiled, made a joke about the thin air in the Mile High City and continued her captivating speech.

Toward the end of the Q&A session, Chris hurried down the staircase, leaned against a pillar near the Grand Street entrance and pretended to text on his cell phone. He watched the senator leave and get into a car with her assistant and another woman. Then he discreetly followed them to the Denver World Trade Center[81] where he monitored a packed room of businesspeople during her speech and a reception.

It was already impossible to remember all the faces. Chris vowed to spend part of his evening downloading facial recognition software to identify and cross reference people from different venues. Their assumption was there was only one silentcide asset assigned to kill the senator. That assumption could be a costly mistake.

That evening, the threesome tag-teamed surveillance of two private fundraisers at the homes of wealthy constituents and later the senator's residence until dawn. The rotation was working well.

One would always be near the senator, one would monitor the laptop feeds, and the third would sleep. However, frustration was growing. At the end of day one, there was no evidence of the asset. The assassin's ability to avoid detection was a testament to their training, skill and deadliness.

◆◆◆

Early the next morning, Chris talked to Michelle while following a mile behind the senator's car using the GPS on his cell phone. His sister sounded giddy, a refreshing emotion he hadn't heard in months. She planned to spend the next several hours shopping for a formal dress, plus rent a tux for him, even though both would be returned on Monday. She thanked him profusely for using the malware to get them on the senator's guest list for the charity ball. At least for the moment, Michelle seemed as excited as a teenager going to a high school prom, an event she never experienced on the Amish farm.

Protecting Rosa Phillips was a potential disaster the moment she was greeted by the vice chancellor of Student Affairs in front of Norlin Library.[82] The senator's morning itinerary began with a walking tour of the old campus of University of Colorado Boulder. Norlin Quadrangle was packed with students and young adults, many carrying signs and banners in support of their gender identity or sexual orientation.

The senator was in her element. She kept stopping to talk, shake hands, sign autographs and pose for selfies. Chris fixed his zoom lens on her purse, watching for the slightest hint someone was switching inhalers. People consistently obstructed his view. Too many times the exchange could have happened undetected. As he inched closer, he began sweating beneath the black wig, both from the heat and anxiety.

Near the steps of Old Main,[83] CU Boulder's oldest building, the unexpected happened. Senator Phillips approached Chris, stared at his press credentials, and said, "Impressive, young man. You flew all the way from DC to photograph me?"

"Yes," he said. "The editors are considering running a feature story about you."

"I'm flattered," she said, "but newspaper circulation is so low, I'm surprised they want to risk a further decline by printing an article on me." The self-deprecating remark was followed by a charming grin. "I've seen you take a lot of photos of me on that fancy camera of yours. If you manage to get a flattering one, send it to my press secretary, will you?"

"Yes, ma'am," he said with genuine respect.

"And knock off that ma'am stuff. Just call me Rosa. All of my friends do."

"Okay," Chris said with a smile. He really liked her.

"And just among us friends," she said with a twinkle, "you'd be so much more handsome with a haircut. I'll bet your mom would agree."

After her good-natured poke, she turned around and engaged with someone else. For a moment, he was distracted by his thoughts. *This wonderful woman deserves to live.*

The senator was the keynote speaker at the Celebrating Life Choices event inside the Macky Auditorium Concert Hall.[84] He knew she was safe while standing in front of the podium but worried a lethal inhaler was now in her purse. When she returned to the speaker's table on stage and took two puffs to open her lungs, Chris breathed a sigh of relief. He was happy to see her drive off campus an hour later. She hadn't died on his watch.

Ansel had the afternoon shift, observing the senator through binoculars while she attended a backyard barbeque for her nephew's birthday party. Later, Ansel watched the video feeds back at the hotel while Chris and Michelle strolled arm-in-arm into the cancer research charity event at the Colorado Convention Center.[85]

The ballroom was packed with tables of eight for Denver's social elite. The cost per plate was two thousand dollars. Plenty of hefty checks were written after the silent auction. The bar was free but effectively lubricated the donations.

Michelle was stunning in a black designer gown. Other than a long auburn wig, she wasn't disguised. But judging from the stares at her long legs peeking out from the thigh-high slits, and the ample cleavage exposed by the plunging neckline, few people would be looking at her face. In contrast, Chris felt like a dork in a monkey suit that was two sizes too big and wearing the Ted Collins disguise.

The evening was enchanting with Michelle, despite their constant vigilance of Senator Phillips sitting at the head table. Chris especially enjoyed the dancing after dinner. For fleeting moments, he forgot about his litany of problems and savored the rare closeness with his sister.

The only frustration was there was still no positive identification of the assassin. Chris was beginning to wonder if they were mistaken about the senator being the target. Or maybe the commission was canceled or postponed. More likely, the silentcide asset was waiting for the opportune moment. For the senator's sake, the three of them could not let down their guard.

◆◆◆

At 8:10 Sunday morning, Rosa Phillips and her husband walked up the steps of the Cathedral Basilica of the Immaculate Conception.[86] They were greeted at Denver's oldest church by the archbishop of Denver's Archdiocese. A few worshippers clamored for the senator's attention. Michelle's role was to follow close behind, remain vigilant, and select a pew with a good view of the senator.

Chris slipped through a side door. He was impressed by the stunning interior featuring grand arches and columns crafted from Carrara marble. Equally marvelous were the seventy-five stained glass windows, the most in the United States. He selected the last row of a shortened side aisle. This gave him excellent visibility of the main nave plus allowed for a quick exit if needed.

Ansel's voice boomed through the earbud. "Michelle, can you readjust the camera at the end of your pew? That big man holding the baby is blocking my video view of the senator."

She did not respond.

A moment later, Ansel said, "That's better. Much better. We're good to go."

Chris could count on one hand how many times he had attended a Catholic Mass. The music and singing were good, but the ritual was painstakingly slow. He frequently made a clandestine glance toward Phillips and the surrounding people. No one seemed threatening.

About a half hour into the ceremony, the baby started crying. The father attempted to soothe the child, became frustrated and embarrassed, excused himself, awkwardly stepped over people's legs, then rushed down the center aisle.

Chris maintained an eagle eye on the senator. A moment of crowd distraction like this would be the ideal opportunity to switch the inhalers in the senator's purse sitting behind her on the wooden bench. He relaxed when nothing obvious happened.

Twelve minutes later, the father sheepishly returned carrying the sleeping infant. People shifted toward the middle of the pew, allowing him to sit at the end. Ansel's voice returned to the earbuds. "Michelle, that guy is blocking everything again. Can you reposition the camera?"

At that moment, Chris thought he saw in his peripheral vision a swift movement by the elderly woman kneeling behind the senator. He risked a prolonged stare. The woman was deep in prayer with her eyes closed and hands folded. She seemed innocuous, but his instincts were on fire. Something definitely felt wrong, but he couldn't pinpoint the problem.

During communion, he watched, waited and worried. When an usher reached the senator's row, everyone stood and filed into the line headed toward the altar. The old woman sat and allowed others to pass when the usher signaled them to join the line. Then she slowly stepped into the side aisle, genuflected, made the sign of the cross and struggled to walk toward the back of the church.

Two rows behind, Chris noticed the plainclothes guard from the State Capitol Building. The man watched the woman pass before casually standing and entering the aisle. It seemed unlikely he was sneaking out of Mass early like some other parishioners. Had he seen the woman do something suspicious to the senator that Chris missed?

Chris heard coughing. The sound was muted at first before becoming louder, followed by a rattling wheeze. The senator's husband tried to help as she frantically dug through her purse, stuck the inhaler between her lips and pushed the plunger twice. During the violent hacking, Senator Phillips was in obvious agony. She clutched her chest, gasped, stumbled and tried grabbing her husband's arm before crashing to the floor. Her face looked clammy. Her lips were turning blue. People rushed to help while others gawked.

Chris was certain she was dying. He had failed her.

He bolted out of the pew and down the aisle to confront the old woman when he heard the guard shout, "Stop!" while running out the door with a pistol. Chris retrieved his Glock from behind his back. By the time he got outside, the man was giving chase. "Stop! Police!" he shouted again.

The old woman clearly wasn't old. She was sprinting toward the parking lot. The assassin suddenly turned and began aiming her SIG P229 when two bullets erupted from the guard's gun. The first was errant. The second slammed into her chest. Her head bounced off a car door as her legs crumpled. When she tried raising her gun, a third bullet crushed her skull.

Chris concealed his weapon and walked away.

Chapter Thirty-Four: Denver and Boulder, Colorado

Photos 79–86

THIRTY-FIVE

Seville, Spain

Sunday

"You're an idiot," Irene belittled Jacob Conners. "How do you expect to be worth a damn if you can't even control an old dog?"

The eighteen-year-old orphan flinched at the scolding, tugged on the leash and said "Heel" repeatedly but was being dragged by Brutus toward another dog in the historic El Centro neighborhood of Seville. Brutus won the tug-of-war and was soon wagging his tail while sniffing a female Spanish pointer. Conners watched helplessly.

Irene couldn't stand the kid. The teenager was training to be a silentcide assassin. He was unjustifiably cocky, strong yet not street-wise, self-absorbed and moody. His lips were too big and pouty, a gargantuan nose dominated his oblong face, and black caterpillar brows gave his hazel eyes a distrustful glare. The hideous bowl haircut he wore at the now-defunct Amish farm had been replaced by a buzz cut.

Irene mostly resented Jacob Conners for putting a bullet in Lionel Jørgensen's head three weeks ago. Sure, the kid was following her orders. The mercy killing had been a test to see if Conners had the gonads to pull the trigger up close and personal. The test had been a mistake. Having Lionel alive as an unresponsive vegetable was better than having him dead. She ached for her former husband and lover every day.

The dogs continued to frolic at the base of a tall monument in Plaza Nueva,[87] a two-acre public square. Ferdinand III looked regal perched on top as an equestrian statue. She resented the thirteenth-century king of Castile and León. His military prowess over the Muslims created a massive Christian empire and earned him sainthood. There was no way he would have accomplished any of that as a woman.

She had become the head of a major prestigious law firm and created an international network of assassins. A huge success. Her achievements rivaled the top half percent of female titans. Yet when she died – and that time was on the horizon – there would be no monuments or statues, only an enormous pile of unspent money without heirs. If only she had been born a man, imagine the conglomerate, power, fame and trophy wife she would control.

Going forward, perhaps the best she could hope for was to be reincarnated as a rich woman's dog. Then she could be loved and pampered while sniffing or peeing anywhere, anytime. Better yet, come back as a male champion purebred with an active life as a stud service. Now that would be nirvana.

Until then, she'd have to tolerate the incompetent idiots she employed and hope they could follow orders and satisfy her clients while keeping her alive and out of prison. That wasn't asking too much, was it? She feared those minimal expectations were a pipe dream.

"Goddamn it, Conners!" she yelled at the teenager. "Let's go. It's five o'clock and I'm missing cocktail hour."

The Afghan hound galloped with enthusiasm as they walked past the Plateresque reliefs on the façade of City Hall,[88] an architectural jewel dating back to the sixteenth century. The dog's long glossy coat waved in the breeze while the teenager's enormous feet clumped along. What a hideous mismatch.

Wolfgang had insisted on bringing the worthless teenager to Spain after closing the farm where Rachel and Mamm were killed.

Irene had hoped Conners could, at the very least, groom and walk Brutus. The time-consuming labors of love were becoming physically demanding for her. Yet after this maiden outing, she questioned whether Conners was competent enough to manage a dog. She had to find some meaningful role for the inept teenager.

After they took the private rear lift up to her penthouse apartment, Irene was thrilled to discover her manservant had graciously set out a bowl of water for Brutus and a chilled oshibori towel for her. On the antique table in front of a Spanish salon sofa was a pitcher of dry martinis, a bowl of stuffed olives on ice and a tray of hors d'oeuvres. Pierre was consistently competent.

The first sip was delightfully refreshing. The second was ruined when Wolfgang König entered the Mudéjar-style living room. The man had an irritating habit of interrupting life's simple pleasures.

Irene demanded, "Don't you dare say a word unless you have good news for a change."

"I do," he said without inflection or emotion while standing at attention. His fierce, inset eyes were raised yet difficult to read. "Very good news, in fact ..."

"Excellent," she said but remained leery.

Then he finished his statement. "... except for a couple of asterisks."

"Goddamn it," she bellowed with disgust. "Are you incapable of delivering good news without some kind of caveat?"

"No, Ms. Shaw," the head of Thanatos said, showing no reaction to her chastisement.

"Well then, try it sometime, because I can't remember it ever happening."

"Yes, Ms. Shaw."

"*Yes, Ms. Shaw. No, Ms. Shaw. We screwed up again, Ms. Shaw.*" Irene was tired of this crap. She missed the days when she, Lionel and Nathan Yasin succeeded together as a high-functioning team. Those glory days were gone forever. Age and greedy expansion had robbed them of their perfect formula. Lowering her head and rubbing her forehead in exhausted abhorrence, she reluctantly said, "Okay, tell me the good news, and make the rest of it painless."

Wolfgang spread his legs apart with his arms behind his back, the stance he normally assumed when delivering a report. "About an hour ago, Senator Rosa Phillips died of a severe asthma attack."

"That's excellent," she declared, raising her glass before finishing the first martini with an unladylike gulp. She might as well savor the headline. The rest of the conversation was certain to go downhill. "Where did it happen?"

Wolfgang replied, "In the center aisle of Denver's cathedral during Sunday Mass."

"That's perfect," she said with zeal. "Right in the middle of a crowd. That'll get a lot of tongues wagging." The successful silentcide also meant she didn't have to accept Wolfgang's offer to be shot if he failed the commission. She couldn't afford to lose his leadership and affinity for managing the nasty details. Irene leaned back into the sofa. "I'm assuming that completes the extent of your good news. So pour me another drink before you screw up my mood."

She chewed a stuffed olive while he refilled her martini, then used the toothpick to dig out a hunk of something wedged in her bicuspid. After taking a sip from the refreshed glass, she said, "All right, dear, let's hear the shitty asterisks."

With a continued monotone, he said, "After the senator's inhalers were exchanged, our asset was leaving the cathedral when confronted by what appeared on the bodycam to be a plainclothes guard or cop. There was a shootout. She's dead."

"For Christ's sake," Irene screamed. "How many assets have we lost in the last three weeks?"

"A lot," was Wolfgang's evasive answer, or maybe he had lost track of the body count.

"Too many," she said in a rage.

He nodded in agreement, taking no responsibility for their dwindling inventory of people, then said, "The upside is I'm assuming the senator's good inhaler was still in our asset's pocket. As a result, your client will be very pleased. There will be no question that Phillips was assassinated. That should create an indisputable link to the other senators."

That was perfect, a fact she would leverage for a higher fee. "What nationality was our dead asset?" she asked.

"Eastern European," he answered. "And don't worry, there's zero chance she can be identified."

That nationality would really get the rumor mill buzzing about a foreign conspiracy. This was getting better and better, vastly more than the client bargained for. Irene could spin this to the client as part of her master plan to exceed expectations leading up to the grand finale. A hefty bonus was almost certain.

"Wolfgang, dear, you've earned yourself a drink. Pour yourself a double and have a seat."

Both suggestions were a first in their relationship. Irene had never treated him as a quasi-partner. Although Wolfgang would never reach the status of Lionel or Nathan, he might come close someday. She watched as he poured three fingers' worth of Jack Daniel's from a Waterford crystal decanter at the bar. His choice of liquor made her smile. The whiskey had been Lionel's favorite.

He pulled up a hand-carved walnut armchair from the mid-nineteenth century, crossed his legs, took a long swig and seemed to be waiting for the right moment to explain something else.

Irene said, "Is the next asterisk stuck in your throat and just waiting to come out?"

"Yes, Ms. Shaw."

She liked the formality of being addressed as Ms. Shaw. He hadn't earned the privilege of calling her Irene. That time would probably never come. "Go ahead, dear. Spit out the furball."

Wolfgang took another slug of Jack. "The asset's bodycam caught a familiar face running out of the church at the time of the shootout." He paused. "Ted Collins."

Irene was pissed but not surprised. At this point, Chris would probably do almost anything to get his revenge. "Is Chris still wearing that ratty disguise? What an idiot. Is there any reason to believe the plainclothesman was working with him?"

"I'm guessing no, but we'll learn the shooter's identity when the media stories start coming out. I also believe if Chris was there, then the rest of the foursome were in Denver too. I promise to personally review other bodycam videos to see if I can spot them trailing our asset."

"That's fine, but they probably were. They travel together like a pack of rabid wolves. Any chance you can take care of those nasty pests in Denver?"

"No, Ms. Shaw. If they're smart, they're gone by now. I know I would be."

"You're probably right," she said with disappointment. "Give me a second to think. While I do, have one of those lovely anchovy sandwiches."

Wolfgang cringed while looking at the dead fish tails protruding from small bread triangles.

"Go ahead, dear. They're delicious." Irene resisted the urge to laugh when his thin lips pursed with disgust.

Then, like a master chess champion, she took ten minutes to consider the pros, cons, and risks of various tactical moves until confident of a decisive checkmate. She finished the second dry martini before saying, "The only way Chris and the gang could have identified Senator Phillips is if Yasin tipped them off. Isn't that right?"

"I agree," he said with certainty. "That means our suspicions are confirmed. The doctor's disloyal to you. Do you want me to have him and his family killed?"

"No, he can still be useful. I'll call him later and give him a fake assignment. The ruse should send the annoying Good Samaritans on a wild goose chase while the main event happens at the end of the week."

"I like that," he said.

Of course he did. It was her idea. She continued, "I'll also devise a way to leverage Yasin to lure the foursome into the open. It'll be subtle, but Chris is a smart boy. He'll figure it out. When they're dead, let's reward Yasin for his cooperation by giving him that permanent retirement he's always wanted. Yes, this will work beautifully."

"What do you want me to do?" he asked.

"For now, stay focused on the last stage of this senator commission. It has to happen flawlessly. Understood?"

"Yes, Ms. Shaw," he said, then gulped down the balance of the whiskey. He could sense the meeting was coming to an end and knew he would be quickly dismissed.

Irene said, "One more thing before you go. Is that idiot Jacob Conners a virgin and functional?"

Wolfgang's reaction was priceless. He seemed surprised and perplexed. "As far as I know. Why?"

"After my call with Yasin, send him to my room. He's got to be good at something someday. I'll teach him a few fun things that you can't."

Chapter Thirty-Five: Seville, Spain

Photos 87–88

THIRTY-SIX

Colorado and Salt Lake City, Utah
Sunday

Chris, Michelle and Ansel reconvened in their downtown hotel minutes after Senator Phillips was killed. They quickly agreed the best course of action was to get out of Denver fast. Flying to the Twin Cities was ruled out; the airport might be monitored and their home turf was probably a hunting ground for Irene's henchmen. Ansel suggested making the eight-hour road trip to Salt Lake City. He said, "There's something poetic about escaping persecution like a Mormon pioneer." Chris lobbied for a photography detour to visit Arches National Park[89] near Moab, Utah. He was overruled. Their compromise was a side tour of the towering sandstone monoliths in Colorado National Monument[90] during their drive on Interstate 70.

They had just made a pit stop in Vail,[91] and were traveling through a scenic valley flanked by snow-capped mountains in White River National Forest[92] when Michelle's cell phone rang. Dr. Yasin's voice boomed through the car's speaker. Without a salutary greeting, he said, "I hear Senator Phillips died of an acute asthma attack in Denver."

Michelle asked, "How'd you hear that?"

"It's breaking news on every TV and radio station, plus all over the internet. There's lots of finger-pointing at foreign enemies." His anger was escalating. "What really ticks me off is I gave you the information five days ago. I also took a huge risk confirming Phillips was the target by contacting my pharmacist crony in Denver. Did you even bother trying to save her?"

"Yes, we flew to Denver and were tracking her ..."

Dr. Yasin cut Michelle off. "But you failed, right?"

She was offended. Yasin was giving them no credit for their valiant effort. But rather than push back, she kept trying to defend herself. "I'm sorry, but the inhaler switch happened too fast to stop it."

Yasin shrieked, "Is there any way this can blow back on me and my family?"

"No," she said with confidence. "The assassin was killed by a cop or guard. We had nothing to do with the asset's death, so Irene can't blame you or us."

"Are you sure?"

Ansel leaned forward over the car's front seat and said, "We're absolutely positive."

Michelle gave him a menacing stare, a clear signal he was on the precipice of being a jerk.

"Who's that?" the doctor asked with suspicion.

"It's Ansel," she answered. "You saw him at Fort Snelling. Chris is also here."

"That's great," Yasin said sarcastically. "Just great. There's nothing safer than having a clandestine discussion with a gaggle of people."

Michelle needed to deescalate the conversation before it became adversarial. "I'm assuming you didn't call just to scold us, did you?"

A gasp of exasperation traveled over the Bluetooth. Yasin was obviously trying to lower his temper. "No, you're right. I called to tell you I talked with Irene about an hour ago." The three of them sat up with interest. "She gave me another assignment and profusely promised it would be the last one and then my grandkids would be safe." He sighed again. "I've known that woman for far too long. Whenever she assures you'll get something you desperately want, it's time to be worried."

Michelle and the two men nodded their heads in agreement. They knew exactly what he meant. She asked, "Can you give us the assignment details?"

"Of course," he said with a lingering bite of irritation in his voice. "I'm supposed to prescribe a lethal combination of blood thickeners and coagulants concealed inside twenty-milligram doses of rosuvastatin. And before you ask your question, Ansel, it's a reductase inhibitor or statin designed to slow the production of cholesterol."

Michelle sensed Ansel taking offense at the condescending tone. An index finger to her lips stopped him from saying something stupid. Michelle asked the doctor, "Did Irene tell you anything else that might be helpful?"

"No, that's it."

Chris whispered to his sister, "Ask him if he knows where Irene is." She repeated the question out loud.

Yasin got furious. "What's wrong with you people? Don't you think I'd tell you if I knew? I want her dead more than you do. Now do something about it and fast." He hung up.

Ansel was the first to speak. "What are we supposed to do with that golden nugget of information? Follow all the fat senators?"

Michelle leaned back to give him an icy look. "It's not just fat people who have high cholesterol."

"Then I know," Ansel continued the sarcasm unabated. "We'll run all their credit cards looking for expenses at steakhouses and fast-food joints."

Chris verbally jumped into the fray. "He's right. Our only chance is to hack into the congressional health system and find out who's taking that dosage of drug. And we already tried that, remember? And even then, it might be a needle-in-a-haystack kind of thing."

Their collective silence of discouragement lasted several mile markers. This new assignment seemed challenging, maybe hopeless. Michelle's shoulders flinched when Chris's cell phone rang. He struggled to dig it out of his pocket while driving, put it on speaker and stuck the phone in a cup holder. "Hello?"

Anna's opening question was, "Were you planning to call and tell me what happened?"

He said sheepishly, "You heard about Senator Phillips, huh?"

"Of course I have. The news is everywhere."

In her seemingly endless role as peacemaker, Michelle said in a pleasant way, "Hi, Anna. Where are you?"

"Hi, Michelle. I'm sitting in front of the Beetle Lighthouse in Portland."

Chris instantly said, "I think it's called Bug Light."[93]

From the backseat, Ansel whispered with a giggle, "That sounds like a beer name."

Anna had no patience for either of them. "Thanks, Chris. Of course you couldn't resist correcting me. Just tell me what happened."

They took turns describing the events from the charity ball the night before through their discussion with Dr. Yasin. Anna listened patiently before asking a question, as if she assumed everyone was ready for another rescue attempt. "So how are we going to find this next senator? I'm willing to help with the research again."

No one had the courage to admit they were not up to the task. So they spent the next half hour again discussing how each person would help identify the next target.

After a frustrating and unproductive evening in front of their laptops in a Salt Lake City hotel room, Michelle told Ansel she was going to sleep. He mistakenly took that as a cue. He turned off his computer, got undressed, and was waiting for her under the covers as she exited the bathroom. When she crawled into bed, he slid over to get frisky.

"Not tonight," she announced, the first time she had shunned his advances since they had become partners.

"Why not?" he asked. She sensed him pouting.

"Because I'm tired, it's been a crappy day, and we need sleep so we can get an early start again tomorrow."

Ansel rubbed his eyes as if calculating what to say or do. He gently probed, "Does it also have something to do with the fact that Chris's room is right next door?"

"I suppose," she admitted. "In a way, I still feel a bit guilty."

Ansel sat up, reached for her hand and asked with concern, "You feel guilty about us? Why?"

"I don't know," she said evasively while looking blankly at the ceiling. "You've seen the way Chris looks at us. He's trying to accept us being together, and he's putting on a brave face, but I know it's eating him up."

Ansel's comeback was not very empathetic. "Tell him to get over it."

She laughed softly. "You have no idea how many times I've told him that."

After a moment's thought, Ansel asked, "Do you think Chris would feel differently if he and Anna were still together?"

"Maybe. I don't know."

"Does he still have feelings for her?"

"Of course he does," Michelle said emphatically. "He'd do anything for her. But deep down, he knows they were never meant to be together. The best we can do for both of them, besides getting Irene of course, is to save at least one senator. But after today, I have little to no hope we're going to succeed." Hearing herself admit that was depressing. "Good night," she said, then reached over the nightstand to turn off the light.

Ansel lay down, fluffed the pillow and adjusted the blanket. After a few seconds, he snuggled into a spooning position and kissed the back of her head with tenderness. Having his strength and acceptance beside her was comforting.

Chapter Thirty-Six: Colorado and Salt Lake City, Utah

Photos 89–93

THIRTY-SEVEN

SALT LAKE CITY, UTAH

Monday – Thursday

O n Monday morning, while Michelle and Ansel were working and nibbling on a room-service breakfast, the cavalry unexpectedly came over the hill.

Ansel got a call from Tonya, his facilitator friend. She said the major commission she was supporting in the Middle East had been abruptly canceled, and the Phonoi asset was immediately reassigned to the United States. She had expected to create support files for the new commission because she was always assigned to this asset. However, she was told via an encrypted text that her assistance wasn't required. In short, she now had plenty of time to help them if they still needed her.

Ansel was ecstatic. He explained what they were looking for, asked her to hack into the DC Health Nexus database, then screen all senators' prescription histories. Tonya was up for the challenge.

Two days later, hope springs eternal turned into a dry gulch of failure. Despite countless hours of toil, the five-member team wasn't remotely close to identifying the next targeted senator with any degree of confidence. The mission appeared to be a bust. Another senator was going to die. There was nothing they could do to stop it.

Late Wednesday afternoon, Chris knocked on their hotel room door. He was sweaty, flushed, and his beloved camera hung around his neck.

Michelle asked with disapproval, "Where have you been?"

"Photographing Salt Lake Temple[94] and the LDS campus,[95] plus the state capitol,"[96] he said matter-of-factly.

Michelle was perturbed. "So you've been out frolicking around the neighborhood with that stupid camera while the rest of us are working our asses off?"

"It's not that," Chris said. "I had to get out of that stuffy hotel room to think. And my conclusion: this is a fool's errand. We're never going to figure this out in time. We should be focusing on Irene. She's our primary target, and we're doing absolutely nothing to find her."

Ansel said, "I don't disagree, but how do you propose we do that?"

Chris raised a hand toward Michelle as if to ward off a verbal attack. "Sister, I don't want you going ballistic on me when I say this, but I think we should call Yasin again and ask him."

Michelle tried not to be confrontational, but self-control was difficult. "Haven't you heard a damn thing? Every time we ask him where Irene is, he gets super pissed. Do you actually think he's holding something back?"

"No, not intentionally," Chris said.

Ansel asked, "Then what are you driving at?"

"I don't know, grasping at straws, I guess. But Yasin keeps talking with Irene, right? Maybe if we ask him enough questions about those conversations, he'll remember a clue that'll lead us to her."

"It's a long shot," Ansel said. "But maybe the best one we got." Looking toward Michelle, he asked, "What do you think?"

"Maybe," she said. "But only under two conditions. One, I do all the talking because I have the rapport with him. And two, Ansel, you're nowhere near the damn phone. No offense, but he has a rather low opinion of you."

Ansel seemed offended but reluctantly agreed.

Chris said, "That's fine by me. When are we going to do this?"

"How about right now?" Ansel chimed in.

Michelle was hesitant. The last thing she wanted to do was further upset Dr. Yasin. She reached for her cell phone, pushed his number, put it on speaker and, during the first ring, she said to Ansel, "Now absolute quiet, remember? Don't screw this up."

"What now?" was Dr. Yasin's opening question. "I hope you have something good to tell me for a change."

Michelle responded, "No, I'm sorry, we're still trying to identify the right senator."

"It's been three days already," he exclaimed. "What the hell are you waiting for? To learn the name in the obituary column?"

Michelle ignored the accusatory questions and tried pacifying his frustration. "Doctor, you've always trusted me, right?"

"Yes, of course."

"Then trust me when I say we're doing everything we can to find the right senator. But our other priority is finding Irene, and we're hoping you can help."

Yasin bellowed, "You haven't been listening to me, have you? How many times must I tell you I don't know where she is?"

"I believe you. But we're thinking maybe, just maybe, Irene said something during your conversations that could give us a hint of where she is."

He sounded insulted. "Michelle, I've been in this business a few years, frankly going back to before you were born. Don't you think I would've been listening for clues about where she is?"

Unexpectedly, Chris did the unthinkable. He interrupted. "Hi, Doctor. This is Chris."

"What do you want?" Yasin asked. "I suppose this call was your bright idea. Well, blow it out your ear."

In response, Chris was conciliatory and soothing. "Doctor, you have every reason to be frustrated and angry. And I assure you, we're doing everything we can to protect you and your grandkids. So just hear me out, please."

"You've got two seconds," the doctor said.

"Okay, thanks. By any chance have you recorded your conversations with Irene?"

"I'd never dared do anything like that in the past," Yasin said, then admitted, "but yes, since she started threatening my family, I've recorded them as potential leverage against her."

"Would you be willing to send them to Michelle?"

"I could, but you're not going to find anything."

As soon as Chris received the audio, he retreated to his room. About two hours later, he knocked on their hotel room door. He was visibly excited, but Michelle said with a finger to her lips, "Shh. Ansel's on the phone. Give him a sec, will you?"

The siblings watched as Ansel concluded his call by saying, "That's a tall order, but let me see what I can do, then I'll call you back, okay?"

When Ansel pocketed his phone, she asked him, "What was that all about?"

Ansel said, "Remember that Phonoi asset Tonya was supporting in the Middle East? Well, apparently, he called her in a panic. It seems the new facilitator he's working with can't find his own butt. The asset needs to get his hands on an LAOP-500 by Friday morning. I agreed to call my arms dealer in my hometown of Baltimore to see if he can arrange a delivery."

Michelle was confused. "What's an LAOP?"

Ansel said, "It's the Russian equivalent of a Switchblade 300."

"Of course," she said with sarcasm. "That explains everything."

"Okay, it's a very portable munition – less than six pounds, if I remember correctly – with foldable wings and fits in a backpack. It takes one person less than two minutes to launch and delivers a hell of a wallop."

Chris piped in, "So basically, you're saying it's a small suicide or kamikaze drone."

"Exactly. And after everything Tonya's done for us, I figured I could return the favor." Ansel switched gears. "You look all happy-face for a change," he said to Chris. "What's up?"

"Great news! I heard something on Yasin's tape from Sunday. It took a lot of filtering and enhancing, because at first it seemed like background static, but I isolated what sounds like a horse and buggy. That noise is seared into my memory after years on the Amish farm. Then six repetitive chimes, followed by lots and lots of bells playing all at once. Simple math of when Yasin got this call on Sunday morning suggests Irene made the call at six o'clock at night in the Central European Summer Time Zone."

"That's great work," Michelle said.

Ansel was less enthusiastic. "I don't mean to rain on your parade, buddy. But all that means is Irene was near a church or cathedral someplace in Europe. That hardly narrows it down."

"I know," Chris said. "But when I said a lot of bells were ringing, I mean a lot of bells, too many for me to count. So I sent the tape to Anna. I'm hoping her piano talent can help me identify the exact number of bells. I'm going to keep working with her on it tonight. If we succeed, then maybe I can figure out what cathedral it was."

♦♦♦

Early Thursday morning, there was insistent knocking on their hotel room door. Michelle and Ansel were still recovering beneath the covers. "Oh, shit," she whispered, debated whether to pretend they weren't in the room, worried it might be important, then yelled out, "Just a sec. We can't come to the door right now."

Chris bellowed from the hallway. "Get your damn clothes on and meet me in my room. Pronto!"

With a concerned look, Ansel asked her, "Do you think he heard us and is pissed?"

"I don't know," Michelle said. "If he did, I doubt he'd try barging in on us. Besides, he didn't sound angry, just urgent. We've got to move. Get dressed."

Ten minutes later, they entered her brother's room. Michelle felt like they were doing the walk of shame.

With a mischievous smirk, Chris said, "Stop worrying, sis. I'm over it." He added a wink to dig the tease deeper.

Trying to act guilt-free, Ansel asked, "So what's so important?"

"Sit," Chris said. "I've got two big pieces of news."

They sat together on the unmade bed while Chris began pacing the room during his announcements. His hands and expressions were animated. "First, we've found Irene."

"Are you kidding?" Michelle asked with thrilled disbelief.

"Awesome," Ansel echoed her sentiment. "How'd you do it?"

"We did it," Chris said to share the credit. "Anna and I. I can't tell you how many times we listened to that tape. At the end, I figured there were at least twenty bells on the recording. She heard twenty-two. It didn't take long to screen European cathedrals with that many bells. The answer is La Giralda."[97]

"What's that?" Ansel asked.

"It was a grand minaret built in the late twelfth century alongside the former Aljama Mosque in Seville, Spain. Since the Christians converted it into a cathedral in the mid-thirteenth century, it has eighteen bells and six clappers, among the most in Europe."

Ansel said, "Thanks for the history lesson, but how can you be so sure that's the one?"

"Confirming it was the easy part. I compared the tape to an online video. The pealing is identical. I also found an image on the Encircle Photos website showing a horse and buggy[98] out front. There's no question about it. Irene made the call to Yasin within earshot of La Giralda next to the Seville Cathedral."

"That's spectacular," Michelle exclaimed while rushing over to give her brother a big hug. "Congratulations."

After savoring her embrace, he stepped back and said, "Now,

for news flash number two. I was thinking about Tonya's request to get that suicide drone. Based on my research, when you said it packs a wallop, you weren't kidding. It can destroy an armored tank. I started wondering, why would someone need that kind of explosive power, especially domestically. There's only one answer. To make a very big impact."

"Are you thinking terrorist attack?" Michelle asked.

"I would if it weren't one of Irene's assets. As far as I know, she's not into terrorism. But this is consistent with what Yasin called 'Irene's swan song.' Big and splashy. Then I asked myself, why a Russian drone? The answer seems obvious: to blame the Russians. This has to be political. And this next part I want Tonya to confirm by tracking the asset's T&E expenses, but I'm guessing the attack zone is somewhere in Washington, DC."

Ansel said, "You're onto something. Why didn't I think of that?"

"Because you were too focused on returning the favor to Tonya, so don't beat yourself up. Anyway, I looked for obvious possible targets. The president and vice president are on the campaign trail for the next week, so they're safe until then. And Congress just started summer recess, so they're all out of town. That's when I found the answer. The asset needs the drone by Friday because on Saturday morning there's a major rally on the National Mall in front of the Lincoln Memorial. Thousands of people are expected to attend."

"What's the rally?" Michelle asked.

"Does the phrase 'Keep America Safe' sound familiar?"

"You mean Senator Vickie McLoren's slogan?"

"Yup, the one and only. It's her event. She's the hostess and keynote speaker."

Ansel had listened intently and was thoughtful but finally spoke up. "So someone's hired Irene to kill Senator McLoren in retaliation for all the rumors she's spreading about the dead senators?"

"That's my guess, plus kill and maim countless other people at the same time. And someone wants to make sure Russia gets the blame."

Ansel concurred. "That makes perfect sense. So what do we do about it?"

"I asked Anna the same question. I said we can't do everything at once, so she had to choose two options from the following list. One, keep looking for the senator with high cholesterol. Two, stop the attack in Washington, DC. Or three, go to Seville and kill Irene. Her two picks were obvious."

Indignant, Ansel grumbled, "Since when did Anna become the decision-maker?"

Michelle snapped back, "Shut up, Ansel."

Chapter Thirty-Seven: Salt Lake City, Utah

Photos 94–98

THIRTY-EIGHT

PORTLAND, MAINE

Thursday

A nna was exhausted while walking on a redbrick sidewalk through the charming Old Port District of Portland.[99] None of the boutique stores or bustling plazas had appeal. She was oblivious to the historic surroundings while deep in thought.

Helping Chris decipher the cathedral bells the night before had been a good distraction from her isolation. Although the task was tiring, identifying Irene's location in Seville was initially gratifying. She remained doubtful, however, that Chris, Michelle and Ansel would ever succeed in killing their adversary. Wishing someone was dead was a morbid thought that would have never occurred to Anna before this endless ordeal. She was equally doubtful they could stop the attack in DC. And deciding to let the senator with high cholesterol die because they were too busy with the other priorities was disheartening.

Anna was depressed. While unconsciously cradling her stomach, she wondered if she would ever be free. If liberation came, would there be anything recognizable of the old Anna Monteiro going forward?

Her cell phone rang. She was reluctant to look at caller ID. It was probably Chris wanting to disclose another plan or explain why the last one failed. The endless cycle was dreadful.

"Hi," Liz Walker said when Anna accepted the call. "You're never going to guess what happened." Her best friend and former boss was bubbling with excitement.

"What?" Anna asked, stepping away from the noisy crowd of summer tourists.

"Remember when you were in my office a week ago and I said I refused to give up on Longfellow if there was even a faint pulse?"

"Sure, but I assumed you were in serious denial," Anna said.

"You're right. I was. But … wait for it …" Liz made the sound of a trumpet. "Our prayers have been answered. Longfellow BioSciences has been saved!"

Anna asked in stunned disbelief, "You're kidding, right?"

"No, it's for real. Honest."

"That's amazing. How'd that happen?"

Liz's rapid-fire explanation was gushing with enthusiasm. "Well, for weeks I tried to get one last-ditch audience with Robert Nole, the president of Fármaco, hoping I could reverse his decision to close us down. His guard-dog assistant kept saying no. Then, out of the blue, she scheduled a meeting for last Friday. I was so nervous. I created this huge PowerPoint stuffed with every fact, figure and projection to try to convince him."

Anna laughed. "Of course you did. He must've been impressed."

"Well, no. Frankly, we never got that far. He said he had been studying our company for a couple of weeks. The more he learned, the more he became convinced Longfellow deserved to be part of Fármaco's cancer platform of the future."

"He actually said that?"

"Yes, and it gets better. On the spot, he invited one of his top pharma executives into the room. His name is Jim Thomas. You'll like this guy. Anyway, Nole looked at us and said, 'I want you two to rebuild Longfellow BioSciences and make it an integral part of this company's success. Are you willing to do that?'"

Anna laughed again. "Did you embarrass yourself by how fast you said yes?"

"Yup, I was like a puppy grabbing a bone. I even kissed his ring. And then … you're going to love this part … he made Jim the new Longfellow CEO and president and me the chief operating officer."

Anna was thrilled, but Liz should have been named CEO. "That's so exciting. Congratulations. You deserve it."

"Thanks," Liz said in her characteristic modesty.

"What happens to our current beloved president?"

"In Nole's words, 'the incompetent ass is out on his ass.'"

"Couldn't happen to a nicer guy," Anna said sarcastically. "So then what happened?"

"Well, Jim and I spent the weekend creating a long-term strategy for Longfellow. It included a huge infusion of capital. After we presented it to Nole Monday morning, he made a few changes, then announced his commitment in a press release that afternoon. Since then, Jim and I have been working out the steps needed to restart Longfellow's engine."

"Do you really think that's possible?"

"I'm not naive," Liz said. "I know it'll take a year or more to rebuild what our idiot ex-president destroyed in two weeks. But we have a chance if we can rehire most of the old team."

Anna was skeptical. "Why would anyone come back after the way they were treated?"

"Realistically, many won't. But for the others, they'll get paid for the time since they were fired, plus be given a very attractive signing bonus. Together with their severance, they'll get a huge payday for taking some of the summer off."

"I doubt they'll see it that way."

"I know," Liz admitted, "so I'll have to entice them with my charm." She giggled, then became intense. "Listen, Anna, I know we can renew our dream and make it happen."

"What's this 'we' part?"

"I want you back," Liz said. "You'll get a big bump in pay, more stock options, and be part of the executive team as chief marketing officer. What do you say?"

Under normal circumstances, Anna would've accepted in a millisecond. But nothing about the status quo was normal. There were too many potential disasters ahead before she could put the nightmare behind her and go back to work. "Let me think about it."

"What's there to think about?" Liz asked, sounding crestfallen.

"I don't know," Anna said evasively. "I'm doing lots of soul searching lately, trying to decide what I really want to do when I grow up."

"But I thought this was it, realizing our shared dream together."

"It was. No, I take that back. It still is. Just, I don't know, give me some time to mull it over, okay?"

"Sure," Liz said with reluctance. "Take all the time you need, as long as you call me back in ten minutes with a yes."

Anna gave a half-hearted laugh before answering, "Will do."

"By the way, where are you? I hear lots of crowd noises in the background."

Anna couldn't say Portland for fear that Liz's phone was tapped by Irene's goons. "Traveling around New England and visiting lots of historic sites. It's fascinating."

"Good. I'm glad you're making the most of your vacation. I'll need you rested when you come back to work."

"Not very subtle, my friend," Anna teased. "Stop selling me. I got your memo."

"Okay. Oh, one last thing. Sergeant O'Neill from Boston police called."

"Did she say what it was about?"

"No, just that you should call her back. Do you want her number?"

"I've got it. She's the one who was investigating George Henniker. Thanks."

Liz paused, then said with concern, "You're sure getting lots of calls from the police lately."

"What can I say? I'm a popular girl. Okay, Liz, I'll be in touch soon. And congrats again. I couldn't be happier for you."

As soon as Anna pushed End Call, a flood of conflicting thoughts assaulted her. Had Robert Nole independently made the decision to recommit to Longfellow? Or had Chris used blackmail again like – as Michelle had told her in confidence – he did to force Nole to purchase the company? She sensed Chris's heavy hand was steering Longfellow's fate.

Sergeant O'Neill's call to the office was also disconcerting, especially following her emails and voicemails that went unanswered. O'Neill must believe Anna was involved in the shootout at the brownstone, just as the San Francisco police suspected her in Jessica's death. How much longer could she ignore them before they assumed she was guilty? Maybe they already did. Maybe they had issued a warrant for her arrest.

All she wanted was to get her life back and go to work with Liz. Neither seemed viable.

Anna sat on a bench in the middle of Moulton Street, lowered her head and cried.

Chapter Thirty-Eight: Portland, Maine

Photo 99

THIRTY-NINE

BALTIMORE, MARYLAND

Friday

"Move! Move! Move!" Ansel screamed at the windshield while stuck in rush hour traffic along Cal Ripken Way into downtown Baltimore.[100] Chris, Michelle and Ansel should have had plenty of time to spare. But their red-eye flight from Salt Lake City was almost ninety minutes late arriving at BWI Airport. Baggage claim was excruciatingly slow. The line for rental cars was atrocious. Now they risked missing the drone delivery if they couldn't get to Little Italy soon.

The day before, Ansel had the great idea to circumvent the attack in Washington, DC, by confronting the Phonoi asset when he picked up the Russian LAOP-500 this morning. Tonya had vouched for the guy. She had been his facilitator for over eight years and claimed he hated Irene as much as they did. Their ultimatum was going to be simple: the Middle East asset could either join their crusade to kill Irene or be killed. Ansel's arms dealer was fully supportive of the plan.

Everything was in jeopardy, however, if they didn't arrive by nine. The dashboard clock read 8:45. The downtown high-rises were in sight. The cars ahead were gridlocked. Ansel cursed profusely before deciding to drive down the narrow breakdown lane. Horns blared. Angry fingers flashed from open windows. Ansel ignored all the road rage as he wedged the rental between stopped cars and the concrete barrier. Michelle braced herself in the backseat. Chris tightened his grip on the grab handle above the passenger door.

At Camden Yards[101] ballpark and the Baltimore Convention Center, Ansel took a right, wove among cars, blew through an amber light, then braked hard. Traffic was hopelessly stalled. Yanking the steering wheel, he careened down a side road, turned right onto East Pratt Street, and was making progress until stymied again at the National Aquarium.[102]

Five minutes to nine. Six blocks to go. Maybe there was still a chance to intervene, but prearranged munitions pickups typically happened fast. They were going to miss this easy opportunity to prevent the assassination of Senator McLoren at tomorrow's rally.

Michelle pulled out three pistols hidden below the front seat. She handed Chris his Glock 19, gave Ansel his Glock 17 and chambered a round into her SIG P229. The last thing any of them wanted was a firefight. But you had to expect the worst when cornering an asset trained as a violent killer.

"Come on. Move, damn it," Ansel yelled until the light turned green. Using the bus lane to jackrabbit ahead, Ansel accelerated past the old piers facing the Inner Harbor. The rental car raced into The Neighborhood, a haven for generations of Italian Catholic immigrants since the late nineteenth century. Ansel zigzagged through a labyrinth of small Italian restaurants[103] until slamming on the brakes in front of a brick rowhouse.[104]

They were too late. The body of a rotund elderly man was slumped in the open front door of his house. His eyes had a lifeless stare. Blood trickled down the stairs. Ansel bolted out of the car, gun in hand.

"Ansel! Stop!" Chris yelled. "There're probably security cameras everywhere."

Ansel ignored the warning. He checked the arms dealer's neck for a pulse, stepped over the corpse and ran inside.

"What do we do?" Michelle asked her brother.

"Follow him," Chris said while jumping out the passenger door, disregarding the risk of being videoed. Backing up Ansel was the priority.

By the time the siblings reached the front steps, Ansel was coming out with the Glock at his side. He shook his head with angry disgust. "The bastard killed the wife too. Why the fuck did he do that? Just take the damn drone and leave. Why kill them both?"

The rental car interior was deadly quiet when the threesome drove away. A myriad of possible scenarios of what had gone wrong swirled in Chris's mind. There was time to sort those out later. For the moment, the right thing to do was let Ansel mourn.

Within a couple of blocks, Ansel made an abrupt stop at an old Catholic parish church. "I'm going inside Saint Leo's,"[105] he said without explanation before bolting up the steps.

Chris and Michelle followed. Ansel stuffed a twenty into the offering box near the door, approached a rack of flickering votive candles, lit a wick, made the sign of the cross, then knelt before a prone statue of the slain Jesus. The siblings silently joined him. After five minutes, Michelle placed a comforting hand on Ansel's shoulder but said nothing.

When Ansel was ready to speak, he said, "His name was Luca Amadio. He was an instructor on the Phonoi farm and my mentor when I was assigned to live in Baltimore. As an arms dealer, he was ruthless." With a fond chuckle, he added, "As a teacher, he was a brutal bulldog. But as a man ..." Ansel choked up. "He always cherished his family. I often felt that included me."

Ansel exhaled a deep sigh, then faced Michelle with misty eyes. "Luca was my equivalent of your Dr. Yasin. He meant the world to me. And what did I do to repay him? I got him killed for doing me a favor."

"No, you didn't," Michelle said with compassion to try easing his guilt.

"Yes, I did. It's my fault, as if I had pulled the trigger. I'm sure

Luca was trying to stall handing off the drone until we arrived. The asset probably got suspicious and fired the shot, then killed Luca's wife to cover his tracks. Or maybe Irene ordered the asset to eliminate all loose ends."

Ansel bolted upright with a horrified stare while digging through his pants pocket for his cell phone. "Tonya!" he exclaimed. "Maybe she's another loose end. I've got to warn her."

The facilitator didn't answer during the first or second phone call. Nor did she respond to Ansel's text.

"This doesn't make sense," Ansel said in denial with dread contorting his face. "Tonya always answers her phone. Always! What the hell have I done?" he asked in angst, then dropped his head into Michelle's comforting arms. "What have I done?"

Chapter Thirty-Nine: Baltimore, Maryland

Photos 100–105

FORTY

I f they had prevented the drone delivery, Ansel had planned to show Chris and Michelle some Baltimore highlights, as well as visit his house located a few miles from downtown. No one was in the mood. The atmosphere was somber. Repeated failure weighed on everyone. Irene was winning every encounter. The evil woman seemed invincible.

From behind the wheel, Chris interrupted the quiet tension during their ninety-minute drive from Baltimore to Washington, DC, by asking, "Mind if I call Anna?" No one objected. "Hi," Chris said when she answered.

Anna's voice was cautiously optimistic. "How did it go?"

"Not well," he admitted, then explained how their goal to intercept the drone pickup was foiled and the arms dealer was killed. "Now we're on our way to DC. Hopefully we can prevent the attack at the rally tomorrow."

"And what makes you think that?" she asked, sounding callous.

Chris was taken aback at Anna's abruptness, but her skepticism was warranted. "Okay, yes, stopping the asset tomorrow will be difficult, but we'll do the best we can."

"Uh-huh," she muttered. "Your best hasn't been good enough lately, has it?"

The harsh criticism stung, but she was right. There was no sense defending himself. In fact, his self-criticism was more damning. He tried changing the subject. "Any media news about the senator with high cholesterol?"

"If you mean has another dead senator been added to the pile, then no, not yet anyway."

That was good to hear, however temporary it might be. Chris said, "Let's hope the increased security all the senators are getting keeps him alive until we can put an end to this thing."

Anna's perturbed retort was, "How 'bout just putting an end to this thing … period. Too many people have died already. Way too many. So, for god's sake, save a life for once." She hung up.

Ansel said from the backseat, "Wow, she sounded nasty. What's gotten into her?"

"The truth," Michelle said, sitting next to Ansel. "Anna didn't say one thing we're not all thinking."

"I agree," Ansel said. "But we're doing all the hard work and taking all the risks. So why is she all pissed off?"

"Because she should be," Michelle countered. "We all should be. Trying hard doesn't mean diddly-squat. Only success does. We must succeed tomorrow."

A collective sense of failure permeated the car interior for the next several miles. Michelle reached for her phone. She told the men, in no uncertain terms, to remain absolutely quiet. Then she called Dr. Yasin with an update and to warn him.

Yasin was furious, more irate than Anna. His last words were melancholy about the arms dealer. "Luca Amadio was a mean old cuss, but he had a good heart. And his wife was a sweetie. If Irene has resorted to having innocent people like Betsy killed, then she'll stop at nothing. Please, for the love of god, stop screwing around and kill that bitch soon."

Chris felt like shit and assumed everyone else felt the same way. He decided they could continue wallowing in self-pity or shake it off and get their acts together. He chose the latter. "Okay, now that we're done getting beaten up in the critic's corner, can we get back to business?" He didn't wait for their agreement. He struggled to get papers from his pocket, then tossed them into the backseat.

"What's this?" his sister asked while unfolding the papers and sharing them with Ansel.

"My homework from yesterday. They're maps of the National Mall in DC and the eastern border of Virginia just across the Potomac River. I was trying to figure out where the asset will launch the drone. The rally speakers will be on the steps of the Lincoln Memorial, so the most direct shot would be either at the end of the Reflecting Pool or farther back at the Washington Monument. But that's a bad idea. He'd be caught immediately. The same holds true for a side shot from the Constitution Gardens, the Ash Woods or the Tidal Basin."[106]

Ansel jumped in. "Frankly, I wouldn't dare carry a drone anywhere near the Mall, even if it were concealed in a backpack."

"Neither would I. Too risky."

Michelle asked, "I see you circled a small marina in the Pentagon Lagoon.[107] Do you think he'd use a boat?"

"Unlikely," Chris said. "The Metro Police Harbor Patrol would apprehend him in a heartbeat. I also nixed Theodore Roosevelt Island in the middle of the river because the only way out is a pedestrian bridge."

"Then how about from one of Arlington's eastern neighborhoods?" she asked.

"Maybe that'd work," Ansel said as if thinking through the logistics. "The munition is designed to hit targets up to six miles away. But if I remember correctly, its top cruise speed is only about sixty miles an hour."

Chris added, "Meaning, the longer the flight time, the better the chance that NASAMS would blow it out of the sky."

"Exactly," Ansel confirmed.

Confused, Michelle asked, "What's that acronym?"

Chris answered, "It stands for the National Advanced Surface-to-Air Missile System. It protects all the airspace around DC."

Ansel said, "And from what I've heard, the system can stop low-flying threats like the Russian drone." He asked Chris, "So what are you thinking?"

"One theory for a fast escape is he'd launch from a westbound van or truck on either the Arlington Memorial Bridge or the George Mason Memorial Bridge."

"Nope," Ansel said. "Too difficult to control the shot and the rocket's backblast."

"I agree. That's why I'm guessing the best location is along the walking path on Columbia Island. I've marked the most logical spots on the map."

"Je-sus!" Ansel exclaimed. "That's in the shadows of the Pentagon. Wouldn't that be a ballsy move?"

"Sure, but better than the other options. It also has an easy entrance to the island off either bridge and a direct road out. Remember, he only needs two minutes or less to set up, add the coordinates, launch the drone, then exit. That leaves us a very, very small window to stop him."

No one felt confident. The morose ambiance was stifling for the balance of the car ride.

When they arrived in DC, they dropped Michelle off at one of Ansel's sanctioned resources, then parked on Capitol Hill near the US Capitol Building.[108] The men walked the two-mile length of the National Mall and later drove past the likely launch points marked on the maps. Chris took photos of everything. Along the way, Ansel tried several times to reach Tonya. No response. His worry was growing exponentially. After checking into a hotel, the threesome reconvened to fine-tune their game plan.

Before going to sleep, Chris called Anna again to hopefully make amends and share the details for the next day. She was not impressed.

♦♦♦

As the sun began rising over the nation's capital on Saturday morning, Chris was jogging on the Mount Vernon Trail along the west bank of the Potomac River. His eyes were searching for where the Middle East asset could fire off a kamikaze drone. Fortunately, the vegetation was sparse, so the potential hiding places were few. There were still too many, however, to monitor simultaneously.

Twice Chris acted exhausted and leaned against a tree, pretended to catch his breath, and did leg stretches while placing their two remaining microcameras. They were hardly adequate to cover the mile and a half of the path. At least the live video feeds allowed the threesome to conduct partial surveillance from their cell phones.

Chris paused to savor the view. He wished he had his Nikon camera. The pink-and-purple hues[109] encircling the distant Lincoln Memorial, Washington Monument and US Capitol, plus the rays shimmering across the Potomac River, were gorgeous. Maybe this was a good omen. He hoped so.

Ninety minutes later, the threesome assembled in his hotel room. Chris was disguised as Sully. Ansel resembled a senile old man. Michelle was transformed into a Secret Service agent. Her auburn wig was twisted into a tight bun, with large sunglasses covering half her face. Beneath a black pantsuit was her SIG P229 – the same pistol agents carried – and a fake ID and badge that looked authentic enough to pass a quick scrutiny. After reviewing assignments one last time, they tested their earbuds, wished each other luck, then left to save the life of Senator McLoren. They couldn't fail again.

By eight thirty, Michelle was in position at the Washington Monument.[110] Her job was to stroll down the National Mall while looking for suspects with a backpack. She was also the eyes and ears for accessing ground zero: the Keep America Safe rally.

Ansel sat on a bench at the western base of the Arlington Memorial Bridge.[111] He pretended to read a book, play with his phone and stare at the river. He was actually guarding the most likely place to launch the drone while also monitoring the microcameras. Chris drove a broad loop around Columbia Island in search of the asset. He wanted to pace himself so as not to be seen too often by the same security cameras. That wasn't a problem; traffic was. Too often Chris's foot was on the brake, not the accelerator.

Michelle's fourth report within the hour began as, "Guys, this place is now a zoo. I'll bet ten thousand people are jammed around the Reflecting Pool, and more are rushing in from every direction."

In his earbud, Chris heard the repetitive chant, "U! S! A! U! S! A! U! S! A!" He asked his sister, "Seen anyone suspicious?"

"Yeah, about five thousand of them. The senator's followers are real fanatics. They're either waving banners or signs, or pumping their fists. This could become a riot."

Ansel asked, "How's security?"

"Like an armed uniform convention," she said. "The DC Police, Park Police and Capitol Police are here in spades, plus lots of suits and undercover. The asset would have to be suicidal to try anything here."

The recon confirmed for Chris that the missile was going to be fired somewhere on Columbia Island or deep in an Arlington neighborhood. If the latter, it was game over.

At ten o'clock, Michelle's voice came over the earpiece, "Guys, I think this shindig is getting underway. The senator is walking up the steps of the Lincoln Memorial."

Chris was inching along the George Mason Bridge when he saw a road crew ahead. Two people wearing yellow vests were talking behind orange pylons. A third man was pulling at his pants and smoking a cigarette. A few yards ahead was a flatbed with a flashing "merge" arrow on top. The side rails obstructed the interior. This could be the perfect launch pad.

Ansel demanded, "Where are you, Michelle?"

She said, "Standing at the southwest corner of the Reflecting Pool at the base of the Lincoln Memorial."

Chris scrutinized the road crew, looking for any sign of nervousness.

"You're in the blast zone," Ansel yelled. "Get the hell back, at least as far as the Korean War Memorial."[112]

"Excuse me, miss," Chris heard in his ear. "May I see your credentials please?"

"Of course, officer," Michelle said on the live mic. "But could you hurry? I'm assigned to protect the senator."

While scrutinizing the truck, Chris caught a glimpse through the guardrail of a car pulling over at the trail parallel to the riverbank. A man jumped out of the passenger door with a backpack and sprinted beneath a weeping willow tree. The car drove off. "I've got him!" Chris exclaimed. "The asset's near the Navy and Marine Memorial[113] at Kendall Point."

"I'm coming," Ansel said, sounding as if he was already running. He'd never make it in time.

"Thank you, Special Agent," came the male voice. "You know, I don't envy your job, especially after all those senators have been killed."

Ansel screamed, "Michelle, dump that guy. Please!"

Michelle remained calm. "I suspect your job isn't much easier, Officer."

Chris careened around the dump truck and accelerated toward the off ramp.

"That's true," the male voice said, then laughed, "but having a senator poisoned on your watch probably isn't great for one's career."

Ansel kept shouting breathless warnings while Michelle was doing her best to get away from the chatty policeman. Chris sped toward the asset's position. Senator McLoren boomed over screeching loudspeakers, "Good morning, Americans." A huge round of applause, plus loud hoots and hollers. "Why are you here today?"

The crowd cheered, "To keep America safe."

"I can't hear you!" the senator taunted them.

Thousands roared in unison, "To keep America safe!"

Chris heard sirens. Lots of them. In his rearview mirror, two black sedans with flashing grill lights were racing up behind him. Up ahead, another sedan was approaching from the opposite direction.

Michelle said, "It was nice talking to you too, Officer. Have a good day."

Ansel bellowed, "Michelle. Move. Now, before that goddamn rocket goes off."

Chris was trapped. He reached for his Glock, then reconsidered. Suicide by cop was a bad option. This was where things would end. He screamed to Ansel and Michelle, "I'm being ambushed by cops. I can't stop the launch. I repeat, I can't stop the launch. Run, Michelle. Run."

"U! S! A!" the crowd chanted.

Chris pulled over to the side of the road and waited to be arrested.

"U! S! A!"

The sedans bypassed Chris and came to a screeching halt twenty yards ahead.

"U! S! A!"

Six men with FBI stenciled on their flak jackets leaped from the cars with pistols raised.

Chris bellowed, "FBI are surrounding the asset."

"U! S! A!"

A roar of smoke blasted from the tree line. The Russian LAOP-500 became airborne and extended its wings.

"Michelle, fire in the hole. Incoming!"

The agents fired their handguns. The sleek missile sailed over the Potomac. The rear blade was spinning. The camera scanned for a target. The FBI rushed toward the willow as if hoping to abort the attack. The drone gained altitude to clear the rear of the Lincoln Memorial.[114] Chris assumed it was programmed to explode over the speaker platform, sending a rain of death down on the senator and surrounding crowd. And to kill his sister.

"U! S! A!"

"Michelle!" Chris cried out for the last time.

Chapter Forty: Washington, District of Columbia

Photos 106–114

FORTY-ONE

GRANADA, SPAIN AND WASHINGTON, DISTRICT
OF COLUMBIA

Saturday

rene was nervous, a rare and undisciplined emotion. She contemplated her destiny while standing on an Islamic balcony[115] at the former Monastery of San Francisco in Granada, Spain. Below her feet were terraced botanical gardens. Encircling her were the thirty-five acres of Alhambra.[116] The network of grand palaces was built over one hundred years by Moorish rulers, became the royal residence of the Spanish Crown in 1492, launched Christopher Columbus's discovery of the New World, and was the birthplace of the Spanish Golden Age. Irene was humbled by what she considered to be one of the most revered sites on earth.

She looked at her iced-out diamond watch. Fifteen more minutes of wait time. Anxiousness was eroding confidence. This pinnacle event required flawless implementation. The outcome was binary: either massive wealth and power or devastating ruin. It was an all or nothing big bet.

She closed her eyes to soothe the doubt and felt the comforting presence of her heroine who had been temporarily interred in a chapel a few feet away. Queen Isabella I of Castile was, without question, the most accomplished woman in Spanish history. The fifteenth-century monarch would have understood and approved of Irene's cunning, hunger for riches and quest for dominant political control. Successful women admired and supported each other.

Irene trudged back to her suite in the monastery's bell tower,[117] hesitated to open the door, took a breath, then another, assumed her omnipotent demeanor and walked in. Wolfgang was wearing a headset crouched over a laptop. He was intense despite his reassurance of "Everything's fine, Ms. Shaw. We're right on schedule." She hoped so; otherwise he would earn a bullet to the head from the snub-nosed revolver strapped to her inner thigh beneath the dress.

The hotel room was in a magnificent setting yet cramped compared to her penthouse in Seville or mansion in Philadelphia. Securing it on short notice had cost a fortune. From the window was a spectacular view of a thirteenth-century summer palace[118] of a Nasrid sultan. In contrast, the image quality on the hotel TV screen was crap.

Then she saw a mood brightener on a serving table. Teso la Monja 2015 – a Spanish red reserva wine costing over one thousand dollars a bottle – had been decanted next to a bowl of fresh popcorn. Her manservant always anticipated her needs. Pierre was such a conscientious young man. She savored the aroma, took a sip, noted hints of fruit and spices, then treated her palate to a few kernels of the sugar-covered popcorn. A delicious combination.

"The asset has been dropped off near the Potomac River," Wolfgang announced. "He'll be in position within seconds."

Irene demanded, "Turn up the damn TV volume."

"I can't," he said without making eye contact. "The cameras don't have sound. Sorry."

"Sorry my ass." She fluffed a pillow against the headboard, plopped onto the bed and began watching the split-screen transmission of the Keep America Safe rally from the two cameras the asset had planted on either side of the Reflecting Pool. The crowd seemed to be in a fever pitch. The loudest thing in the room was crunching popcorn.

Wolfgang said, "The asset is extracting the Russian drone."

Irene watched as the pompous Senator Vickie McLoren strolled up the steps of the Lincoln Memorial,[119] wearing a vibrant red blazer and an insipid smile, waving to throngs of roaring fans below her feet. Trailing behind was her worthless husband; he'd make a lovely first lady someday. The senator seemed intoxicated by the manic adoration. Behind the rows of Doric columns was the imposing marble statue of Abraham Lincoln.[120]

Wolfgang's dispassionate voice declared, "The launch tube and tripod are fixed. He's setting coordinates now."

Senator McLoren stood tall and proud, raised her arms as if victorious, and mouthed something. Watching one of the most important events in Irene's life as a silent movie was infuriating. Irene viciously dug at her gumline trying to dislodge a popcorn husk.

"Oh, fuck," Wolfgang grunted before saying, "The drone's airborne."

"What's wrong?" Irene asked as thousands were clearly screaming "U! S! A!" in a frenzied chant.

"Hang on," Wolfgang answered as if struggling to remain calm, then pushed a key on the laptop and said into his microphone, "Senator, the drone is coming. Six seconds to impact."

Irene screamed, "What's wrong, goddamn it?"

Wolfgang winced as he continued the countdown. "Five seconds, Senator."

"Answer me!" Irene demanded in a panic while fixated on the Lincoln Memorial roofline shown from two angles on the TV.

"Four."

A few people pointed upward, followed by more waving fingers as they spotted the incoming missile.

"Three seconds to impact, Senator."

The crowd began to scatter.

"Two."

A stampede of terror ensued. Senator McLoren looked up, then immediately tackled two small children standing on the memorial steps. Irene was spellbound by the drama.

"One."

As planned, the disabled suicide drone splashed harmlessly

into the Reflecting Pool, creating a wave of splashing water. People stampeded in every direction trying to escape. Irene whooped and hollered with delight as the popcorn cascaded to the floor. The mayhem at the rally was a joy to behold.

Police rushed toward the senator, who was lying face down on a young boy and girl. They tried picking her up. Senator McLoren refused to go. She lifted the children, brushed them off, gave them an endearing hug and shed a crocodile tear before being shuffled away.

"What a command performance!" Irene declared. The senator had been brilliant. Within two seconds of staged bravery, McLoren had guaranteed her history-making role as the first woman president of the United States.

Wolfgang did not share her enthusiasm. Instead, he remained fixated on the laptop screen.

"What is your problem, Mr. König?" she demanded to know. "Everything was perfect."

"Not quite," he said as he finished typing, then closed the laptop cover. "It appears our asset was intercepted by the FBI."

In an instant, Irene's mood flashed from elated to livid. "How the hell did that happen?"

"I don't know," Wolfgang said stoically. "But from what I can tell from the asset's bodycam, he was shot multiple times."

"Is he dead?" she asked.

Wolfgang's one-word response was, "Very."

With heightened concern, Irene asked, "Will this expose me?"

"No, Ms. Shaw," he said with confidence. "I just wiped clean his drone-control laptop. His equipment and identity are secure. And after the untimely death of Luca Amadio and his wife, the source of the drone is also untraceable to you."

Irene's anxiety lessened, yet a rapid heartbeat still pounded in her ears.

"In fact," Wolfgang said with a self-satisfied smile as he stood, "the asset's death is icing on the cake."

"How do you figure that?"

He plucked a few popcorn kernels from the bedspread, dropped them into his mouth and said while chewing, "The way I see it, the asset's Middle Eastern nationality will heighten the conspiracy theories. No one will know whether to blame the Russians or some other foreign enemy. There's no question this will mushroom into a full-scale international crisis."

She couldn't resist saying, "Don't talk with your mouth full, dear. It's unbecoming." But his summary was exhilarating. Her fantasy had become reality. "Can you call up the major US news channels on your laptop and patch them into the TV? I want to see the post-game analysis."

"Yes, Ms. Shaw," he said as he sat down again.

On her phone, she scrolled through the live internet charts of stock market futures. They were dropping like a rock. She switched to the leveraged portfolio of inverse ETFs that had been purchased in her name using clandestine offshore accounts. The value was growing about a million dollars a second. Another basket of defense contractor stocks had already increased by ten million. She kicked her feet with delight. At this rate, by Monday morning when the markets opened, her goal of profiting a quarter billion dollars seemed like child's play.

Wolfgang interrupted her ecstasy by saying, "I have CNN coming up, Ms. Shaw."

She shuffled to the end of the bed and fixated on the TV screen. Beneath the commentator in bold red letters was a banner reading, "Breaking News. Major terrorist attack in Washington, DC." The words "Live Interview with Senator Vicki McLoren" flashed in the upper-right corner.

Irene yelled, "Now can you turn up the damn volume?"

The senator was disheveled with torn clothes and rumbled hair yet had a commanding presence, like a general returning from battle. The TV camera zoomed in for a close-up. "This is the biggest attack on American soil since 9/11," the senator said with controlled indignation. "Someone's targeting our senators, our government, our way of life and our freedom. Fortunately, that missile was a dud." Her inflection intensified. "But make no mistake. There will be others. They'll unleash horrific death and destruction. We must defend ourselves against this ruthless evil. We can no longer be complacent against foreign enemies. America's not safe. You're not safe." The senator screamed while pounding her fist, "This is war! We ... must ... keep ... America ... safe. That's my promise as your next president."

Irene concluded McLoren would make an excellent president.

As if staged in advance, two F-16 intercept jets flew overhead. The roar and sonic boom drowned out the interview. The only possible enhancements could have been a waving American flag and a rendition of "The Star-Spangled Banner."

Irene was ecstatic. She had enjoyed her role as kingmaker. Next, she imagined controlling her puppet in the White House. She could also sell that influence repeatedly for millions every time. By early next year, Irene Shaw would become the newest power broker on the world stage. The feeling was orgasmic. Queen Isabella would be so proud of her protégé.

Wolfgang had the audacity to shatter her glorious vision of the future. "Ms. Shaw, before I go, there are three small matters I'd like to discuss."

"Don't screw up this moment," she warned. "Don't you dare."

"On the contrary," he said. "These are pretty ribbons around your victory."

"Go ahead," she said cautiously, then finished the glass of wine.

"First, I assume now is the time to retire Dr. Yasin."

"Absolutely," she said without hesitation. "I don't want anyone alive who has damning evidence against me. But kill his family first. I want him to suffer awhile for his disloyalty to me."

"Consider it done. Second, we located Anna about a half hour ago in Portland, Maine, of all places when she got a call from her former boss."

"Excellent. Have you dispatched someone to finish her off?"

"No, Ms. Shaw. It's not clear if she's still there or just passing through. I still prefer the plan we discussed this morning."

"I agree. But make sure you kill her in front of her family and friends. I want a bloody mess after all the pain she's caused me."

"You have my promise," he said as if taking a solemn oath. "Finally, the whereabouts of the three other irritants remain unknown. With luck, they'll follow Anna to San Francisco so we can take care of them all at once."

"Is there any reason to believe they are in Seville?" she asked.

"No, but I have a team watching for them in case Chris was smart enough to decipher your clue about the cathedral bells and take the bait."

"Thank you, Wolfgang," she said with genuine appreciation. "You were brilliant today. Thanks too for tying up all the loose ends. Your performance has been exemplary."

Wolfgang was open-mouthed and awed by the uncharacteristic praise.

On the spur of the moment, Irene added, "You know what? I've been giving this lots of thought. Starting with McLoren's oath of office in January, I'm going to be very busy with other priorities. How would you like to assume full control of my assassin enterprise?"

His inset eyes were stunned. "You mean that?"

"Yes, you've earned it. I have total confidence you'll take it to the next level of profitability and international scope."

"Thank you, Ms. Shaw. I don't know what to say."

"How about starting with calling me Irene."

He was surprisingly uncomfortable. "Thank you … Irene. I'm honored."

"You're welcome." With a boisterous cheer, she declared, "Let's celebrate! Pour me another glass, and one for yourself." When they both had their wine, she began her short toast. "To our wonderful future together."

The former mercenary had proven himself capable of anything yet seemed speechless at the adoration and promotion. He stuttered a response of, "To us. Cheers."

After they clinked their glasses and took a sip, she patted the comforter next to her on the bed and said seductively, "Join me."

He hesitated. His rigid jawline tightened. Cautiously, Wolfgang crawled beside her. The soft mattress sank from his weight, sliding them together.

"Relax, dear," she cooed while placing a hand on his inner thigh. "Lean back and let me give you another reward."

Chapter Forty-One: Granada, Spain and Washington, District of Columbia

Photos 115–120

FORTY-TWO

Starting at ten o'clock, Anna began surfing the internet for news about the rally in DC. She was initially relieved the Russian drone had been a dud or perhaps defused by Chris and the others. However, she worried what the chaotic event, together with the poisoning of four senators, meant for the country. She sensed public fear would soon escalate into a panic.

Clearly, Irene had orchestrated the chaos. But what foreign country or terrorist group was the mastermind? How many more attacks were planned? What was their endgame? Anna felt sickened and helpless. Why hadn't Chris, Michelle and Ansel prevented all of this from happening when they had the chance?

Equally infuriating, Chris didn't have the common courtesy to call with an update, a pattern he had followed too many times. She was just an afterthought to him; out of sight, out of mind. She'd be damned if she called him first.

Anna had been wandering through downtown Portland for about an hour – trying to manage her emotions – when her cell phone vibrated. She was going to give Chris five seconds to explain himself before unleashing a torrent of anger and frustration.

She smiled. Her best friend Liz Walker's name was on the screen. "It's uncanny you just called," Anna said.

"Why's that?" the newly promoted COO of Longfellow BioSciences asked.

"I just passed the former home of your favorite American poet."

"Really? Oh my gosh. You mean the Wadsworth-Longfellow House?"[121] Liz asked with unbridled enthusiasm. "That's been on my bucket list forever. Did you go inside?"

"Of course. It's filled with original furniture as if he still lived there."

"Awesome. Send me a photo, will you? How long are you staying in Portland?"

Damn it, Anna thought. If Irene's goons were monitoring the call, she just gave away her location. To cover her tracks, Anna said, "I'm already checked out and leaving in about a half hour. I have no idea where I'm going next."

"I'm so jealous of your vagabond adventures," Liz said.

Anna hurried to change subjects. "Say, if you're calling about your job offer, I'm still thinking about it."

Liz unexpectantly became somber. "That can wait, given what's happened. My deepest condolences, my friend."

Anxiety surged through Anna's chest. "Wait, what happened?"

"You haven't heard?" Liz asked with surprise.

"Heard what? Tell me what's going on," she urgently said.

There was an anxious pause. "Paul was found dead last night," Liz declared, referring to Anna's ex-husband. "I'm so sorry to be the one to tell you this."

An avalanche of denial and grief crashed into Anna. She staggered toward a war memorial[122] in a triangular square, held on to a granite base, then lowered herself onto a concrete curb and curled up her legs. Shocked devastation. "How did it happen?" she asked in disbelief.

"I don't know," Liz said. "I just saw the news on Facebook. You have over forty comments of sympathy from people at Longfellow, your family and lots of others."

Anna's mind went blank. She could barely speak. "Thanks for telling me. I've gotta go."

"Of course," Liz said. "Please let me know if there's anything I can do. I mean it. Anything. I'm here for you."

Anna didn't say goodbye. After disconnecting, she stared blankly at the ground, consumed by angst. Although Paul had been estranged since his cheating led to their divorce, she had once loved him. Giddy, infatuated love. They married with plans to raise a family and grow old together. The great American dream. During those eight years, the dream faded, shattered and now was very final. She tried picturing Paul's face, his voice, mannerisms and laugh. They were a disheartening blur.

For years she abhorred Paul's infidelity. Over time, she became calloused and finally indifferent. But she never wished him ill will, and he certainly didn't deserve to die. She cursed herself for being abrupt with him at Jessica's funeral a month ago. If only she had known, what would she have said? It was senseless speculation, yet she felt guilty.

She had to know what happened. She would call her parents, his parents, and his roommates. Attending his funeral in San Francisco was a must. Yes, it would be risky, but she was tired of cowering from Irene. She had little to live for anyway. Almost everything and everybody important had been taken away, except maybe Longfellow. A judge would take that away from her too when she was convicted of being complicit in the crimes of Chris, Michelle and Ansel. Her family and friends would also abandon her.

Anna felt too hopeless to cry.

Chapter Forty-Two: Portland, Maine

Photos 121–122

FORTY-THREE

WASHINGTON, DISTRICT OF COLUMBIA

Saturday

Michelle's gut was twisted. The drone hadn't exploded, nobody was killed, and only a few were injured. Yet Irene had crippled American politics and damaged the nation's psyche. And once again, their nemesis had made Michelle, Chris and Ansel seem inept. Maybe the threesome wasn't as capable as they previously thought. Maybe they were inept.

Senator Vickie McLoren was also a major victor judging from the countless news stories in the eight hours since the rally. "Did you see this one?" Michelle asked Ansel while showing him an article on her phone. The headline read, "Senator Keeps Little Americans Safe," above a photo of the politician clutching two children. In the background, terrified people were running away.

Leaning over to take a look, Ansel said with disgust, "Yeah, that photo's gone viral. I'm already tired of hearing her interviews and sound bites. Commentators keep calling her a national hero. What a joke. Did you also read how her cable news buddy Lyle Mannity says she deserves the Presidential Medal of Freedom for her extraordinary bravery?"

Michelle huffed with disdain. "Fat chance her opponent will award her that during an election year."

Ansel didn't acknowledge her retort. He was clearly distracted by his phone. "Hey, give me a sec, will you? I want to finish this up."

Michelle surveyed Lafayette Square. Normally abuzz on a summer Saturday, the place was nearly empty except for curiosity seekers. There were no lines outside of the Renwick Gallery.[123] Only a few tourists were snapping selfies in front of the heavily guarded White House.[124]

The authorities and the media had warned people to stay away from the city for fear of another attack. An evening curfew had been announced. Capitol Hill, the Mall and the Smithsonian Museums were cordoned off by fencing, emergency vehicles, and police with tactical gear and automatic weapons. Washington, DC, was a scared ghost town.

"Okay," Ansel said while pocketing his phone. He sighed with a blank stare at the statue of Marquis de Lafayette.[125] His expression was tormented. "I just got a text back from Jack," he said with gloom. "He hasn't heard anything from Tonya either."

She wanted to comfort Ansel by saying Tonya was probably okay. But after thirty-two hours of no response, she assumed his facilitator friend was dead, another victim of Irene's manic cleansing. Michelle tried offering support anyway. "I'm sure she's just busy with a commission or unplugged for a long weekend."

"No, you don't understand," he protested. "Tonya, Jack and I were inseparable growing up on the Phonoi farm. She'd call either one of us back in a heartbeat ..." Ansel winced. "If she still had one."

Michelle put her arm around his shoulder, pulled him tight and kissed his cheek. There was little else she could do to ease his sorrow. She remembered all too well the overwhelming sadness she felt when thinking Chris was dead. No words could ease that pain.

After a minute, Ansel broke the uncomfortable silence. "By the way, Jack reports no sighting of Irene near the cathedral or anywhere else in Seville. After two days of recon, he's questioning whether we should bother coming."

Michelle refused to weigh in on that advice. "That's a decision we need to make with Chris," she said. "But I already know how he's going to vote."

Her brother rushed up to the rendezvous point ten minutes later. He was perspiring profusely from the oppressive heat and humidity. "Sorry I'm late."

"No problem," Michelle said. "Ready for some dinner?"

"Not yet." His demeanor was serious and fervid. "Before we go, I've got something to tell you."

Ansel sniped back, "Now what?"

To his credit, Chris didn't escalate the strained nerves. They were all on edge. "I got a call this morning from Anna telling me Paul is dead."

"Her ex-husband?" Michelle asked.

"Yeah."

Ansel questioned, "How'd that happen?"

"She didn't know at the time. But after some digging, I learned his body was found late last night behind a dumpster in the Tenderloin District of San Francisco."

Ansel's knee-jerk response was judgmental. "That's probably no surprise. You said he was gay, right?"

Michelle bristled. How could Ansel be so damn insensitive, especially while suffering his own grief? Michelle shunned him by turning toward her brother. "How'd he die?"

Chris explained, "From an apparent overdose. There was a heroin needle stuck in his arm."

Ansel chimed in, "I hear that neighborhood is littered with discarded needles."

Again, Michelle ignored his obnoxious commentary. "Did Anna ever mention her ex was an addict?"

"No," Chris said. "She told me lots of his faults but never once mentioned drugs."

"But people change," Ansel said.

"Sure they do," Chris agreed, "because Anna also never figured he was capable of having her murdered."

"What!" Michelle exclaimed.

"Yeah, Paul's the one who contracted with Irene to have Anna killed."

Michelle was shocked. "You mean to tell me it wasn't George Henniker all along?"

"No," Chris said. "I'm sorry to say I failed at that version of the Name that Client game."

Michelle bellowed in rage, "You're sorry?" She punched him hard on the shoulder. "Is that all you've got to say? You're sorry?" When she tried punching him again, he held her wrists but couldn't contain her fury. "That wasn't some little oops. Do you realize all the pain and death you caused during the last – what's it been, six weeks? – by making that stupid assumption?"

Ansel pulled her off Chris. "Okay, okay, he knows you're pissed." He tried shuffling her into a neutral corner, but she shook him off and stood firm. With clinched fists and rigid jaw, she seemed ready to lunge again when Ansel asked, "So how did you figure this out?"

"It was simple, actually. I used Anna's old email account to find Paul's address. I assumed one of his partners would be monitoring his account after his death. I created a malware inside an email called 'Funeral Arrangements.' Once somebody clicked, I had full access to Paul's computer."

Ansel asked, "What did you find?"

"Well, among the interesting things was Paul had several emails titled 'Life Policy Expires Soon.' The policy was underwritten a month before they were married. It's a first-to-die, whole life policy for two million. The premiums had never been paid except from a sizable start-up cash value, so it was set to expire this month. Seeing that the policy was issued by the insurance company where Anna's father was president, I assume it was a wedding gift. Two million bucks seems like a big enough incentive to have someone killed."

Michelle wasn't convinced. She refused to let Chris jump to another erroneous conclusion. "Did you actually find any email exchanges with Thanatos?"

"Of course not, but I didn't expect to find any. You know how heavily encrypted their phantom communications system is with clients."

Her temper flared. "So this is all speculation again?"

"Maybe I could find another smoking gun if I had Paul's computer in hand. Then I'd use data recovery software to read any documents he deleted from the Recycle Bin that had not yet been overwritten by his hard drive. But that's not going to happen."

"Besides," Ansel piped in, "a couple-million-dollar jackpot seems incriminating enough to me."

"I agree," Chris said, "especially when I also learned the dumb bastard's been jobless for three years, heavy in debt and had top club memberships at two casinos."

Ansel asked, "Then how did he pay for Irene?"

Chris shrugged and laughed. "I don't know, GoFundMe maybe? Seriously, I'm guessing from a loan shark or maybe one of his bed partners."

Trying to be empathetic, Michelle said, "You're not going to tell Anna, are you?"

"No, why break her heart? She's been through enough already."

She nodded in vigorous agreement.

Ansel kept pressing. "Are you guessing Irene had someone lure Paul into the Tenderloin District?"

"No, it seems he arranged a date with a young dude online. Kid looks about sixteen. I'm guessing Irene's people just took care of Paul before or after the date."

Ansel concluded, "And the police will never bother to investigate the death of a junkie."

"Exactly," Chris said. "Another perfect silentcide."

Michelle remained worried about Anna. "How did she sound during the call?"

"Traumatized. She's flying to San Francisco tomorrow and plans to attend services for Paul."

"That's risky," Ansel said.

"That's what I told her, but she wouldn't listen. She also made it very, very clear that I was not invited this time."

Michelle's expression softened into concern. "Shouldn't you go anyway to protect her?"

"Listen, Michelle, I can't keep doing that if she doesn't want it. From the very beginning, I told her she was free to go anytime. Well, now's that time. Besides, the best thing we can do is finally focus on Irene."

"About that," Ansel interjected. "My farm roommate Jack says he's seen no sign of Irene in Seville, so he's wondering if we should go."

Chris's temper flared. "That's bullshit! I'm going."

"That's what I told him you'd say. But he suggested we monitor the cameras he's set up around the cathedral plaza for a couple of days, then make the decision."

"If you want to sit around watching home movies, be my guest. I'm leaving as soon as possible, with or without you."

Chapter Forty-Three: Washington, District of Columbia

Photos 123–125

FORTY-FOUR

Seville, Spain
Tuesday

How ironic. Michelle had barely slept during the sixteen hours of travel time from Washington, DC, to Seville. Yet after storing their luggage with the hotel bell captain, she nodded off during their short cab ride to meet Jack Olson. He was the childhood roommate of Ansel's while training to be Phonoi assassins. It was only a few minutes before noon, and she was beyond exhausted.

She, Chris and Ansel were dropped off at the spectacular centerpiece of Maria Luisa Park. Plaza de España[126] was stunning. The sweeping, crescent-like pavilion was, according to Chris, built for the Expo Sevilla in 1929, was a masterful blend of three design styles and measured almost a half million square feet. The men barely noticed the grandeur in their rush to get to the rendezvous point beneath the south tower.[127]

Jack was notable from a distance. His strong, diamond-shaped face with a prominent chin was accented with wavy brows canopying powerful brown eyes. Below his thick brown hair were permanent scowl lines. He was about Ansel's age and height yet, in comparison, had an aura of menacing confidence.

"Toad Head!" Ansel shouted as he ran to greet Jack. The former foster brothers hooted while slapping each other's back. After sharing their close bond, Ansel said, "I'd like to introduce you to the dynamic sibling duo of Chris and Michelle."

"Thanks for helping us," Chris said. "We really appreciate it."

While shaking hands, Jack responded, "My pleasure. It's great to finally meet you both. I feel like we're extended family. And in case he's never told you," Jack added with a wink, "Ansel's nickname on the farm was Clown Face."

Everyone laughed at Ansel's expense. Michelle was enchanted by Jack's row of perfect white teeth, brightened by his rugged tan. The broad smile was transformational. He exuded a warm, endearing charisma.

The tempo quickly changed from levity to seriousness when Ansel asked Jack, "Any word from Tonya?"

Jack's expression became mournful. "No. Nothing."

No one wanted to say what they were thinking, but everyone was clearly thinking the worst. Chris interrupted the somber mood. "Any sightings of Irene?"

"Sorry, but no to that question too. I've had facial recognition running since I placed the camera on Friday, and I watch the live video when I can. I've also walked around the cathedral a few times a day. But nothing." He turned toward Ansel. "Like I said before, I think this might be a bust."

Chris was fast to counter. "I'm positive Irene's hiding within earshot of the cathedral."

Ansel said with a patronizing inflection, "Frankly, all we know for sure is Irene was here – what was it? – nine days ago when she made a phone call."

"That's not very reassuring," Jack said. "She could be anywhere by now."

"I'm sure she's still here," Chris said emphatically. Michelle could tell her brother was fuming and struggling to remain civil.

"Well, if she is, we'll find her," Jack said with a hint of doubt. "That's why we're all here." Then he faced Ansel. "Oh, by the way, I recruited another Irene hater for our search-and-destroy mission."

"Oh yeah? Who's that?"

"Sam Lincoln. He told me he was recently added to Irene's shit list after helping you. He's thrilled to help again."

Ansel blanched and shuffled uncomfortably. "Why didn't you ask me first?"

"Because you were thirty thousand feet in the air. What's the problem?" Jack's deep scowl lines reappeared. "I thought you'd welcome the extra manpower."

Michelle asked, "Who's Sam Lincoln?"

Jack answered, "He's a Phonoi asset that Ansel and I've worked with before. He's very capable. But now I'm confused. I thought you both knew him."

"Never heard of him," Chris blurted out. In an accusatory fashion, he asked Ansel, "Who is this guy?"

Ansel was speechless. His eyes darted back and forth as if struggling for something to say. Words weren't necessary. Michelle immediately recognized the out-of-shape body and bald head as Sam Lincoln hustled and huffed toward the group. He was the man who saved them from being killed while having dinner in Montreal.

"What the hell is going on here?" Chris demanded. "You knew this guy before Montreal?"

"Yes," Ansel admitted, then continued as if carefully choosing his words. "I recognized him based on your description of the assassin you let live in Québec City. So I asked him to protect us in Montreal."

"And I was happy to return the favor," Sam said with a yellow-stained grin while trying to catch his breath.

"Thanks for that," Chris said, then confronted Ansel again. "But how did you know we needed protection? I'd covered our tracks."

Ansel grew increasingly nervous while saying defensively, "I was just trying to be cautious."

Chris studied Ansel's face for an intense second, then Sam's, before screaming, "That's bullshit! You told Irene where we were having dinner, didn't you?"

Ansel's silence was an admission of guilt.

Chris lunged toward Ansel and landed a double blow to the face before Jack yanked him aside. Chris squirmed, shook off the restraint and squared off in front of Ansel again. "Have you been Irene's mole this entire time?"

"No. I mean, yes, initially, but I stopped after we left Niagara-on-the-Lake."

Michelle was in stunned disbelief. "Why'd you do that?"

"Because she'd have killed me if I didn't." Ansel's eyes implored for understanding and forgiveness. "Besides, it was the only way I could always know her next moves and keep you alive." To Chris, he added, "Just think of how many times I saved your life."

"That's a load of crap. I'm supposed to be grateful for being set up and then so-called saved? Does that make you some kind of hero? You're a lying coward."

"It wasn't like that at all," he weakly protested.

Michelle's heart ached from the betrayal. "Why did you stop being her spy?"

Ansel's expression softened. "Because I was falling in love with you."

Chris delivered a savage blow to Ansel's jaw, sending him reeling before falling down. Chris pulled back his leg as if to kick him, reconsidered, gave a look of total disdain, spit, then stomped off.

Jack and Sam struggled to pull Ansel to his feet. He stumbled while trying to stand. "You okay, man?" Jack asked.

"Yeah, I'm fine," Ansel answered but clearly wasn't.

"Your lip is bleeding. Badly."

Ansel sucked on the split lip and winced. "I said I'm fine." Then he turned toward Michelle. Her arms were folded tight. Her face was twisted with disgust. "You've got to believe me, Michelle. I was only doing what I thought was best. And I did stop reporting to Irene after Niagara-on-the-Lake."

"You said the same thing after we faked my death in Minneapolis," she said. "I believed you then. I don't now. You've been lying all along."

He raised his hand as if taking an oath. "Honest to God, I swear I haven't."

"Your word means absolutely nothing. You said you were falling in love with me? Well, the foundation of love is trust. That's gone. We're done. It's over."

"But what about getting Irene?" he asked in desperation.

"We don't need your help. Chris and I will figure something out." Then she apologized to Jack and Sam. "Guys, thanks for coming. And, Sam, thank you very much for saving our butts in Montreal. You were terrific. But Chris and I will take it from here. Sorry for the inconvenience."

As she left, she heard Jack ask Ansel, "Why the hell did you just stand there and take those sucker punches?"

"Because I deserved them, frankly worse. I fucked up big-time."

Michelle rushed to catch up with Chris as he walked along a groomed trail in the exquisite Maria Luisa Park. She asked with sisterly concern, "How's your hand?"

"Hurts like hell," he grunted. "I think I broke a knuckle. But it was worth it. Good thing I didn't have my gun."

It was challenging to match his stride. "I'm really sorry for trusting Ansel. I should've listened to you in the first place."

"It's not your fault," Chris said sincerely. "He duped us both."

"Then why do I feel so bad?"

"Don't beat yourself up. You did nothing wrong. You can't change it. Only Ansel's to blame. So let it go." After an angry pause, he said, "Hey listen, shush for a minute and give me time to think."

They moved in sync for an awkward five minutes until Chris abruptly stopped in Plaza de América facing the former Mudéjar Pavilion,[128] now the Museum of Popular Arts. He began to rant. "Ansel's betrayal explains everything. The attacks in Québec and Montreal, why Irene wasn't at her mansion and the ambush in Boston. It also explains why we failed in Denver and DC. He played us every step along the way."

"You really blame him for all that?"

"Absolutely!" he barked. His pale complexion was beet red. "I couldn't believe we were that incompetent or unlucky. We're neither."

Thinking there might be some benefit of a doubt, she asked, "Then why'd he say he stopped after Niagara-on-the-Lake?"

"I suppose to try covering his ass."

"But maybe he's telling the truth this time."

"Doubtful. Very doubtful." Chris became confrontational. "Look, you can either be with me or Ansel. What's it going to be?"

"That's an insulting question," she shot back.

His argumentative posture sagged. As his shoulders and eyes lowered, he said with atonement, "It was. I'm sorry. But the shitty thing is he's probably also warned Irene we're in Seville."

"What are we going to do?"

With an uncertain shake of the head, he said, "I don't know. But we're here. The first thing we should do is change hotels. Then let's walk the area. But I suspect Irene's either long gone, or this is a trap." He cradled his injured hand. "Or both."

While wearing disguises, they spent the afternoon doing reconnaissance while pretending to be tourists exploring the iconic landmarks in Casco Antiguo. Chris snapped countless photos throughout Old Town. They visited Seville Cathedral[129] (of course Chris had to see the tomb of Christopher Columbus[130]) and La Giralda (the bells were identical to the tape). They studied the buildings encircling Plaza Virgen de los Reyes[131] and toured Real Alcázar, the epicenter of the city's two-thousand-year history. The palace was still used by Spanish monarchy.

While visiting the seventeen-acre royal garden,[132] Michelle got a call from Ansel. She ignored it. A follow-up text was an apology and an appeal to let him explain everything. She ignored that too.

The afternoon was a bust. No sightings of Irene, with no idea where she was.

The air conditioning felt great when they returned to their shared hotel room. Michelle decided to shower away the day's heat and frustration. Chris wrapped his hand in ice, then opened his laptop to monitor the live video of Plaza del Triunfo near Seville Cathedral. Two hours later, the room reeked of smelly seafood, spicy rice, and gazpacho. No Irene.

Michelle tried reaching Dr. Yasin again. He hadn't answered his phone since their conversation on Saturday. She called his son at the pharmacy and, after some probing, learned he hadn't been to work for two days. Worry compounded stress. She feared the doctor and his family were dead – more victims of Irene Shaw – but refused to express the concern out loud. Somehow saying it would make it real.

Exhaustion was overwhelming. She could no longer fight the jetlag. She had to sleep. As she crawled into bed and said good night to Chris, the cell phone dinged. Another desperate text from Ansel. He apologized again and said he didn't deserve her but at least let him help get Irene. He also wrote that Jack and Sam agreed to stay one more day and then he would leave too.

Tomorrow may be our last chance for freedom and a new life. It's now or never.

Michelle was convinced it would be never.

Chapter Forty-Four: Seville, Spain

Photos 126–132

FORTY-FIVE

San Francisco and Sausalito, California
Tuesday

Being back in San Francisco had been a whirlwind of conflicting emotions since stepping off the plane on Sunday. This was the second time in a month Anna had returned to say a permanent goodbye to someone who had been important in her life. Almost everything good about her past had been chipped away, leaving an uncertain and depressing future.

A night at a bar with her former Wells Fargo co-workers was uplifting, although they had too many uncomfortable questions about the deaths of Jessica and Paul. Giving condolences to his parents was strained. Having lunch with Paul's lovers was awkward but necessary to discuss settling his estate. Selecting photos for the celebration-of-life posters was melancholy. And visiting the alley where Paul died was a huge mistake. Worst of all was the constant fear of being killed by an assassin.

When Liz Walker arrived yesterday, Anna clung to her best friend. Liz was terrific, a bedrock of emotional support. She never passed judgment and never probed for secrets. She just listened and provided comfort until the wee hours of the morning. If only Anna could tell her everything. Anna's mother had been the same way since landing in the morning. These two pillars of strength would prop her up during this ordeal. Would they stand behind her later if her association with assassins was ever revealed?

Several people had agreed to meet on Tuesday after work outside of the Marine Terminal[133] at Pier 41 to take the ferry across San Francisco Bay. The celebration of life was scheduled to take place inside a popular restaurant at the end of a historic pier in Sausalito. It had been one of Paul's favorite places to eat.

This event would be the only large gathering for her ex-husband. According to rumors, his parents were too ashamed of how he lived and died to have a formal funeral in a Catholic church. Their plan was to cremate his remains and have a private interment on an unannounced date. What a horrible legacy to be openly shamed by your parents. That was probably her destiny too.

Most of Anna's friends hustled to the top of the ferry to enjoy the sights of Alcatraz[134] and the fog engulfing the Golden Gate Bridge.[135] Anna sat in the lower deck. The remote bench seemed secluded and safe. Her mother joined her.

"How are you doing, honey?" her mom asked with a pinched expression of concern.

"I'm fine," Anna said woefully, staring at the grimy floor. "As good as can be expected, I guess."

"You look – I don't know how to say this – *miserable* is the word I'm looking for. Did you still have feelings for Paul?"

How could Anna begin to explain the burden she was carrying? Hopefully her mom would never learn about the traumas of the last six weeks. "No, I got over Paul after the divorce, maybe long before then, I don't know. It's just hard to believe he's gone, and Jessica too. It's made me face my own mortality. Does that make sense?"

"Of course," Donna said with a caring pat on Anna's hand. "What you're feeling is perfectly normal. None of us like facing death, but it's inevitable. I get the same feeling when one of my friends dies and, at my age, that's happening way too often. But I'm always here for you when you need it. I hope you know that."

Her mom meant well, but nothing she said or did could solve Anna's problems. She'd be horrified by them. "Thanks, Mom."

"Say, as I told you, your father regrets he couldn't come."

"That's okay," Anna said while picturing her father screaming at the top of his lungs that there was no way he'd celebrate the life of the bastard who cheated on his only daughter by sleeping with a married couple.

Her mom continued, "But he sends his support and love. He also wanted me to give you this."

Anna took the sealed envelope, looked at her mom inquisitively and read her father's letter. She could tell it had been typed by his assistant.

Dear Anna –

I'm sorry I couldn't be with you, but your mom is better at times like this than I am. Be assured your brothers and I send our deepest sympathy and condolences.

I wanted to remind you there was a two-million-dollar life insurance policy gifted to you and your ex-husband. Under the terms of the contract, you will be the sole beneficiary. Processing the claim will begin as soon as the company receives his death certificate. If you can expedite this, it would be greatly appreciated. At least something good came from your former marriage.

I'm confident you can use this money to start a new and better life. Continue your admirable career by finding a new job with a stable company where you can excel and where your employer appreciates your hard work and many talents. Also find a decent man who loves and respects you and makes you as happy as your mother and I have been for almost fifty years. You deserve it.

Love you lots,

Dad

As the letter dropped to her lap, Anna began to cry.

"Touching letter, isn't it?" her mom asked.

No, it was god-awful. Two million dollars was an unbelievable windfall. But money and a man who met her father's impossible standards could never bring true happiness. Curing cancer could. And having a supportive father would be nice. But he'd probably disown her when he learned the truth. "Very touching," Anna said.

"All that money is wonderful, isn't it?" Her mom's eyes sparkled with excitement. "Imagine what you can do with that kind of nest egg. Now you won't have to worry about being unemployed for a while."

"That's awesome, Mom. It really is," Anna said with as much enthusiasm as she could muster. "Thank Dad for me, will you?"

"Give him a call and thank him yourself, honey. He'd love hearing from his little girl."

Anna would call if he ever answered his phone. "I'll do that. Thanks again."

Donna lifted her head, listened to the PA announcement, then handed Anna a wad of tissue from her purse. "Sounds like we're almost at the landing. Why don't you use the ladies' room to freshen up. You don't want everyone seeing you like this."

They stood up. Anna rushed to give her mother a long, emotional hug as uncontrolled tears flowed down her cheeks. This might be the last time to say what was in her heart. "I love you, Mom. You're the best mother a daughter could have. Thanks for everything."

As people disembarked from the ferry,[136] Anna's friends scattered to explore nearby Viña del Mar Plaza, stroll the harbor sidewalk, or browse in the quaint boutique shops. Anna and Liz sat along the rocky edge with a view of Richardson Bay.[137]

Liz asked, "How are you holding up?"

God, I wish people would stop asking how I'm doing. I'm a goddamn basket case! "Okay, I guess," she answered, but knew she wasn't fooling her friend.

"Good talk with your mom?"

"Yeah, you know how those things go," Anna said with a shrug. "She means well. I just want to get through this. And your being here means everything to me."

Liz smiled while trying to manage her curly red hair blowing in the breeze. "That's what buddies are for."

Anna needed a distraction from her troubles and a ray of hope. "So, I've been thinking about your job offer. Tell me everything that's been happening, and the chance for really reviving Longfellow."

Liz's passion was unleashed. As she talked incessantly, Anna occasionally scanned the surroundings. Most people were casual while savoring the seaside scenery. Sitting on a bench was a man in a black suit with a well-trimmed beard and sunglasses. He seemed out of place. She couldn't tell if he was watching her or if she was being paranoid. She tried to dismiss him as a commuting business-man unwinding before going home.

After fifteen minutes of Liz's monologue, Anna suggested they walk toward the restaurant. A sizable group of people was clustered at the pier entrance.[138] A sign read: "Restaurant Closed on Tuesday. Private Event at 6:30."

Anna looked at her watch. Ten minutes before the gate opened. She looked at her fingernails. There was nothing left to bite off. She searched for the man in the suit. He was moving toward her with his arm behind his back. The hair on her neck tingled. Her pulse pounded. A car in the parking lot backed up, raced forward and screeched to a stop within feet of the waiting crowd. The busi-nessman raised a gun. Both car doors flew open. Two more men raced out with pistols.

Anna was surrounded. Trapped. She screamed.

This was it. This was where she would die. She should've listened to Chris's warning.

Chapter Forty-Five: San Francisco and Sausalito, California

Photos 133–138

FORTY-SIX

C hris tried sleeping but failed. After three hours of a restless battle against troubling thoughts, he got out of bed, returned to his laptop in the dark hotel room, turned the bright screen away from Michelle so as not to wake her, and went back to work. Doing something felt better than doing nothing, but he didn't expect to learn much of anything. He had failed too many times to be hopeful.

He processed five days of video from the cathedral plaza through two new versions of facial recognition software. Each time a potential likeness of Irene was flagged, he got pumped. Each time, the match was a false positive. He then spent hours identifying tenants and property owners of buildings within blocks of the cathedral. None produced a clue of where Irene might be staying. He checked a final time to see if Anna had returned his emails or texts. She hadn't. That wasn't surprising. She had justifiably written him off.

As the sun rose on a new day, frustration was his only companion. His hand was swollen, stiff and hurt like hell. He stood up, showered, donned a disguise, left his sister a note, grabbed his camera and quietly closed the door as he left. He walked randomly as Old Town began welcoming an influx of tourists. Most were eager to explore the grand historic sites. Chris was defeated and depressed.

He was about ready to return to the hotel when a commotion in front of the Central Post Office[139] diagonal from Seville Cathedral caught his eye. Two dogs were engaged in a frantic sniffing and yelping dance while the owners tried pulling them apart. The bigger dog was an Afghan hound. The teenager yanking the leash was vaguely familiar.

Chris photographed the scene while racking his brain. He zoomed in for a close-up. Could that be Irene's dog and Rachel's orphan roommate from the Amish farm? Chris had only seen the kid once about a month ago, and the teen looked a bit different than Chris remembered, but it could be what's-his-name.

Chris discreetly followed the teenager and dog as they walked behind the General Archive of the Indies,[140] into the cathedral plaza, down an alley, and slipped through a back door of a building beneath the shadow of La Giralda. Hot damn! Was Irene inside? Raging adrenaline and dopamine screamed yes.

He hustled back to the hotel and burst into the room. Michelle bolted upright in bed. "Jesus. You scared me. Is everything okay?"

"Better than okay," Chris said. "I may have found her."

"Irene? That's awesome!"

"Yeah, but before you get too excited, I need to verify a few things. Go back to sleep."

"How can I after you scared the hell out of me?" she asked while absently combing her tangled hair with her fingers. "Tell me what's happening."

"I will soon," he said with animated focus as his laptop booted. "I just need a minute. Please."

A minute dragged into sixty. He started by pulling up the security camera video he stole from the Amish farm after Rachel and Mamm died. Fortunately, the file included three days of history. He scrolled through the tape until finding a good image of the teenager. A comparison to the photo taken outside the post office was a match except for the boy's short haircut.

Michelle was now dressed and idling away the time on her phone when he asked her, "What was the name of that kid who almost killed me on the farm and then shot Lionel?"

"You mean Jacob Conners?"

"Yeah, that's it. Thanks." He ignored her follow-up question.

While the facial recognition software compared Jacob's photo with the crowds who'd passed through the plaza since Friday, Chris turned his attention on the dog. He retrieved the video from the hummingbird assassination attempt, scrolled to the section when it hovered over Irene's mansion, took a freeze-frame of the dog in the courtyard, then exclaimed, "Holy shit!"

Michelle dropped the fork onto the plate filled with breakfast from room service. "What is it?"

His outreached palm stopped her from running up to him. "I need a few more seconds."

She was getting irritated. "You keep saying that."

"I know. I know," he said. "I just have to check out one last thing."

By the time he pushed back the desk chair and took the first sip of the cold coffee Michelle had poured a half hour ago, she was irate. He had seen that exasperated expression many times. She seethed, "Are you finally going to tell me what's going on?"

"Yup," he said proudly. "I've positively ID'd the Jacob kid with Irene's dog."

Michelle jumped up and clapped. "Did you see where he went?"

"I sure did. He went through the back door of a building directly across from the cathedral. Using facial recognition, I also discovered his pattern. Like clockwork, Jacob walks the dog every four hours starting at eight. The next time should be at noon."

"That's great," she said, reaching for the cell phone. "I'll call the boys and tell them to get ready."

"Like hell you will," he spat.

"Why not?"

"First of all, I don't trust Ansel."

"I realize that but …"

He cut her off mid-sentence. "Hear me out before you try defending that son of a bitch. The big question right now is whether Irene is really there."

"But you just said …"

"I know what I said, but Irene never showed up in the plaza in five days. That's real suspicious. I also doubt she'd let anyone walk her beloved dog, let alone some pimple-faced teenager."

"But that's not really true," Michelle pushed back. "You said before the body double at her mansion was walking the dog on her patio. Unless you're claiming the dog is a body double too."

"That's a distinct possibility," Chris said with a straight face.

Michelle laughed. "Now you're being ridiculous."

"Am I? Would you put anything past Irene's ability to deceive us?"

"No," she said solemnly.

"Okay, and here's something else to consider. Doesn't it seem unlikely – highly unlikely, in fact – that Irene would be so sloppy to allow background noise like cathedral bells to give away her location?"

"But you worked for hours figuring that out."

"Exactly. And it's just the kind of subtle clue she'd use to bait us."

"What are you saying?"

"I'll put it this way," Chris said with hands on his hips and a dejected voice. "At the least, Irene's not here. At the most, this is a trap."

"But we've got to do something," she countered. "This is our best lead."

"No, I think I know where she might be."

"Where?"

"Do you remember seeing the Courtyard of the Maidens[141] during our tour yesterday of Real Alcázar?"

"Kind of," Michelle said, meaning she was clueless.

"Well, the lower half of the palace's inner courtyard had exquisite Islamic multifoil, horseshoe arches. The Mudéjar design resembles Irene's courtyard at Elkins Park."

"If you say so. What's the point?"

"The point is, I took a frame from the hummingbird video of her courtyard, downloaded it into Google Images and found a match. And I mean an exact match. It's called the Court of Lions[142] at Alhambra in Granada, Spain. That's about two hundred fifty kilometers from here."

"That's interesting but proves nothing."

"Sure it does. Imagine the cost to duplicate this," he said while turning his laptop screen toward Michelle showing the elaborate courtyard of Palacio de los Leones. "Irene's mansion courtyard is a perfect replica, right down to the dozen white lion sculptures holding up a marble fountain. She must be enamored with the place. I'll bet that's where she is."

Michelle assumed her worried maternal expression. "Chris, brother of mine, you're delusional. You also look like crap. Have you gotten any sleep?"

"No," he said with a hint of exhausted desperation, "but I can't until I figure this out."

"What's to figure out? You're way overthinking this. It's simple as one, two, three. One, you've seen Jacob. Two, you've seen Irene's dog. And three, you've seen where she's hiding. What more proof do you need? So stop dinking around. Let's round up the posse and take action."

Chris rubbed his bloodshot eyes. Maybe Michelle was right, at least partially. "I'm not sure that's wise."

She said emphatically, "Yes … it … is!"

He begrudgingly acquiesced. "Okay, fine. But we don't need them. We can do this ourselves."

"Are you kidding me? For all we know, that building's an armed fortress. Five of us stand a chance in a shootout. Two of us alone will be slaughtered."

Chris pushed back, hard. "We'll all be slaughtered if Ansel warns her we're coming in with guns blazing."

"That's not going to happen."

"But he ..."

She screamed, "Chris, shut up for one second and listen to me."
He stood in respectful silence.

"Did Ansel betray us? Yes. Did he lie about it? Yes. Do I forgive
him? No. But he did save your life multiple times. And he could have
ratted out our location countless other times. And I highly doubt
he's capable of sending us all into a death trap. Three of us are his
only family. And he said he's falling in love with me."

"Don't bring that up again," Chris warned her.

"Fine. All I'm saying is he wouldn't let me die. I believe that in
my soul. So here's what's happening. I'm going to call Ansel, tell him
to get Jack and Sam ready, then we're going to kill Irene. After that,
we never have to talk with him again. Got it?"

"I still think it's a bad idea."

"So noted. But when it comes down to it, we have no choice."
She took a deep breath as if trying to calm the tension. "Look, Ansel
said it best in yesterday's text, 'It's now or never.' I say it's now. If
you'd rather sit here playing with that goddamn laptop, that's fine.
But I'm going."

Chris almost immediately regretted agreeing. While struggling
to put on a middle-aged Spaniard disguise – his swollen right hand
had limited dexterity – he considered backing out. Which decision
would he later regret for the rest of his life? That assumed he survived the day.

Michelle was the designated go-between with Ansel because
Chris refused to talk with him. Jack and Sam were all in and eager to
go. The game plan was simple. Chris and Michelle would discreetly
wait in the plaza facing Irene's building. The others would hide in the
cobblestone alley near the back entrance. If they saw Jacob walking
the dog at noon, it meant he hadn't been spooked earlier by Chris
and presumably Irene's guards wouldn't be on high alert. But if no
kid, no attack. That was an ironclad rule.

Chris and Michelle were pretending to wait in the long ticket line for Real Alcázar[143] when a bell inside La Giralda began striking twelve. Each peal sounded like a death knell. Chris suppressed the screaming warnings of his instincts by continuing to assess the people at Plaza del Triunfo.

A pair of Policía Municipal were patrolling the area. They appeared bored in idle chitchat but may be a problem later. A man near the cathedral's front gate seemed suspicious, but his owllike swivel suggested he was waiting for someone. Two stationary men resembling mercenaries – big muscles, grim faces – had stood too long in one place. Three people wearing business attire were too quiet while eating their lunch. The only activity on the rooflines was disgusting pigeons. Who else posed a threat? It was the ones Chris didn't see that worried him most.

The heat was oppressive, made worse by the spring jacket he had to wear to conceal the Glock 17 wedged in his belt. Michelle sweltered inside the modified Doris Mathews disguise. The black synthetic wig, full-facial latex mask, and inflated bodysuit stuffed inside a size-sixteen dress made her unrecognizable. Large circles of sweat dampened her armpits.

They both flinched when Ansel's voice boomed through their earbuds. "The kid and the dog have left the building. They should be headed your way."

"Got it," Michelle said.

The siblings waited patiently as Jacob emerged from the alley, lollygagged across the plaza and headed toward the post office. Chris kept discreetly watching the suspected enemies. They hadn't moved yet appeared to show no interest in Jacob Conners as he struggled to manage the Afghan hound. They were either very good at covert surveillance or harmless. The odds were fifty-fifty.

As planned, Chris and Michelle drifted toward the Monument of the Immaculate Conception.[144] The final staging area was about seventy-five feet from the entry point. They would burst through the front door, while Ansel and his team breached the rear. Chris began managing his heart rate and breathing.

Ansel's commanding voice filled their ears. "Okay, guys. This is it. Are you ready?"

"Hold on," Chris protested. "I thought we agreed to wait until that Jacob kid returned."

"We had," Ansel answered. "But we decided he's one less combatant to deal with. We're moving on three."

Chris fumbled to retrieve the loaded Glock. His fingers struggled for a firm grip on the handle.

Ansel began the countdown. "One!"

"I can't do this, Michelle," Chris said defiantly. "I know it's a trap."

"Two!"

With eyes ablaze, she chambered a round and barked, "I'm going in, with or without you."

"Three!"

Chris grabbed Michelle's shoulder to restrain her. During the struggle, he dropped his gun. As he reached to pick it up, he spotted a construction van concealed inside an archway. The side doors swung open. A police tactical unit jumped out and sprinted toward them. They brandished heavy firearms.

"¡Congelar! ¡Policía!" the lead policeman shouted, scattering the crowd of terrified tourists.

Chris tried warning the others. "Get out! It's a …" The attempt was stopped by a submachine gun pressed to his face. He was forced to spread-eagle.

Simultaneously, Michelle screamed, "Ansel …" before being knocked to the ground. She was winded as a heavy boot pressed against her neck.

They were handcuffed, frisked and stripped of their weapons and earbuds. Once secured, the three businesspeople who had been eating lunch casually approached. The eldest had a shit-eating grin while flashing his FBI credentials. He asked with arrogance, "Daniel and Sarah Ritchie?" as his associates pulled off the siblings' disguises. "Oh, there you are," he said in mockery. "I knew it was you fun-loving kids."

How the hell does he know our real names? Chris wondered. No one had called them that in twenty-six years.

The FBI agent continued, "I'm going to let the local authorities have the pleasure of arresting and processing you. But soon you'll be FBI property," he said with a cocky smile. "There are several special agents back in the States who have waited a long time for this moment."

Irene's building exploded. A deafening roar. Then another blast. A torrent of debris scattered in billowing black smoke as the top floor was consumed by an inferno. The heat was intense. A cloud of embers seared Chris's scalp. The façade buckled, twisted, then collapsed into a thundering avalanche of broken stones, glass and rubble. No one inside could have survived.

Chapter Forty-Six: Seville, Spain

Photos 139–144

EPILOGUE

PHILADELPHIA, PENNSYLVANIA

Eight Weeks Later

With impatience, Chris tapped his bright red fingernails on the steering wheel of the stolen car. He hated waiting. But he had already waited decades. What was a few more minutes? He cranked up the A/C, leaned back against the headrest and recalled the events during the last eight weeks since Seville leading up to this decisive day.

Ansel had died instantly in the explosion of Irene's penthouse apartment. Michelle was still mourning the loss. She obviously had developed strong emotions for him. Maybe not love, but deep affection. She regretted doubting Ansel's motives for lying. She blamed herself for not heeding Chris's warnings of a trap. Grief and guilt were a toxic mix. Hopefully, time and lots of brotherly support would ease her depression.

Ten other people were killed in the blast. Jack Olson was among the wounded and faced a long recovery. By the time Sam Lincoln died four days later, Chris and Michelle were in FBI custody[145] back in Washington, DC. They were imprisoned without bail facing several life sentences. The death penalty was a distinct possibility if convicted in federal court of espionage, terrorism and multiple capital murders, including the death of a US senator and the attempted murder of another.

The FBI had started tracking Chris after taking over the investigation of the shootout at his Saint Paul house. They had evidence of his involvement in the Québec City and Montreal firefights, DNA from the Amish farm and the Mazda in Elkins Park, prints in the Denver Cathedral and his bullet-riddled car in Boston, plus security cam footage near the DC drone launch. They also had rudimentary evidence of his silentcide career. Michelle was implicated in several of the crimes. Fortunately, they hadn't uncovered the killing of George Henniker or Jessica Daly. But adding two more murders would hardly make a difference.

After Chris and Michelle were arrested, he tried for two days to convince the FBI and Spain's National Police Corp that Irene might be in Granada near the Alhambra. By the time a team was dispatched to follow up, all they learned was a sophisticated, senior-aged woman with an Afghan hound had checked out of the former Monastery of San Francisco the day before. Irene was gone.

Jacob Conners eluded authorities in Seville. Wolfgang apparently tried to shut everything down and destroy all evidence of Irene's assassin network. He wasn't fast enough. The FBI had been building a case against Irene for over two years. During a coordinated raid, they seized her law firm, mansion, farms in Lancaster County, domestic bank accounts and every electronic device they could find. Analysts were still scrubbing her records for information. Sometime in the future, her assets would be sold and profits surrendered under civil forfeiture laws.

A handful of assassins and sanctioned resources were also arrested in four countries, including the US. Many took plea deals in exchange for testimony. Chris imagined those awaiting trial would have loved having Irene's superior legal skills to defend them in court.

Chris remembered laughing when he first reviewed the short list of those apprehended, then tossed the paper back across the table inside an interrogation room. "You proud of yourself?" he jeered at the FBI senior special agent. "You arrested just the tip of a very big iceberg. What's below the surface could sink several *Titanics*. And you have far too few lifeboats."

Chris laughed again inside the car. Upon reflection, that taunt of the lead investigative agent may have changed the course of his life. He looked at his watch. Twelve minutes before game time. Dwelling on the plan could cause anxiousness. The best distraction was remembering what got him here.

Dr. Yasin was among those captured in the sweep. He didn't resist. He was devastated after learning his son, daughter-in-law, and twin grandsons were dredged out of the Mississippi four days after disappearing. Police recently closed the case. Their investigation concluded the car swerved off a winding road late at night before plunging off a river bluff. The tragedy was declared an accident. Trying to blame Irene for the deaths was fruitless. Yasin had resigned himself to life in prison. He would probably die soon from a broken heart.

One of the biggest surprises was when Tonya resurfaced. Apparently, during a confirmation phone call with the arms dealer in Baltimore, she heard Luca Amadio and his wife being shot. She got spooked, didn't trust anyone, including Ansel, and went underground. Unfortunately, Tonya was caught up in the FBI net while staying with an assassin friend who was arrested at his home.

Chris checked out his disguise in the car's rearview mirror. He looked hideous. A mop of stringy gray hair. A face marred by a checkerboard of wrinkles and brown spots. Pale brown contacts concealed his aquamarine eyes. He rubbed pink blush across his cheeks and added a coat of red lipstick to his dry, cracked mouth. With a tissue, he formed a kiss mark.

Until recently, the huge victor appeared to be Senator Vickie McLoren. She rode the wave of her DC heroism into a tsunami of public admiration and support. She easily won the Republican nomination during the national convention in August. Her Keep

America Safe theme was pounded into Americans' psyches during a whirlwind campaign tour, plus endless advertisements, interviews and broadcasted sound bites. She decimated the sitting president during the televised debates. Entering the last month of the race, polls projected a commanding lead and commentators predicted she'd become the first woman to be elected president of the United States.

The FBI believed Chris when he claimed Irene was responsible for the DC attack. But they initially thought he was withholding information when he couldn't name a client or motive. After no additional drones or senator deaths, the official position to the public was the Denver and DC assassins were the sole instigators, so the threat had died with them. Yet rampant speculation fueled by the senator blamed Russia for everything.

Senator McLoren's downfall came from an unlikely source in an unlikely location. A cub reporter – fresh out of grad school – at the *Des Moines Register* was assigned to write a routine story about the senator's stopover visit. During her research, the reporter uncovered an obscure interview with McLoren saying she felt blessed the Russian drone was a dud. The drone may have been a dud, but her comment was a smoking gun; there was no way McLoren could've known the munition's origin within an hour of the attack. Her editor called the speculation baseless, then fired the reporter for insubordination when she began arguing.

Kathy Linhoff was motivated by the setback. She generated boxes of research. Among her findings was that two of the poisoned Democratic senators were on the Senate Appropriations Committee and strong advocates for further slashing the defense budget. After their deaths, and with the country's fear of attack by foreign powers, the government was now poised to rebuild their war chest and spend lavishly on national security.

With money borrowed from her parents, Kathy became a political groupie at the Republican National Convention. Late one night, she snapped a grainy photo of Senator McLoren passionately kissing someone as a hotel elevator closed. The mystery man was an aerospace president. His company had an eighteen-billion-dollar contract at risk if the current administration kept orchestrating world peace. Fabricating a large-scale foreign threat benefited him and Senator McLoren.

On a lark, Kathy decided to test her hypothesis. She drove to the battleground state of Ohio, cornered McLoren's campaign manager during a rally and confronted him with the conspiracy theory. He panicked. Despite his vehement denials, his facial expressions on her cell phone video were priceless.

When the story broke two weeks ago, Kathy became famous. The reporter turned down a *Washington Post* job offer to start a podcast. Over seven million people downloaded her initial episodes in the first few days. She was rumored to be a shoo-in for the Pulitzer Prize for investigative reporting.

Senator McLoren was villainized in the court of public opinion. Her arrest in the Senate Wing of the US Capitol Building was sensationalized. The Republican party appealed to the Supreme Court to delay the November election. And the aerospace president resigned to spend more time with his family. His arrest seemed imminent.

Chris laughed. Payback was a bitch. He looked at his watch. Seven minutes to showtime. He yanked on his pantyhose. *Why in the hell do women wear such a hideous garment?*

Anna had ignored his repeated phone calls until four days ago. The conversation was civil yet strained. She described her disgrace when led off by the FBI outside the Sausalito restaurant. She also called it a blessing because the special agents unknowingly thwarted an assassination attempt by the man in the black suit.

At FBI headquarters, she was told she wasn't under arrest, only brought in for questioning. Anna was petrified they were going to accuse her of Jessica's death or implicate her in the Boston brownstone shooting. She was relieved when their first question was, "How did you know in advance about the poisoning of Senator Phillips in Denver, an attempt on another senator with high cholesterol, and the approximate location of the drone launch in DC?" As Ansel had warned her, they had traced her anonymous tips and used them to try preventing the crimes.

On the spot, she decided to explain the five-week ordeal she had suffered. Included in her information was where to find Chris and Michelle near the Seville Cathedral. This led to their arrest.

Anna apologized to Chris but said she didn't have a choice. He said he fully understood and forgave her. She owed him nothing. Why ruin her life for theirs? Then he apologized for subjecting her to so much trauma, wished her the best of everything and teared up when saying his only regret was not being part of her future.

Their conversation ended with an update. Anna had initially been charged with aiding and abetting criminals, conspiracy to commit murder, second-degree murder, and terrorism. After her father hired the best defense team in Boston, the lawyers made the claim she suffered from Stockholm syndrome. They brokered a plea deal for a minor misdemeanor and a small fine in exchange for her ongoing cooperation and testimony.

Anna was now back at Longfellow BioSciences with a promotion and sizable compensation package. She used some of the life insurance money to pay off her ex-husband's debts and donated a million dollars to a children's hospice center in memory of her deceased brother. She was excited about looking to buy a modest house in the Boston suburbs.

At the end of their conversation, she emotionally said, "Chris, I'm not sure how to say this so you know how much I mean it, but thank you for keeping me alive. I'll never forget everything you did for me. Deep down, you're a good man."

He would never forget her either. She was the best person he had
ever met. After a deep sigh, Chris patted his eyes with the tissue,
then looked at his watch. Two minutes to go.

Anna's full confession was actually advantageous. She explained
to the FBI how the siblings had been victims since childhood. She
also stressed how they had risked their lives to stop Irene and the
assassination attempts of the senators.

After days of interrogating Chris and Michelle, and a week to
verify their stories, the FBI made a surprising proposal. They would
be given a conditional immunity agreement in exchange for joining
an FBI task team. The mission was to dismantle the rest of Irene's
network within two years, plus identify and prosecute all clients
who ordered hits.

Taking the offer versus dying in prison was an easy decision to
make. The deal also gave the siblings restrictive freedom. That freedom would be short lived, however, if the FBI could ever prove the
crime about to take place. The risk was worth the reward: vengeance.

Beep. Beep. Beep. Chris turned off the cell phone alarm and
turned on the live video of Michelle's bodycam. "You ready?" he
asked.

"Ready," came her voice through his earbud.

"Let's do this."

This was the day they had dreamed about.

Chris reached below the car seat, retrieved a Canik TP9SA,
pulled back the slide and chambered a 9mm round.

He pictured Michelle waddling through the front door of the
plastic surgery clinic with a seven-month baby bump protruding
below a light summer dress. A full facial disguise displayed an ugly
scar across her cheek. Her fingertips had been sprayed with latex
to avoid leaving prints.

The pleasant receptionist asked, "How can I help you?"

"Yes, hi," Michelle responded. "My name's Linda Madison. I have
a ten o'clock appointment."

"Welcome. I see you're here for an initial consult with Dr. Peters." She handed Michelle a clipboard. "Please fill out these forms, then bring them back to the desk along with your medical insurance information."

The bodycam video was a bit jerky as Michelle moved toward the waiting area. As she approached a chair, the pen fell off the clipboard. She strained to pick it up.

With a gracious smile, Irene's chauffeur said, "Here, let me help you." He bent down from his chair.

"That's so nice of you," Michelle said while injecting his neck with the powerful sedative midazolam. As John lost consciousness, she pushed him into a sitting position, sat next to him and began filling out the forms.

"Nice work," Chris whispered in her ear. "Now for step two." He got out of his car and moved toward the clinic's back entrance.

Sixty seconds later, Michelle returned to the front desk. "Sorry to disturb you again. Is there a bathroom nearby?"

The receptionist chuckled. "Of course. When I was that far along, I had to pee every ten minutes." A buzzer sounded. "Go through that door. It's at the end of the hall on the left."

"Thanks." Michelle jammed the door behind her, proceeded down the hall and pushed open another door marked "Not an Exit."

"Hi there," she said to Chris. "You look absolutely marvelous, darling. Not a day over seventy." Her serious voice came thundering back. "I'll see you back here in five."

Chris took the exam rooms, nurse workstations and a breakroom on the left. He methodically threatened, zip-tied and gagged all the patients and personnel he encountered. Michelle used her Canik pistol to accomplish the same on the right. Her last stop was the manager's office to erase the security camera system.

They met back in front of the Procedure Room with one minute to spare. A red sign above the door read "In Use." He checked his phone for a final time. A video of the operating suite showed their timing was perfect.

Chris felt his heart racing. Very unprofessional but totally merited. He savored the rush of anticipation and wallowed in the euphoria. "Ready for step three?"

"I've been ready for a lifetime," she answered with a grin while raising her pistol.

The surgical staff of four was startled. It took less than sixty seconds to contain and render them unconscious. The siblings approached the operating table and stared down at their nemesis. Irene was heavily sedated but awake. She tried screaming. The noise was a raspy garble.

"Hi there, dear," Chris said in mockery. "It says here on your chart you're in for a nip and tuck."

Michelle plucked at the folds on Irene's neck. "Tsk, tsk, tsk. I'm surprised you waited for so long. A most unbecoming look, dear."

Chris continued the verbal harassment. "I'm also surprised you violated your own rule of never being predictable. But we knew you couldn't resist returning to your favorite plastic surgeon. I'm sorry to say he's incapacitated at the moment. So perhaps we can help." He turned toward Michelle. "Scalpel, please."

She taunted Irene by flashing the sharp knife in front of her bulging eyes, then handed it to her brother.

"Now then," he said, relishing the moment, "I promise to make only a small cut so as not to ruin your appearance in an open casket." The blade pressed down on Irene's carotid artery. "Ah, screw it. You'll look good in a turtleneck."

Epilogue: Philadelphia, Pennsylvania

Photo 145

If you enjoyed *Silentcide 2: Vengeance,* then please ...

+ **Write a review** on Amazon, Goodreads, Barnes & Noble, or where you purchased the book. Favorable reviews and ratings are essential to authors.
+ **Tell your friends** and family so they can enjoy the story.
+ **Buy** *Silentcide: The Art of Undetected Killing,* the first novel in the *Silentcide* series.
+ **Send email** to Author@RichardEbert.com to learn about future book releases.

Thank you for allowing me to entertain your imagination.

ACKNOWLEDGMENTS

Being an author requires endless hours at a keyboard with only your characters to keep you company. Then several people help transform the story into a marketable novel. I owe them a huge debt of gratitude.

To my subject-matter experts, especially Tom Emmerich, Matthew L. and Kathy Jonsrud. I appreciate the time and knowledge you invested in polishing passages to add realism, accuracy and excitement.

To my editors Alyssa Matesic and Megan McKeever, plus my copy-editor Lisa Gilliam. As a team, you elevated my early drafts into a cohesive novel.

To Kraig Larson for your continued technology and design assistance for Encircle Photos and Encircle Books. Your ability to convert my raw concepts into stunning creative is admirable.

To my loyal beta readers. I am always impressed by your observations and suggestions. Thanks for your insightful contributions to my novels, both published and unpublished.

To relatives and friends who showered me with congratulations for my debut novel, then eagerly promoted it. Your endorsement was the foundation for my initial success.

To the booksellers who shelved my first novel, hosted book signing events and offered their advice and encouragement. Your warm welcome to a rookie author was inspiring.

To Michelle, Bobby, Ali, Charlie and Daniel. I am blessed to have such a wonderful family.

And to Mary Beth. Your love, companionship and support for over five decades is the essence of living happily ever after. I love you always.

ABOUT RICHARD EBERT

Richard Ebert started as a photographer and cinematographer. Then he was president of two advertising agencies before becoming president of a consulting firm serving Fortune 500 companies in the US, Canada, Mexico and Chile. Since retiring, Richard has pursued three passions: writing, travel and photography. He lives in Saint Paul, Minnesota, with his wife and has two adult children plus two grandsons.

Contact the Author

Author website: RichardEbert.com
Travel guides website: EncirclePhotos.com
Author Facebook: Facebook.com/EncirclePhotos
Author email: Author@RichardEbert.com

Send an email to Richard for updates about new book releases.

Made in the USA
Middletown, DE
02 October 2024

61818998R00203